HAND OF THE MORNINGSTAR

Resurrection

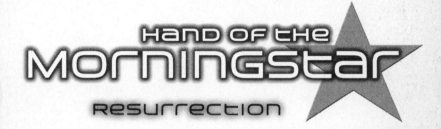

 ZONDERVAN®

Resurrection
Copyright © 2007 by Lamp Post, Inc.

Requests for information should be addressed to:
Zondervan, *Grand Rapids, Michigan 49530*

Library of Congress Cataloging-in-Publication Data

Miller, Mike S.
    Resurrection / written and illustrated by Mike S. Miller; edited by Brett Burner.
        p. cm. -- (Hand of the morningstar; v. 2)
        ISBN-13: 978-0-310-71370-8 (pbk.)
        ISBN-10: 0-310-71370-6 (pbk.)
        1. Graphic novels. I. Burner, Brett A., 1969- II. Title.
        PN6727.M555R47 2007
        741.5'973--dc22

                                            2007003147

This book published in conjunction with Lamp Post, Inc.; 8367 Lemon Avenue, La Mesa, CA 91941

Series Editor: Bud Rogers
Managing Editor: Bruce Nuffer
Managing Art Director: Sarah Molegraaf

Printed in the United States of America

---

07 08 09 10 11 12 • 8 7 6 5 4 3 2 1

HanD OF tHE MORNINGStar

Resurrection

series EDITOr: BUD ROGErs
STOrY BY BrEtt BUrnEr anD MIKE MILLEr
art BY MIKE MILLEr

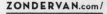
ZONDERVAN.com/
AUTHORTRACKER
follow your favorite authors

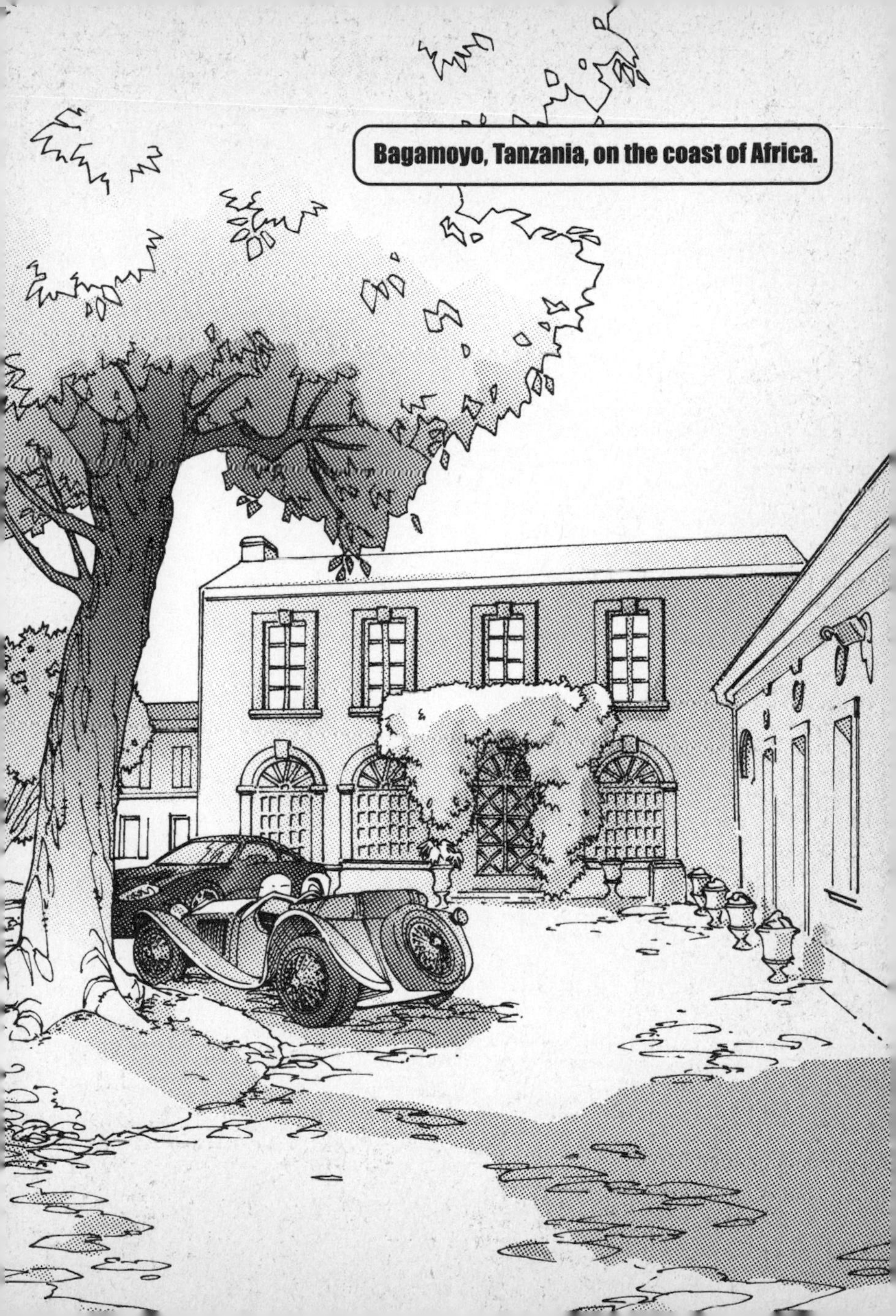
Bagamoyo, Tanzania, on the coast of Africa.

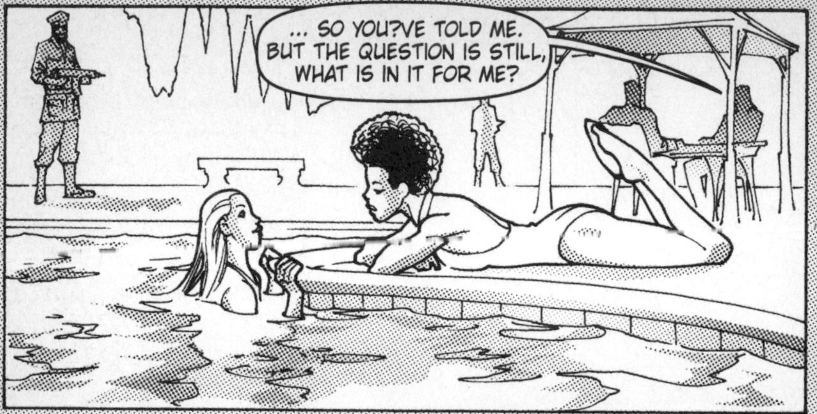
... SO YOU?VE TOLD ME. BUT THE QUESTION IS STILL, WHAT IS IN IT FOR ME?

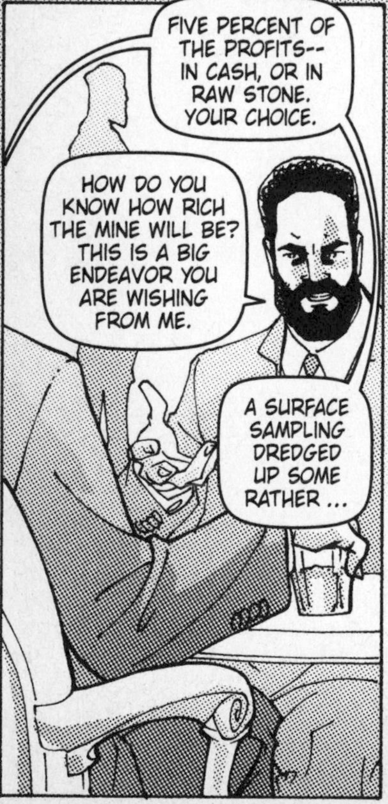
FIVE PERCENT OF THE PROFITS-- IN CASH, OR IN RAW STONE. YOUR CHOICE.
HOW DO YOU KNOW HOW RICH THE MINE WILL BE? THIS IS A BIG ENDEAVOR YOU ARE WISHING FROM ME.
A SURFACE SAMPLING DREDGED UP SOME RATHER ...

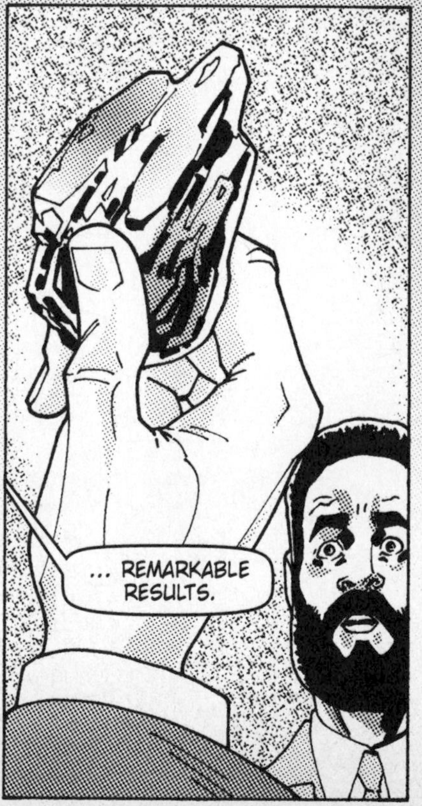
... REMARKABLE RESULTS.

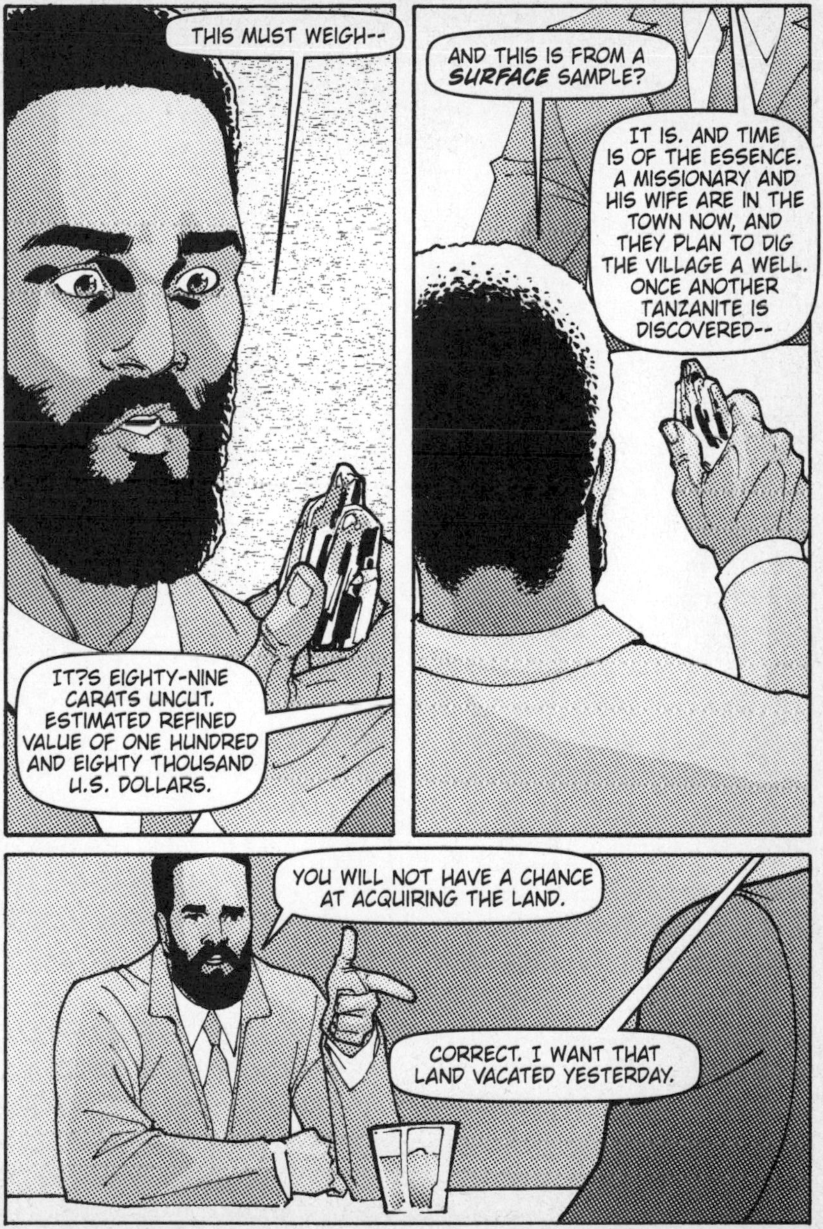
THIS MUST WEIGH--
IT?S EIGHTY-NINE CARATS UNCUT. ESTIMATED REFINED VALUE OF ONE HUNDRED AND EIGHTY THOUSAND U.S. DOLLARS.
AND THIS IS FROM A *SURFACE* SAMPLE?
IT IS. AND TIME IS OF THE ESSENCE. A MISSIONARY AND HIS WIFE ARE IN THE TOWN NOW, AND THEY PLAN TO DIG THE VILLAGE A WELL. ONCE ANOTHER TANZANITE IS DISCOVERED--
YOU WILL NOT HAVE A CHANCE AT ACQUIRING THE LAND.
CORRECT. I WANT THAT LAND VACATED YESTERDAY.

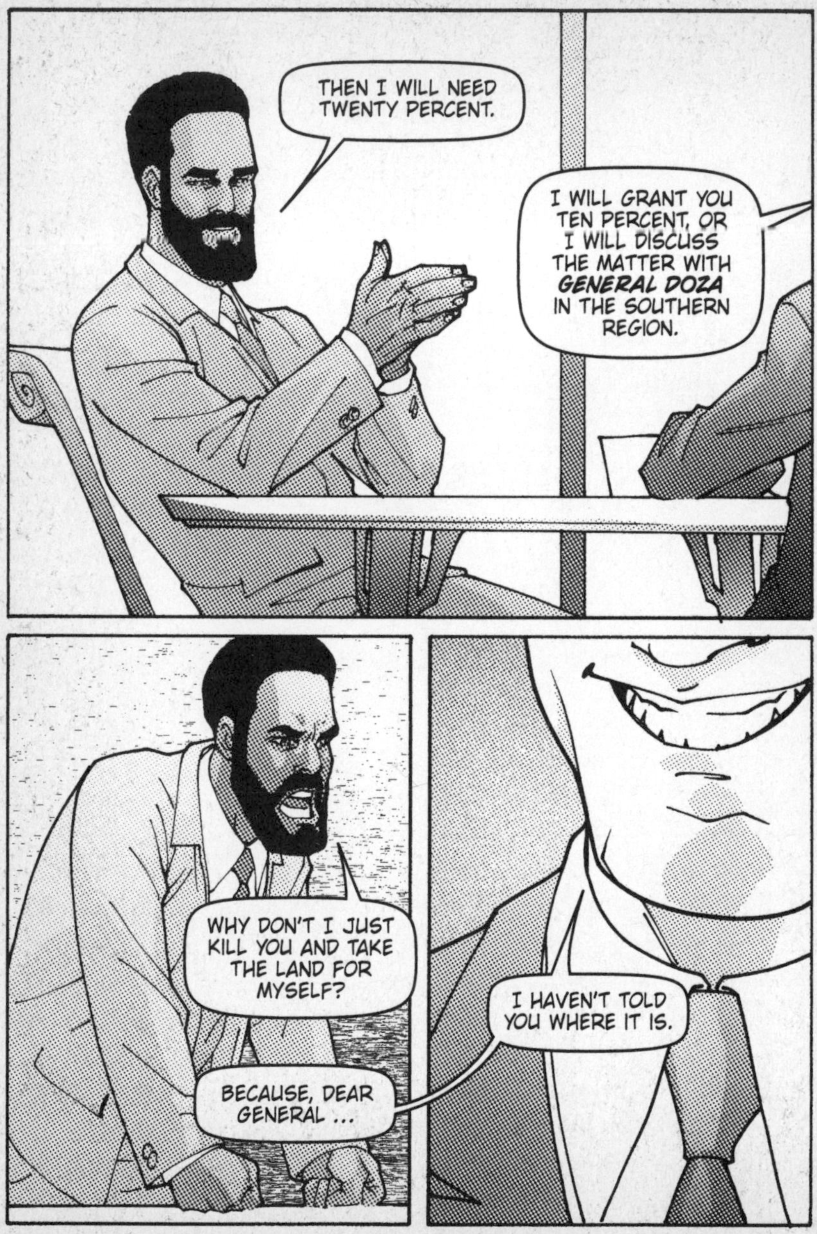
THEN I WILL NEED TWENTY PERCENT.
I WILL GRANT YOU TEN PERCENT, OR I WILL DISCUSS THE MATTER WITH ***GENERAL DOZA*** IN THE SOUTHERN REGION.
WHY DON'T I JUST KILL YOU AND TAKE THE LAND FOR MYSELF?
BECAUSE, DEAR GENERAL ...
I HAVEN'T TOLD YOU WHERE IT IS.

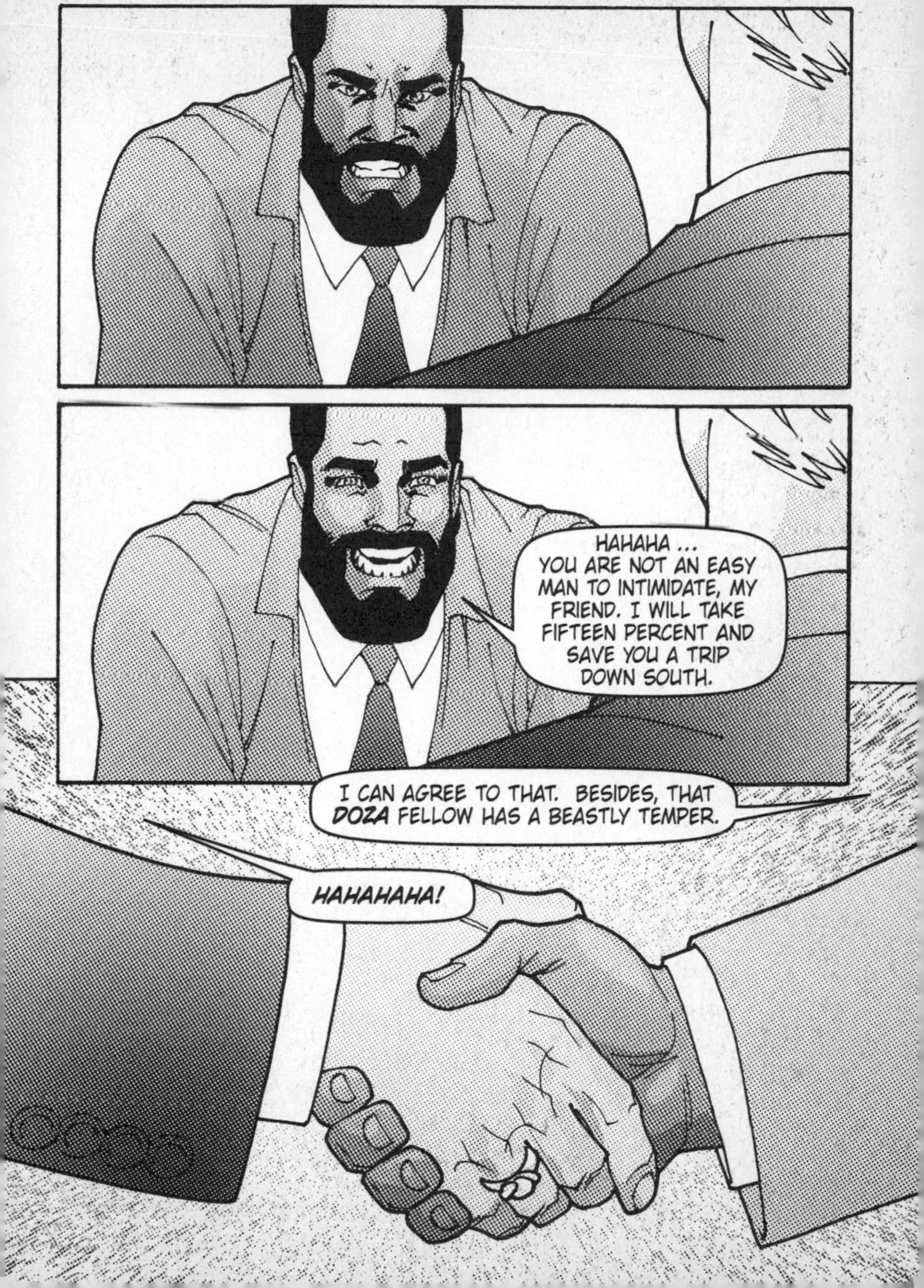
HAHAHA ... YOU ARE NOT AN EASY MAN TO INTIMIDATE, MY FRIEND. I WILL TAKE FIFTEEN PERCENT AND SAVE YOU A TRIP DOWN SOUTH.
I CAN AGREE TO THAT. BESIDES, THAT *DOZA* FELLOW HAS A BEASTLY TEMPER.
HAHAHAHA!

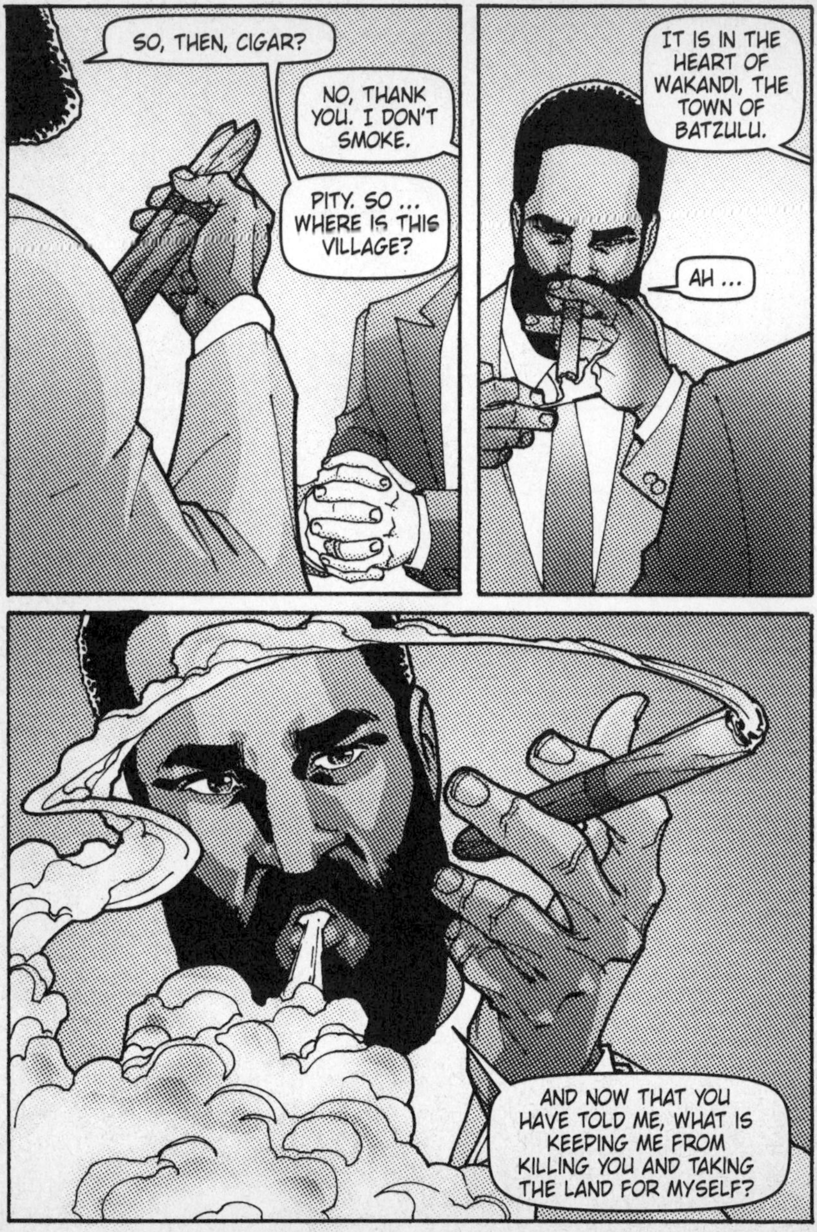
SO, THEN, CIGAR?
NO, THANK YOU. I DON'T SMOKE.
PITY. SO ... WHERE IS THIS VILLAGE?
IT IS IN THE HEART OF WAKANDI, THE TOWN OF BATZULU.
AH ...
AND NOW THAT YOU HAVE TOLD ME, WHAT IS KEEPING ME FROM KILLING YOU AND TAKING THE LAND FOR MYSELF?

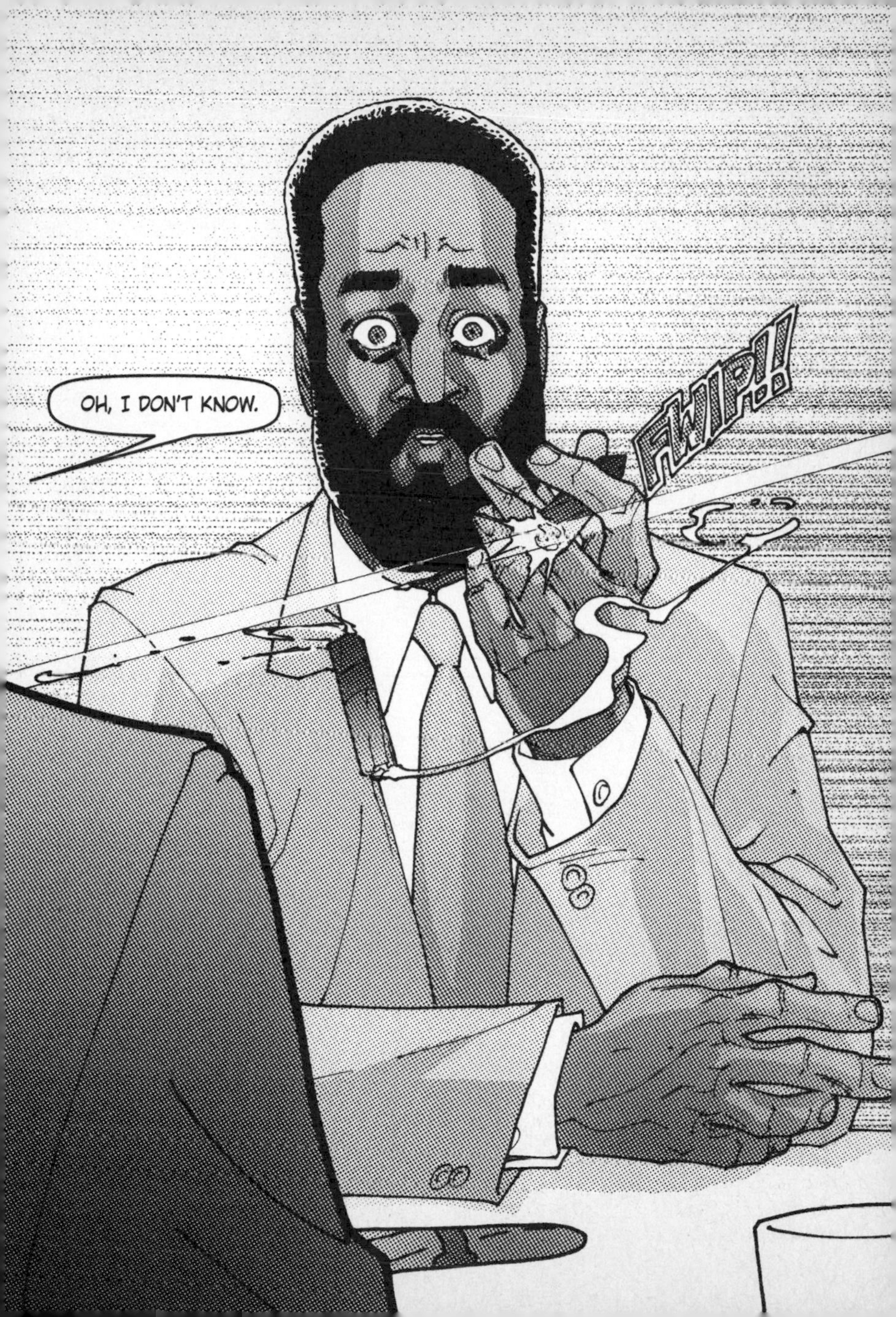
OH, I DON'T KNOW.
FWIP!!

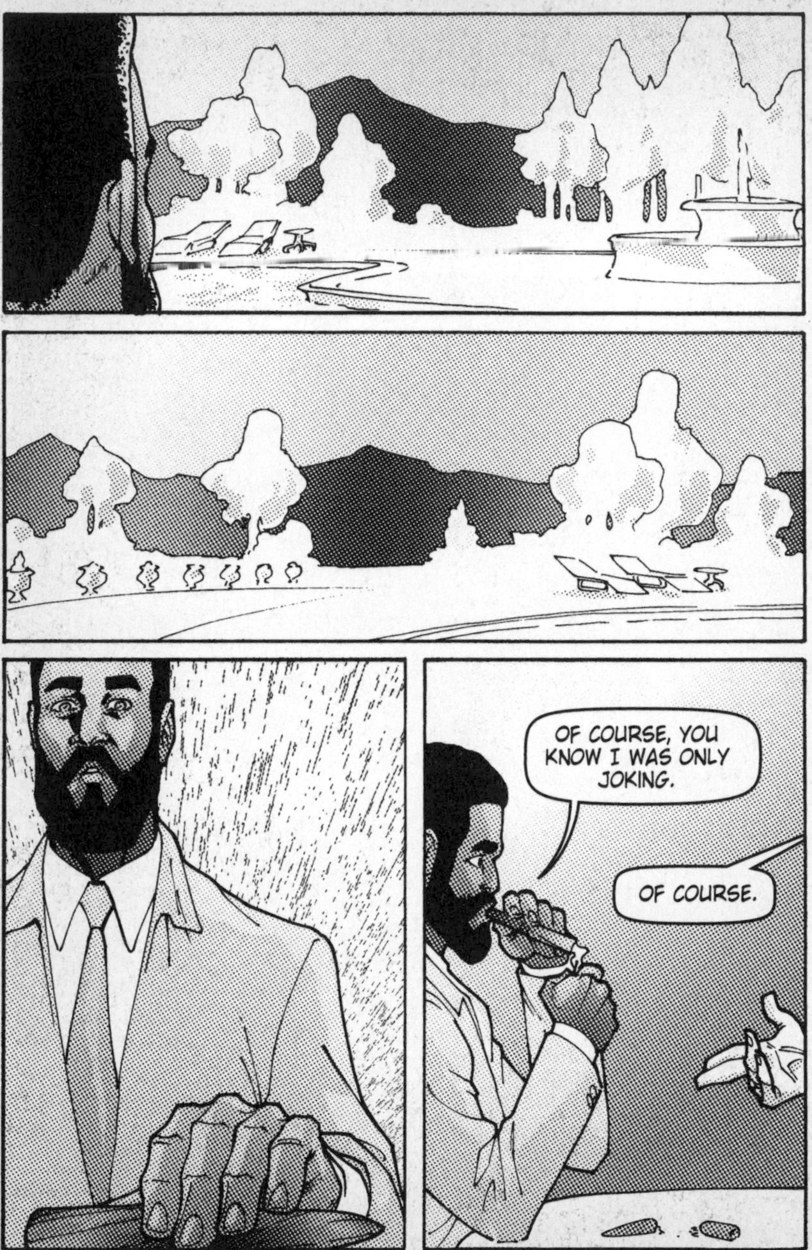
OF COURSE, YOU KNOW I WAS ONLY JOKING.
OF COURSE.

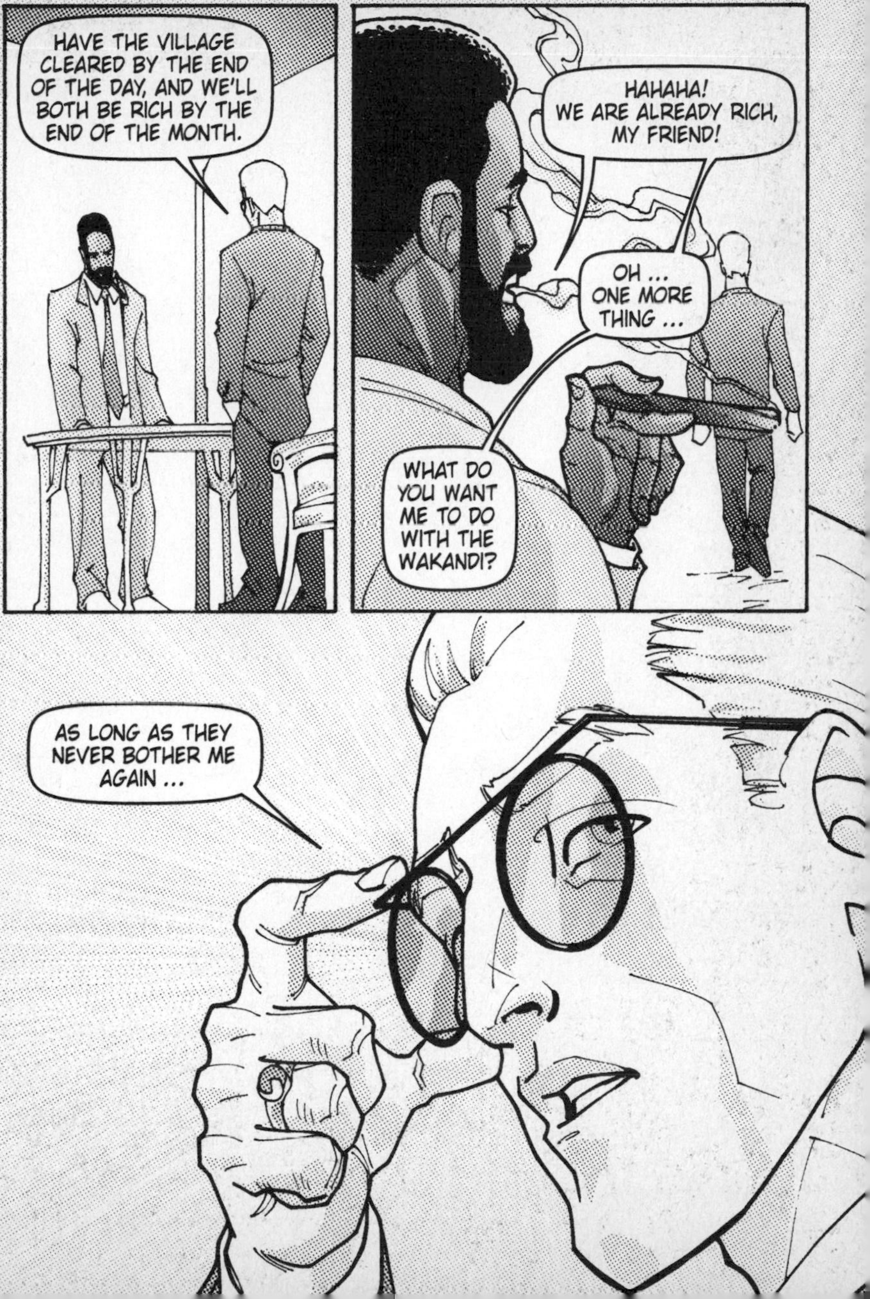
HAVE THE VILLAGE CLEARED BY THE END OF THE DAY, AND WE'LL BOTH BE RICH BY THE END OF THE MONTH.
HAHAHA! WE ARE ALREADY RICH, MY FRIEND!
OH ... ONE MORE THING ...
WHAT DO YOU WANT ME TO DO WITH THE WAKANDI?
AS LONG AS THEY NEVER BOTHER ME AGAIN ...

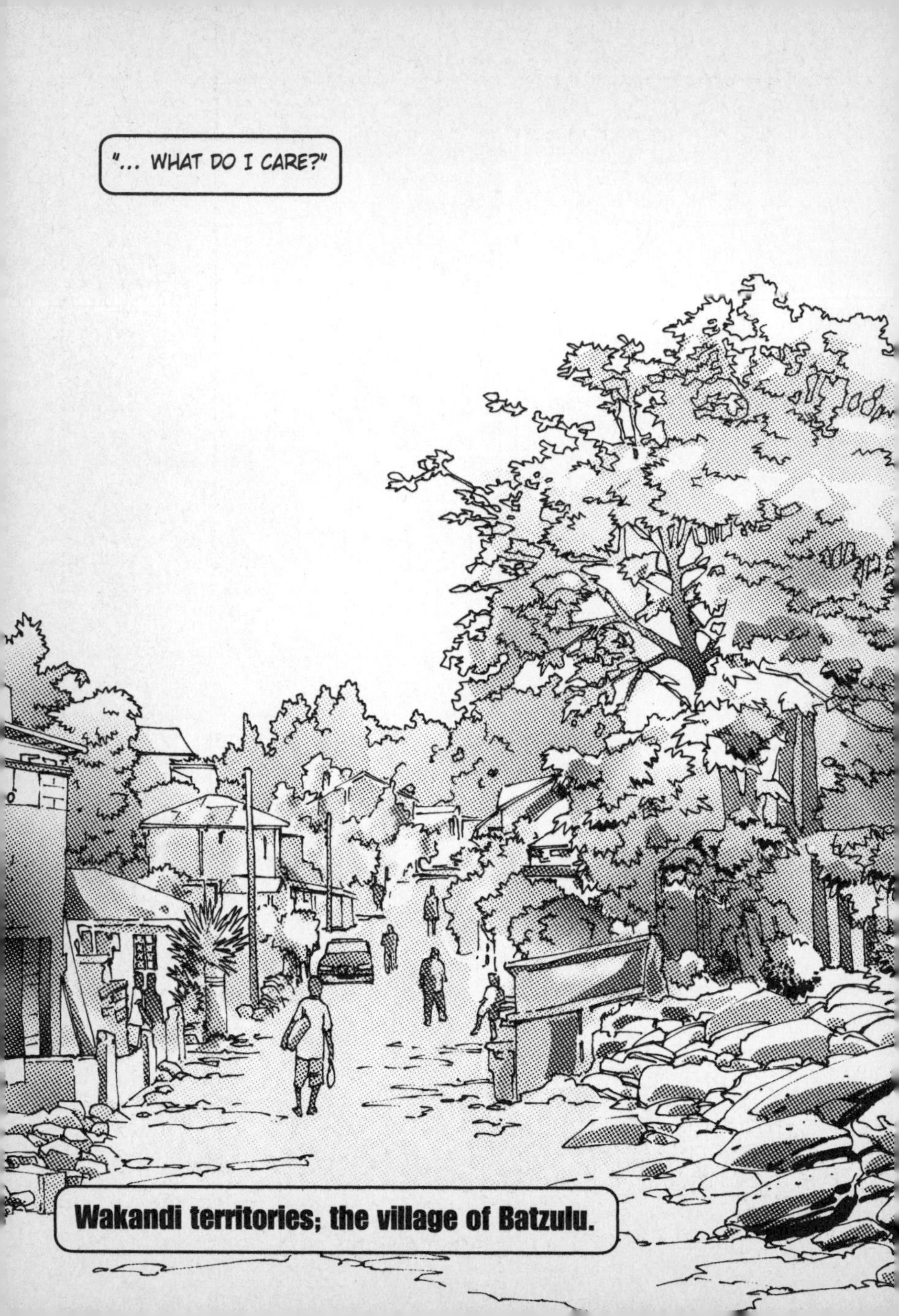
"... WHAT DO I CARE?"
Wakandi territories; the village of Batzulu.

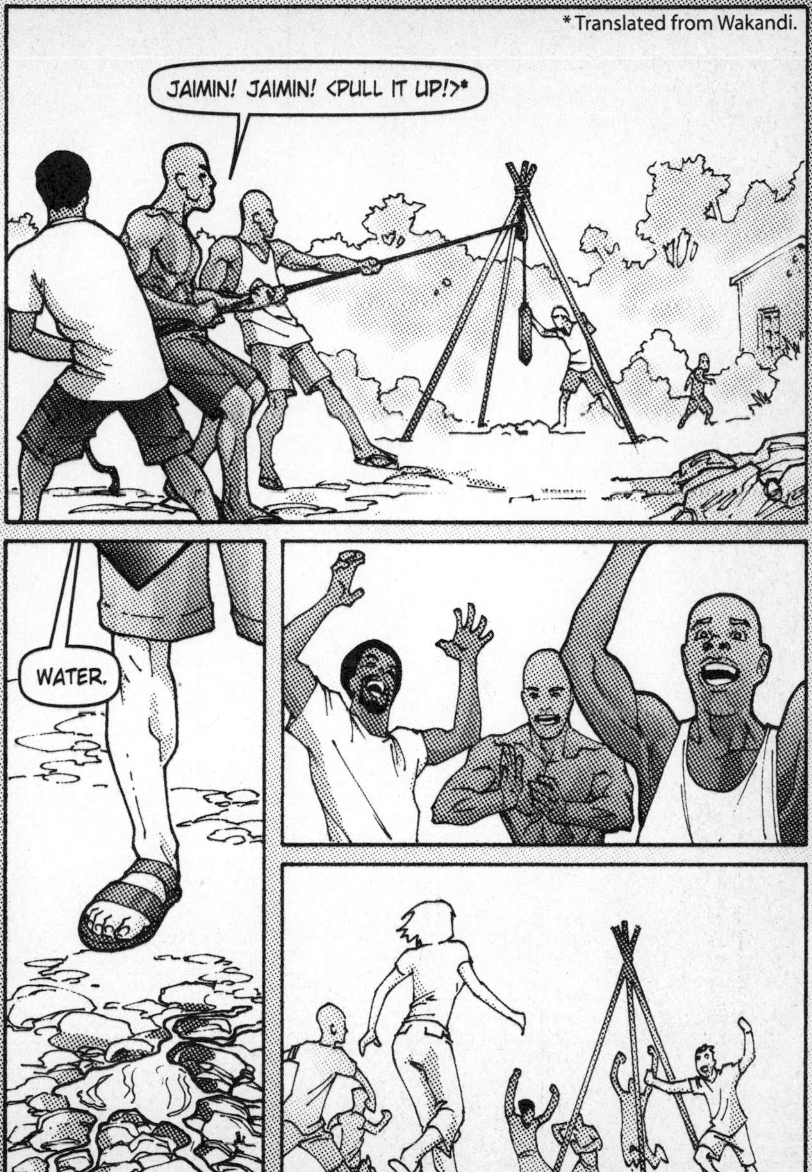
* Translated from Wakandi.
JAIMIN! JAIMIN! <PULL IT UP!>*
WATER.

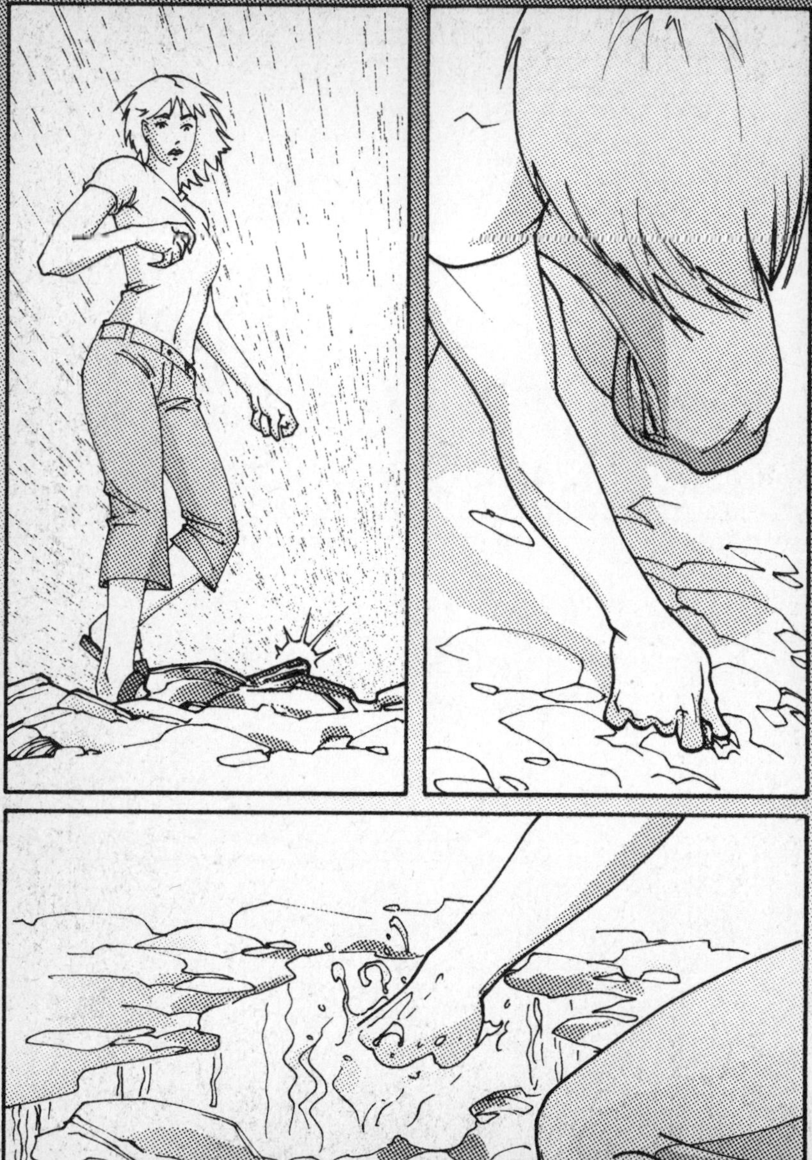

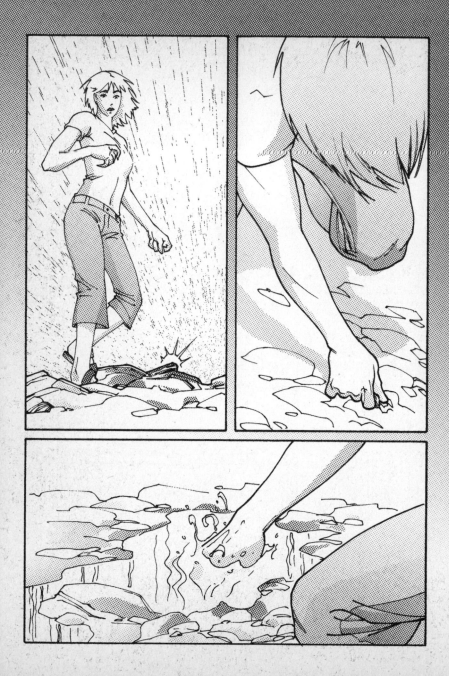

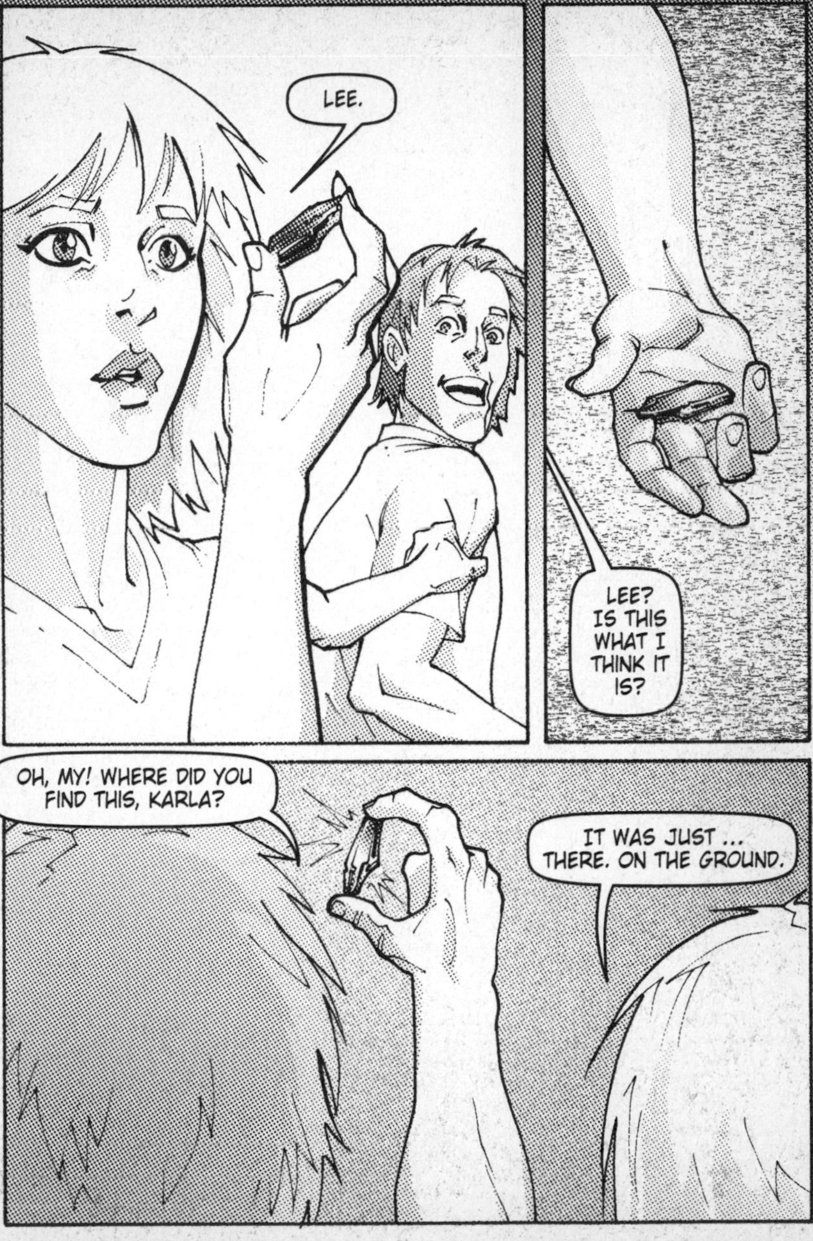
LEE.
LEE? IS THIS WHAT I THINK IT IS?
OH, MY! WHERE DID YOU FIND THIS, KARLA?
IT WAS JUST ... THERE. ON THE GROUND.

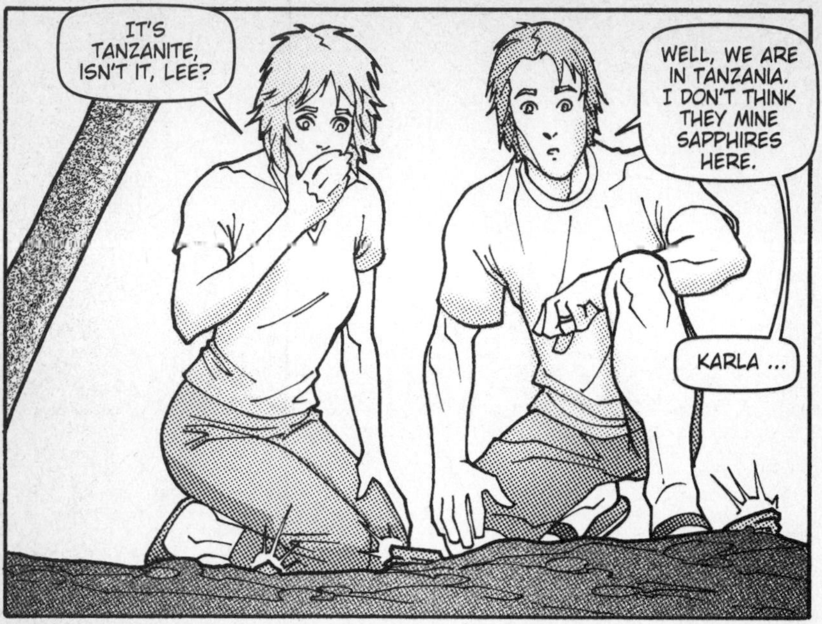
IT'S TANZANITE, ISN'T IT, LEE?
WELL, WE ARE IN TANZANIA. I DON'T THINK THEY MINE SAPPHIRES HERE.
KARLA ...

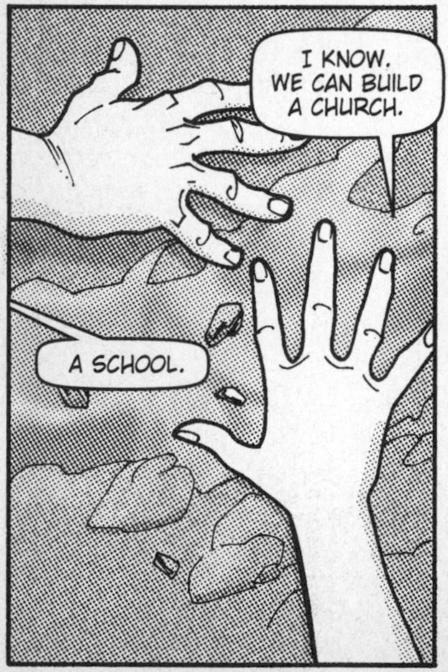
I KNOW. WE CAN BUILD A CHURCH.
A SCHOOL.

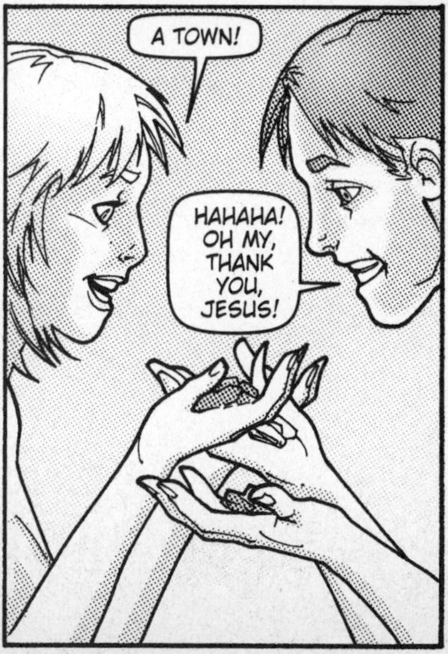
A TOWN!
HAHAHA! OH MY, THANK YOU, JESUS!

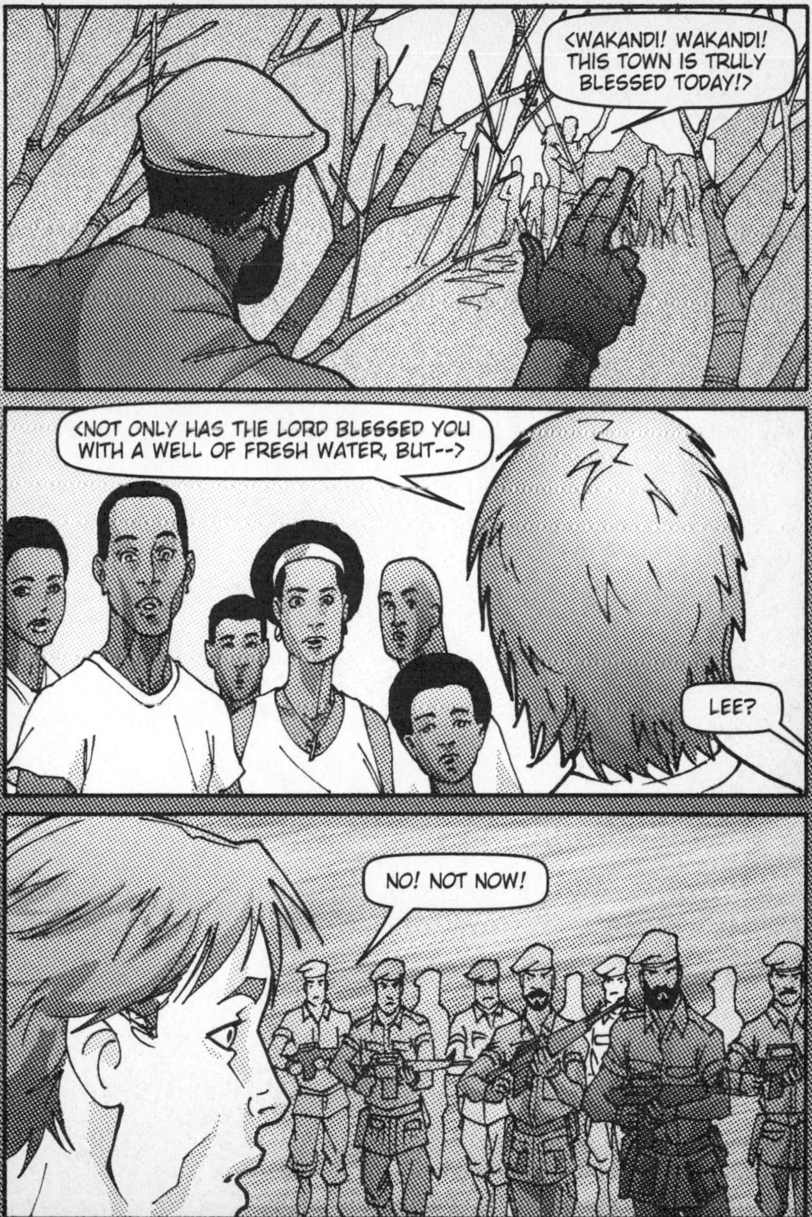
<WAKANDI! WAKANDI! THIS TOWN IS TRULY BLESSED TODAY!>
<NOT ONLY HAS THE LORD BLESSED YOU WITH A WELL OF FRESH WATER, BUT-->
LEE?
NO! NOT NOW!

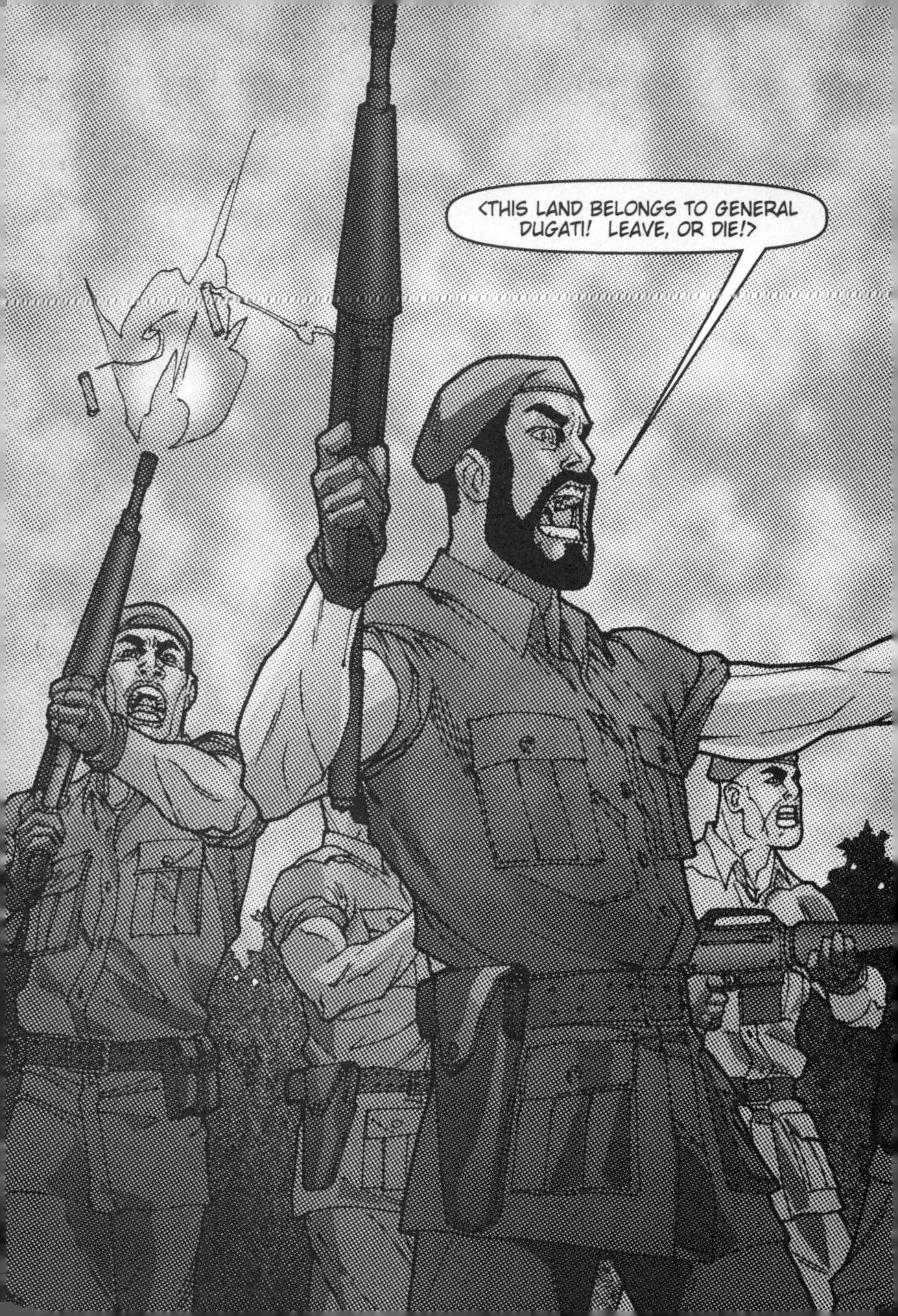
<THIS LAND BELONGS TO GENERAL DUGATI! LEAVE, OR DIE!>

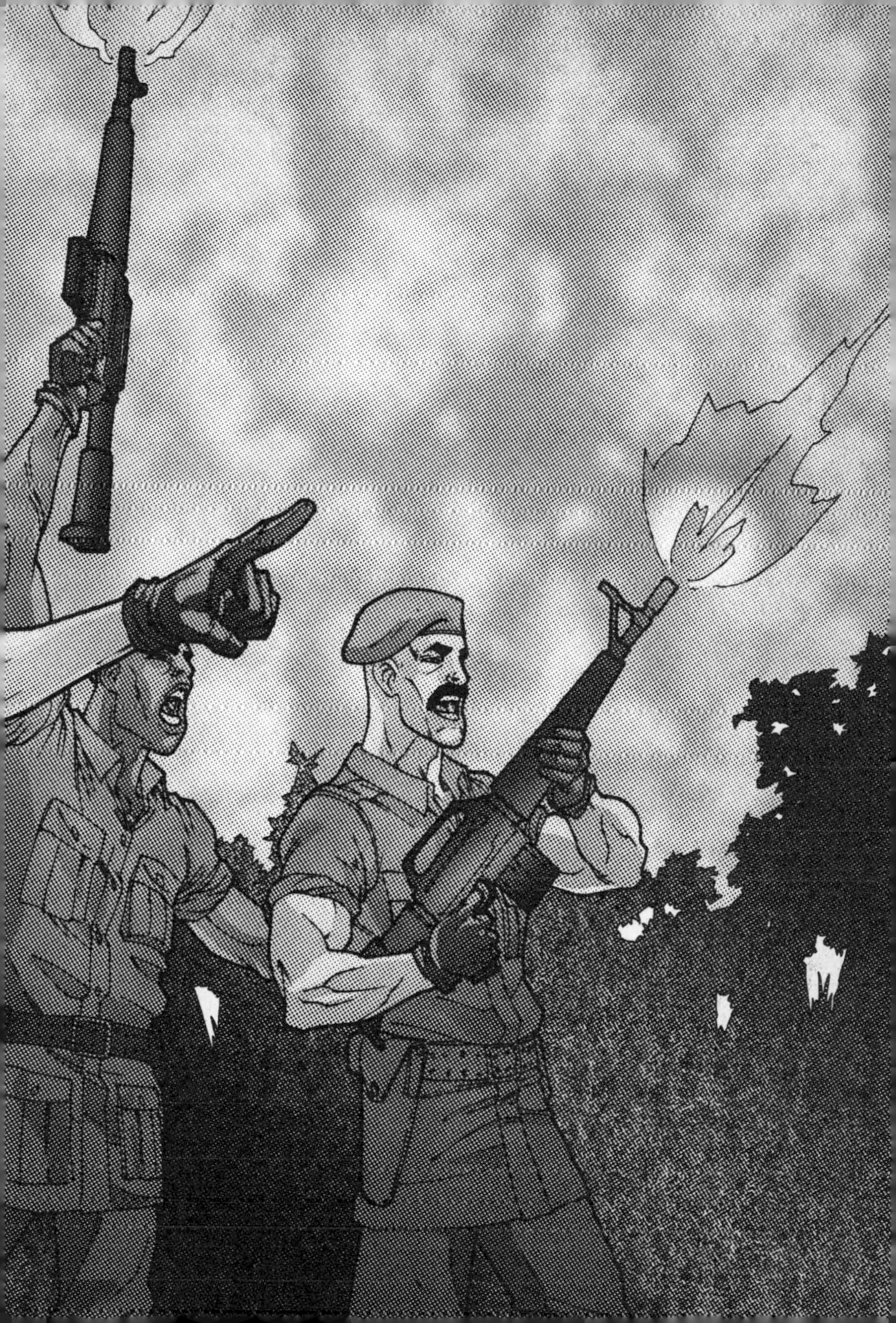

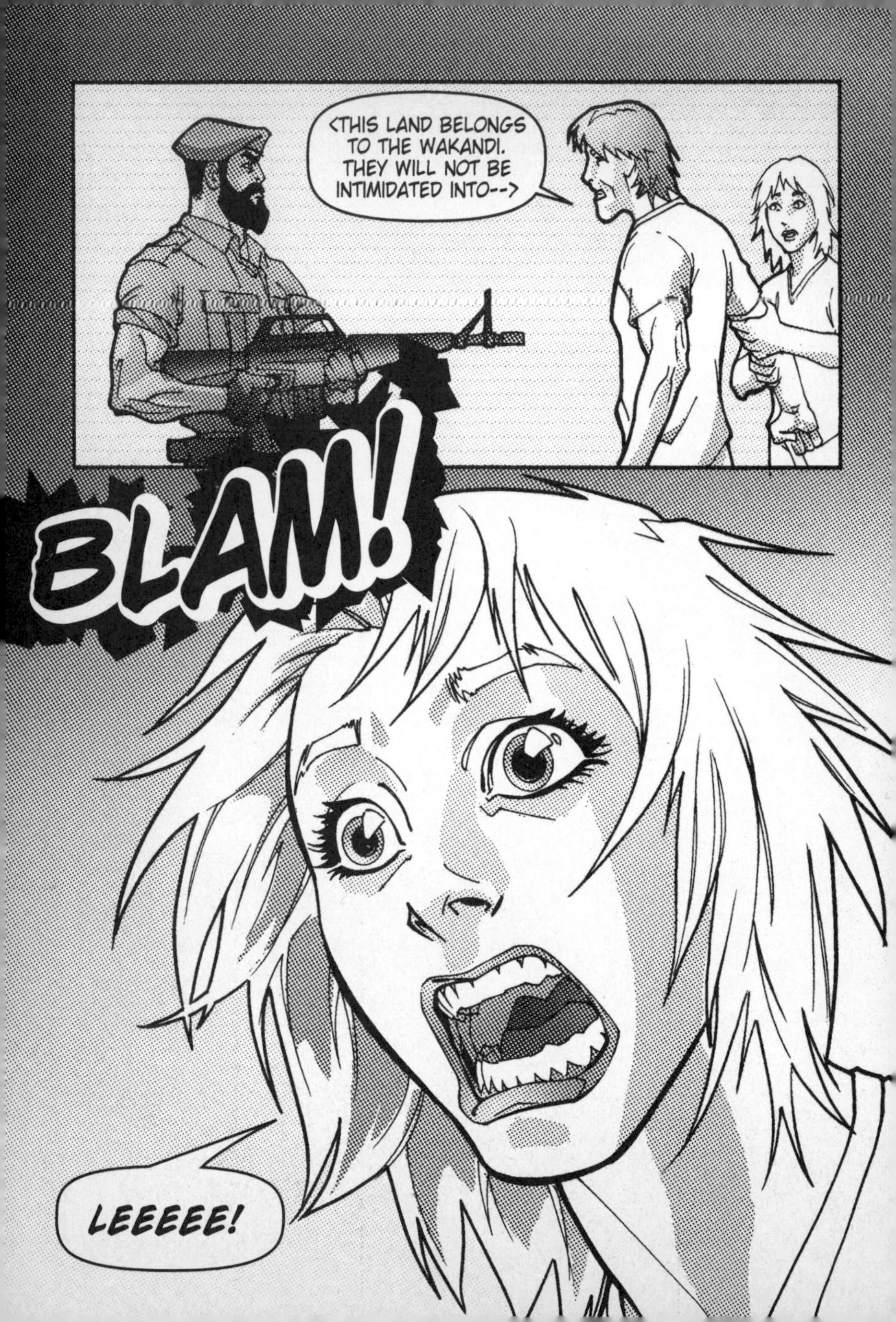
<THIS LAND BELONGS TO THE WAKANDI. THEY WILL NOT BE INTIMIDATED INTO-->
BLAM!
LEEEEE!

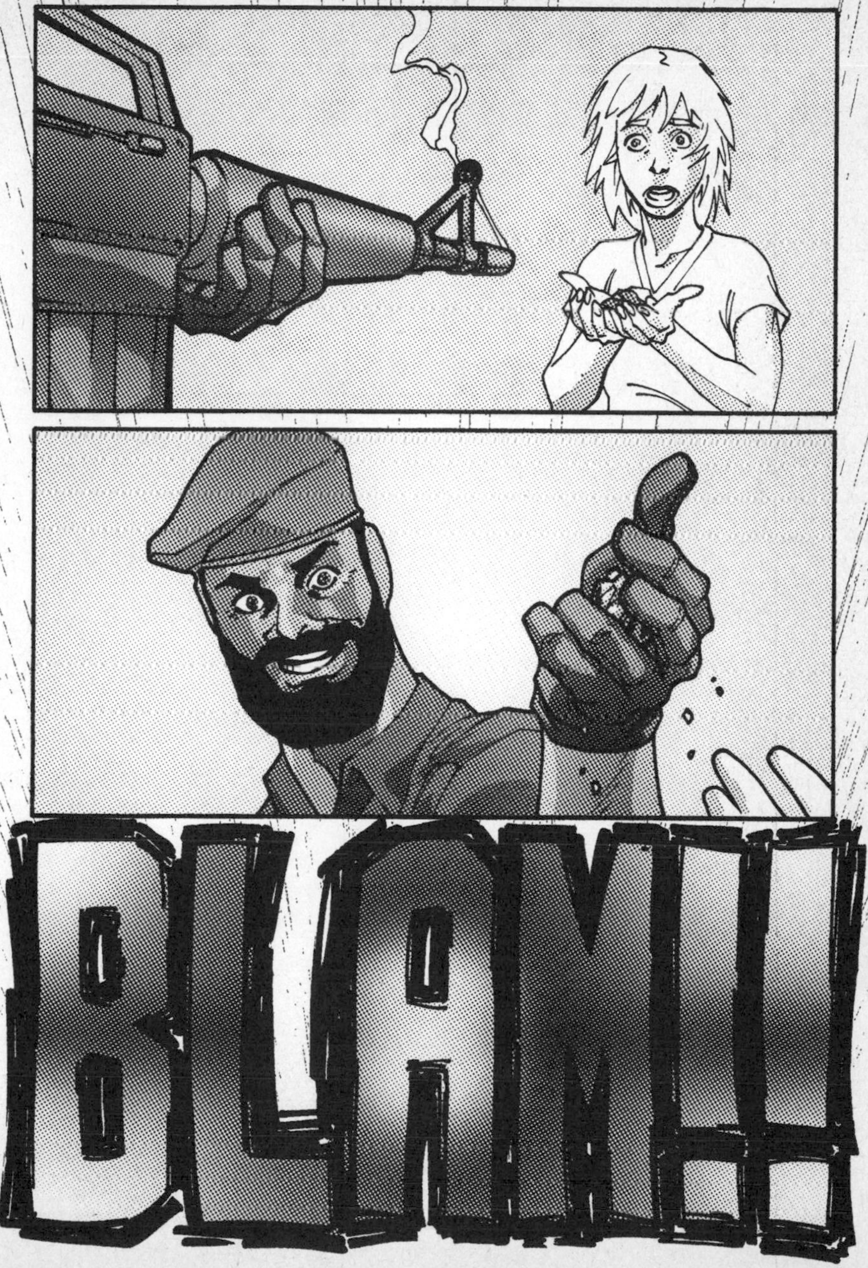
BLAM!!

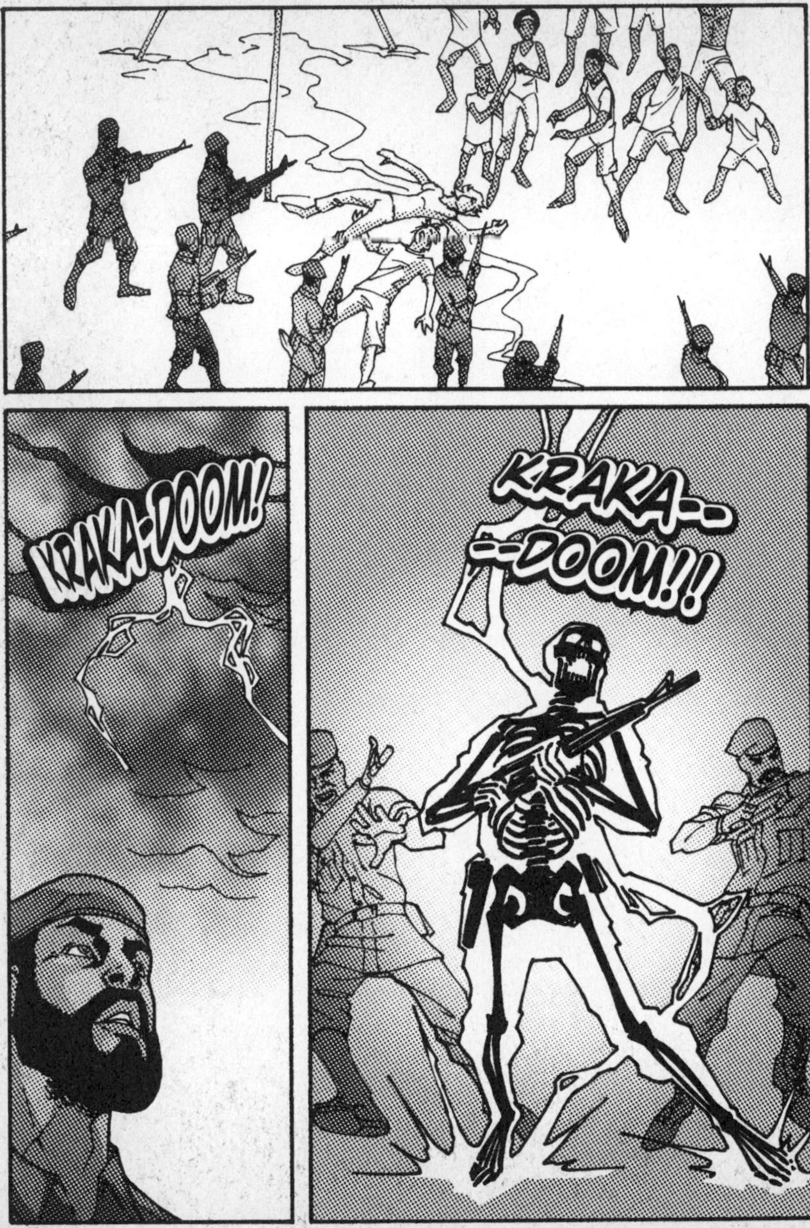
KRAKA-DOOM!
KRAKA--
--DOOM!!!

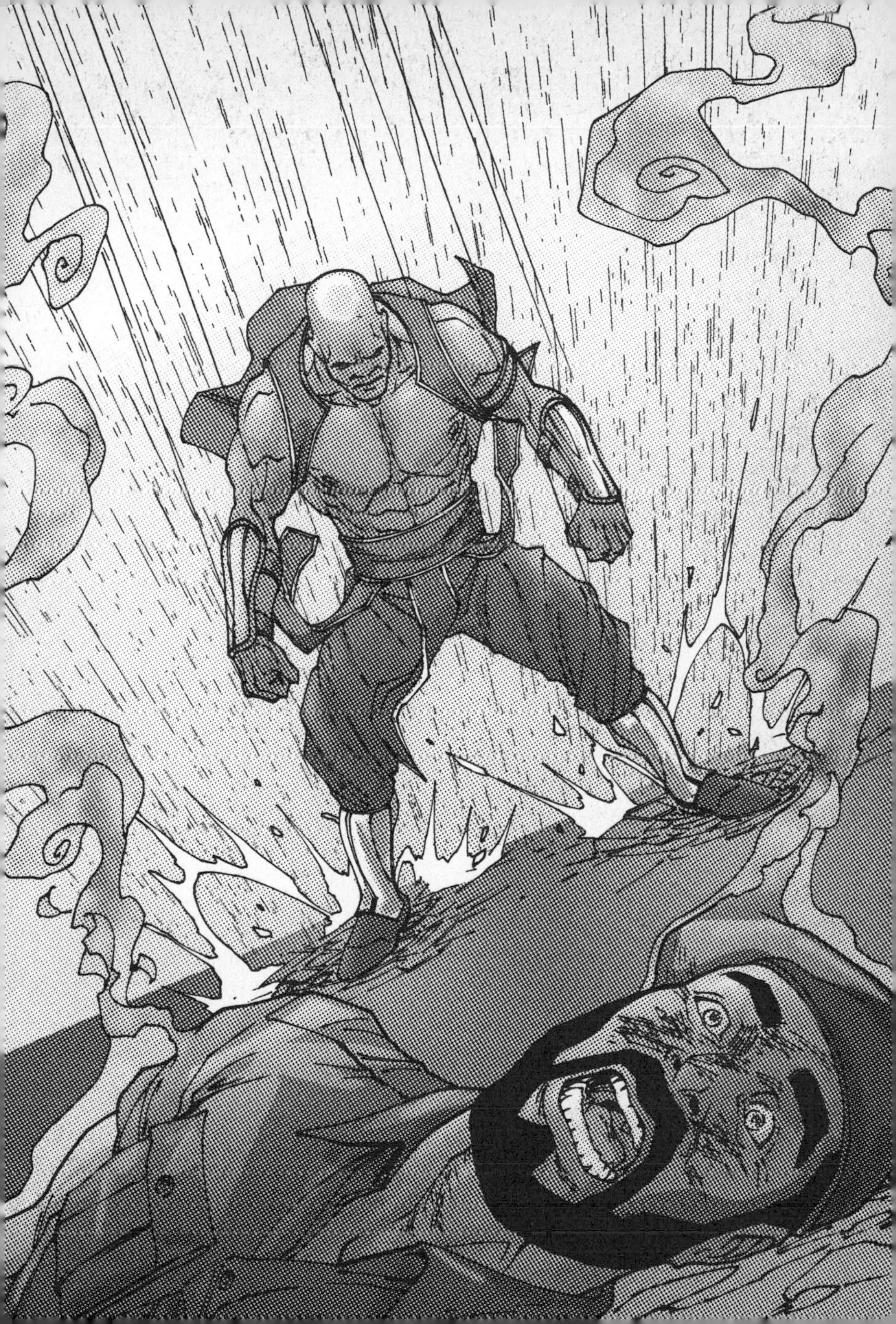

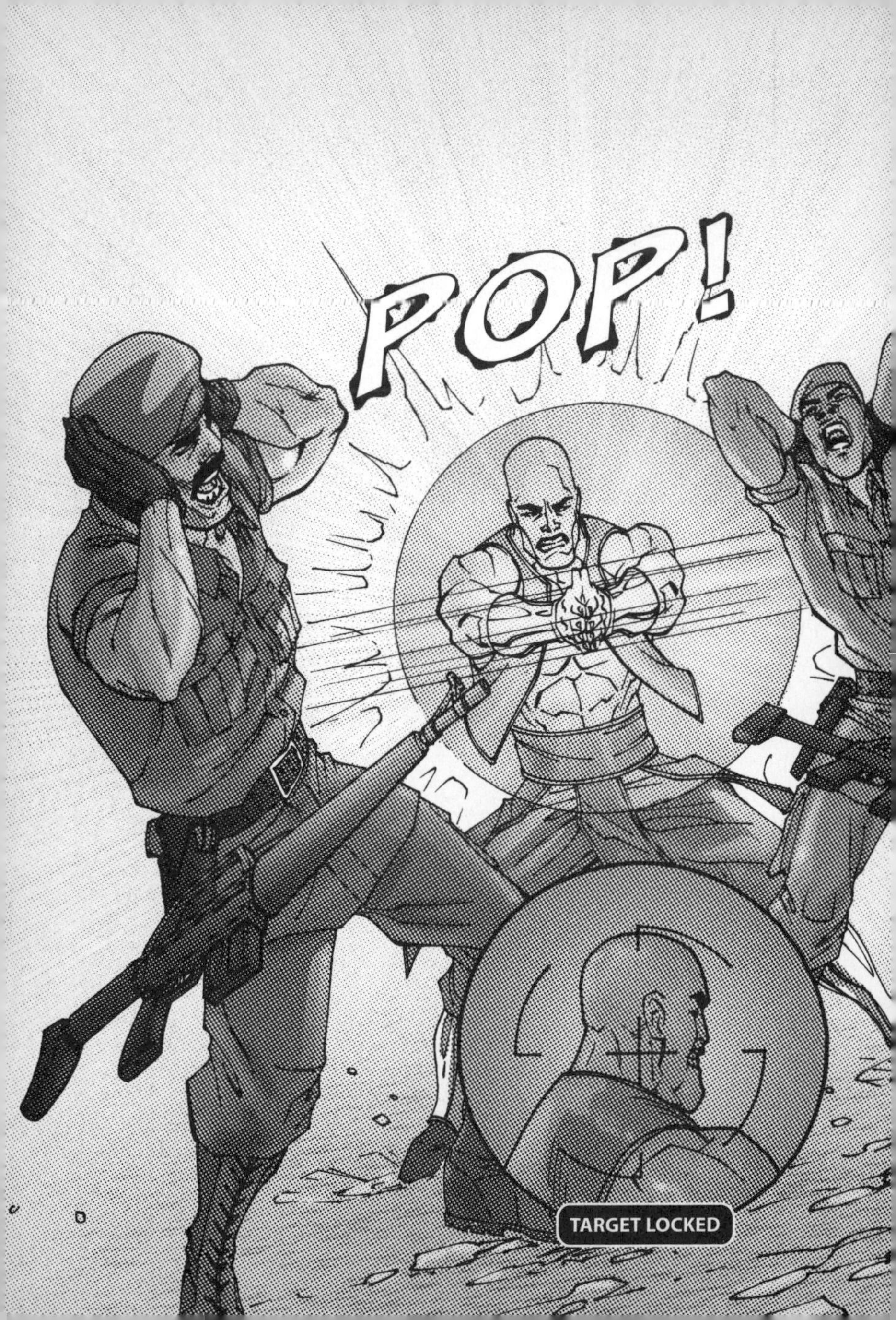
POP!
TARGET LOCKED

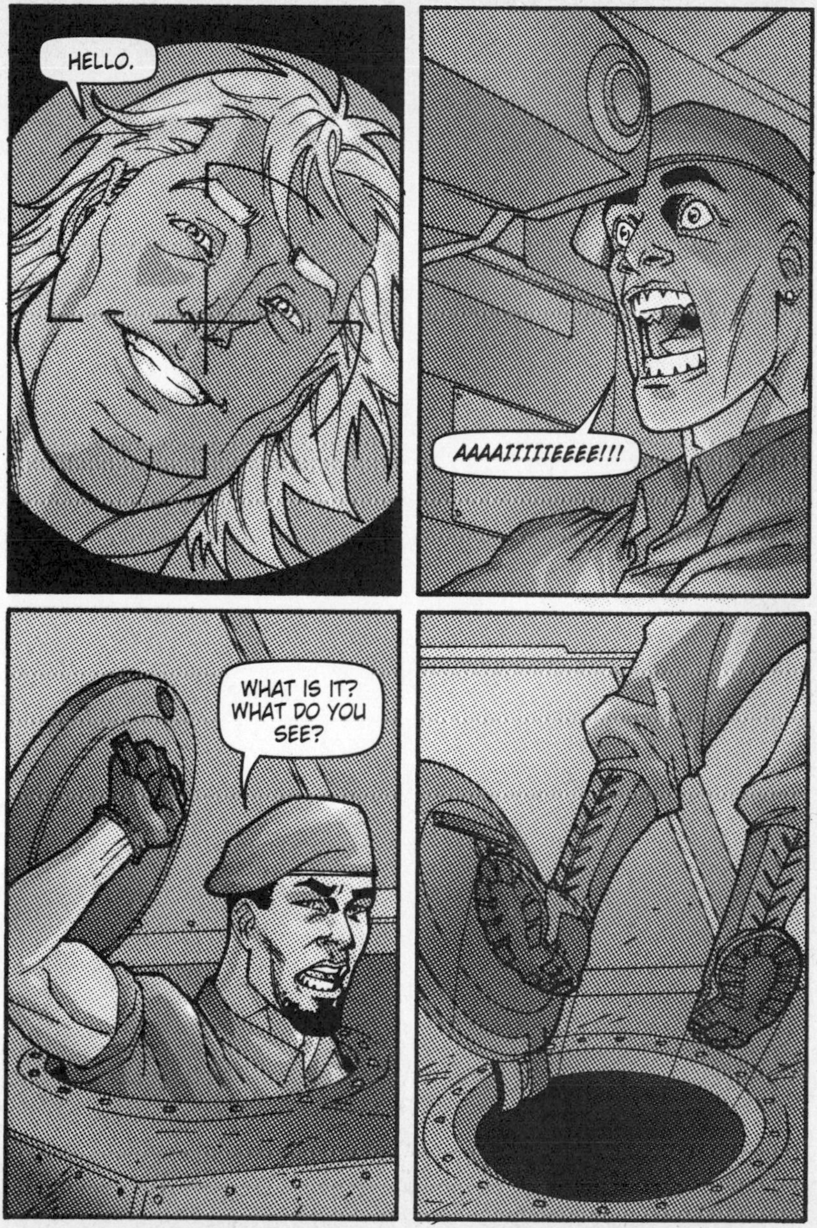
HELLO.
AAAAIIIIIEEEE!!!
WHAT IS IT? WHAT DO YOU SEE?

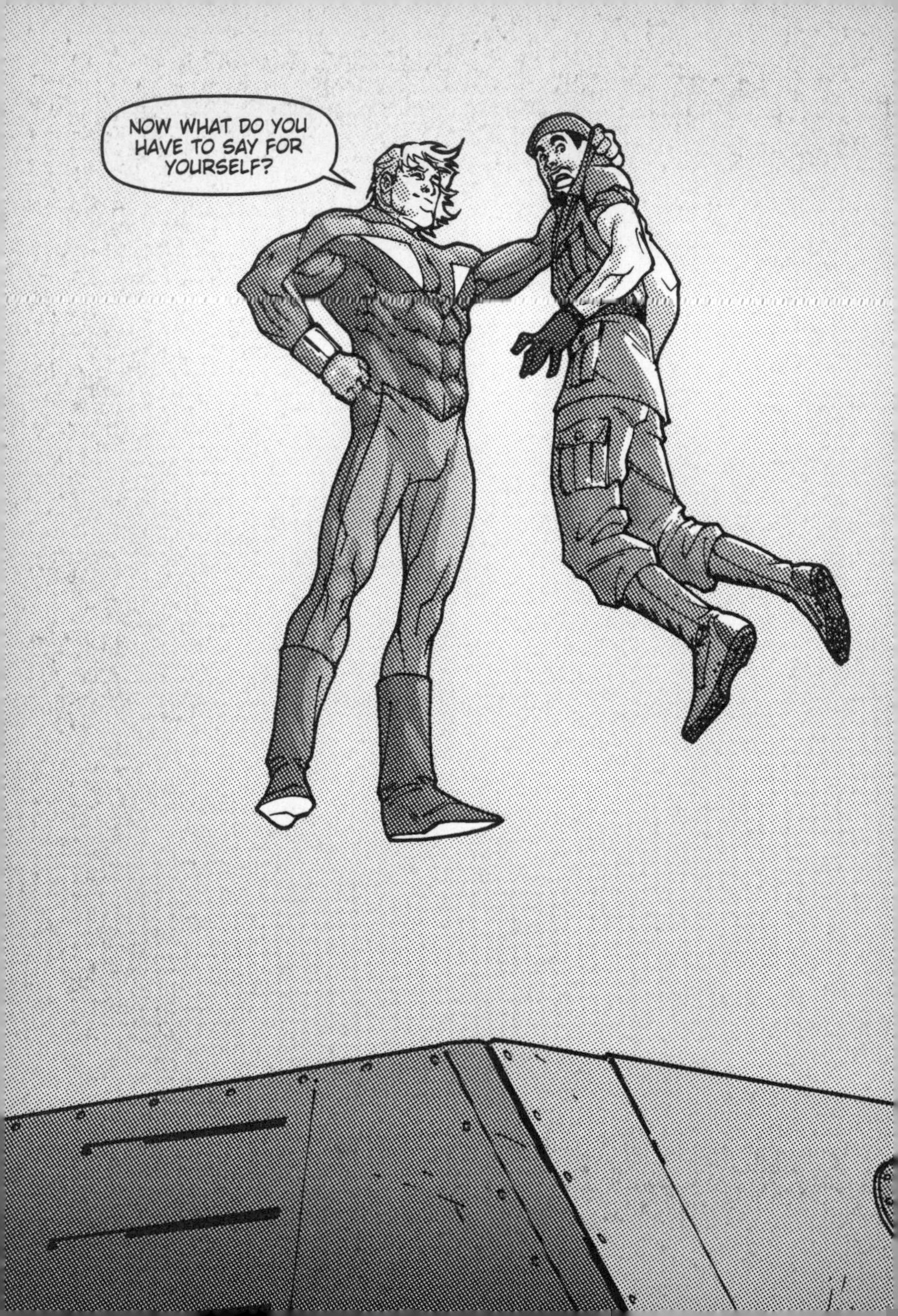
NOW WHAT DO YOU HAVE TO SAY FOR YOURSELF?

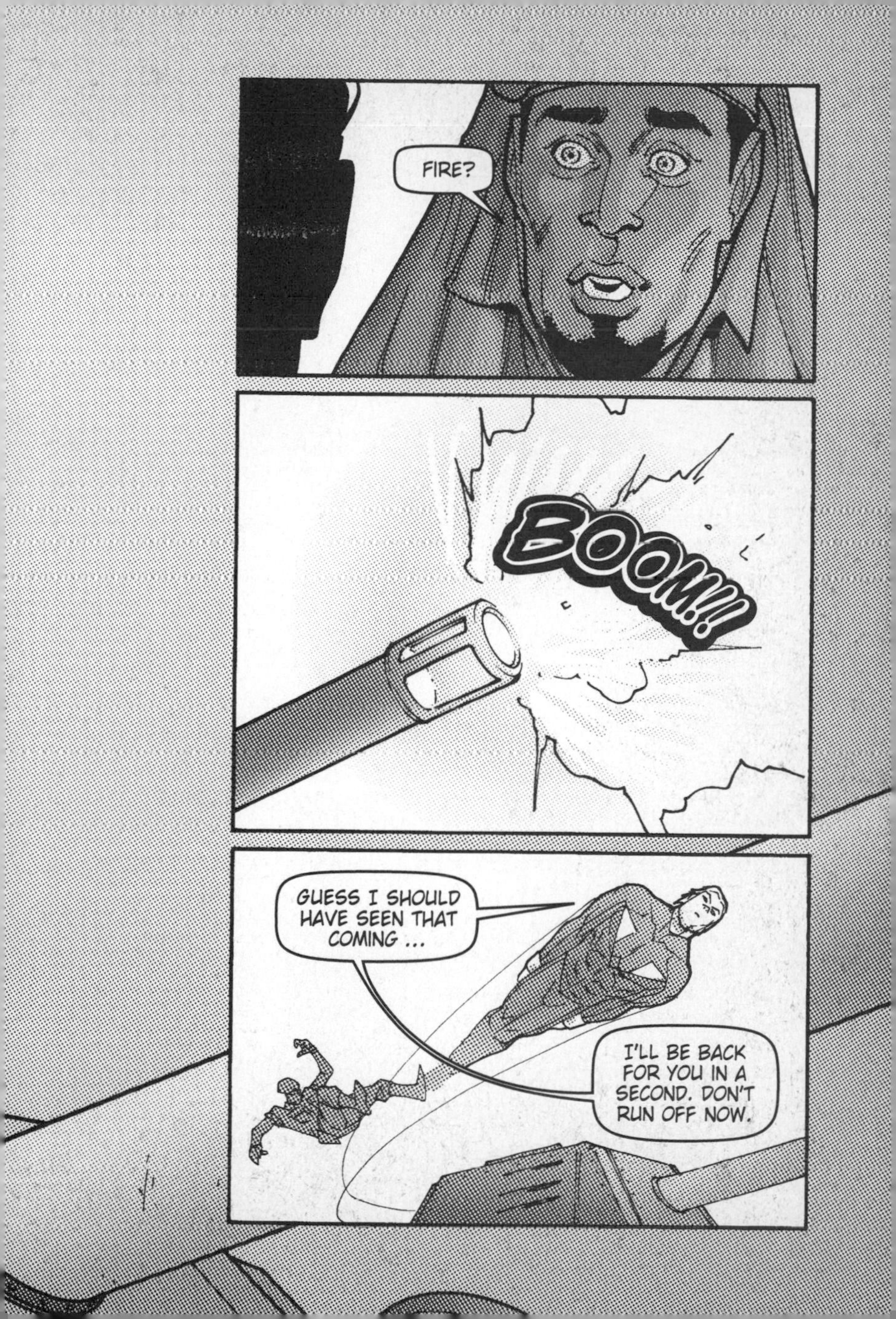
FIRE?
BOOM!!!
GUESS I SHOULD HAVE SEEN THAT COMING ...
I'LL BE BACK FOR YOU IN A SECOND. DON'T RUN OFF NOW.

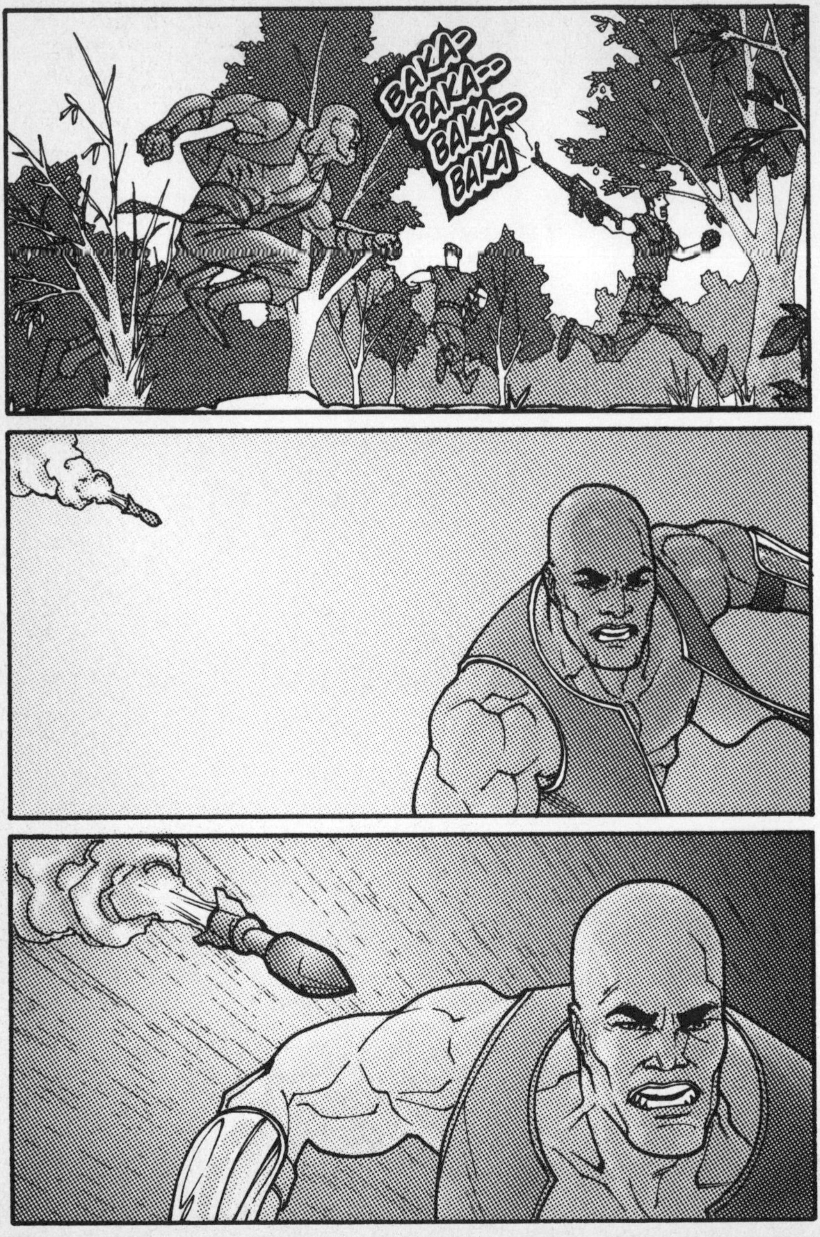
BAKA-
BAKA--
BAKA--
BAKA

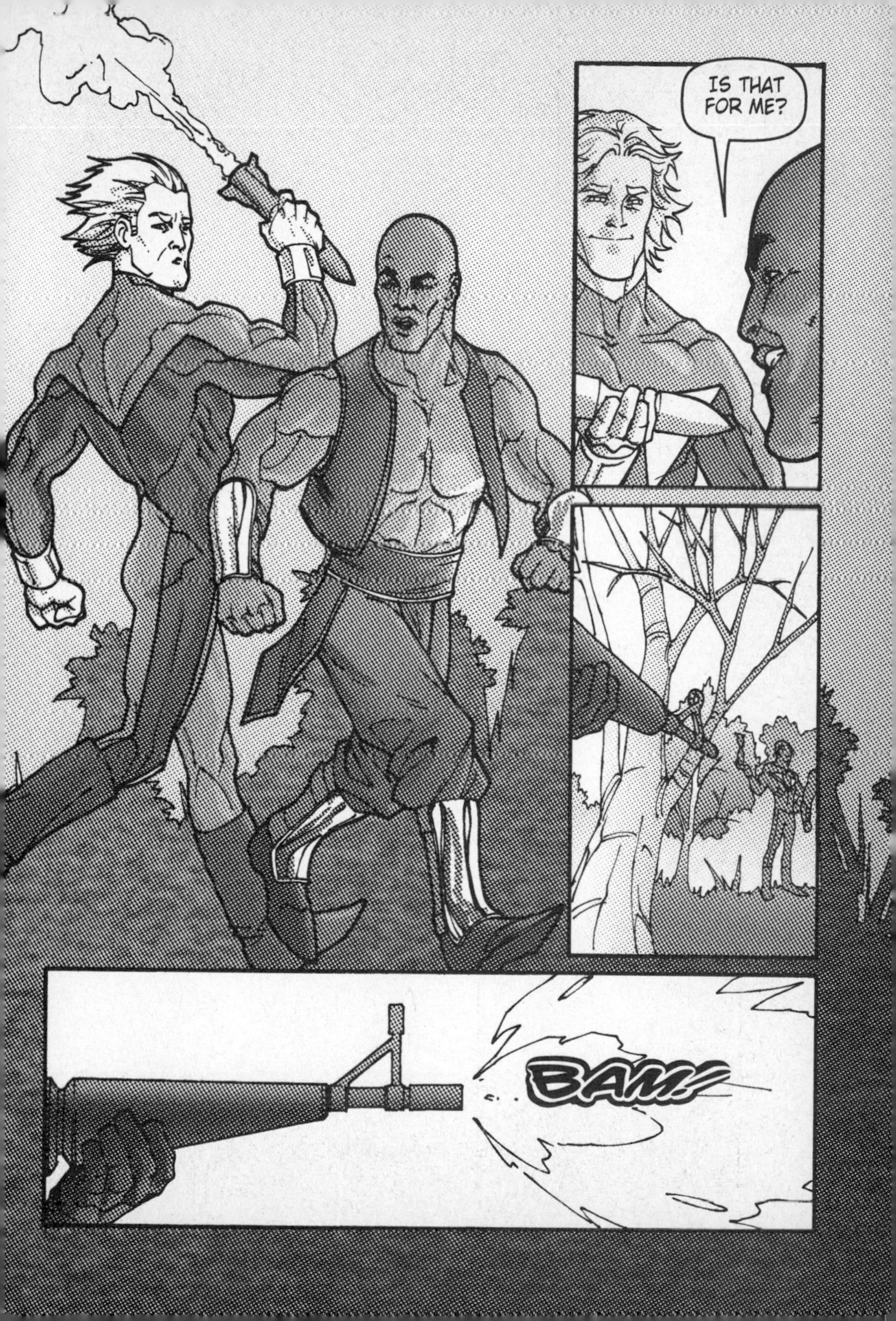
IS THAT FOR ME?
BAM!

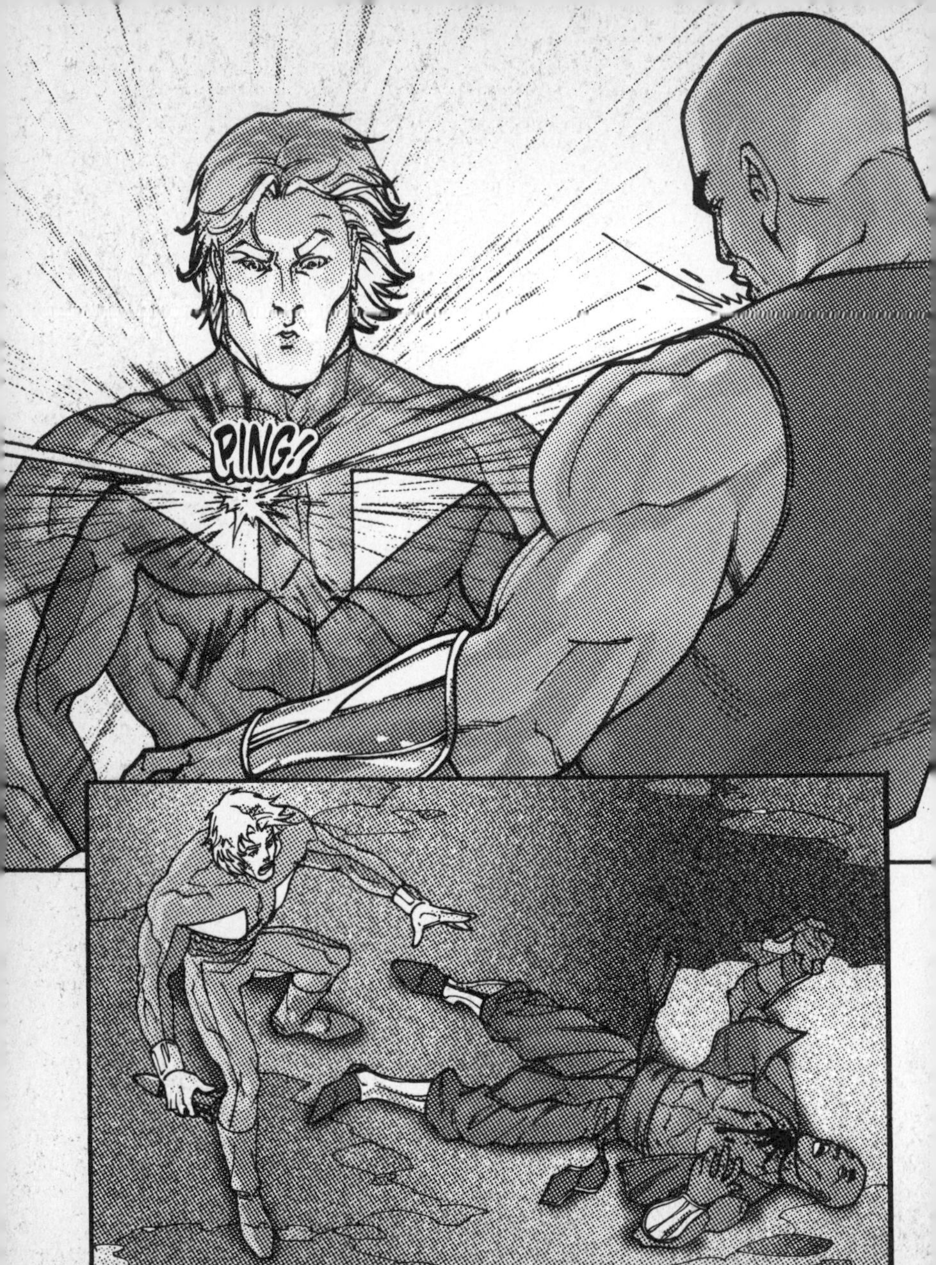
PING!

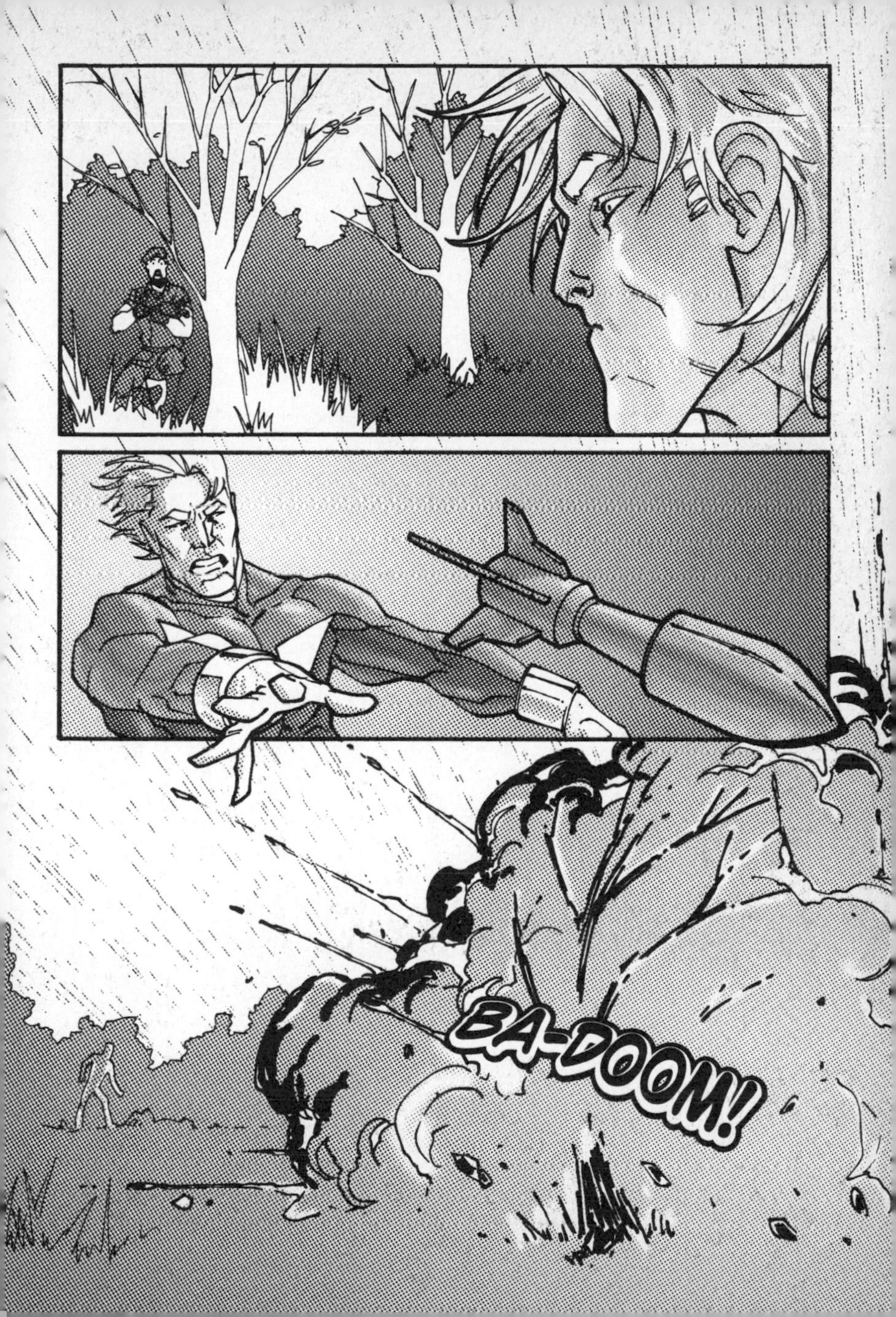
BA-DOOM!

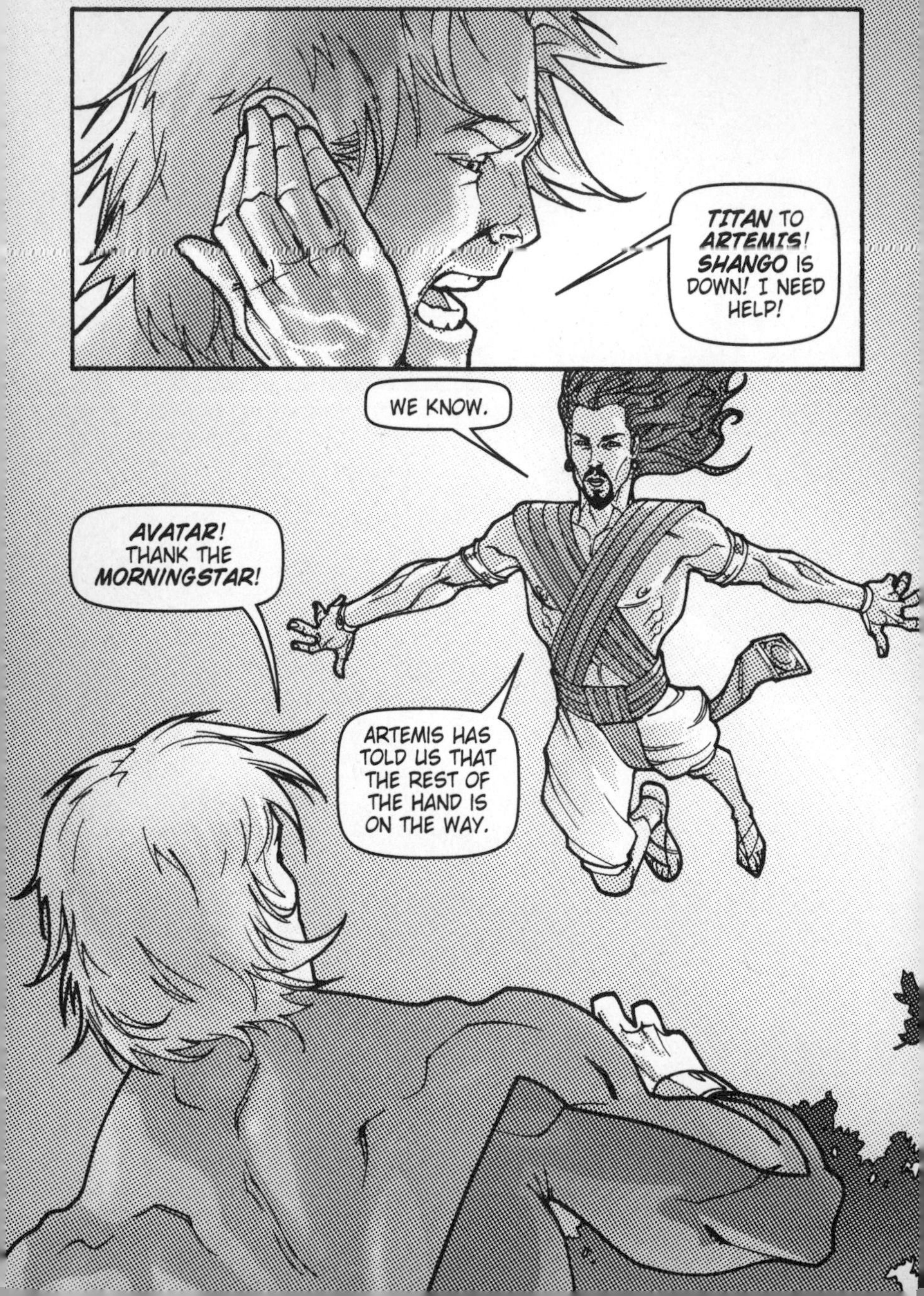
TITAN TO ARTEMIS! SHANGO IS DOWN! I NEED HELP!
WE KNOW.
AVATAR! THANK THE MORNINGSTAR!
ARTEMIS HAS TOLD US THAT THE REST OF THE HAND IS ON THE WAY.

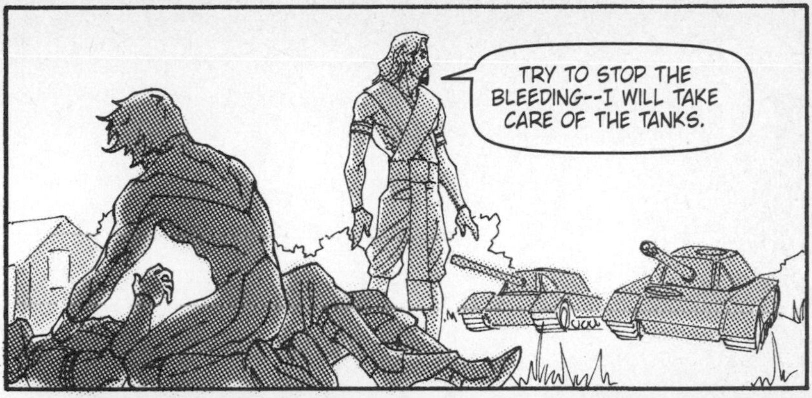
TRY TO STOP THE BLEEDING--I WILL TAKE CARE OF THE TANKS.
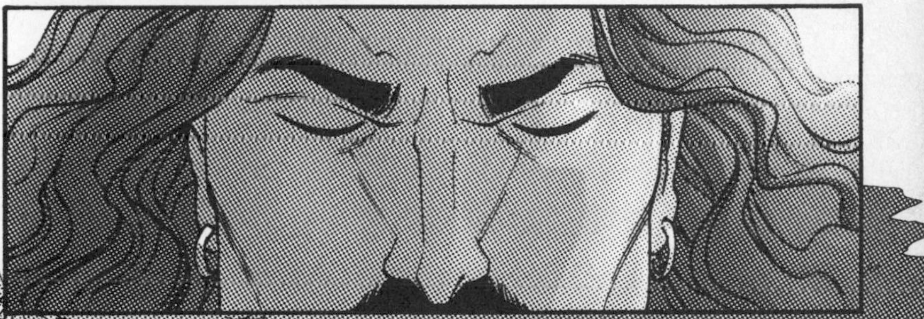
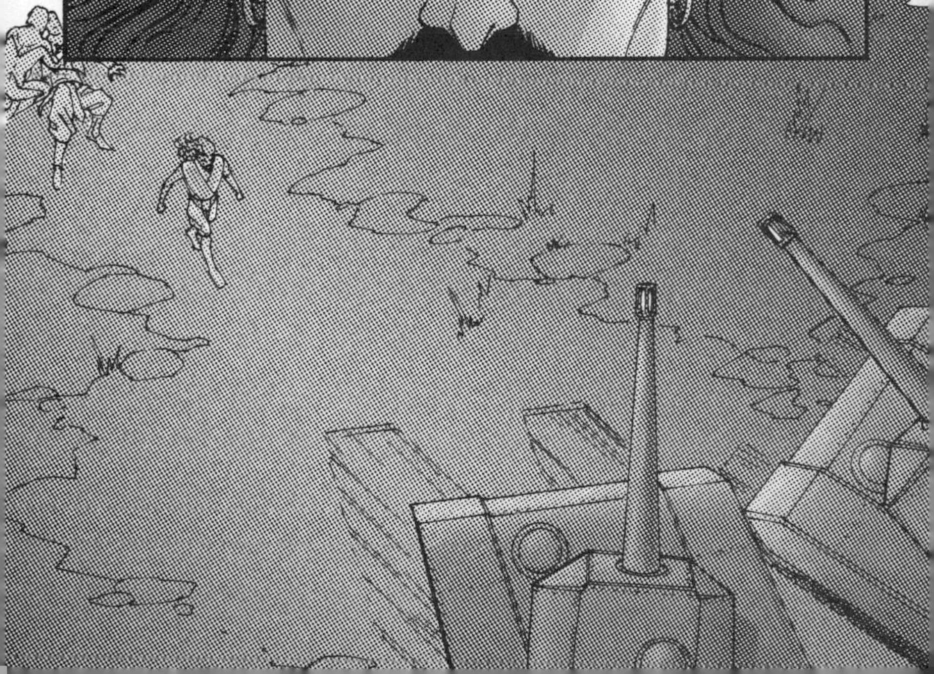

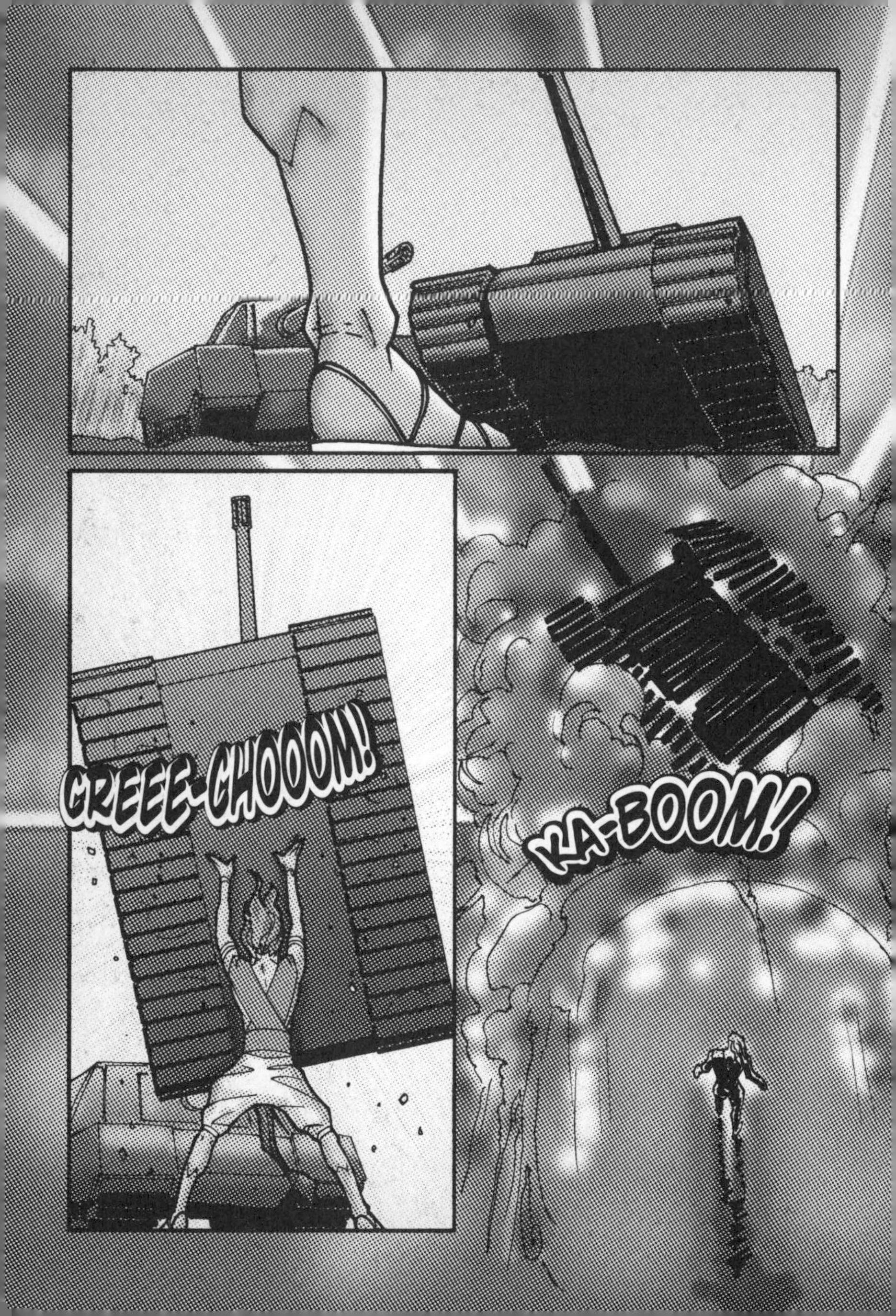
CREEE-CHOOOM!
KA-BOOM!

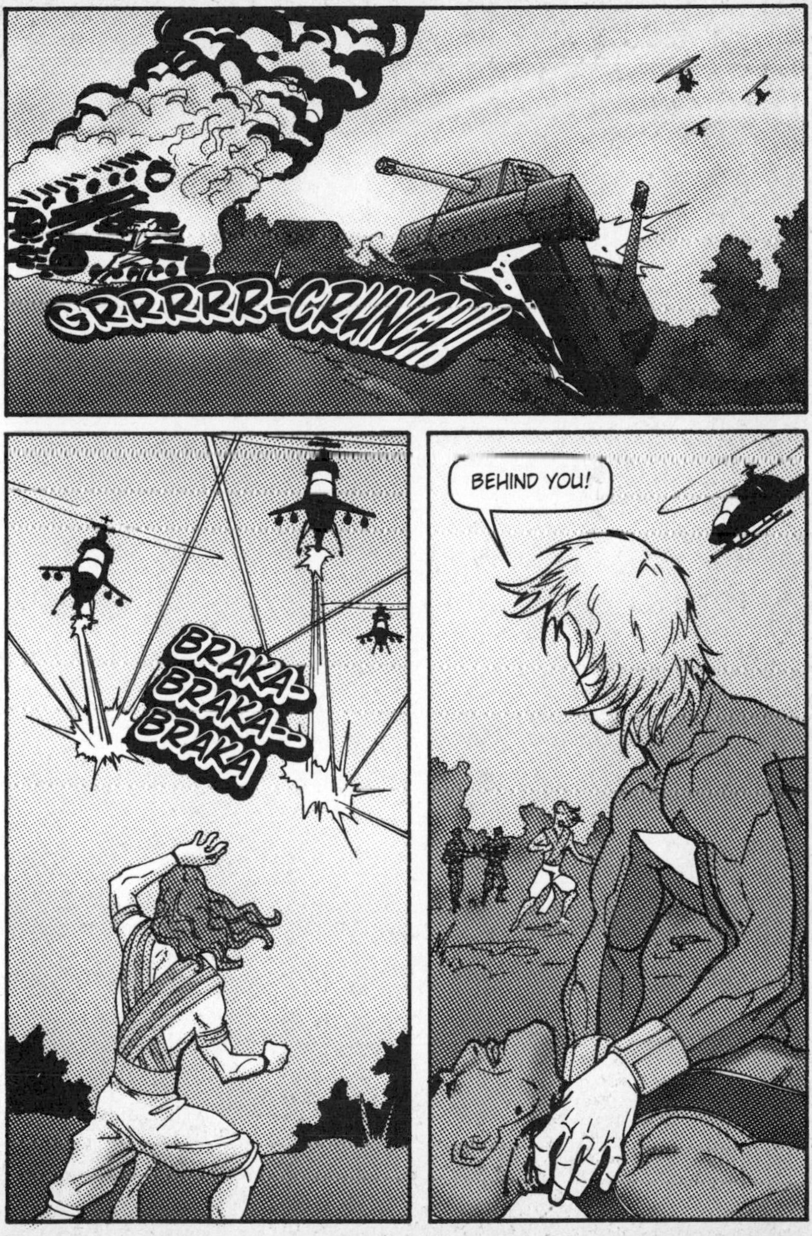
GRRRRR-CRUNCH!!
BRAKA-BRAKA--BRAKA
BEHIND YOU!

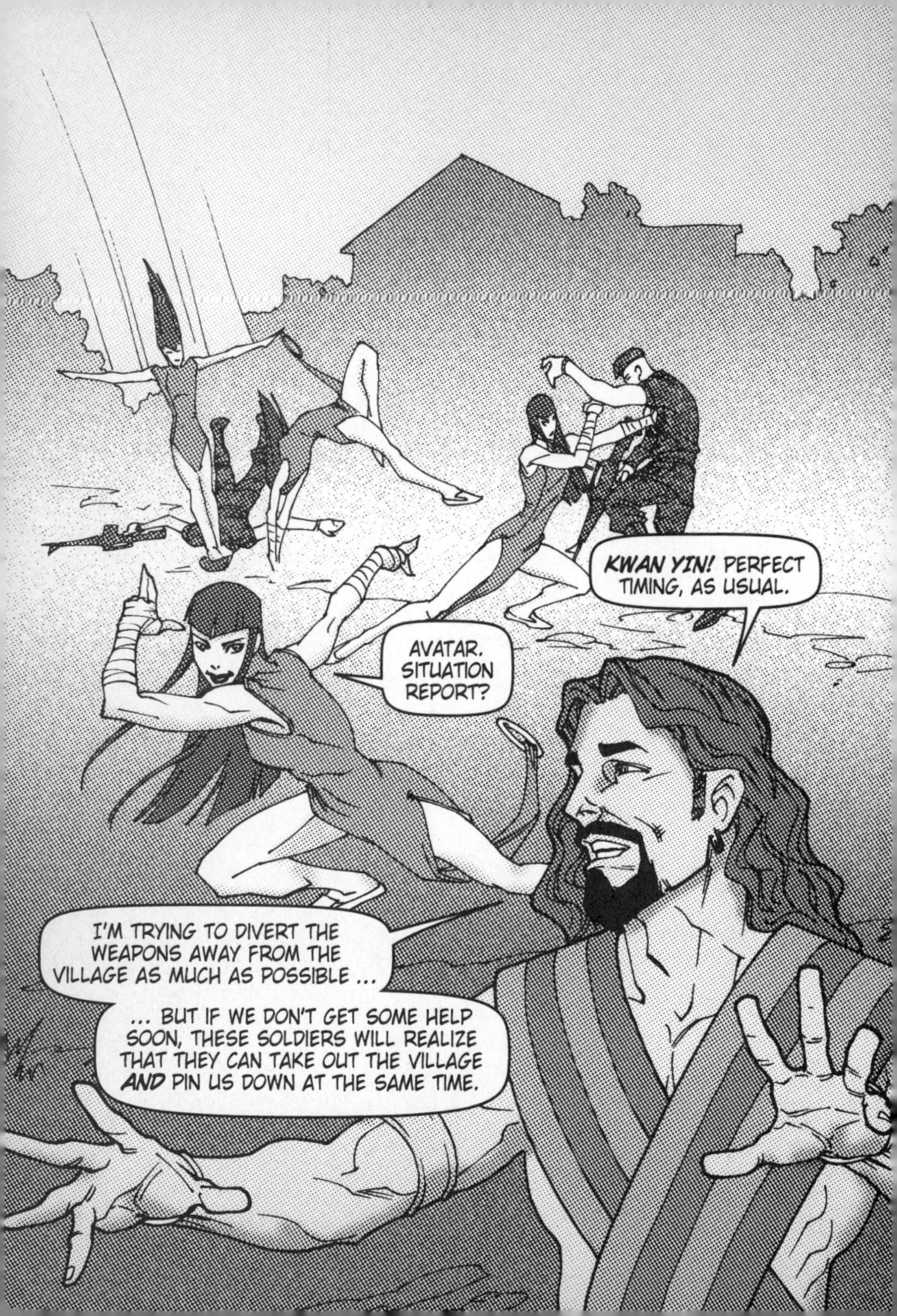
AVATAR. SITUATION REPORT?
KWAN YIN! PERFECT TIMING, AS USUAL.
I'M TRYING TO DIVERT THE WEAPONS AWAY FROM THE VILLAGE AS MUCH AS POSSIBLE ...
... BUT IF WE DON'T GET SOME HELP SOON, THESE SOLDIERS WILL REALIZE THAT THEY CAN TAKE OUT THE VILLAGE AND PIN US DOWN AT THE SAME TIME.

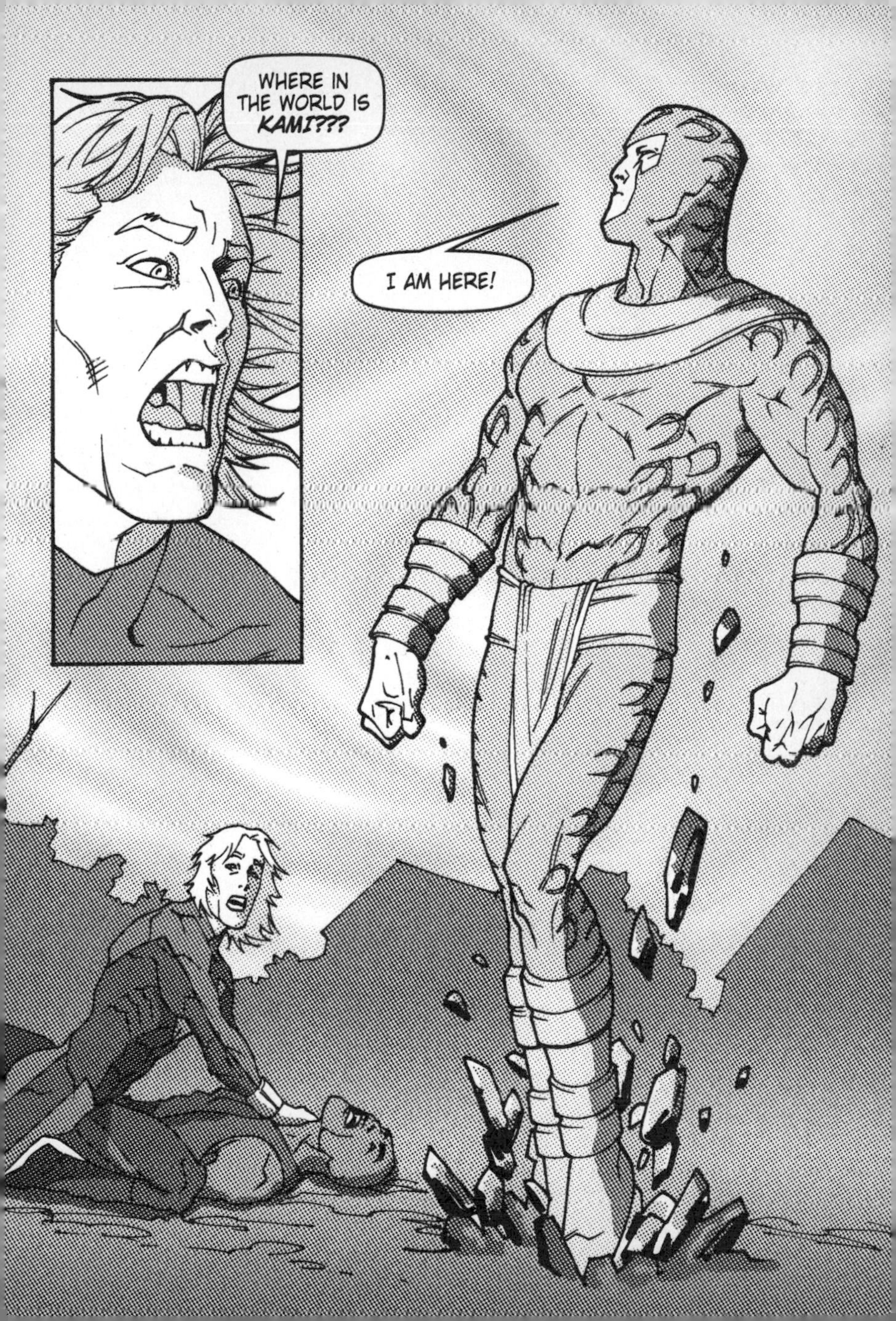
WHERE IN THE WORLD IS KAMI???
I AM HERE!

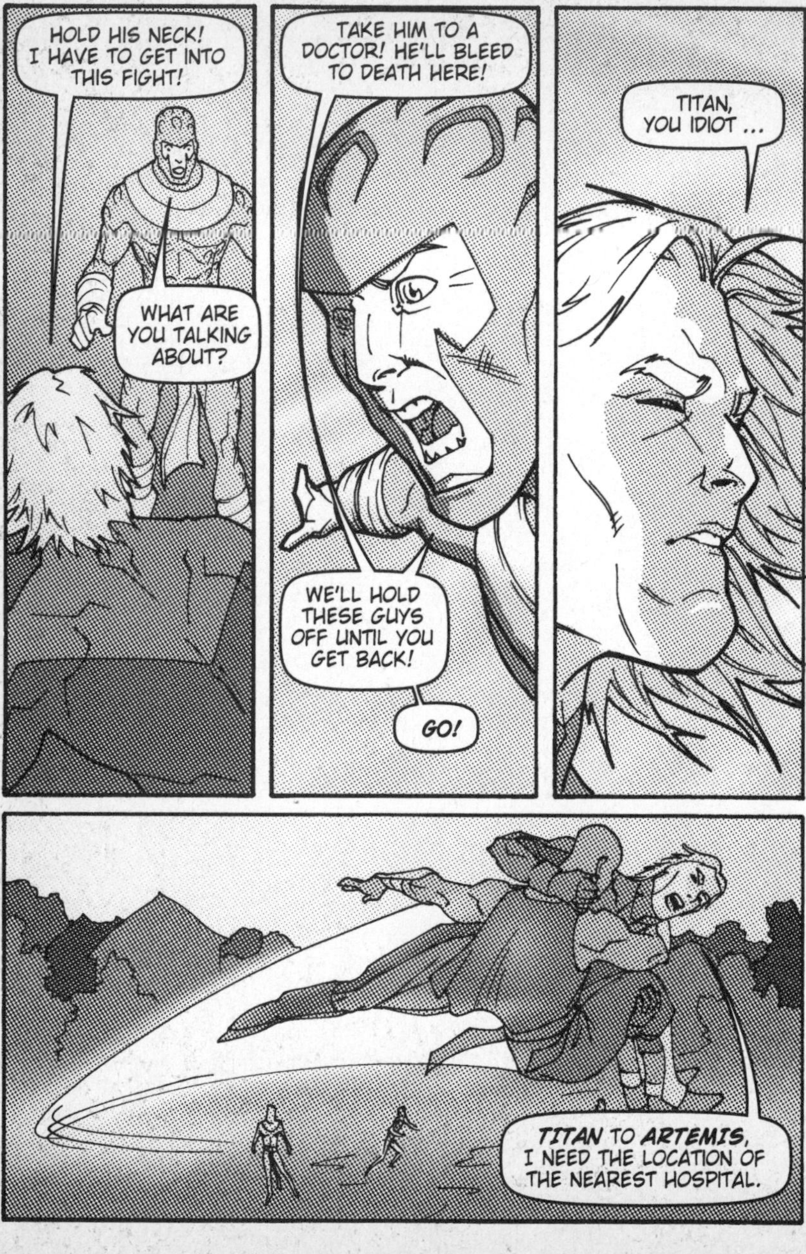
HOLD HIS NECK! I HAVE TO GET INTO THIS FIGHT!
WHAT ARE YOU TALKING ABOUT?
TAKE HIM TO A DOCTOR! HE'LL BLEED TO DEATH HERE!
WE'LL HOLD THESE GUYS OFF UNTIL YOU GET BACK!
GO!
TITAN, YOU IDIOT ...
TITAN TO ARTEMIS, I NEED THE LOCATION OF THE NEAREST HOSPITAL.

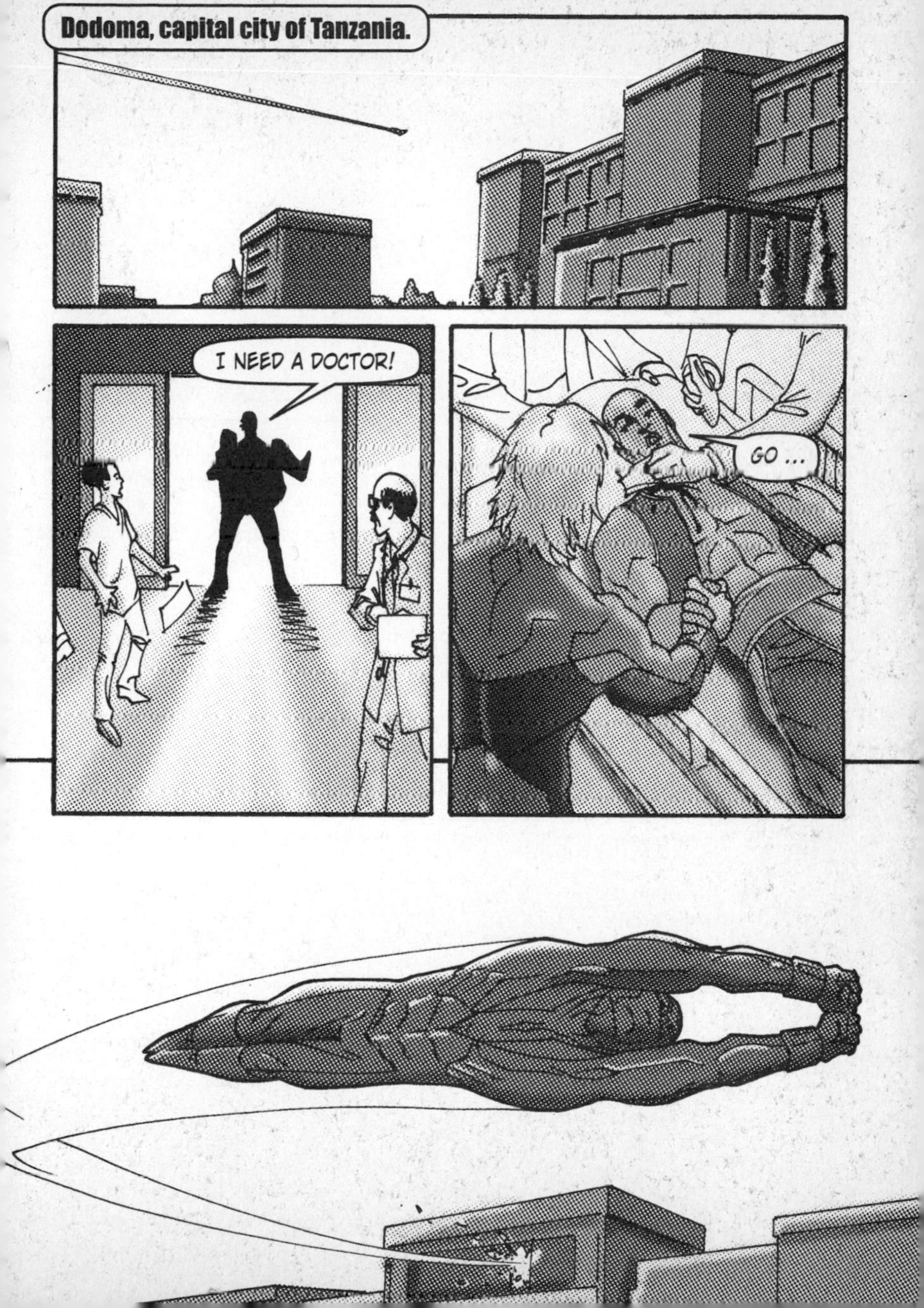
Dodoma, capital city of Tanzania.
I NEED A DOCTOR!
GO ...

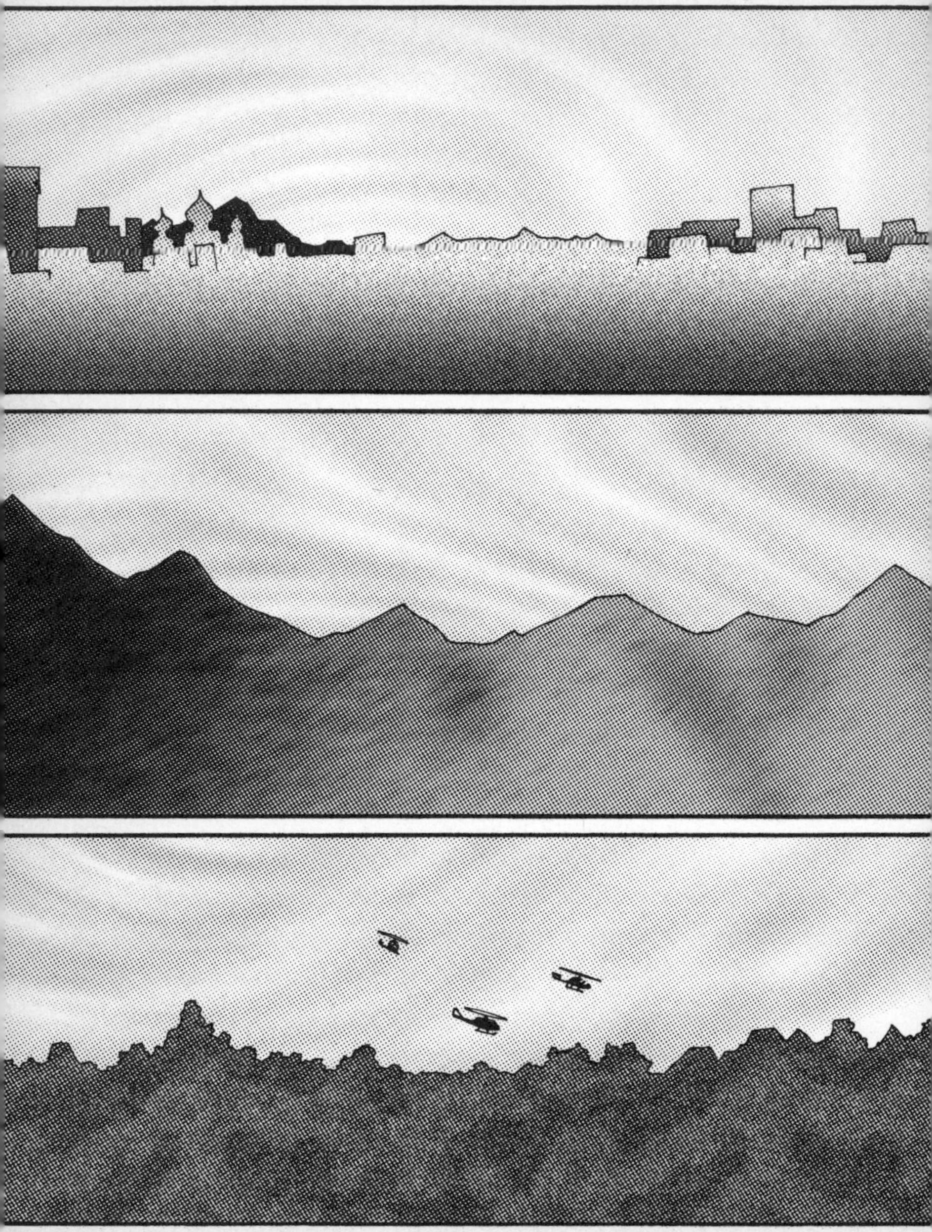

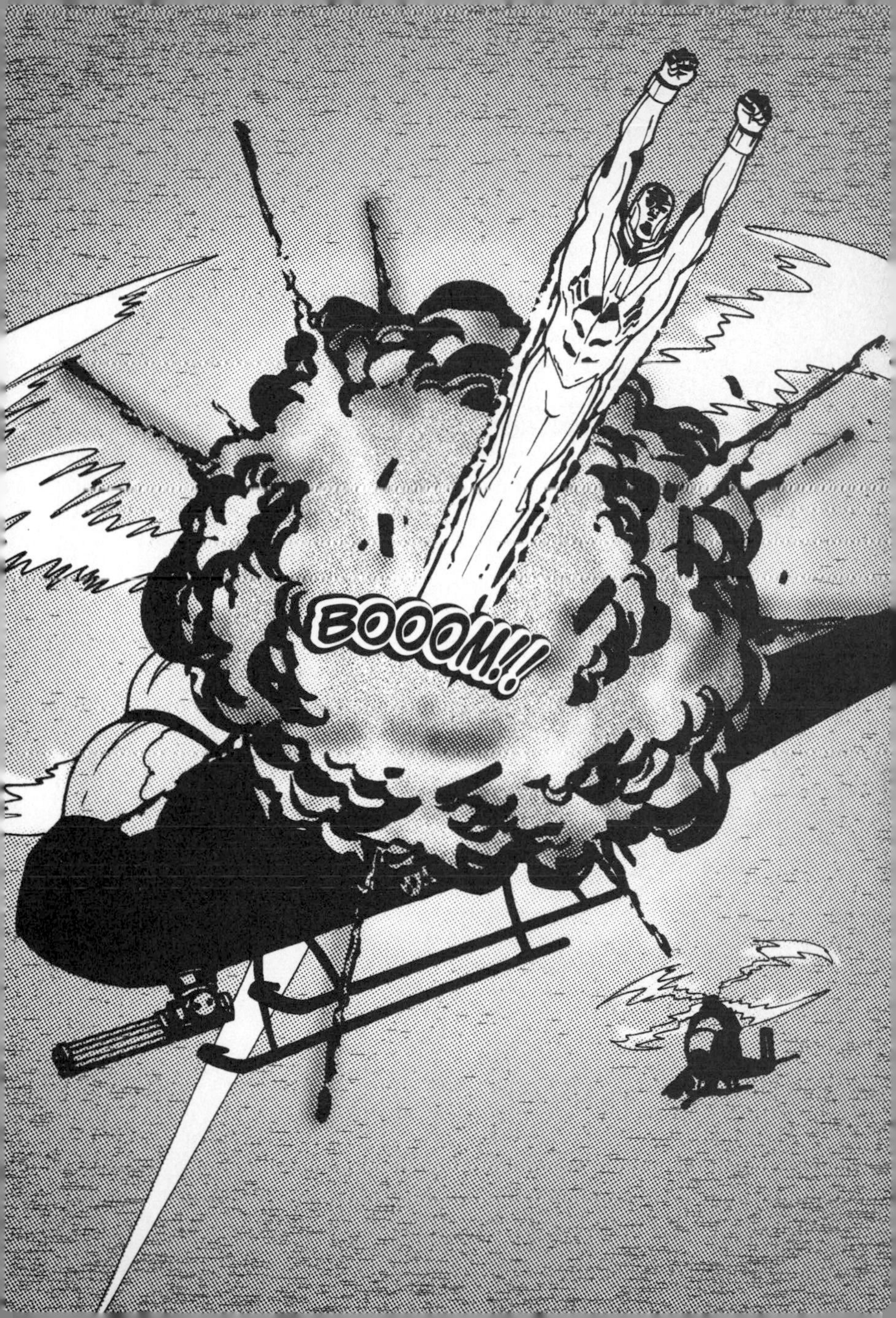
BOOOM!!

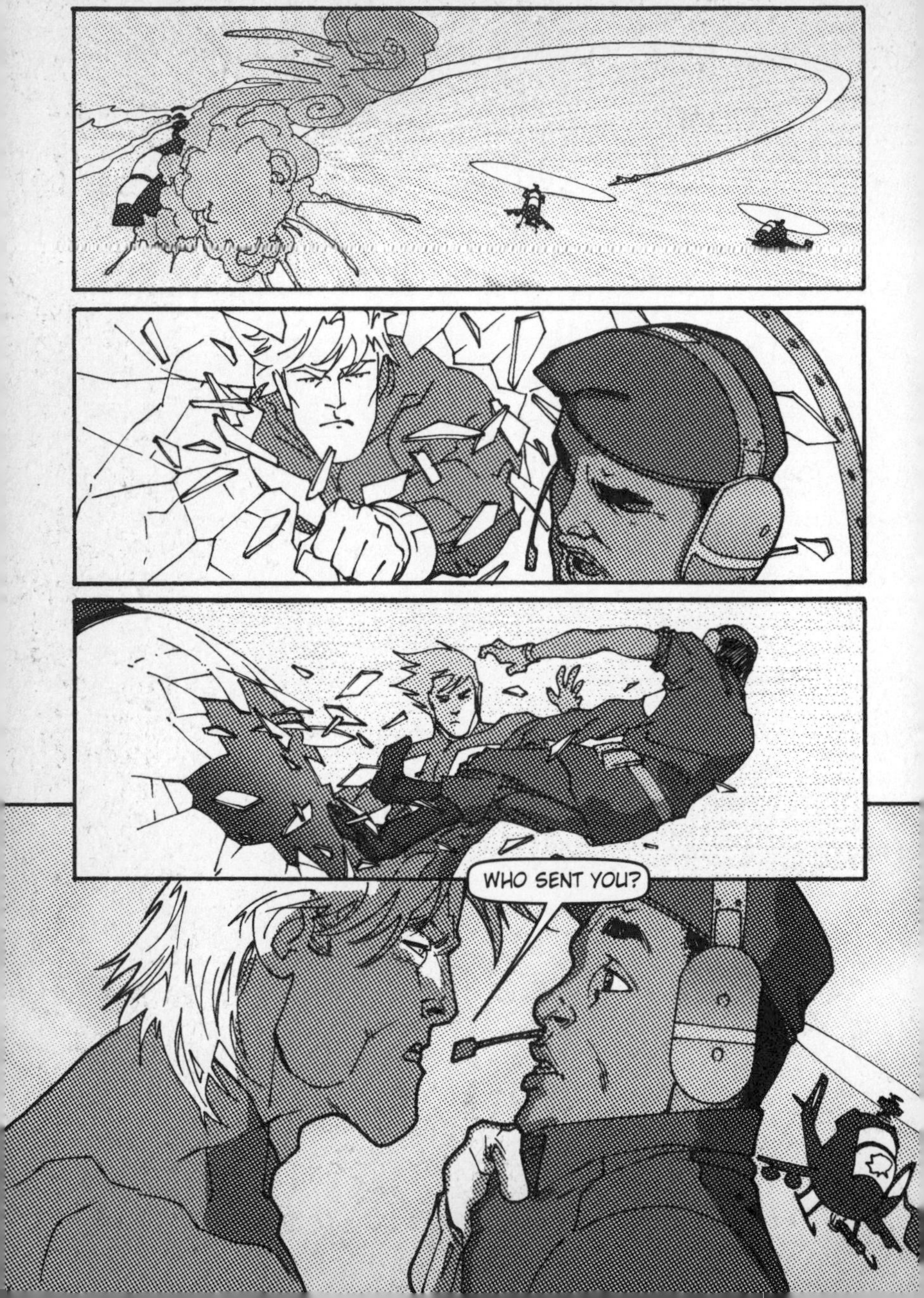
WHO SENT YOU?

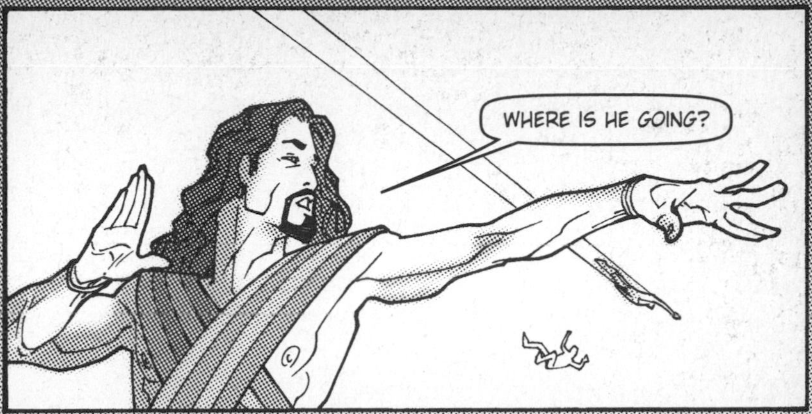
WHERE IS HE GOING?

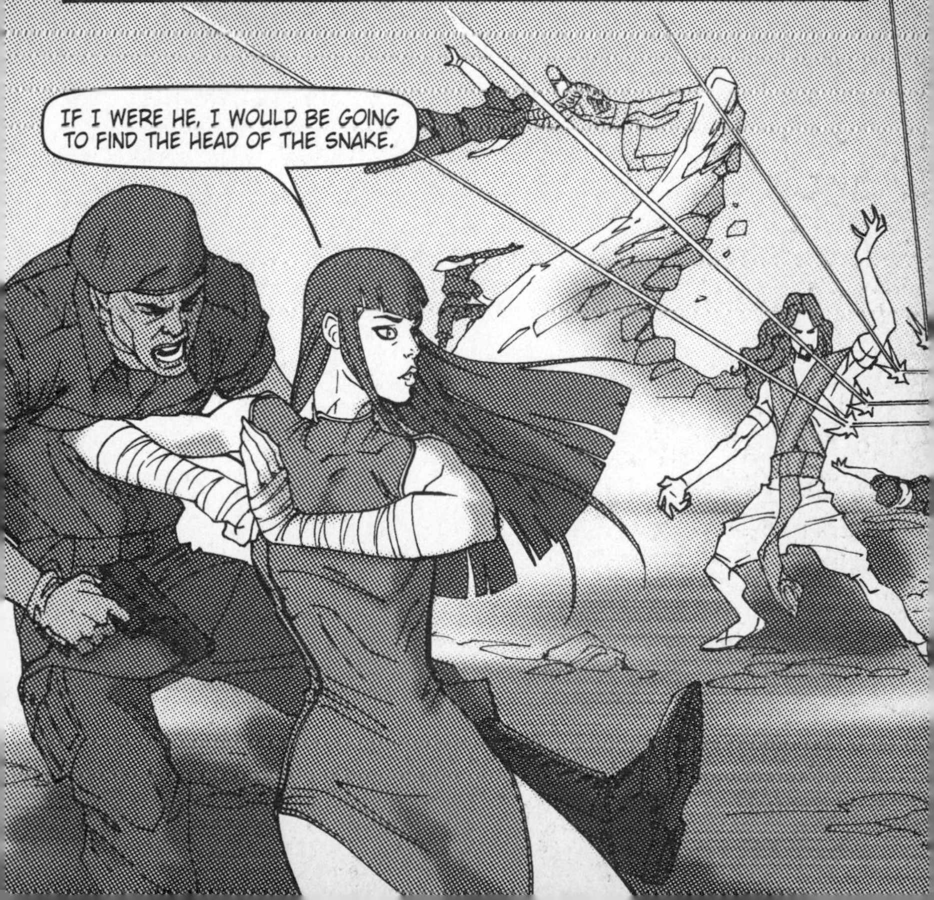
IF I WERE HE, I WOULD BE GOING TO FIND THE HEAD OF THE SNAKE.

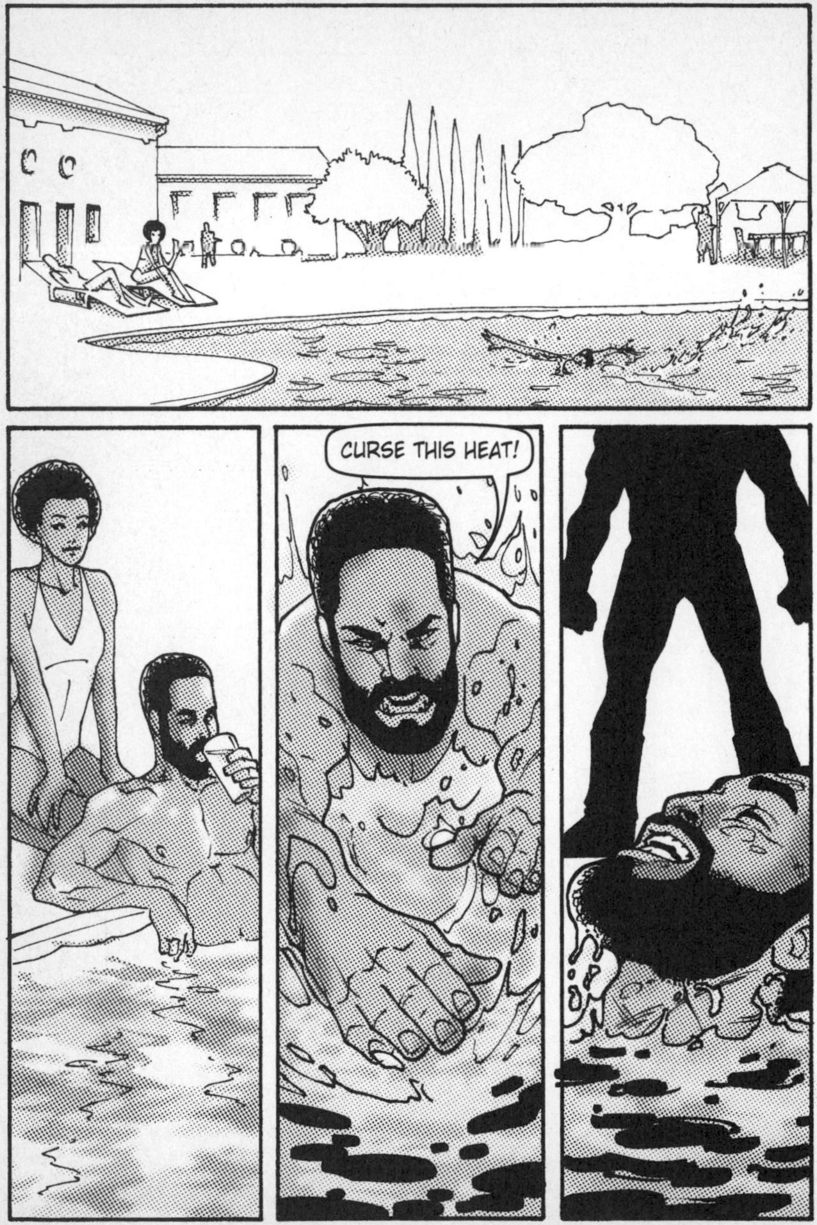
CURSE THIS HEAT!

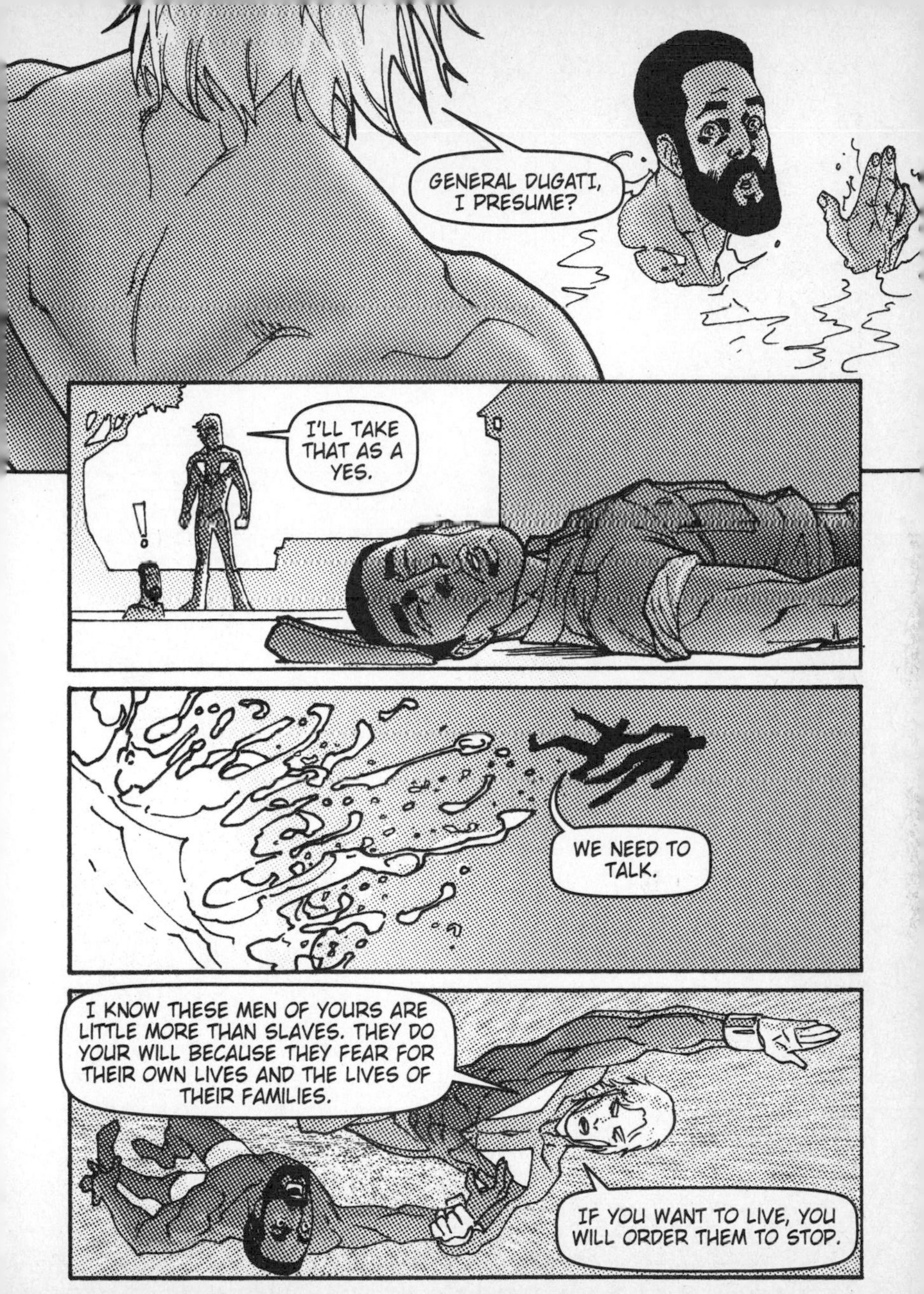
GENERAL DUGATI, I PRESUME?
I'LL TAKE THAT AS A YES.
!
WE NEED TO TALK.
I KNOW THESE MEN OF YOURS ARE LITTLE MORE THAN SLAVES. THEY DO YOUR WILL BECAUSE THEY FEAR FOR THEIR OWN LIVES AND THE LIVES OF THEIR FAMILIES.
IF YOU WANT TO LIVE, YOU WILL ORDER THEM TO STOP.

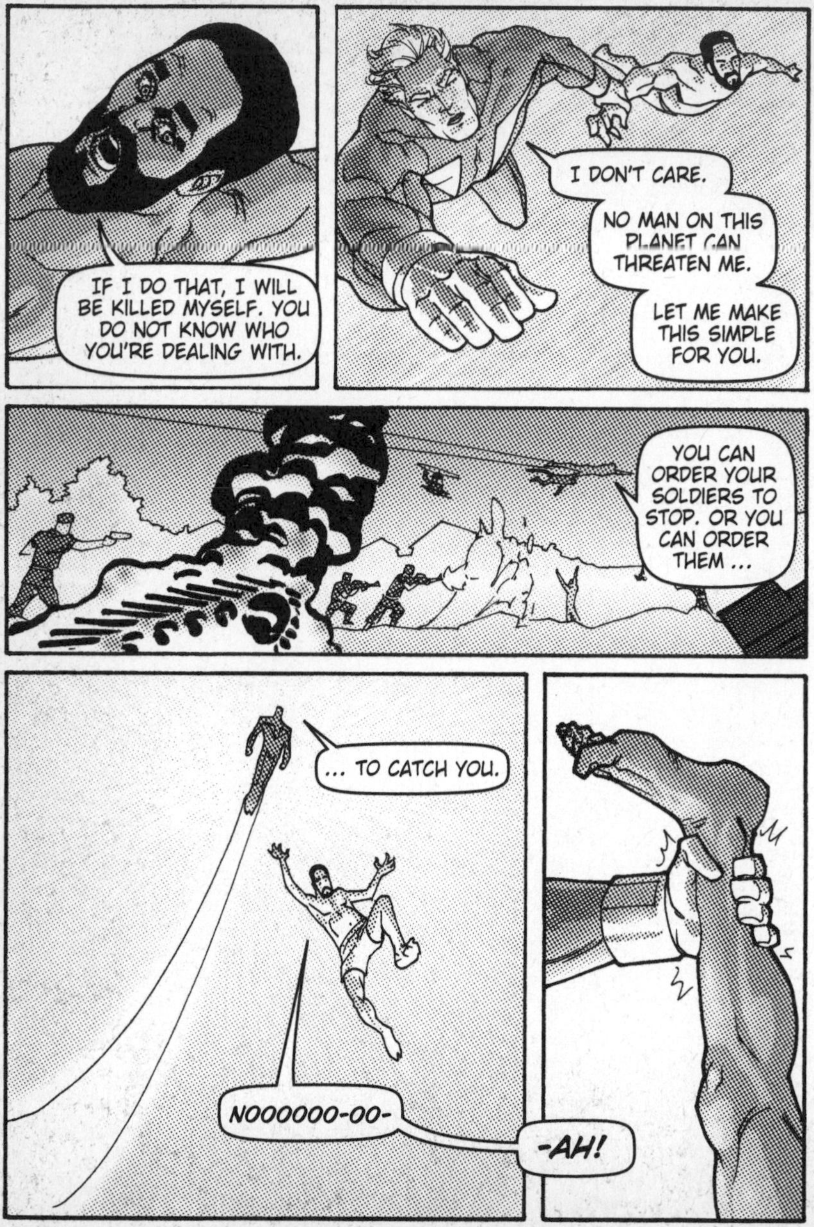
IF I DO THAT, I WILL BE KILLED MYSELF. YOU DO NOT KNOW WHO YOU'RE DEALING WITH.
I DON'T CARE.
NO MAN ON THIS PLANET CAN THREATEN ME.
LET ME MAKE THIS SIMPLE FOR YOU.
YOU CAN ORDER YOUR SOLDIERS TO STOP. OR YOU CAN ORDER THEM ...
... TO CATCH YOU.
NOOOOOO-OO-
-AH!

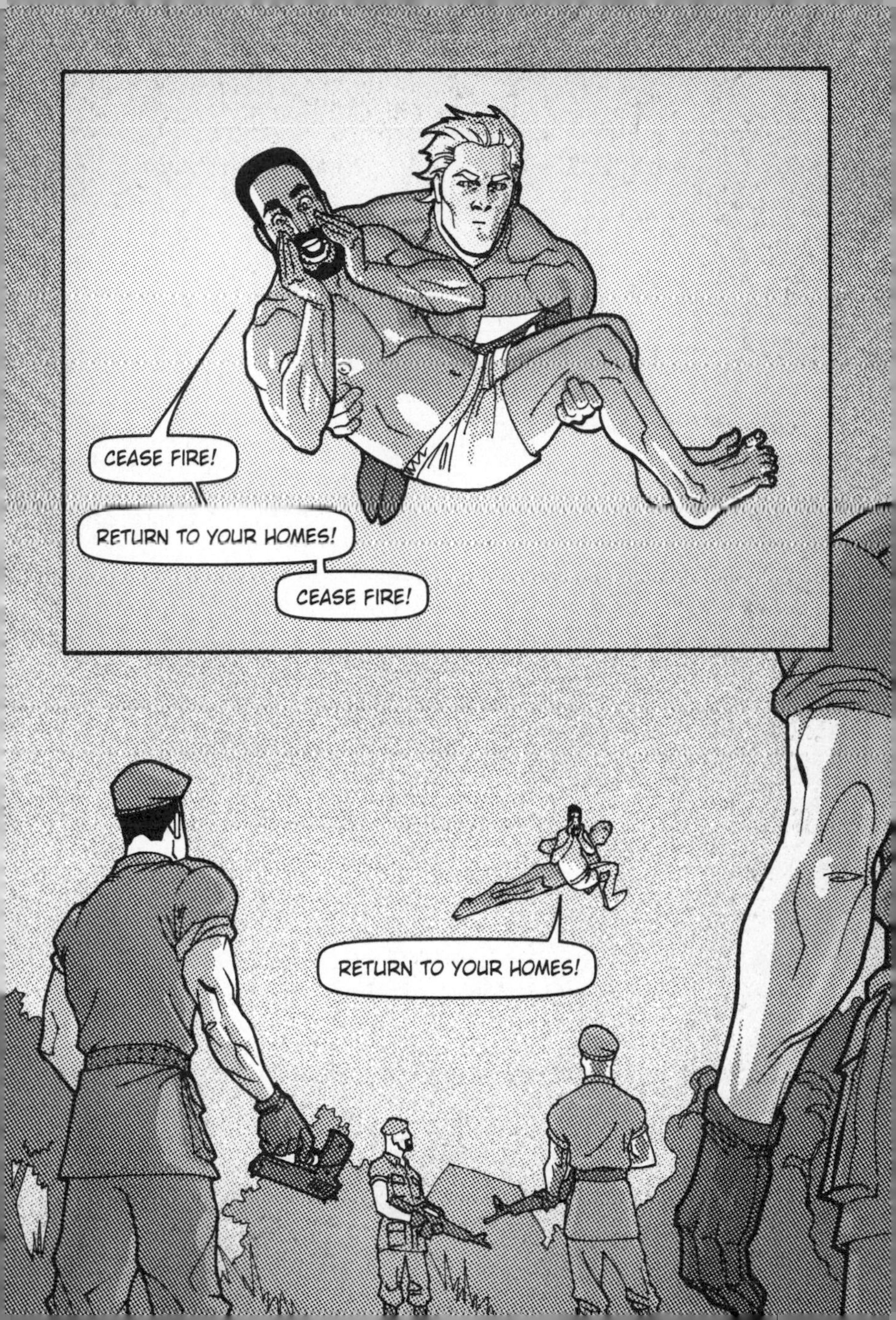
CEASE FIRE!
RETURN TO YOUR HOMES!
CEASE FIRE!
RETURN TO YOUR HOMES!

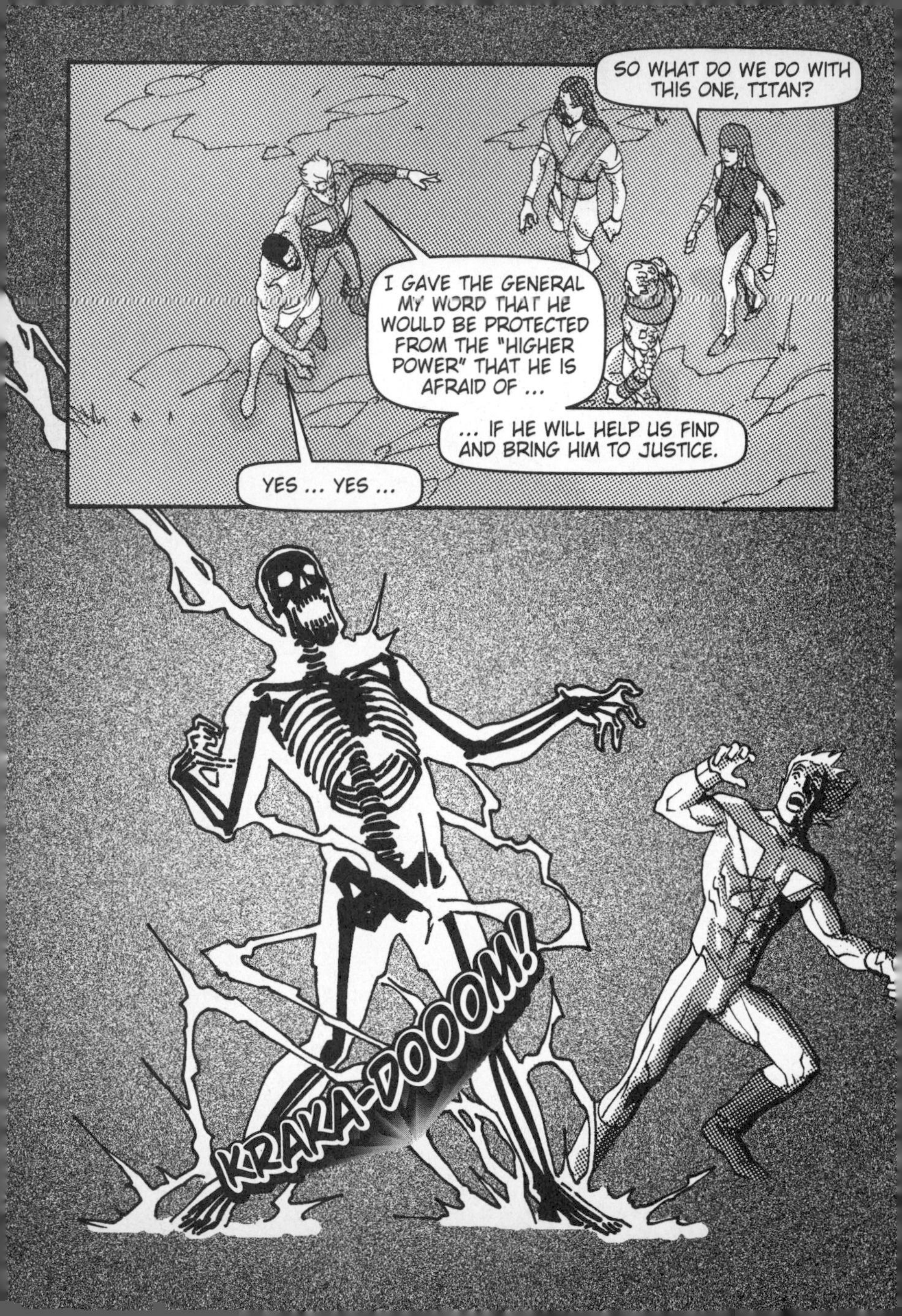
SO WHAT DO WE DO WITH THIS ONE, TITAN?
I GAVE THE GENERAL MY WORD THAT HE WOULD BE PROTECTED FROM THE "HIGHER POWER" THAT HE IS AFRAID OF ...
... IF HE WILL HELP US FIND AND BRING HIM TO JUSTICE.
YES ... YES ...
KRAKA-DOOOM!

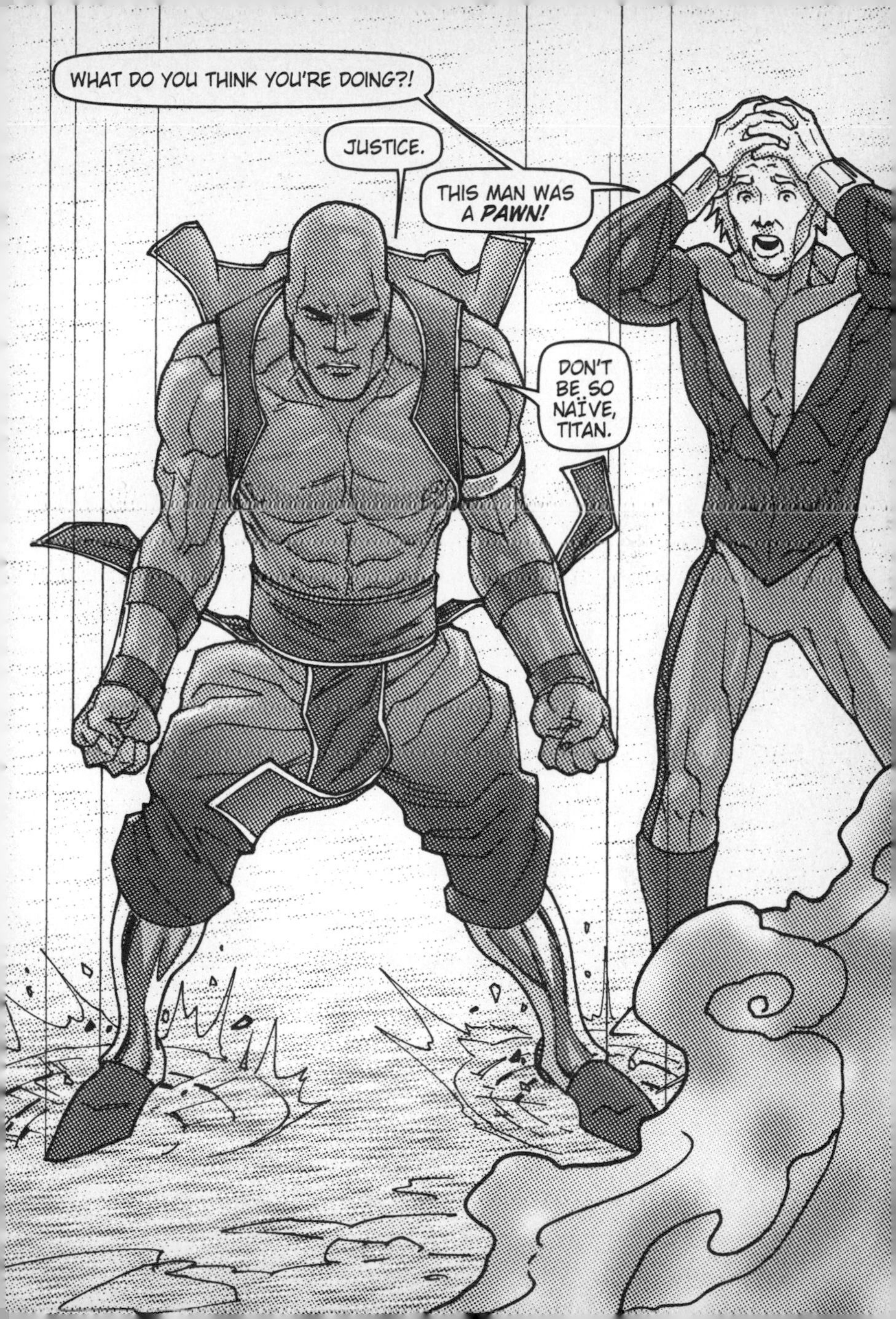
WHAT DO YOU THINK YOU'RE DOING?!
JUSTICE.
THIS MAN WAS A PAWN!
DON'T BE SO NAÏVE, TITAN.

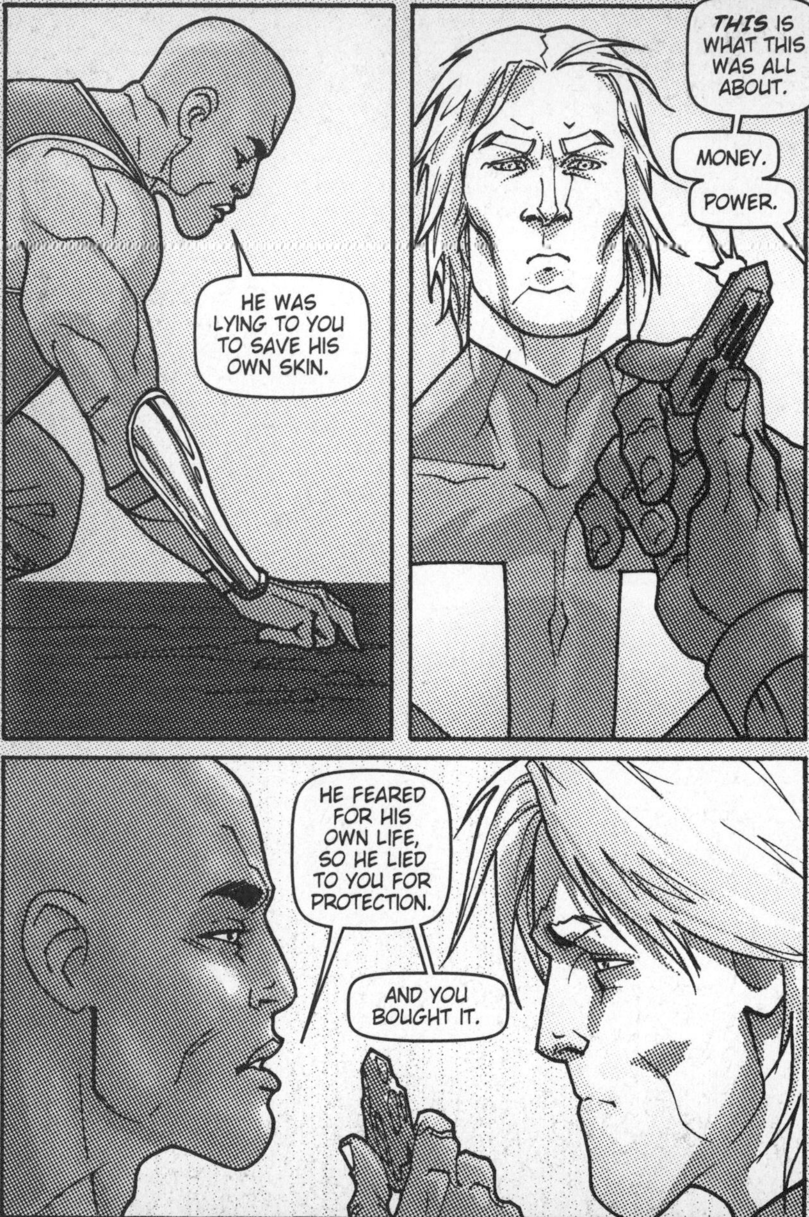
HE WAS LYING TO YOU TO SAVE HIS OWN SKIN.
THIS IS WHAT THIS WAS ALL ABOUT.
MONEY.
POWER.
HE FEARED FOR HIS OWN LIFE, SO HE LIED TO YOU FOR PROTECTION.
AND YOU BOUGHT IT.

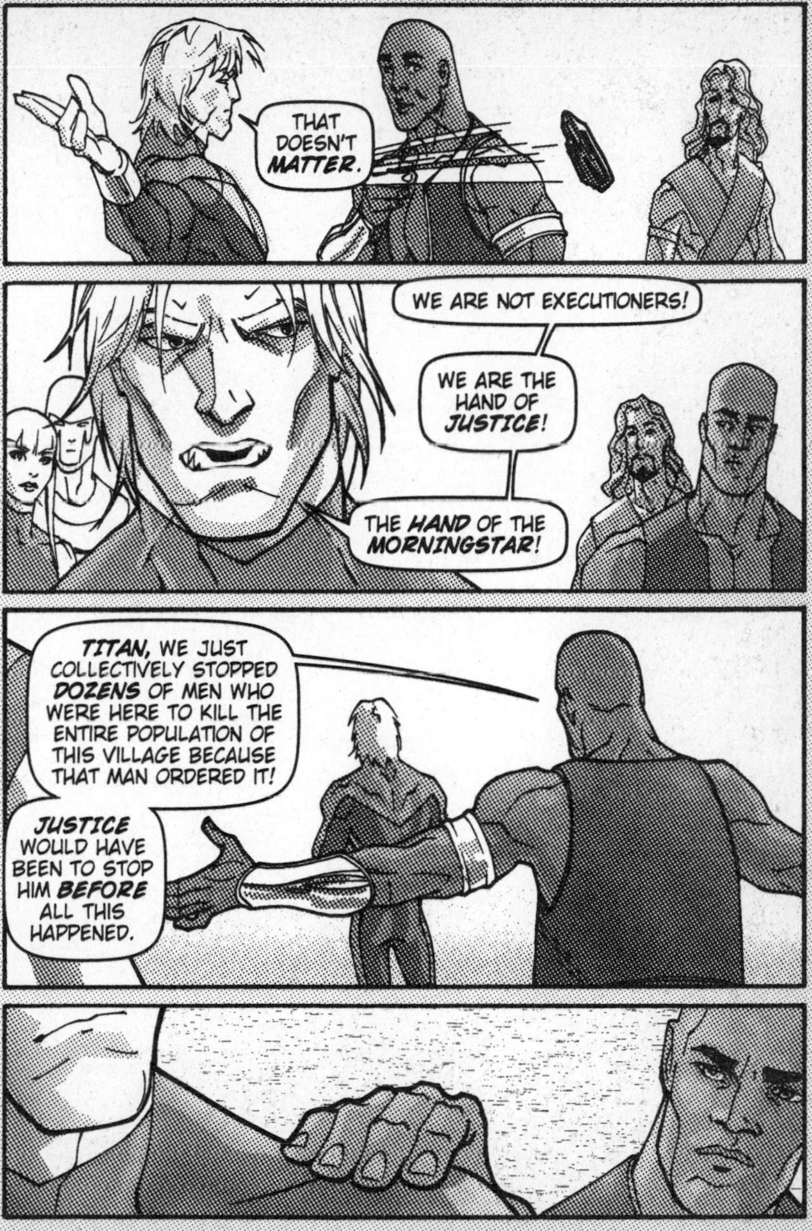
THAT DOESN'T MATTER.
WE ARE NOT EXECUTIONERS!
WE ARE THE HAND OF JUSTICE!
THE HAND OF THE MORNINGSTAR!
TITAN, WE JUST COLLECTIVELY STOPPED DOZENS OF MEN WHO WERE HERE TO KILL THE ENTIRE POPULATION OF THIS VILLAGE BECAUSE THAT MAN ORDERED IT!
JUSTICE WOULD HAVE BEEN TO STOP HIM BEFORE ALL THIS HAPPENED.

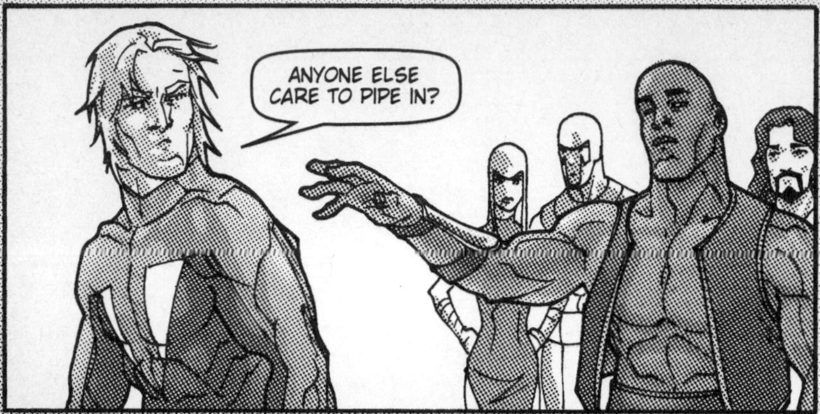
ANYONE ELSE CARE TO PIPE IN?

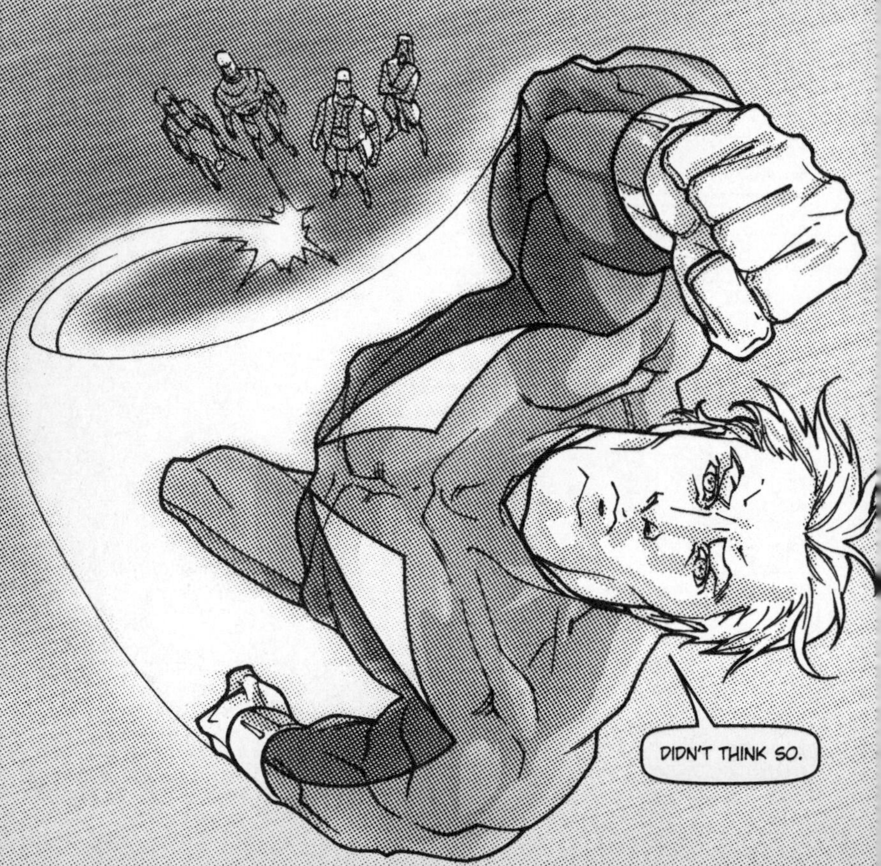
DIDN'T THINK SO.

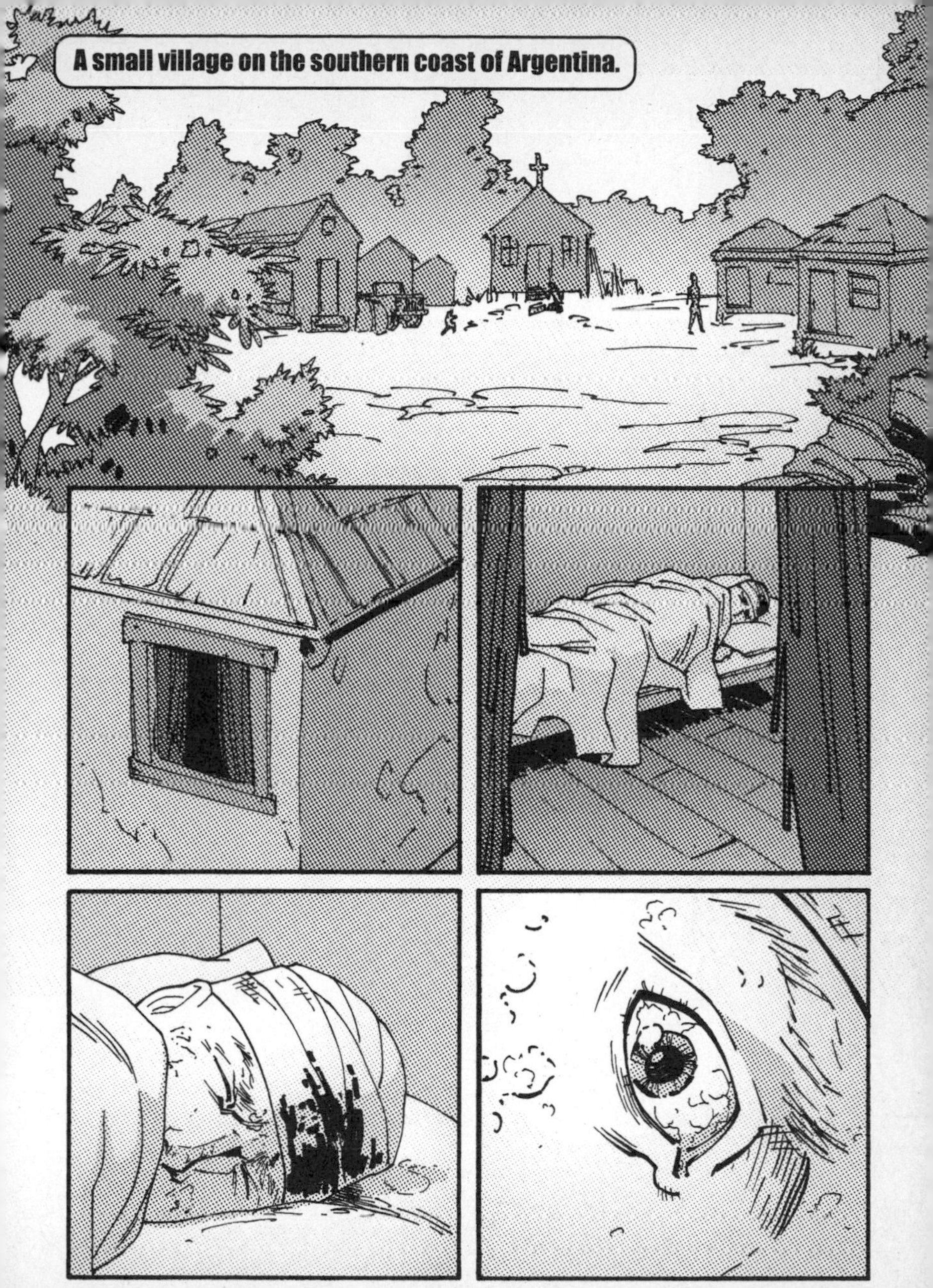
A small village on the southern coast of Argentina.

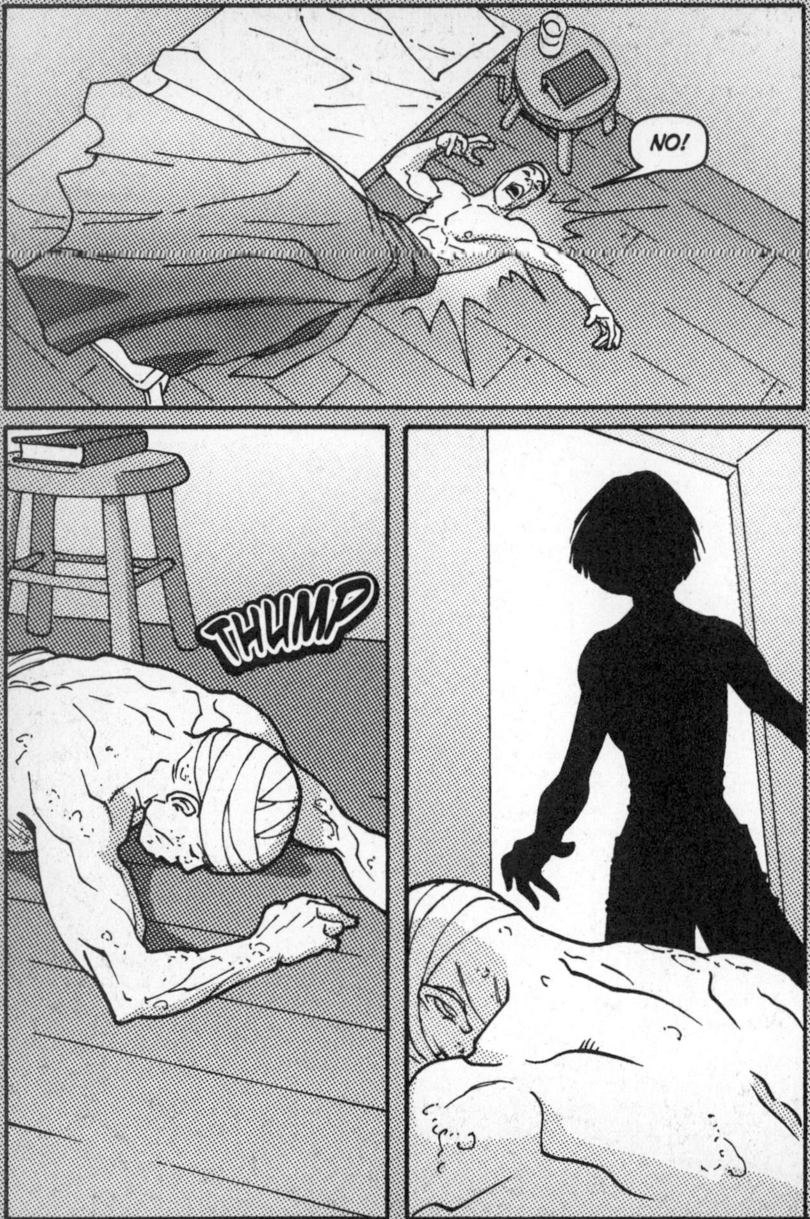
NO!
THUMP

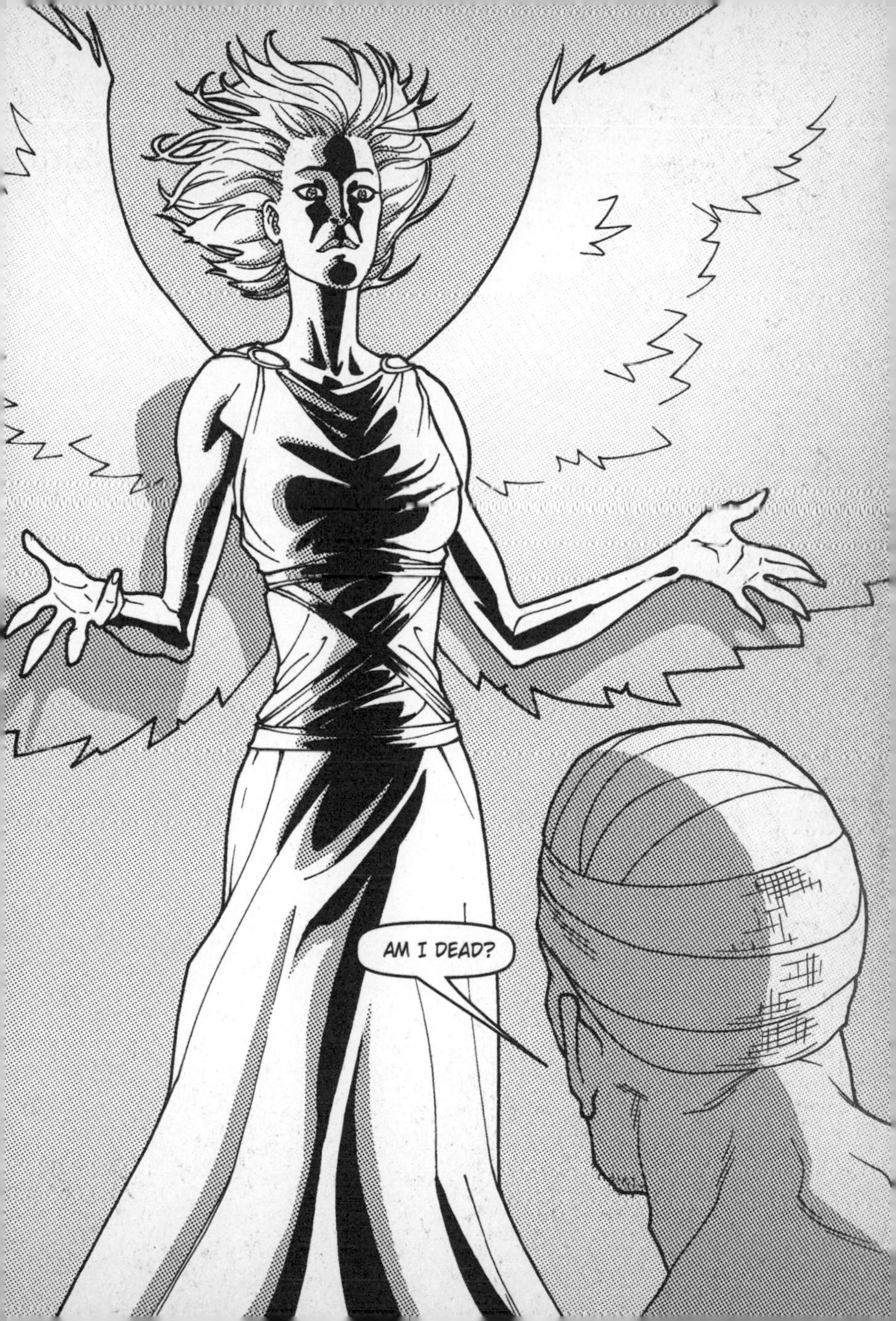
AM I DEAD?

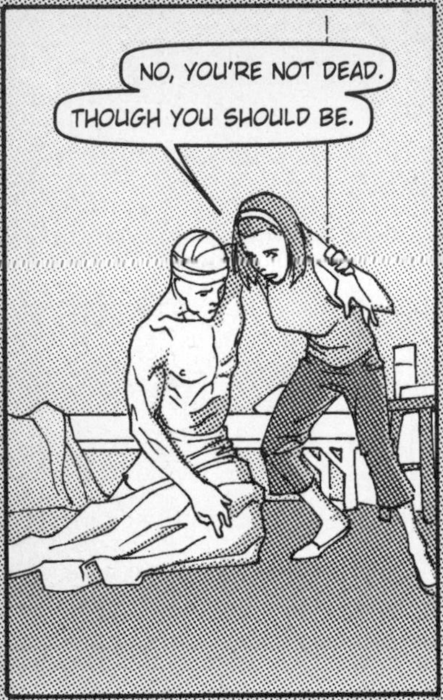
NO, YOU'RE NOT DEAD.
THOUGH YOU SHOULD BE.
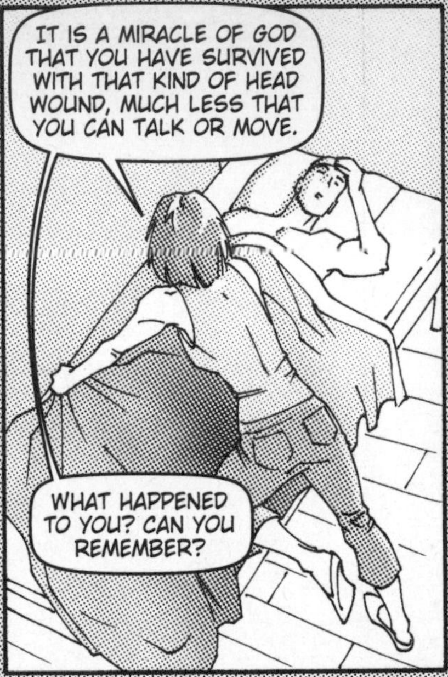
IT IS A MIRACLE OF GOD THAT YOU HAVE SURVIVED WITH THAT KIND OF HEAD WOUND, MUCH LESS THAT YOU CAN TALK OR MOVE.
WHAT HAPPENED TO YOU? CAN YOU REMEMBER?
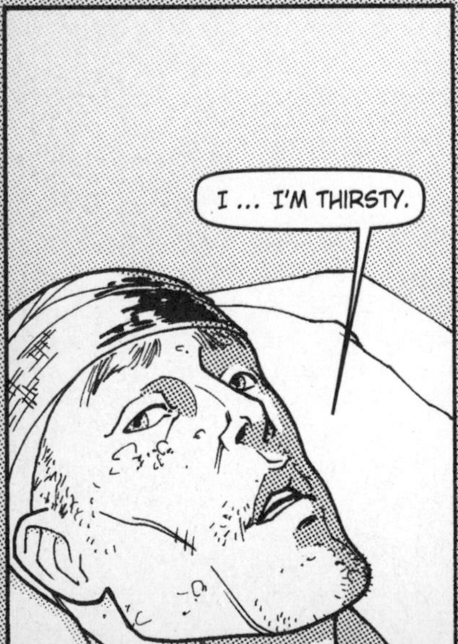
I ... I'M THIRSTY.
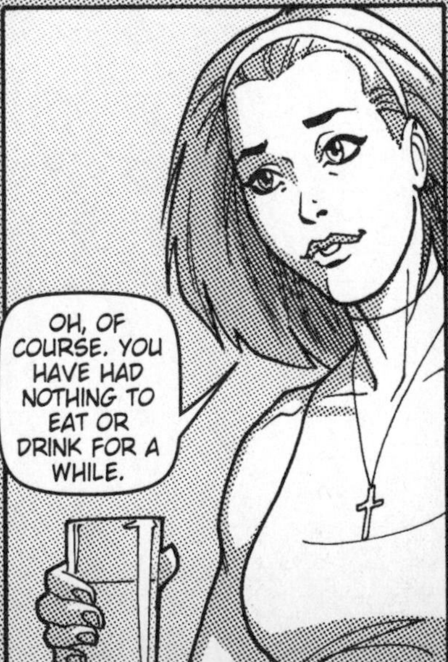
OH, OF COURSE. YOU HAVE HAD NOTHING TO EAT OR DRINK FOR A WHILE.

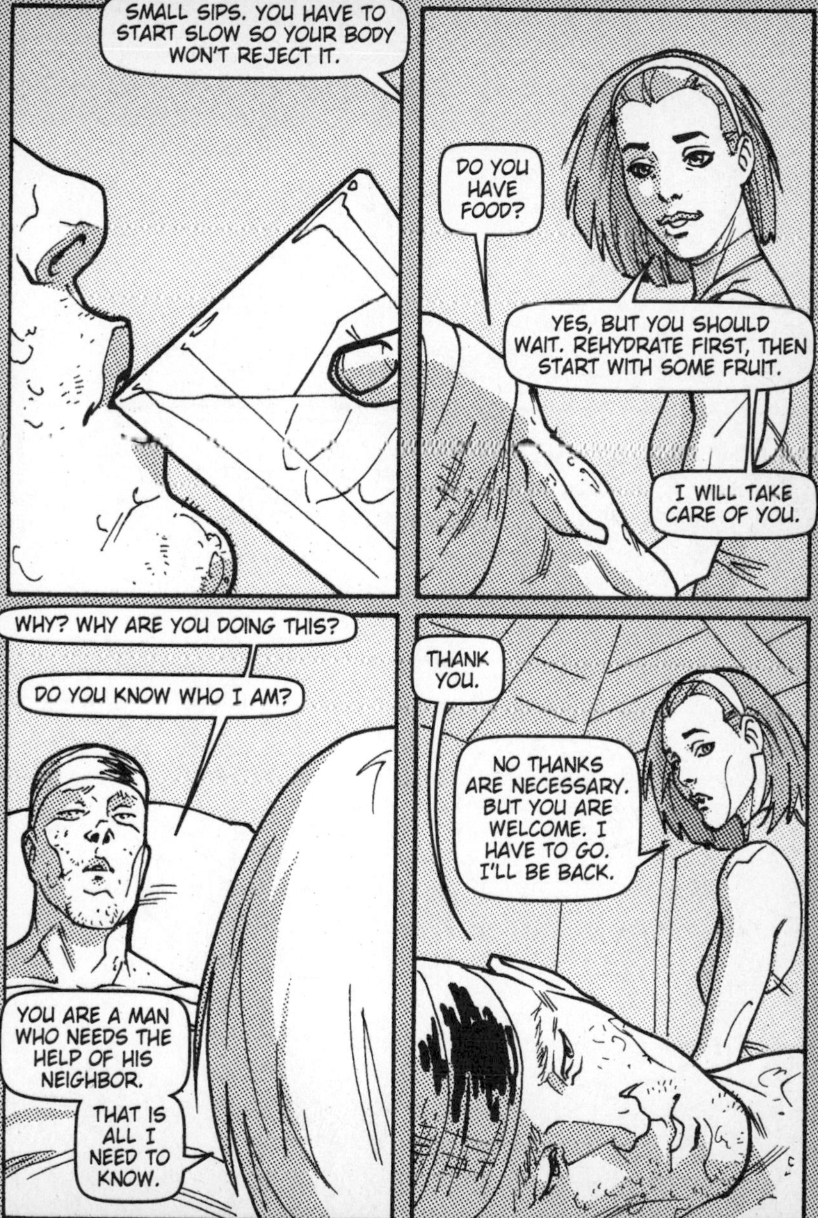
SMALL SIPS. YOU HAVE TO START SLOW SO YOUR BODY WON'T REJECT IT.
DO YOU HAVE FOOD?
YES, BUT YOU SHOULD WAIT. REHYDRATE FIRST, THEN START WITH SOME FRUIT.
I WILL TAKE CARE OF YOU.
WHY? WHY ARE YOU DOING THIS?
DO YOU KNOW WHO I AM?
YOU ARE A MAN WHO NEEDS THE HELP OF HIS NEIGHBOR.
THAT IS ALL I NEED TO KNOW.
THANK YOU.
NO THANKS ARE NECESSARY. BUT YOU ARE WELCOME. I HAVE TO GO. I'LL BE BACK.

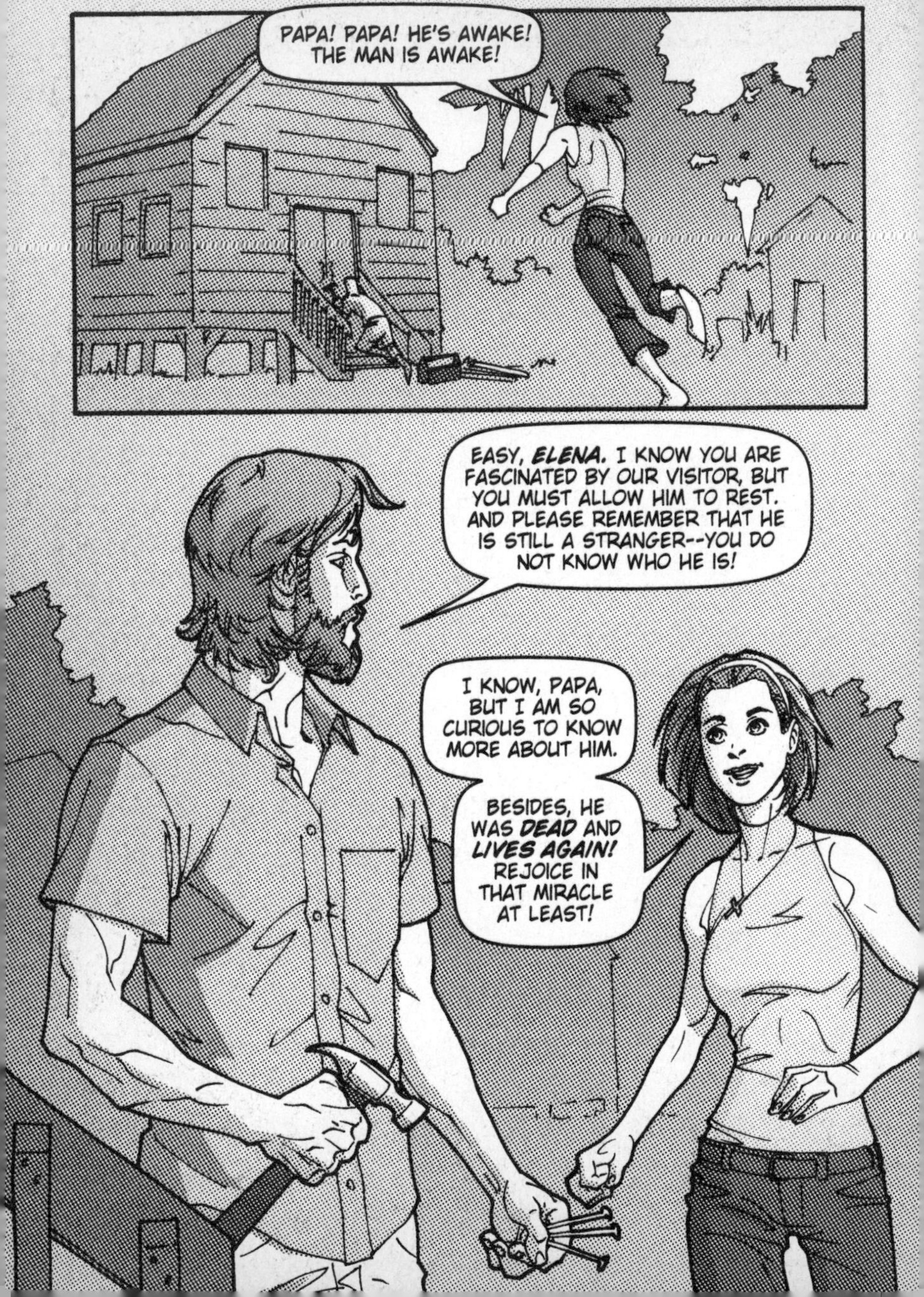
PAPA! PAPA! HE'S AWAKE! THE MAN IS AWAKE!
EASY, ***ELENA.*** I KNOW YOU ARE FASCINATED BY OUR VISITOR, BUT YOU MUST ALLOW HIM TO REST. AND PLEASE REMEMBER THAT HE IS STILL A STRANGER--YOU DO NOT KNOW WHO HE IS!
I KNOW, PAPA, BUT I AM SO CURIOUS TO KNOW MORE ABOUT HIM.
BESIDES, HE WAS ***DEAD*** AND ***LIVES AGAIN!*** REJOICE IN THAT MIRACLE AT LEAST!

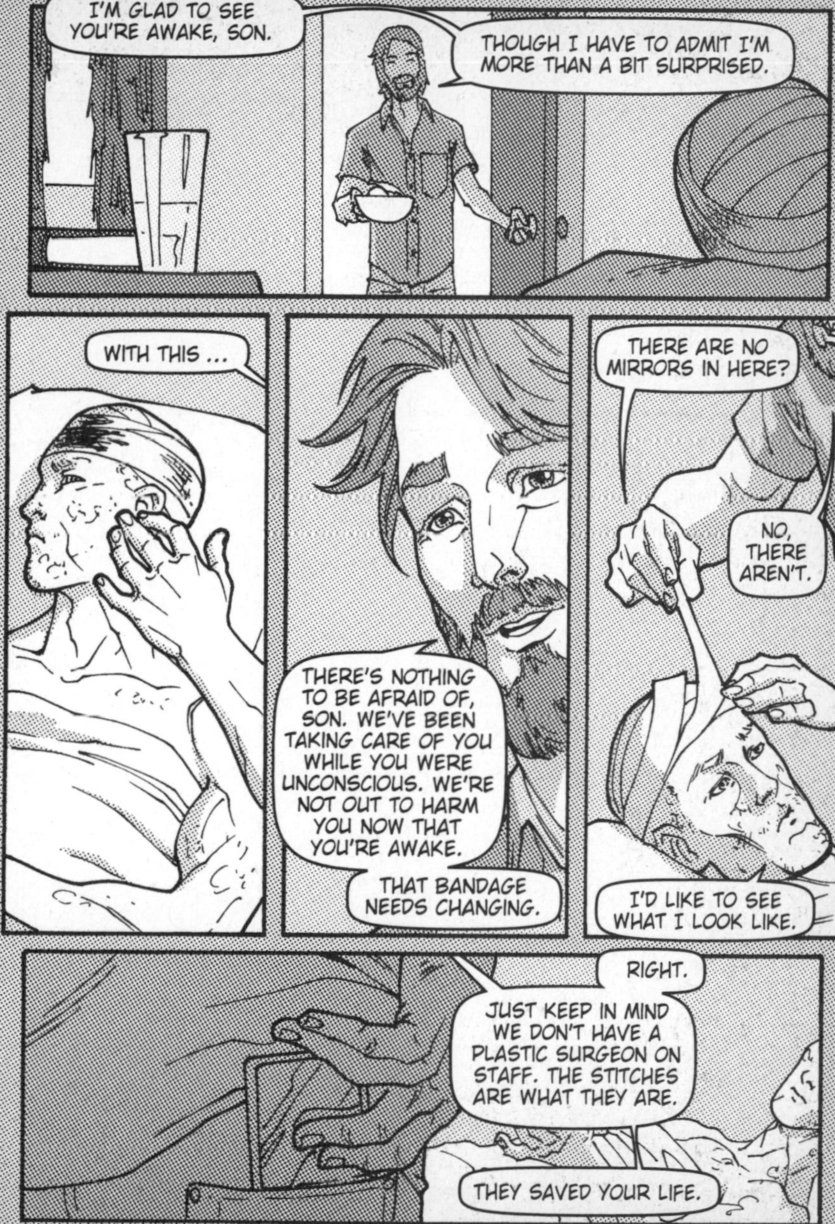
I'M GLAD TO SEE YOU'RE AWAKE, SON.
THOUGH I HAVE TO ADMIT I'M MORE THAN A BIT SURPRISED.
WITH THIS ...
THERE'S NOTHING TO BE AFRAID OF, SON. WE'VE BEEN TAKING CARE OF YOU WHILE YOU WERE UNCONSCIOUS. WE'RE NOT OUT TO HARM YOU NOW THAT YOU'RE AWAKE.
THAT BANDAGE NEEDS CHANGING.
THERE ARE NO MIRRORS IN HERE?
NO, THERE AREN'T.
I'D LIKE TO SEE WHAT I LOOK LIKE.
RIGHT.
JUST KEEP IN MIND WE DON'T HAVE A PLASTIC SURGEON ON STAFF. THE STITCHES ARE WHAT THEY ARE.
THEY SAVED YOUR LIFE.

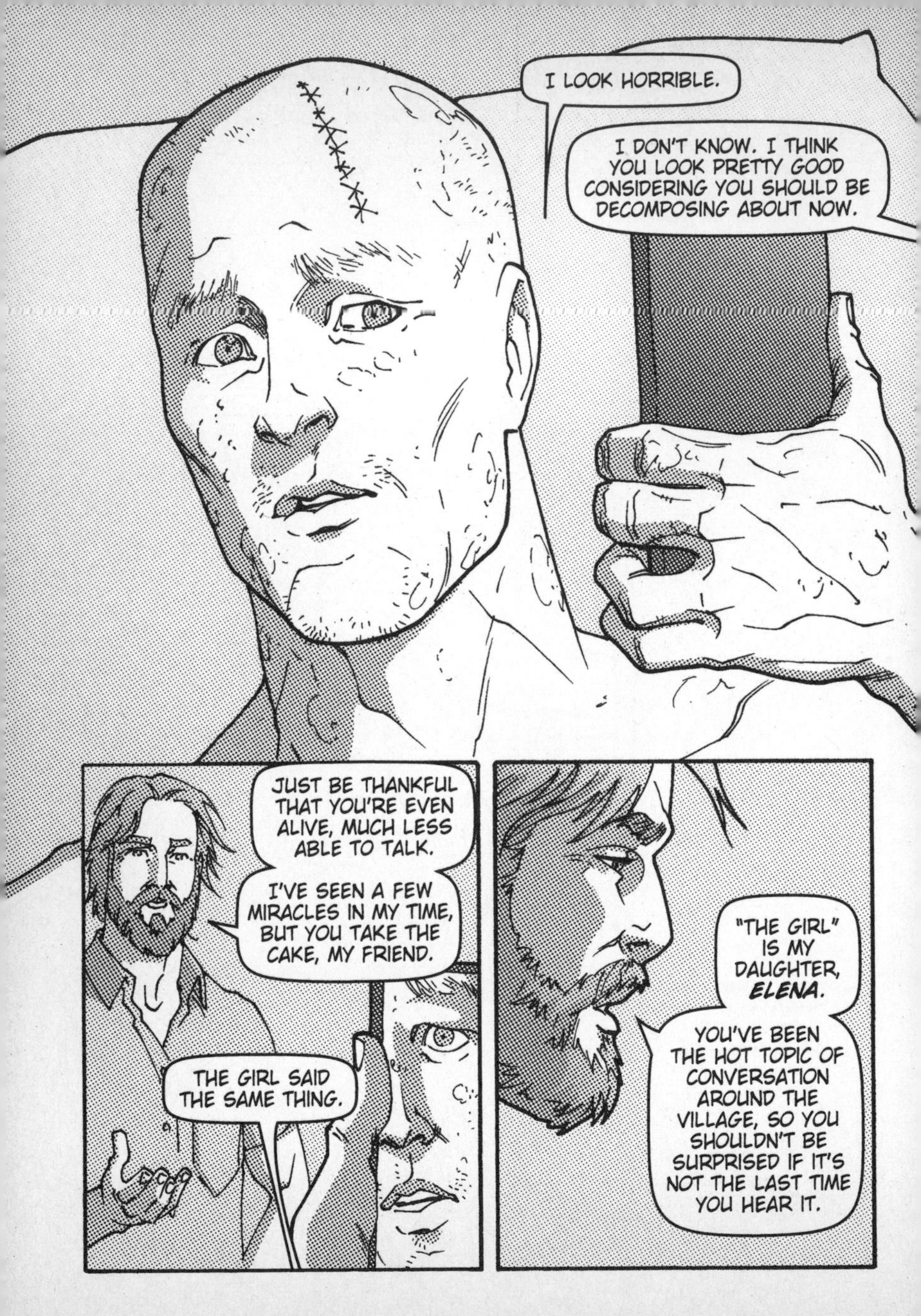
I LOOK HORRIBLE.
I DON'T KNOW. I THINK YOU LOOK PRETTY GOOD CONSIDERING YOU SHOULD BE DECOMPOSING ABOUT NOW.
JUST BE THANKFUL THAT YOU'RE EVEN ALIVE, MUCH LESS ABLE TO TALK.
I'VE SEEN A FEW MIRACLES IN MY TIME, BUT YOU TAKE THE CAKE, MY FRIEND.
THE GIRL SAID THE SAME THING.
"THE GIRL" IS MY DAUGHTER, ELENA.
YOU'VE BEEN THE HOT TOPIC OF CONVERSATION AROUND THE VILLAGE, SO YOU SHOULDN'T BE SURPRISED IF IT'S NOT THE LAST TIME YOU HEAR IT.

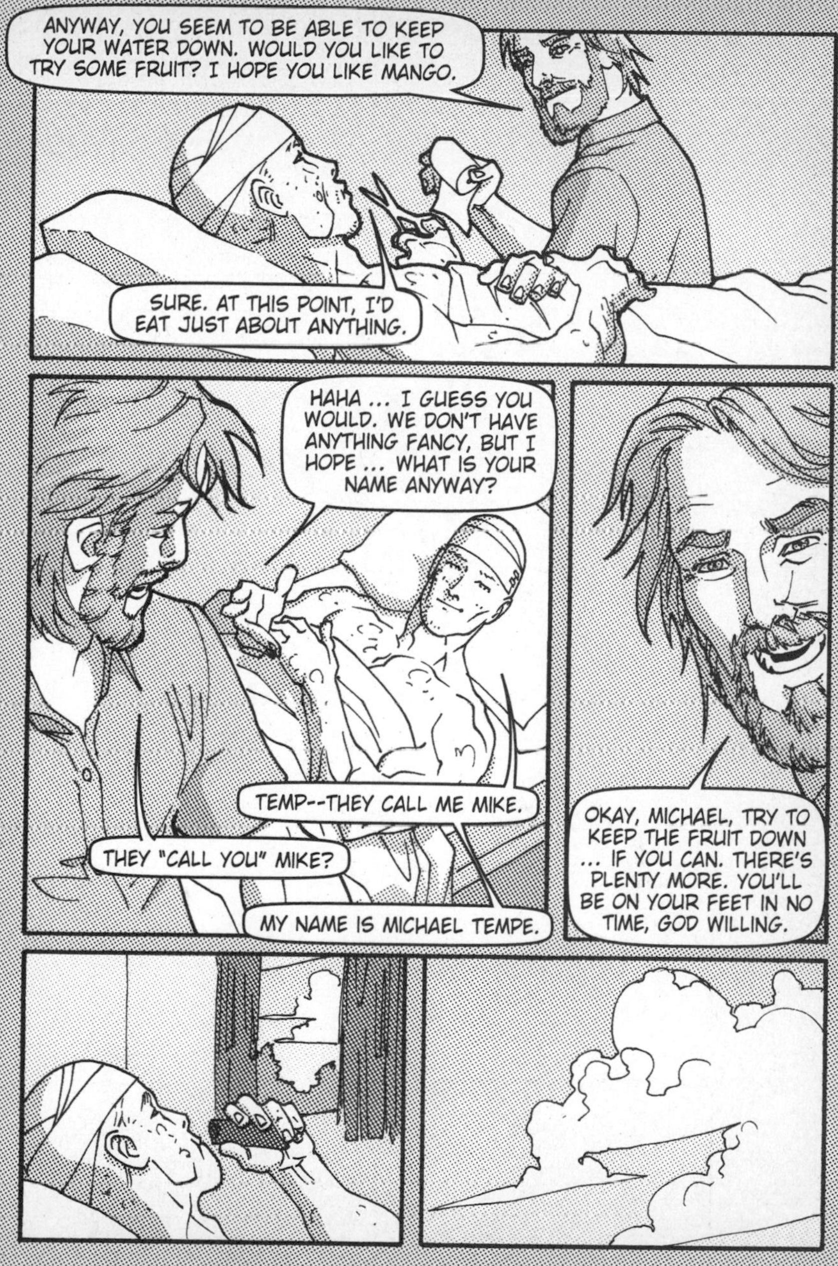
ANYWAY, YOU SEEM TO BE ABLE TO KEEP YOUR WATER DOWN. WOULD YOU LIKE TO TRY SOME FRUIT? I HOPE YOU LIKE MANGO.
SURE. AT THIS POINT, I'D EAT JUST ABOUT ANYTHING.
HAHA ... I GUESS YOU WOULD. WE DON'T HAVE ANYTHING FANCY, BUT I HOPE ... WHAT IS YOUR NAME ANYWAY?
TEMP--THEY CALL ME MIKE.
THEY "CALL YOU" MIKE?
MY NAME IS MICHAEL TEMPE.
OKAY, MICHAEL, TRY TO KEEP THE FRUIT DOWN ... IF YOU CAN. THERE'S PLENTY MORE. YOU'LL BE ON YOUR FEET IN NO TIME, GOD WILLING.

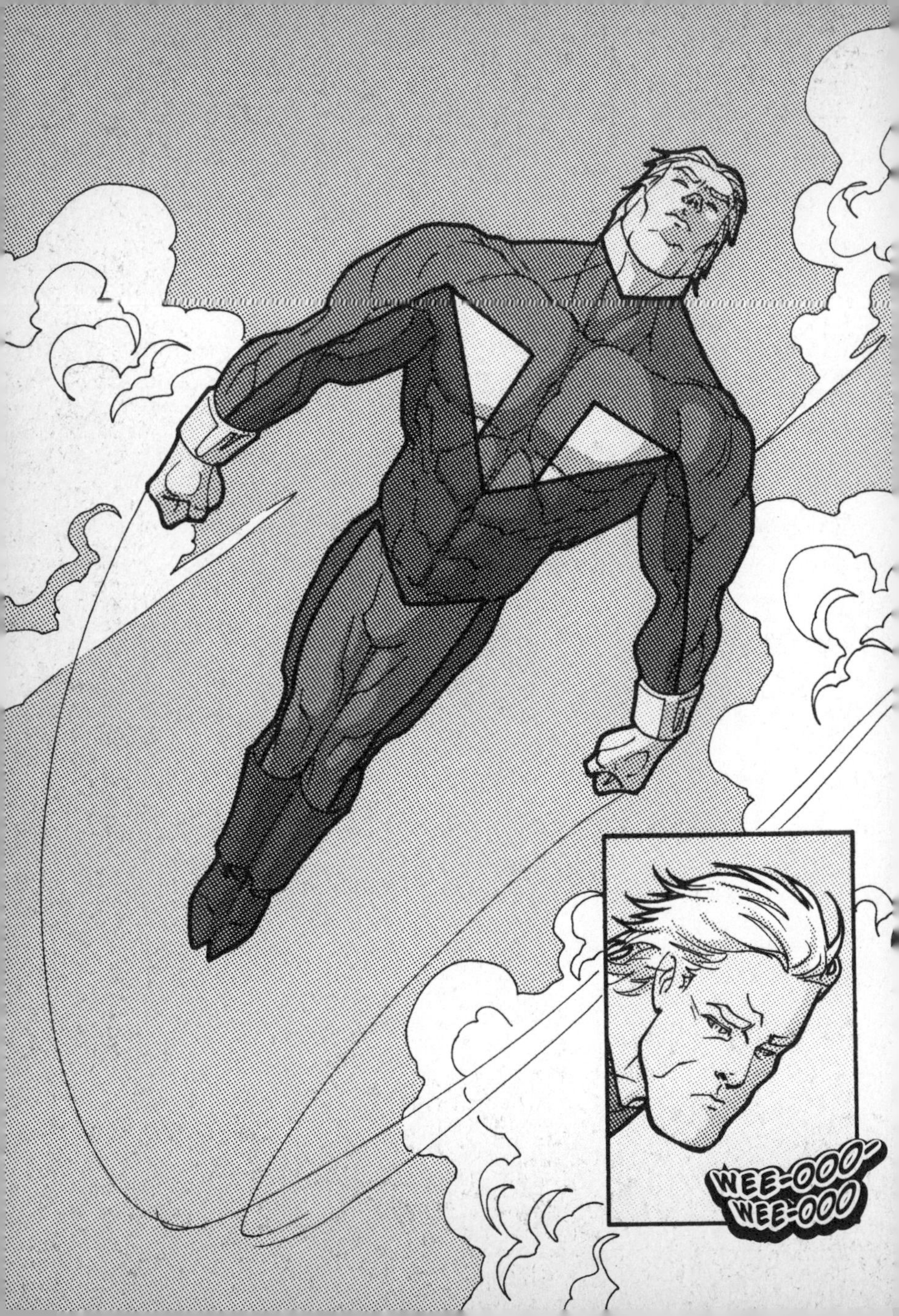
WEE-OOO-
WEE-OOO

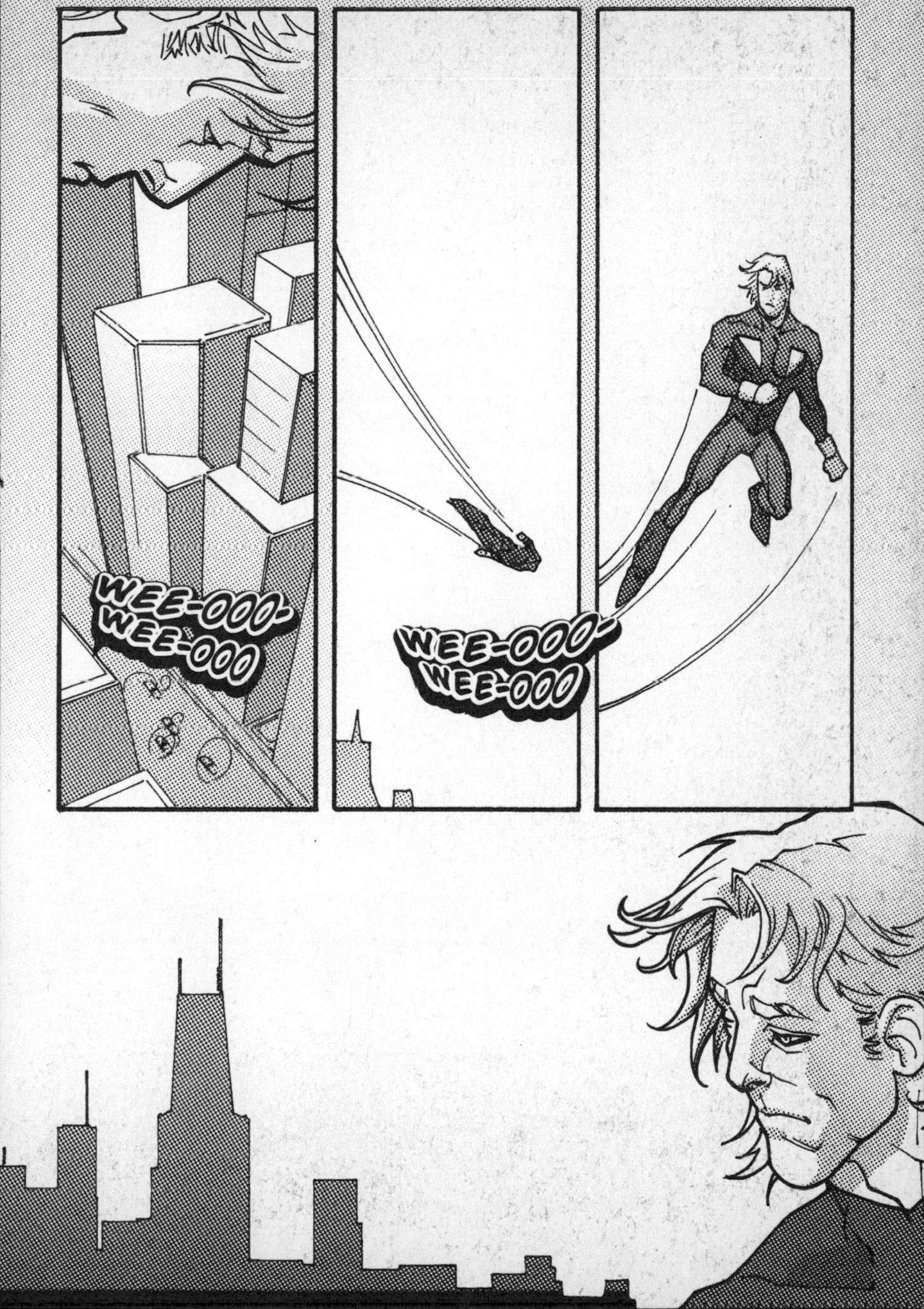
WEE-OOO-WEE-OOO
WEE-OOO-WEE-OOO

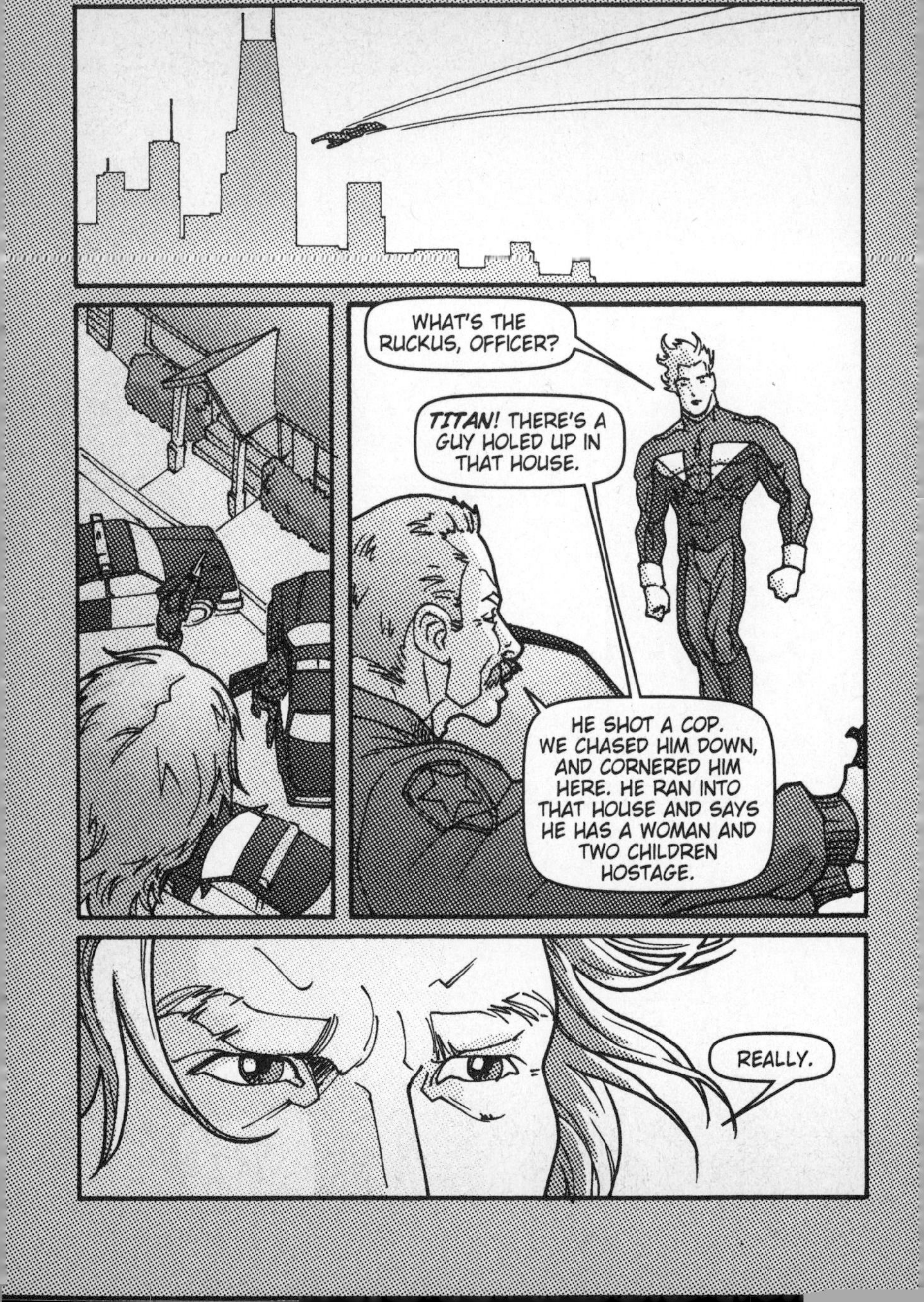
WHAT'S THE RUCKUS, OFFICER?
TITAN! THERE'S A GUY HOLED UP IN THAT HOUSE.
HE SHOT A COP. WE CHASED HIM DOWN, AND CORNERED HIM HERE. HE RAN INTO THAT HOUSE AND SAYS HE HAS A WOMAN AND TWO CHILDREN HOSTAGE.
REALLY.

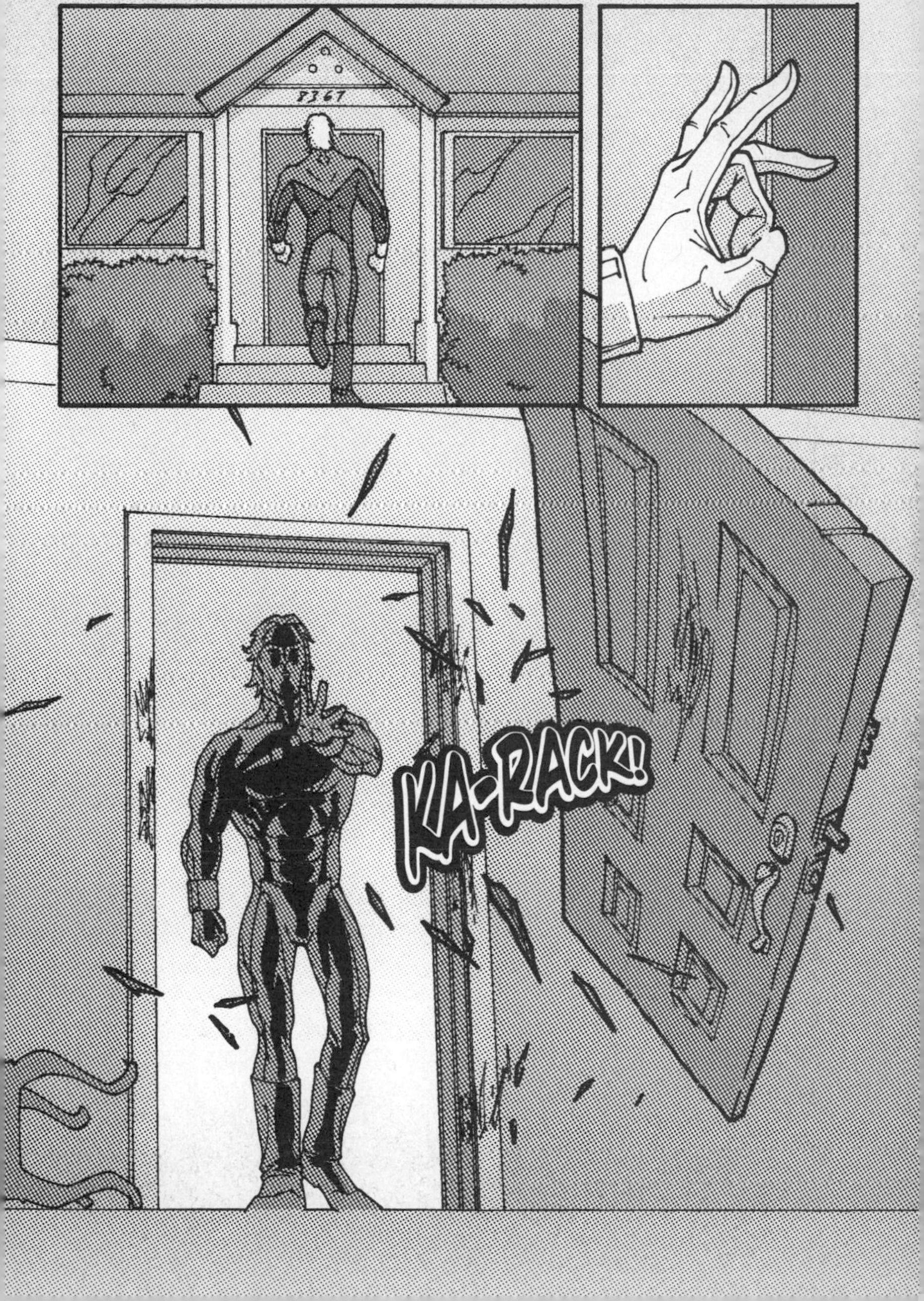
8367
KA-RACK!

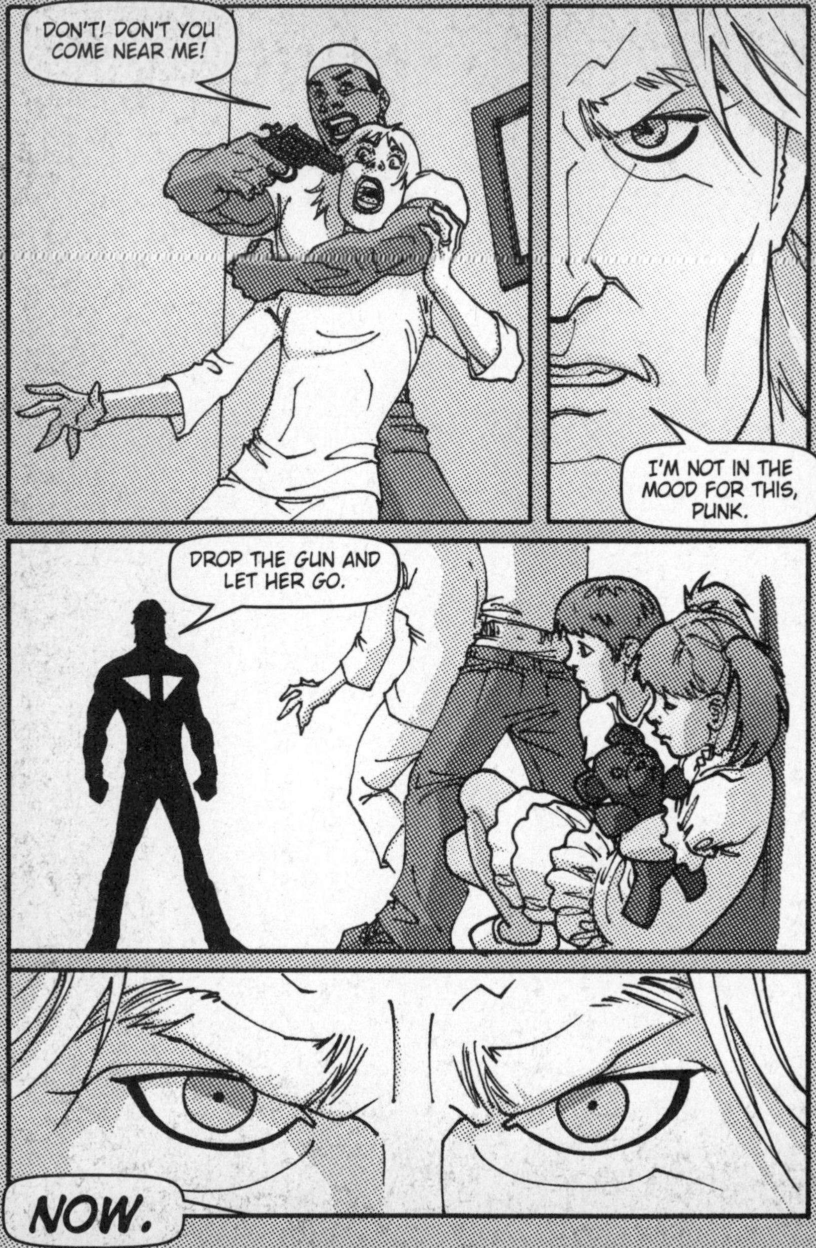
DON'T! DON'T YOU COME NEAR ME!
I'M NOT IN THE MOOD FOR THIS, PUNK.
DROP THE GUN AND LET HER GO.
NOW.

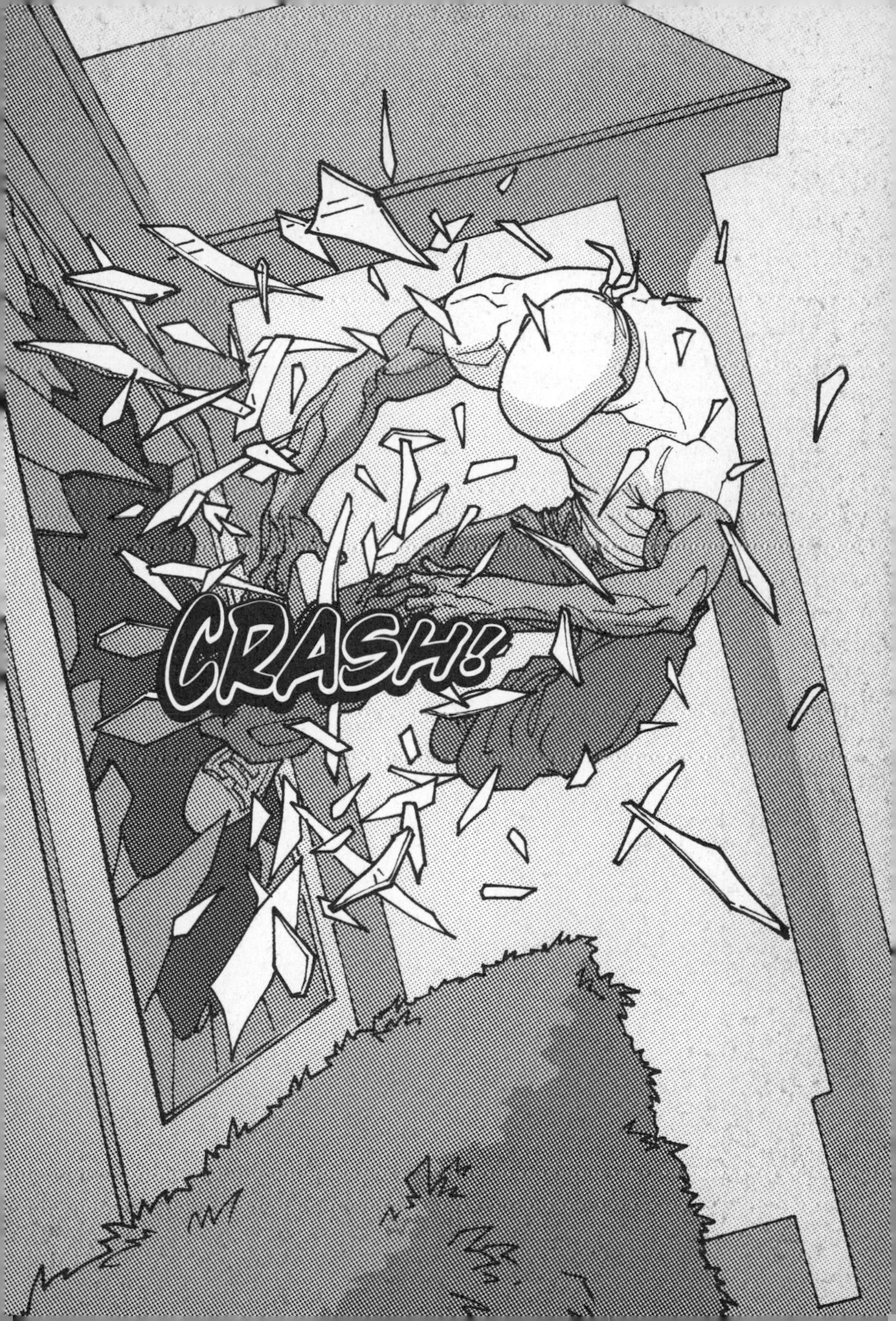
CRASH!

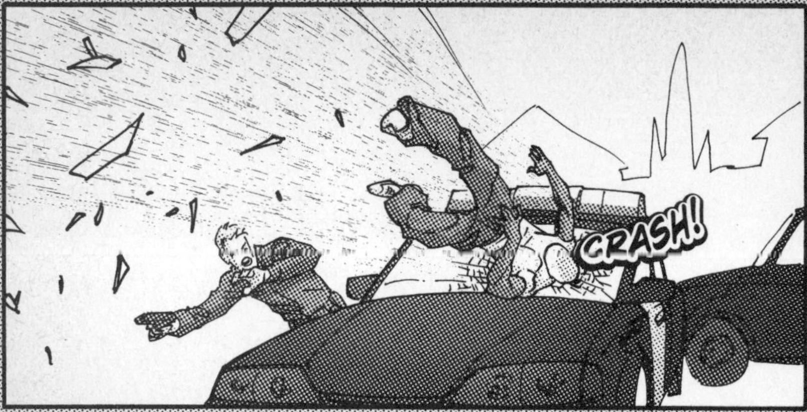
CRASH!
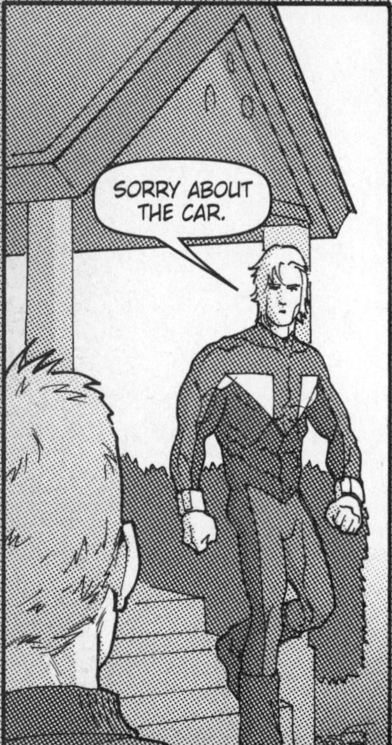
SORRY ABOUT THE CAR.
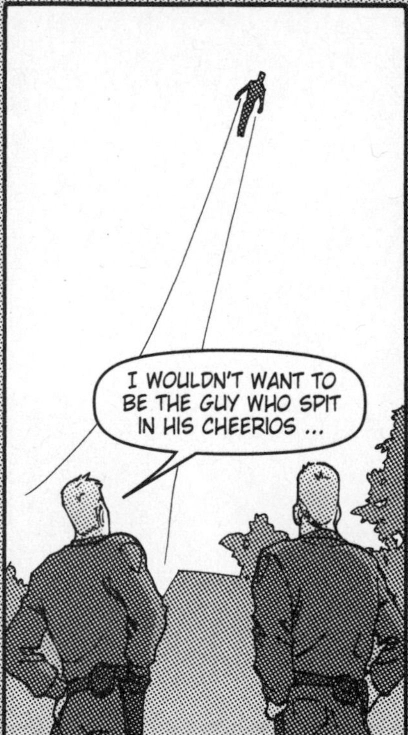
I WOULDN'T WANT TO BE THE GUY WHO SPIT IN HIS CHEERIOS ...

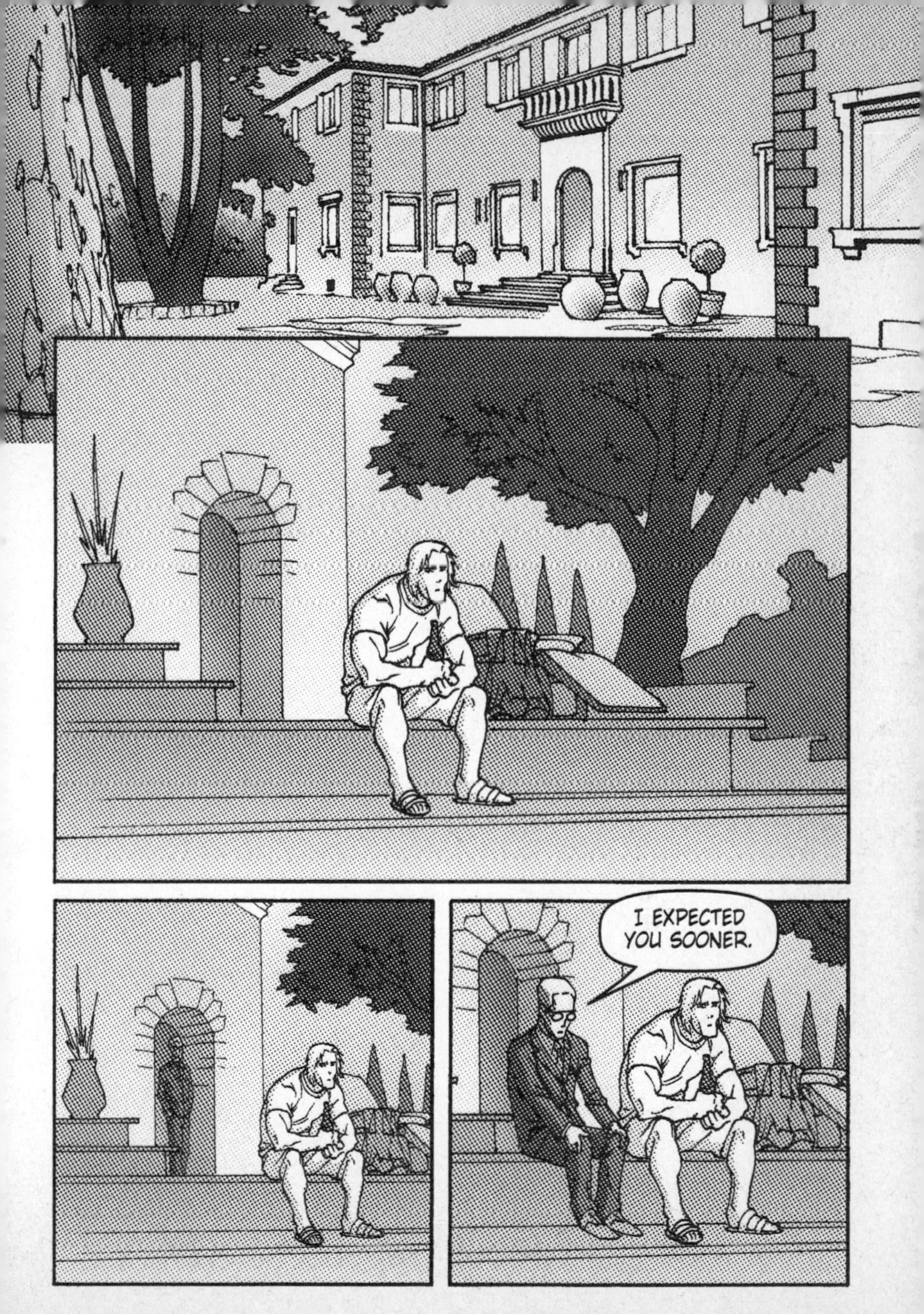
I EXPECTED YOU SOONER.

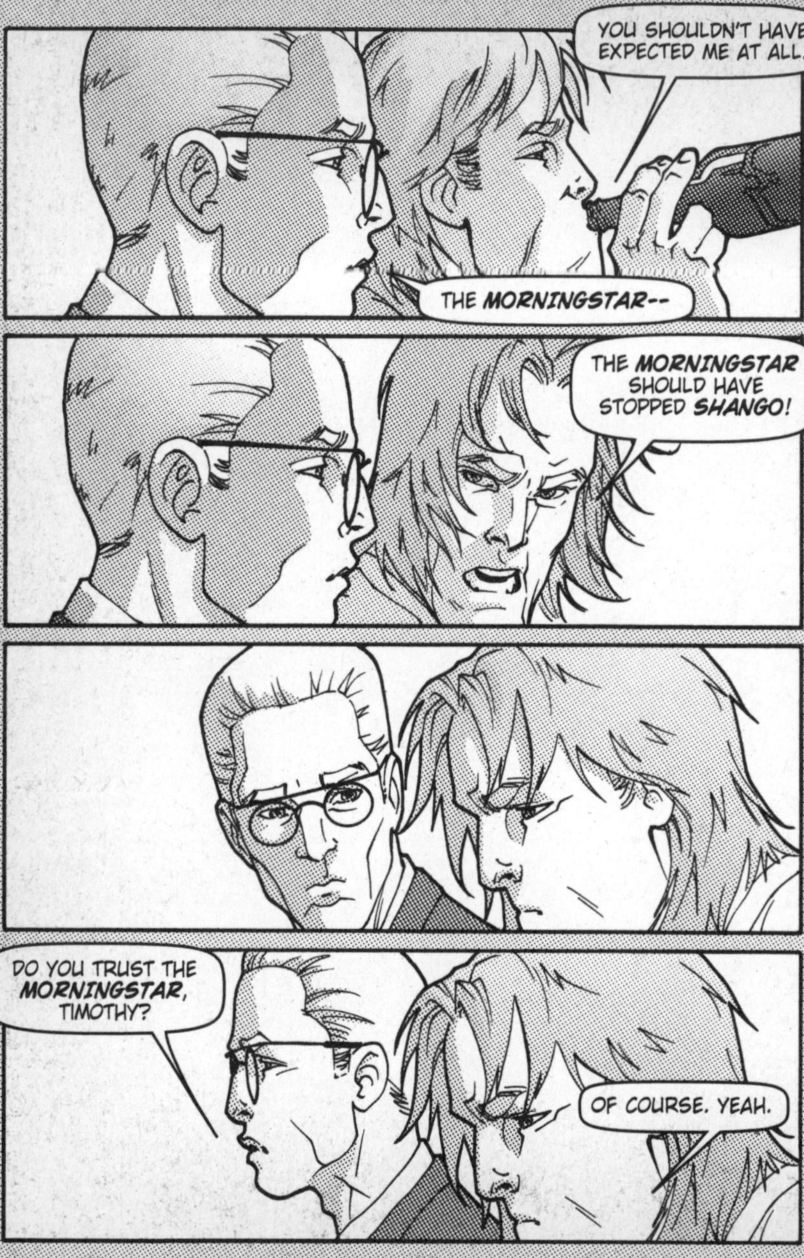
YOU SHOULDN'T HAVE EXPECTED ME AT ALL.
THE MORNINGSTAR--
THE MORNINGSTAR SHOULD HAVE STOPPED SHANGO!
DO YOU TRUST THE MORNINGSTAR, TIMOTHY?
OF COURSE. YEAH.

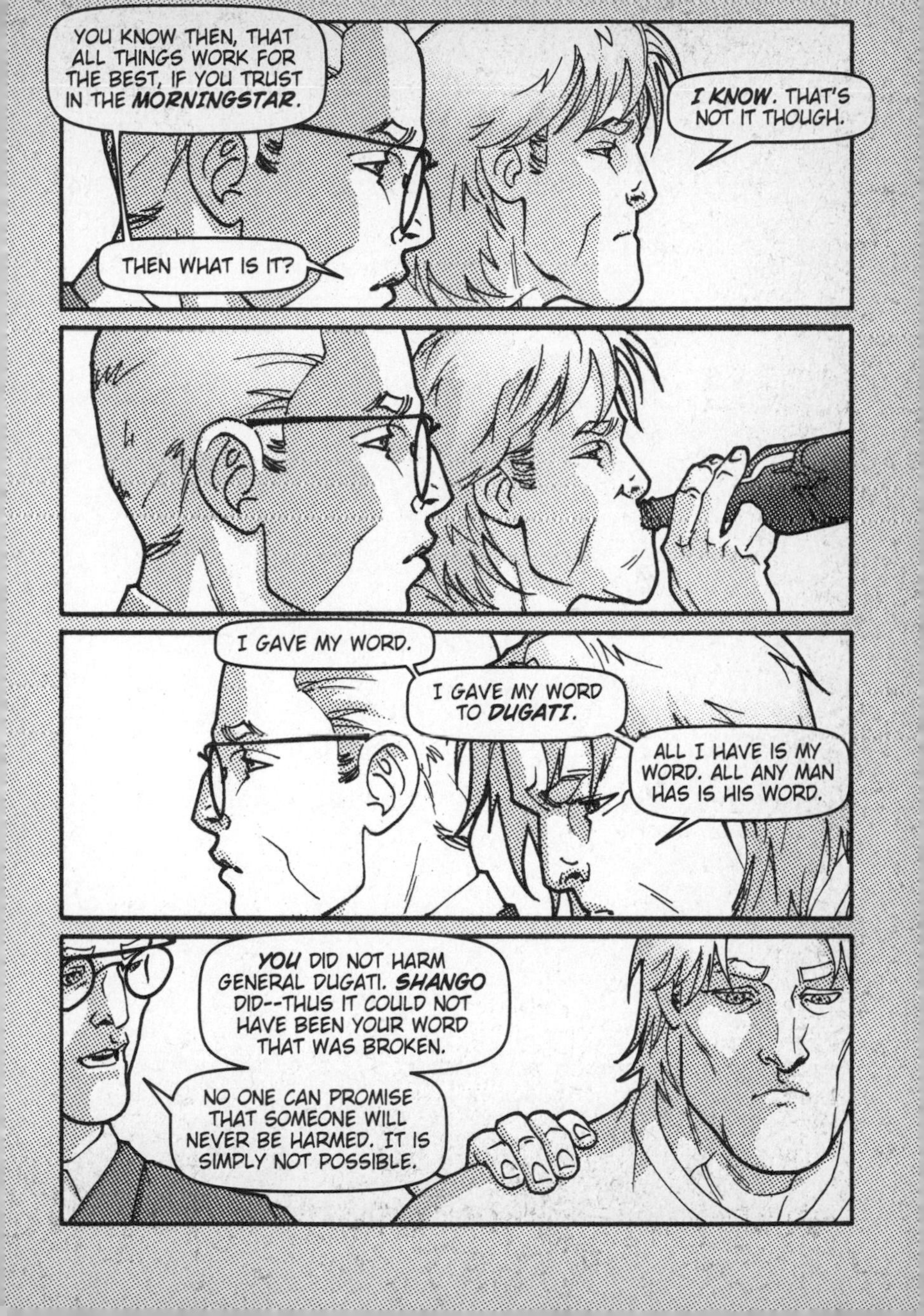
YOU KNOW THEN, THAT ALL THINGS WORK FOR THE BEST, IF YOU TRUST IN THE **MORNINGSTAR**.
I KNOW. THAT'S NOT IT THOUGH.
THEN WHAT IS IT?
I GAVE MY WORD.
I GAVE MY WORD TO **DUGATI**.
ALL I HAVE IS MY WORD. ALL ANY MAN HAS IS HIS WORD.
YOU DID NOT HARM GENERAL DUGATI. **SHANGO** DID--THUS IT COULD NOT HAVE BEEN YOUR WORD THAT WAS BROKEN.
NO ONE CAN PROMISE THAT SOMEONE WILL NEVER BE HARMED. IT IS SIMPLY NOT POSSIBLE.

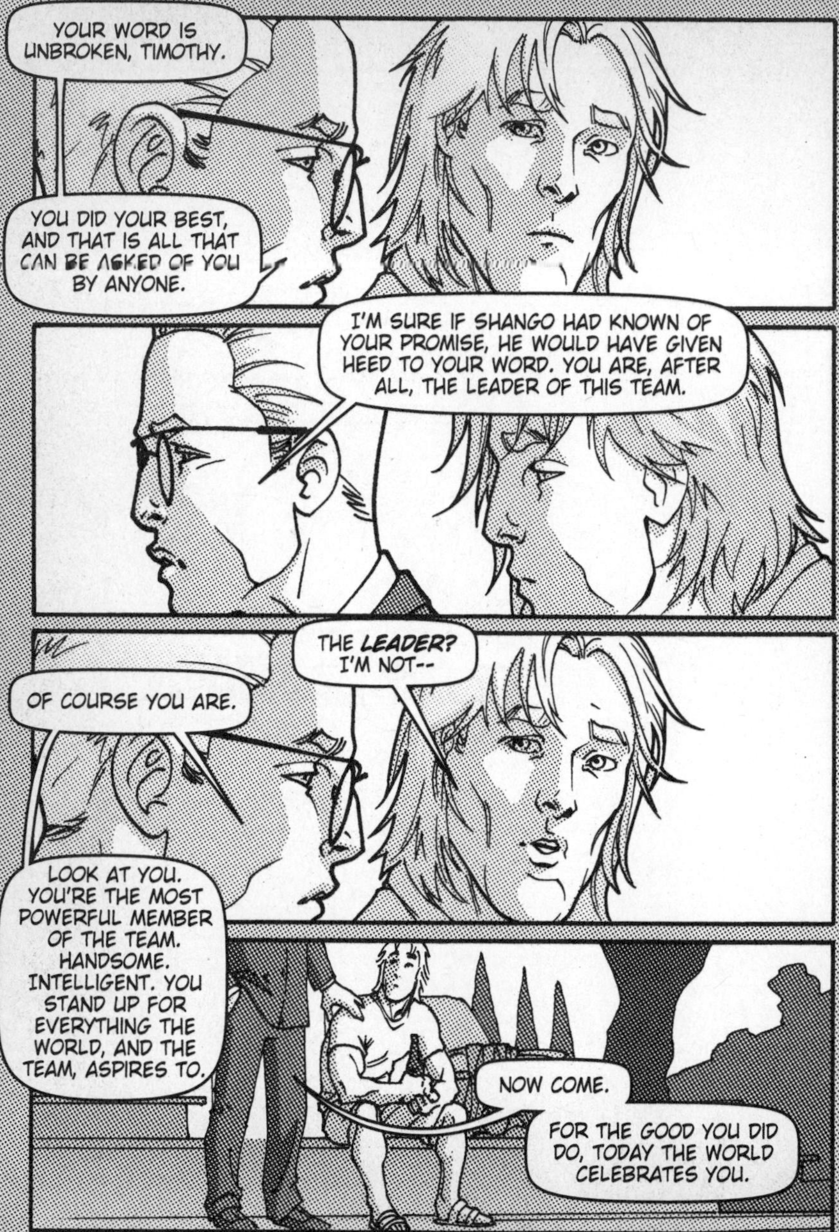
YOUR WORD IS UNBROKEN, TIMOTHY.
YOU DID YOUR BEST, AND THAT IS ALL THAT CAN BE ASKED OF YOU BY ANYONE.
I'M SURE IF SHANGO HAD KNOWN OF YOUR PROMISE, HE WOULD HAVE GIVEN HEED TO YOUR WORD. YOU ARE, AFTER ALL, THE LEADER OF THIS TEAM.
THE *LEADER?* I'M NOT--
OF COURSE YOU ARE.
LOOK AT YOU. YOU'RE THE MOST POWERFUL MEMBER OF THE TEAM. HANDSOME. INTELLIGENT. YOU STAND UP FOR EVERYTHING THE WORLD, AND THE TEAM, ASPIRES TO.
NOW COME.
FOR THE GOOD YOU DID DO, TODAY THE WORLD CELEBRATES YOU.

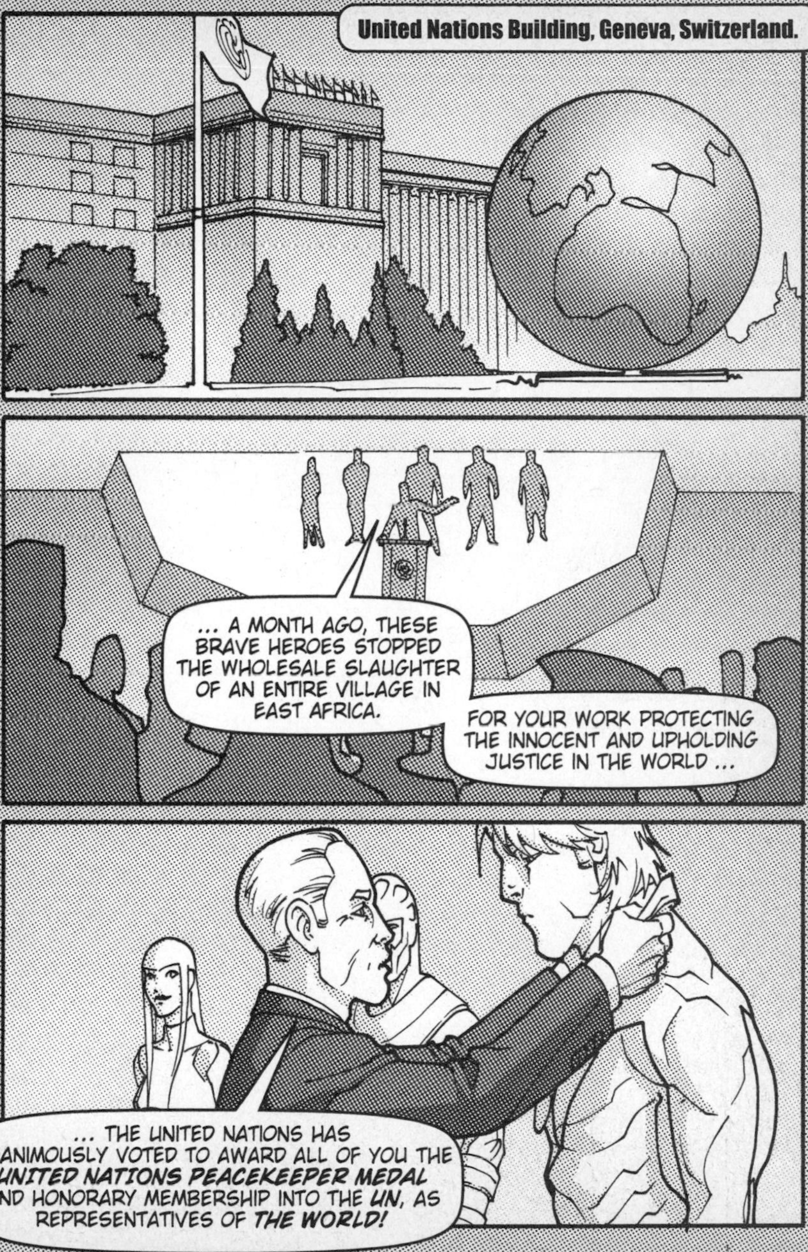
United Nations Building, Geneva, Switzerland.
... A MONTH AGO, THESE BRAVE HEROES STOPPED THE WHOLESALE SLAUGHTER OF AN ENTIRE VILLAGE IN EAST AFRICA.
FOR YOUR WORK PROTECTING THE INNOCENT AND UPHOLDING JUSTICE IN THE WORLD ...
... THE UNITED NATIONS HAS UNANIMOUSLY VOTED TO AWARD ALL OF YOU THE *UNITED NATIONS PEACEKEEPER MEDAL* AND HONORARY MEMBERSHIP INTO THE *UN*, AS REPRESENTATIVES OF *THE WORLD!*

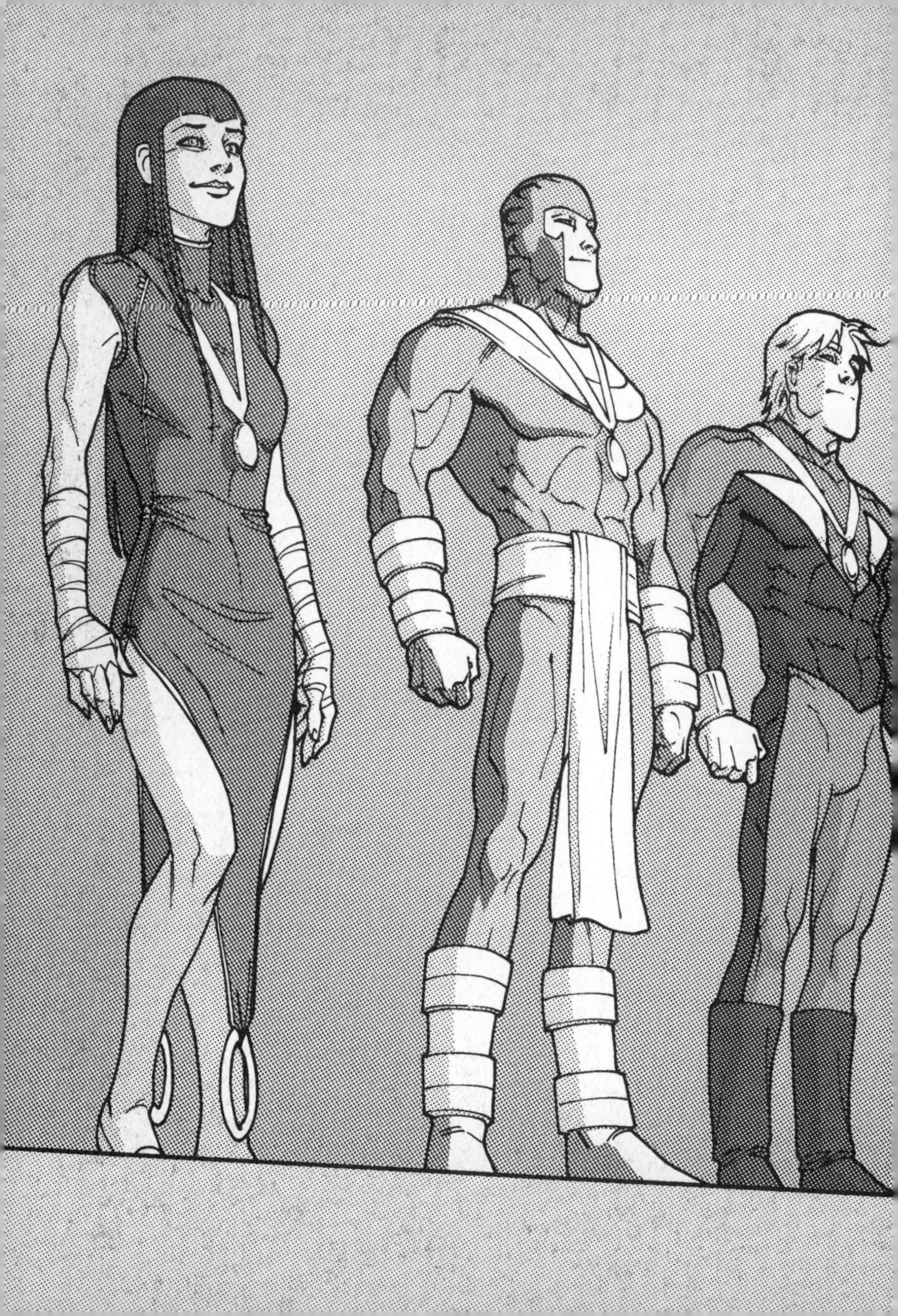

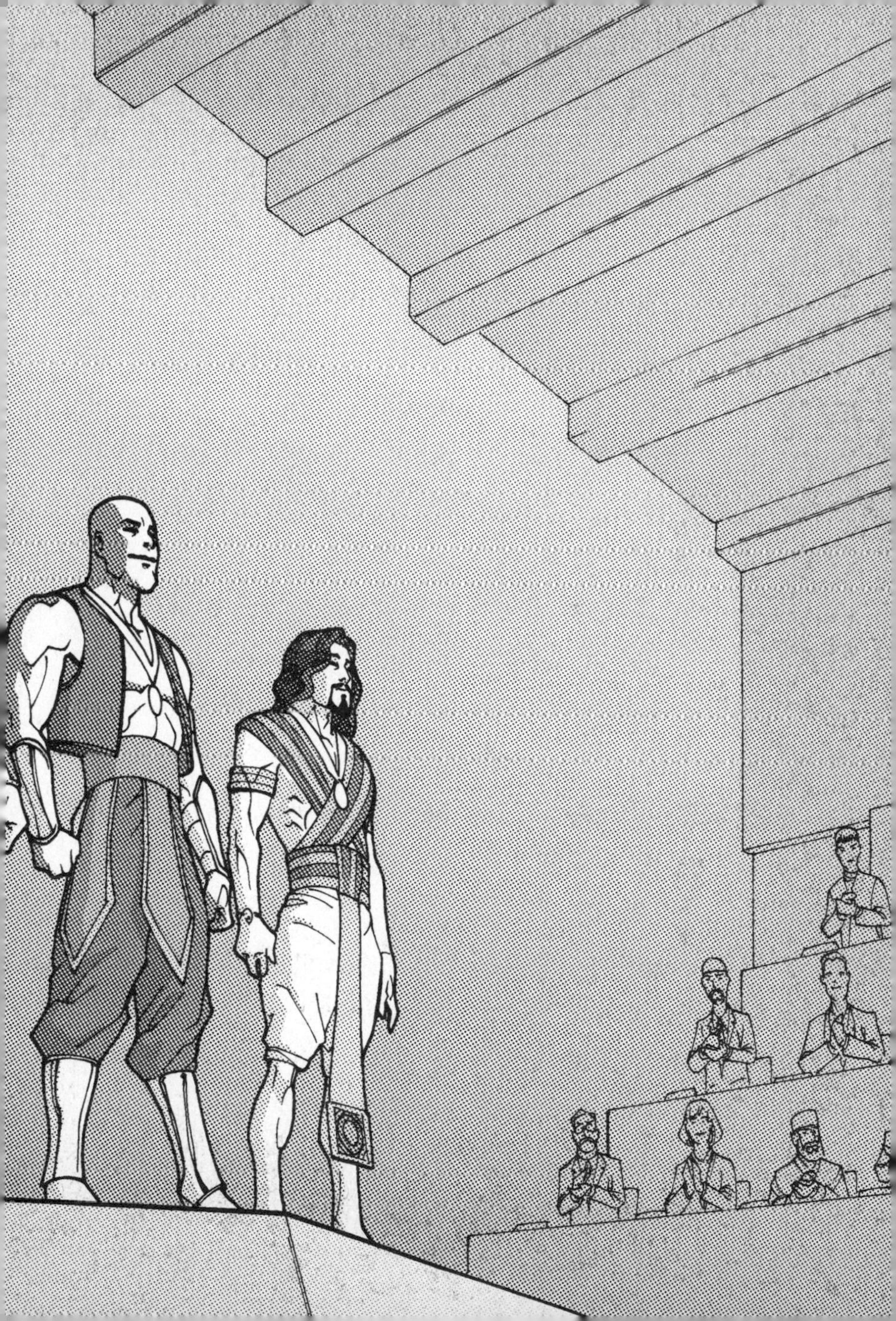

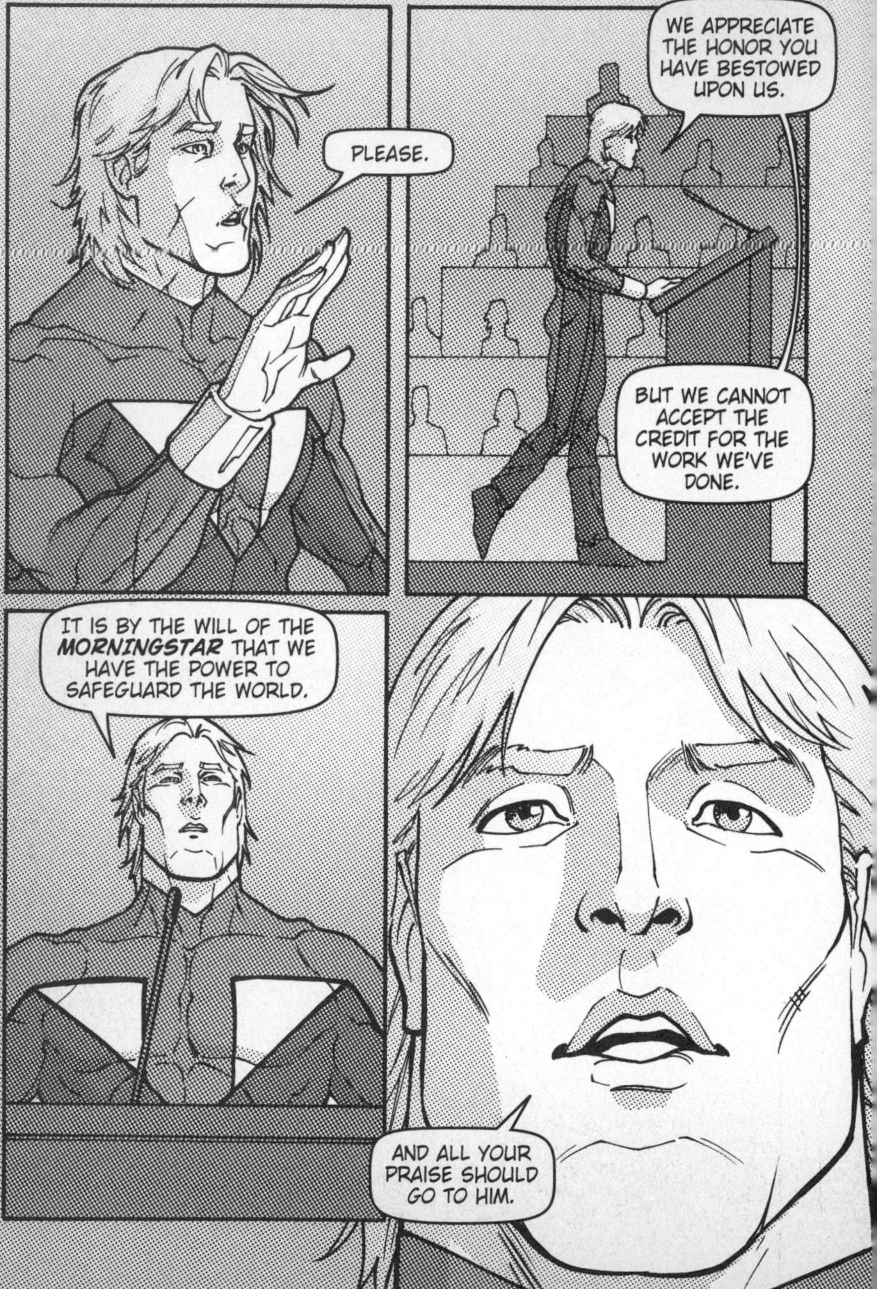
PLEASE.
WE APPRECIATE THE HONOR YOU HAVE BESTOWED UPON US.
BUT WE CANNOT ACCEPT THE CREDIT FOR THE WORK WE'VE DONE.
IT IS BY THE WILL OF THE ***MORNINGSTAR*** THAT WE HAVE THE POWER TO SAFEGUARD THE WORLD.
AND ALL YOUR PRAISE SHOULD GO TO HIM.

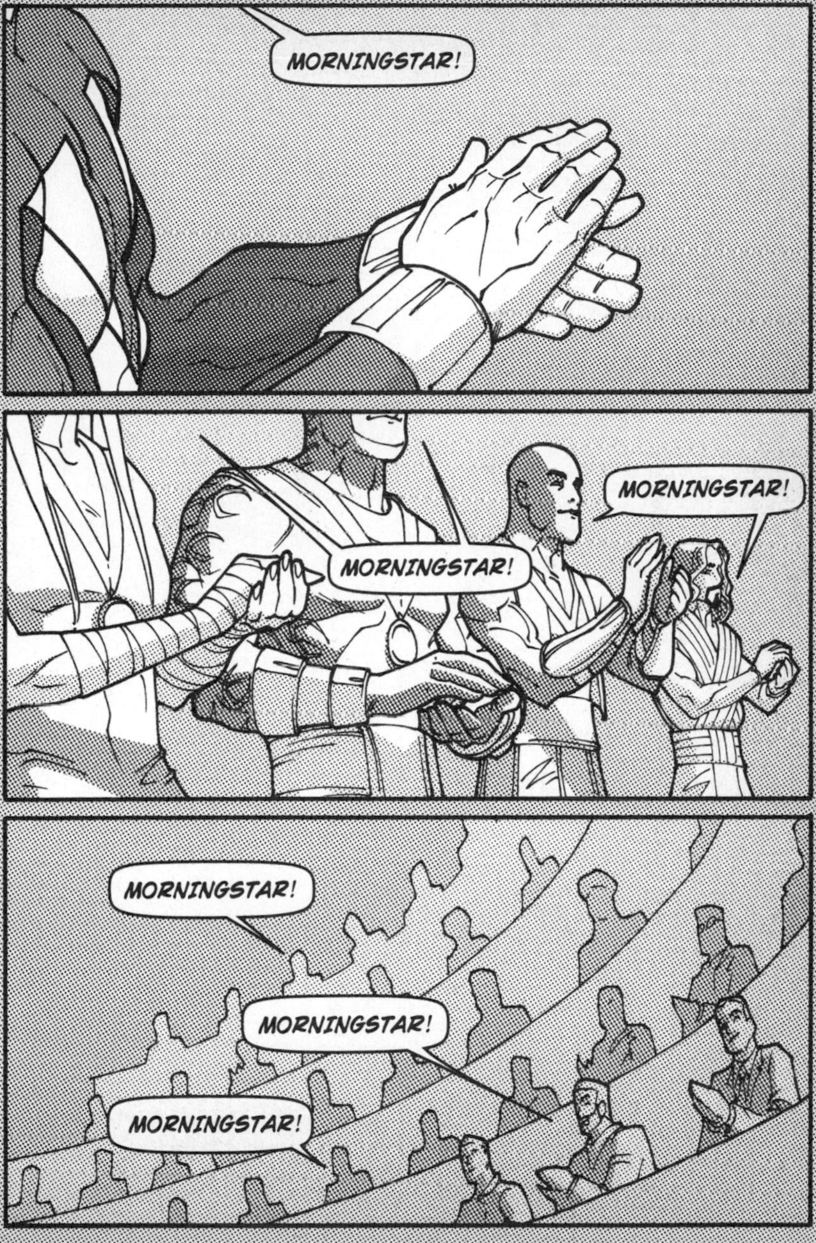
MORNINGSTAR!
MORNINGSTAR!
MORNINGSTAR!
MORNINGSTAR!
MORNINGSTAR!
MORNINGSTAR!

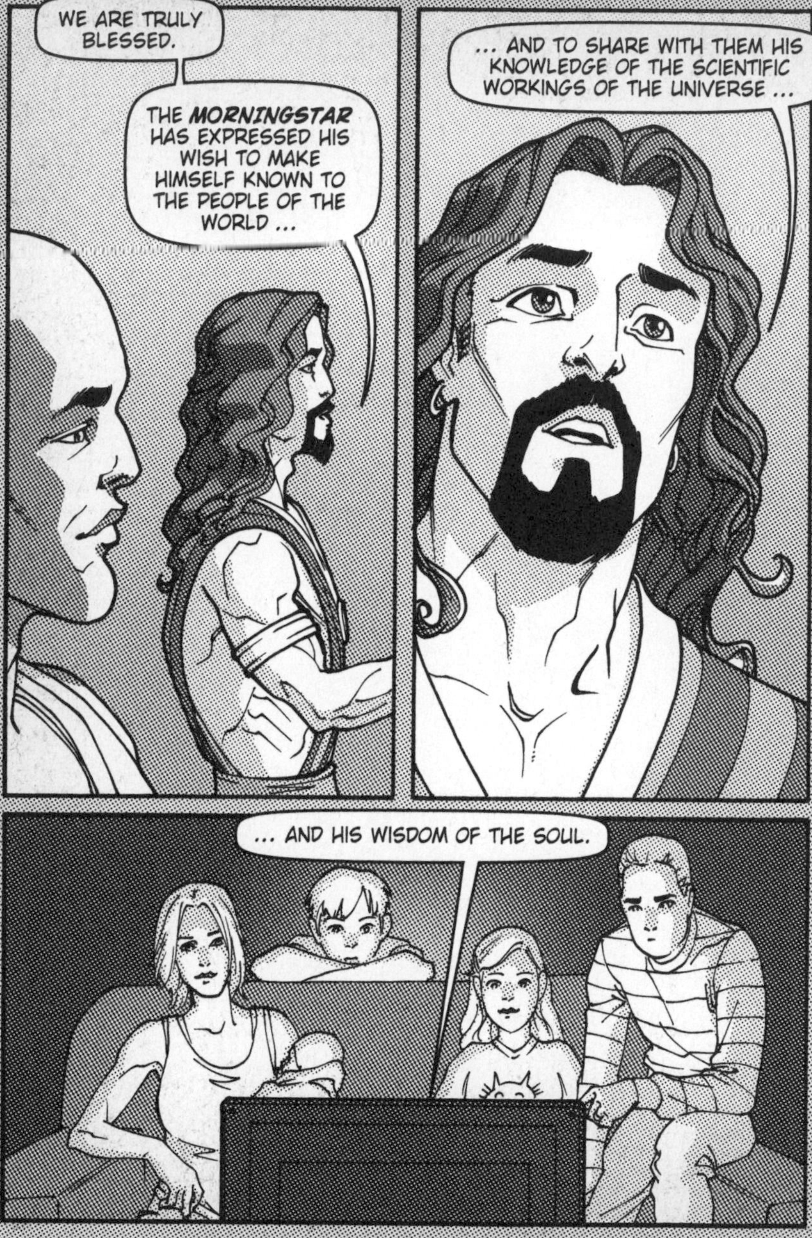
WE ARE TRULY BLESSED.
THE MORNINGSTAR HAS EXPRESSED HIS WISH TO MAKE HIMSELF KNOWN TO THE PEOPLE OF THE WORLD ...
... AND TO SHARE WITH THEM HIS KNOWLEDGE OF THE SCIENTIFIC WORKINGS OF THE UNIVERSE ...
... AND HIS WISDOM OF THE SOUL.

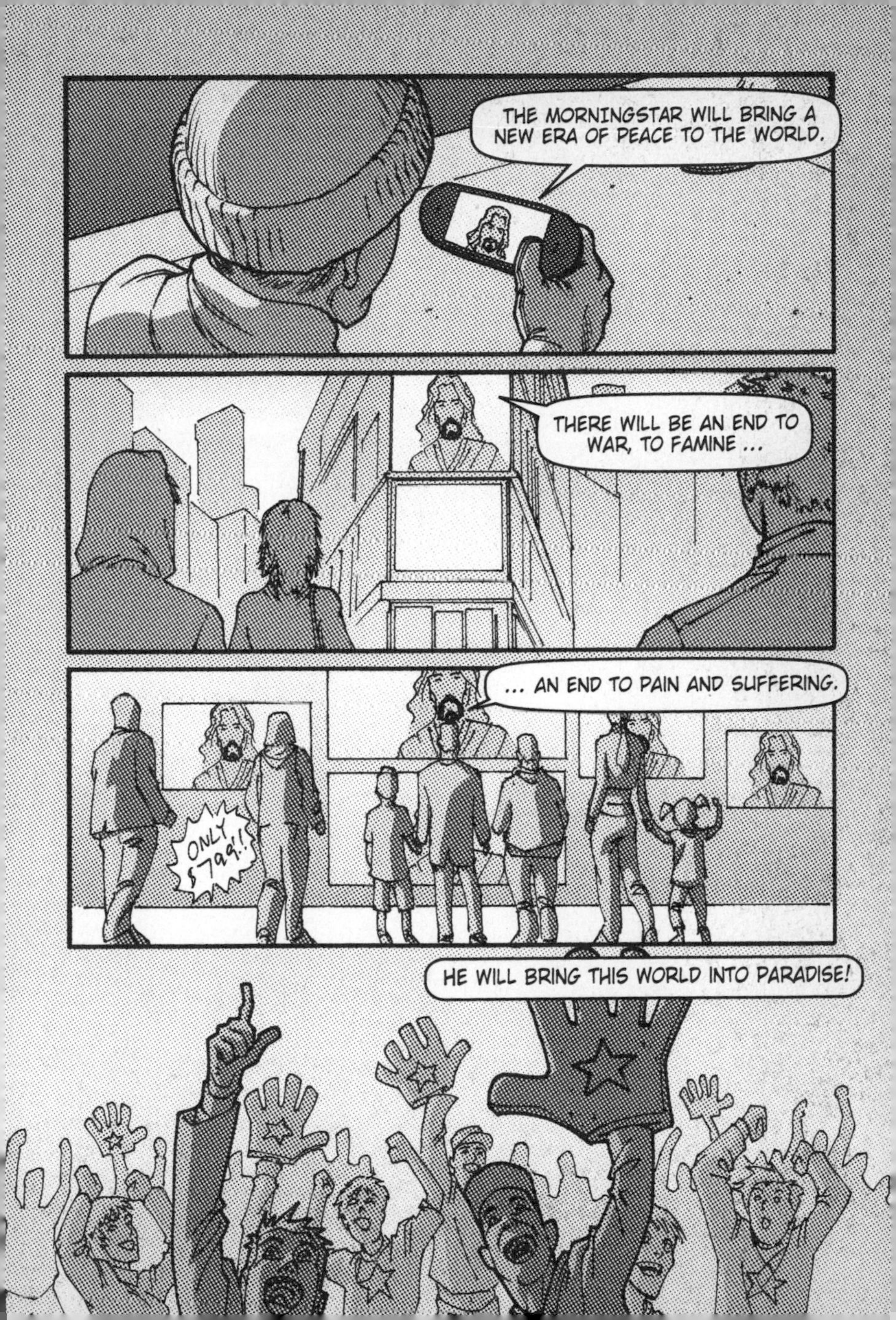
THE MORNINGSTAR WILL BRING A NEW ERA OF PEACE TO THE WORLD.
THERE WILL BE AN END TO WAR, TO FAMINE ...
... AN END TO PAIN AND SUFFERING.
ONLY $799!!
HE WILL BRING THIS WORLD INTO PARADISE!

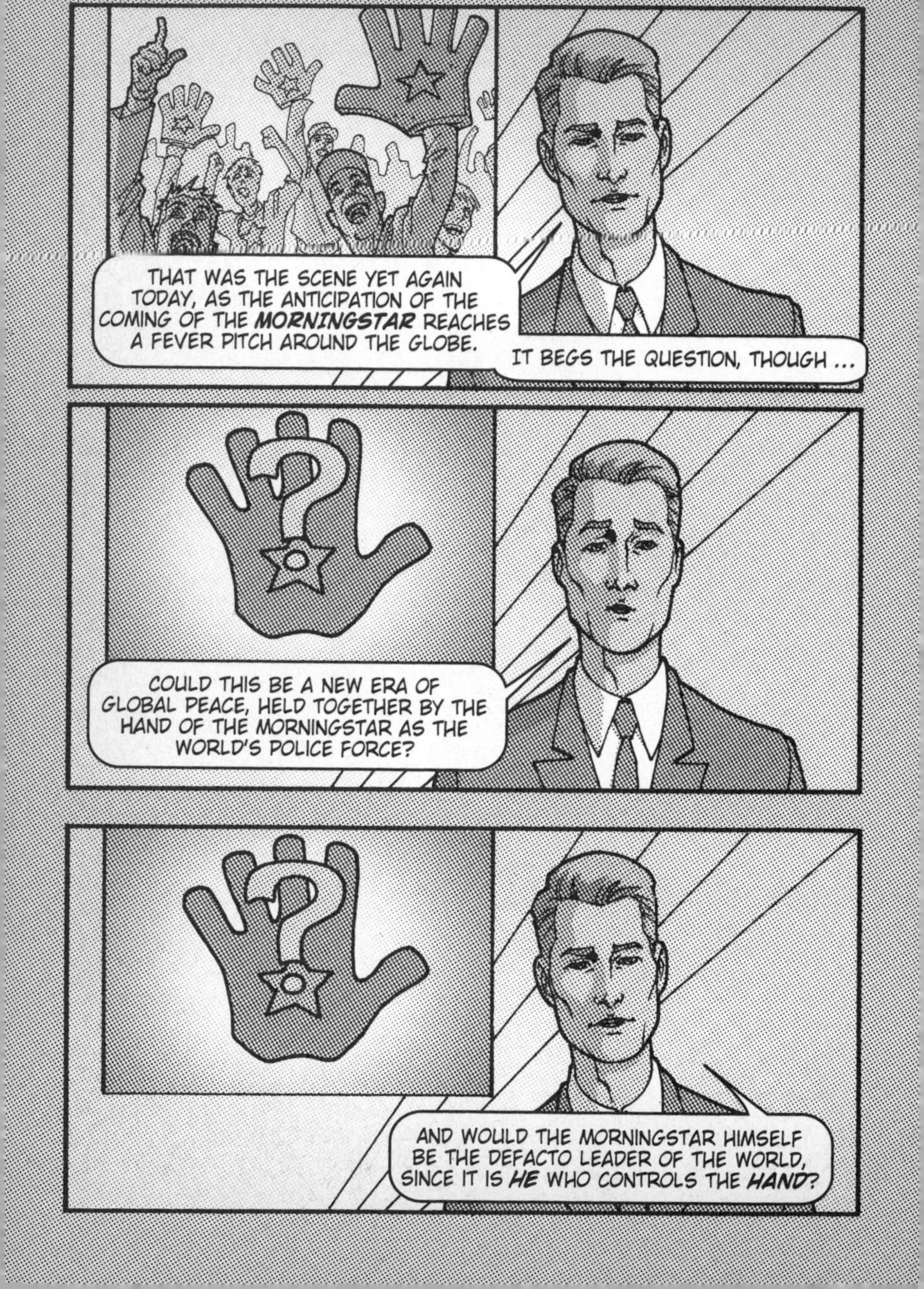
THAT WAS THE SCENE YET AGAIN TODAY, AS THE ANTICIPATION OF THE COMING OF THE MORNINGSTAR REACHES A FEVER PITCH AROUND THE GLOBE.
IT BEGS THE QUESTION, THOUGH ...
COULD THIS BE A NEW ERA OF GLOBAL PEACE, HELD TOGETHER BY THE HAND OF THE MORNINGSTAR AS THE WORLD'S POLICE FORCE?
AND WOULD THE MORNINGSTAR HIMSELF BE THE DEFACTO LEADER OF THE WORLD, SINCE IT IS HE WHO CONTROLS THE HAND?

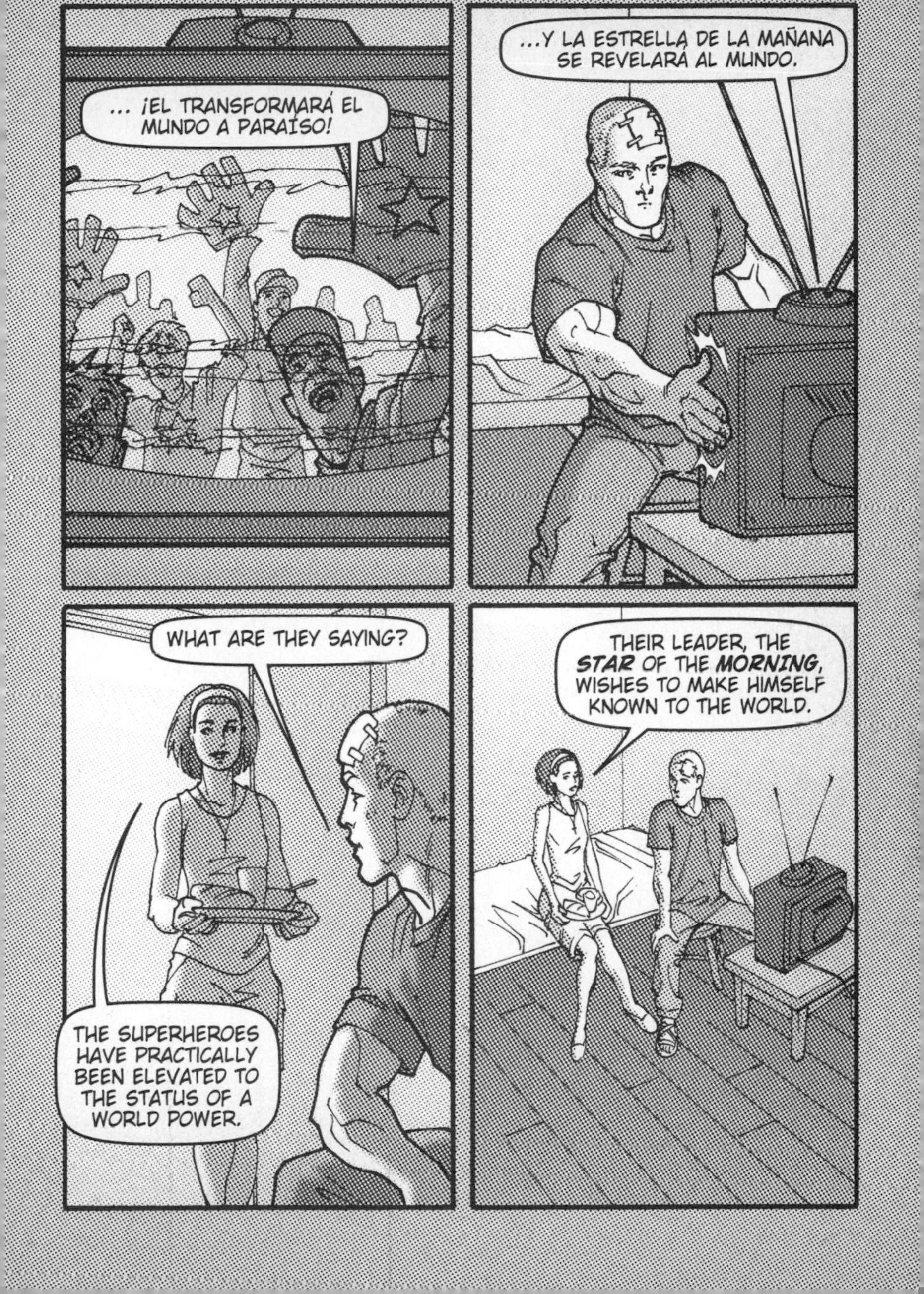
... ¡EL TRANSFORMARÁ EL MUNDO A PARAÍSO!
...Y LA ESTRELLA DE LA MAÑANA SE REVELARÁ AL MUNDO.
WHAT ARE THEY SAYING?
THE SUPERHEROES HAVE PRACTICALLY BEEN ELEVATED TO THE STATUS OF A WORLD POWER.
THEIR LEADER, THE STAR OF THE MORNING, WISHES TO MAKE HIMSELF KNOWN TO THE WORLD.

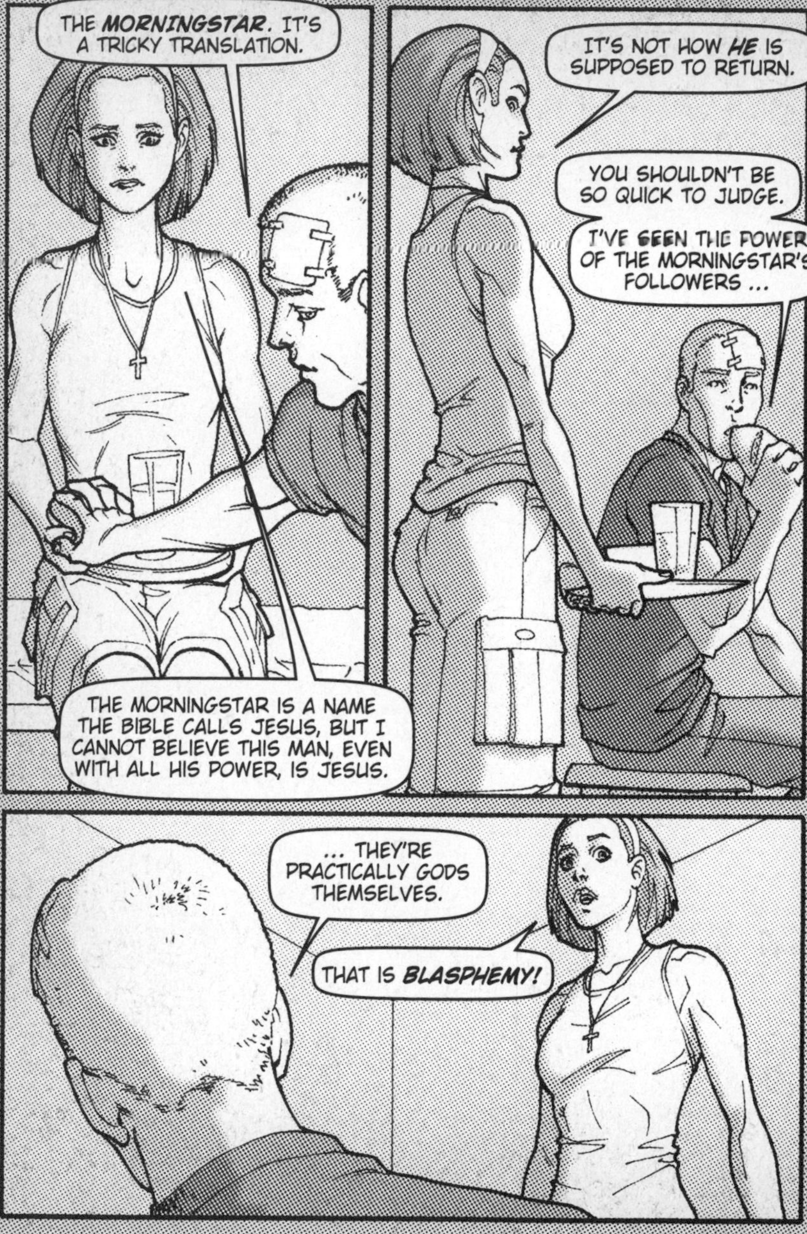
THE MORNINGSTAR. IT'S A TRICKY TRANSLATION.
THE MORNINGSTAR IS A NAME THE BIBLE CALLS JESUS, BUT I CANNOT BELIEVE THIS MAN, EVEN WITH ALL HIS POWER, IS JESUS.
IT'S NOT HOW HE IS SUPPOSED TO RETURN.
YOU SHOULDN'T BE SO QUICK TO JUDGE.
I'VE SEEN THE POWER OF THE MORNINGSTAR'S FOLLOWERS ...
... THEY'RE PRACTICALLY GODS THEMSELVES.
THAT IS BLASPHEMY!

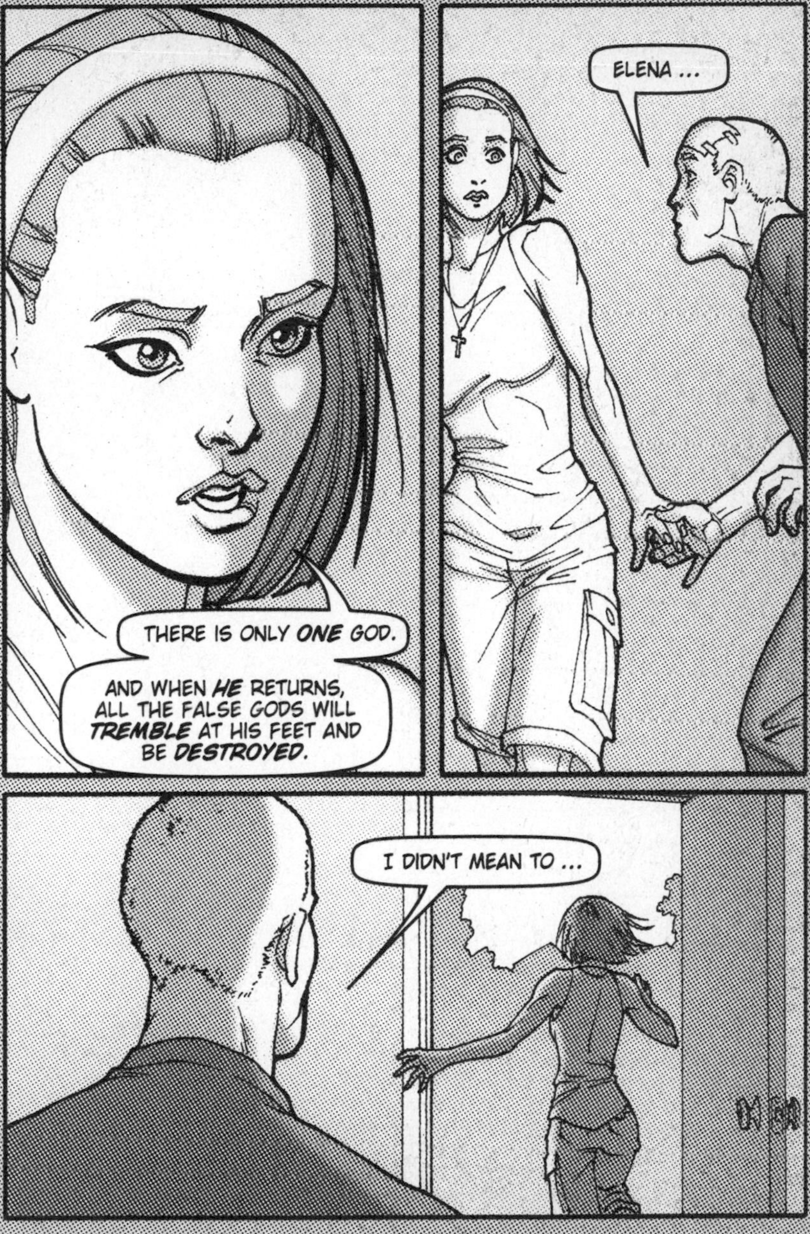
THERE IS ONLY ONE GOD.
AND WHEN HE RETURNS, ALL THE FALSE GODS WILL TREMBLE AT HIS FEET AND BE DESTROYED.
ELENA ...
I DIDN'T MEAN TO ...

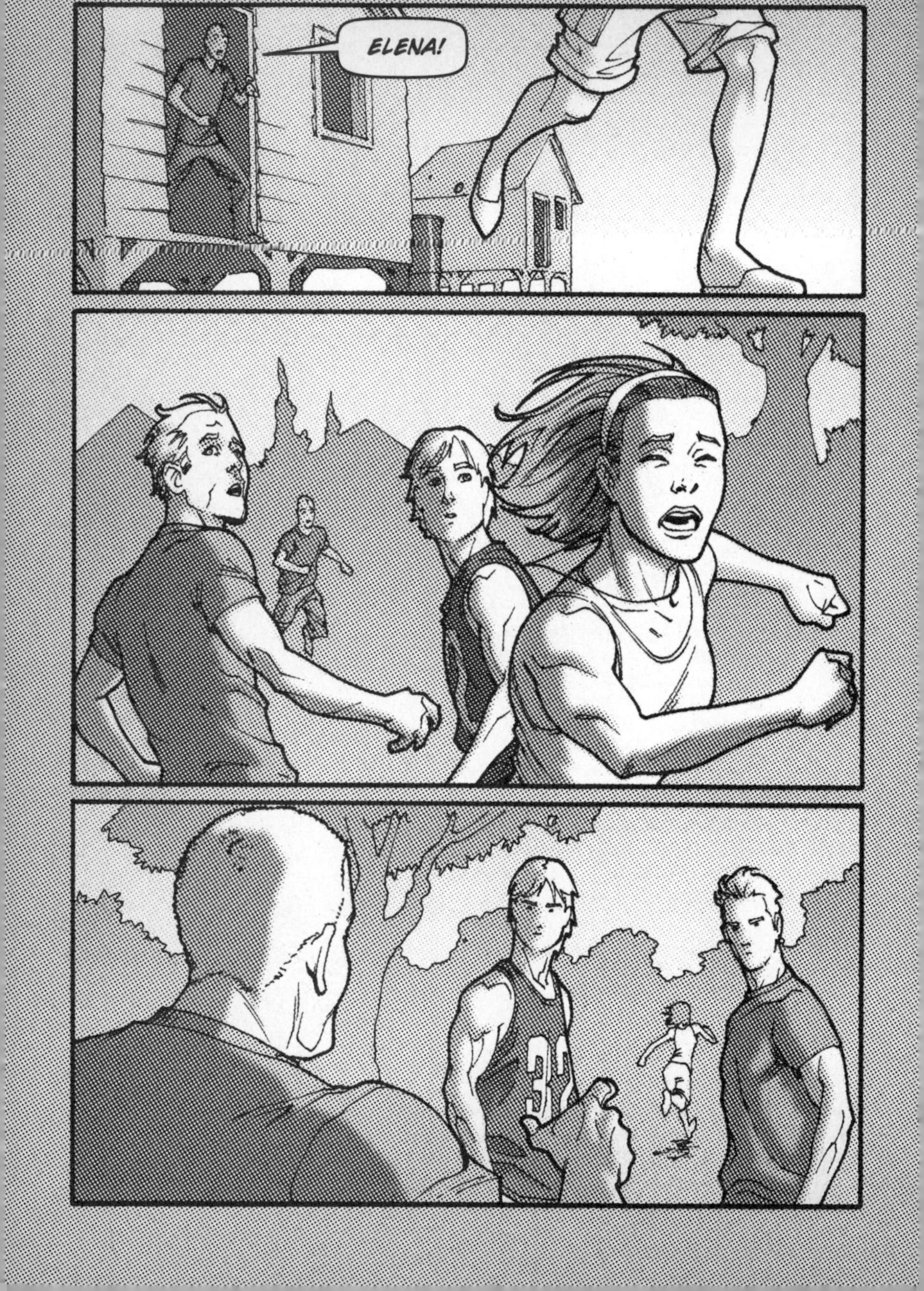
ELENA!

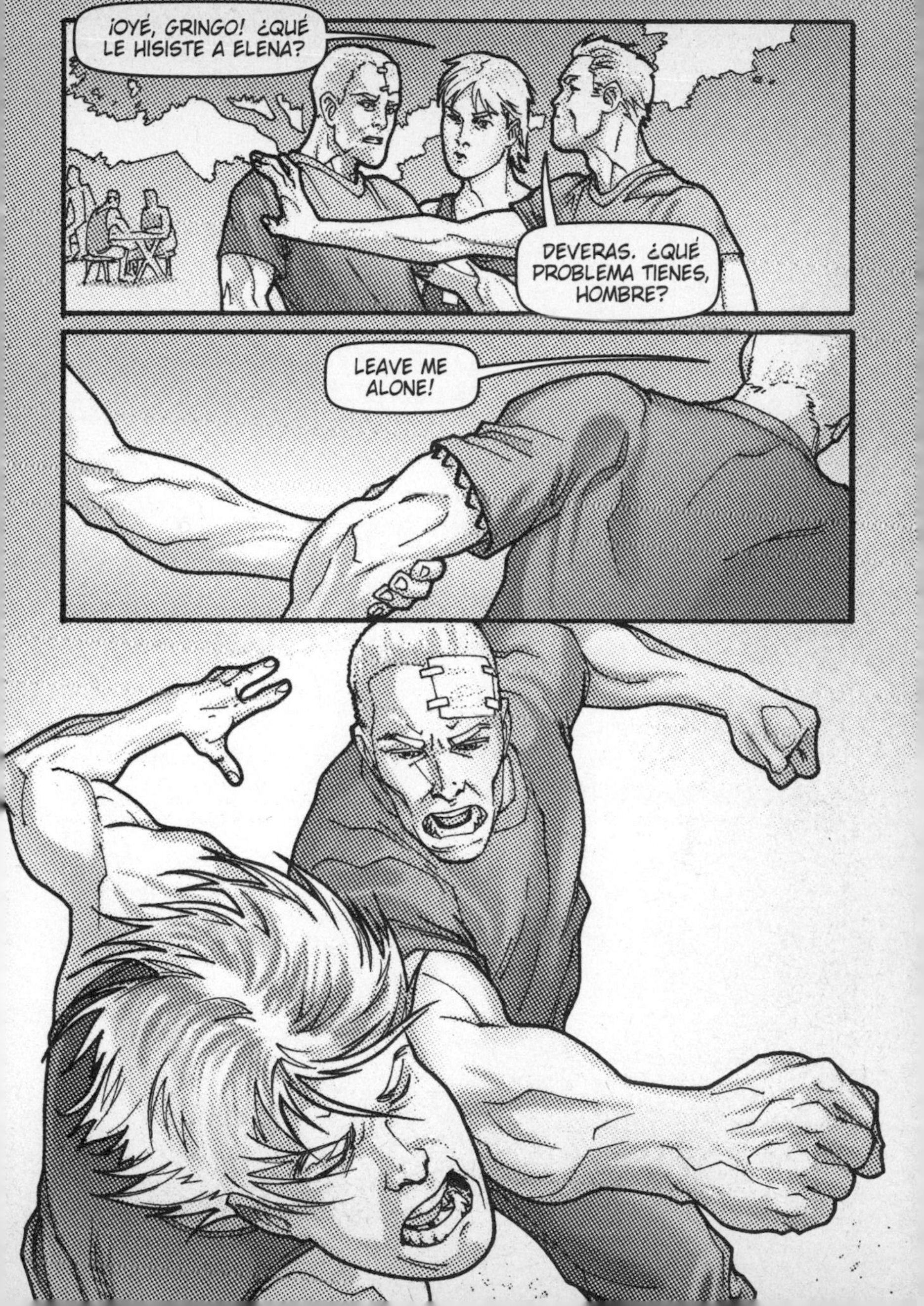
¡OYÉ, GRINGO! ¿QUÉ LE HISISTE A ELENA?
DEVERAS. ¿QUÉ PROBLEMA TIENES, HOMBRE?
LEAVE ME ALONE!

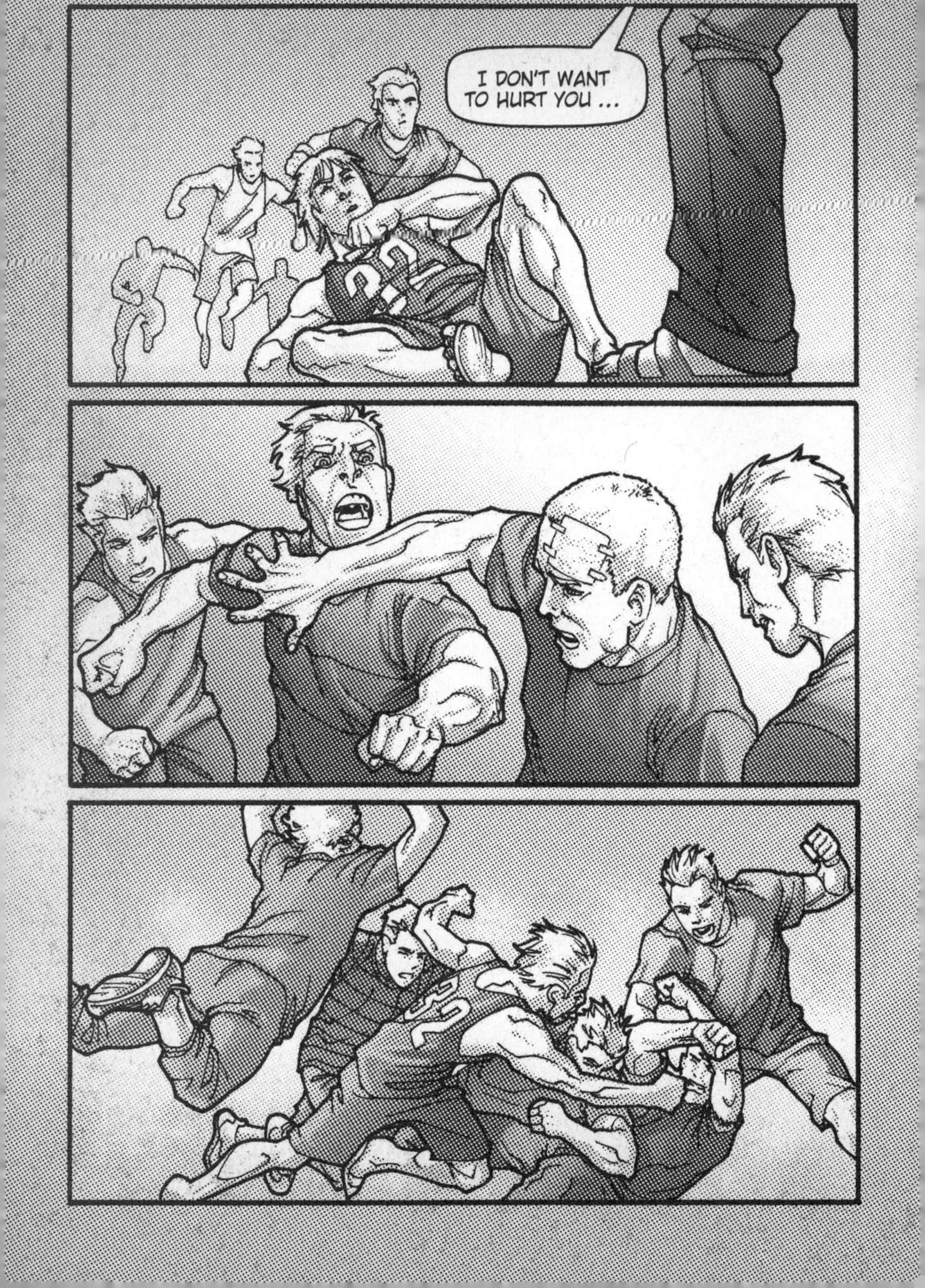
I DON'T WANT TO HURT YOU ...

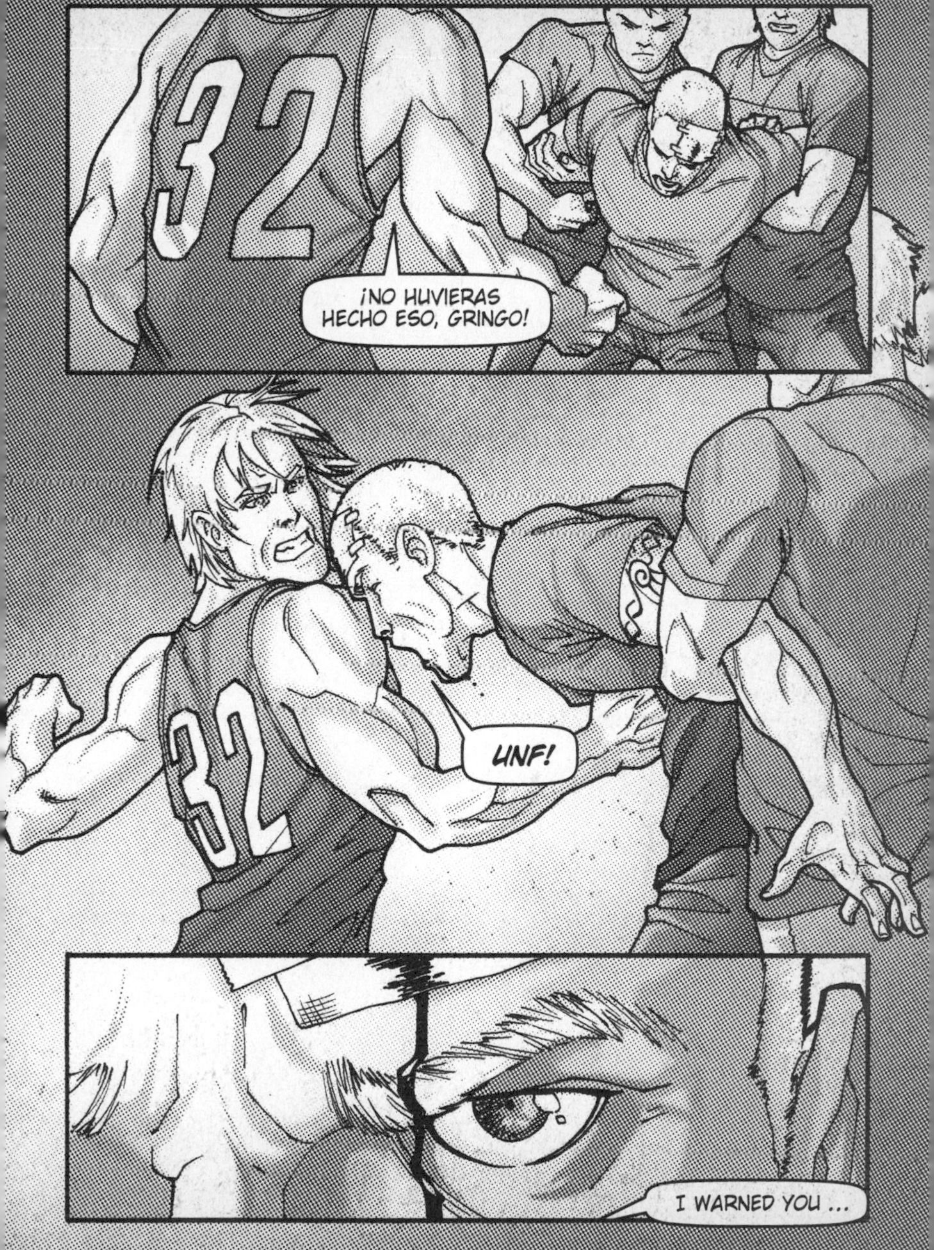
¡NO HUVIERAS HECHO ESO, GRINGO!
UNF!
I WARNED YOU ...

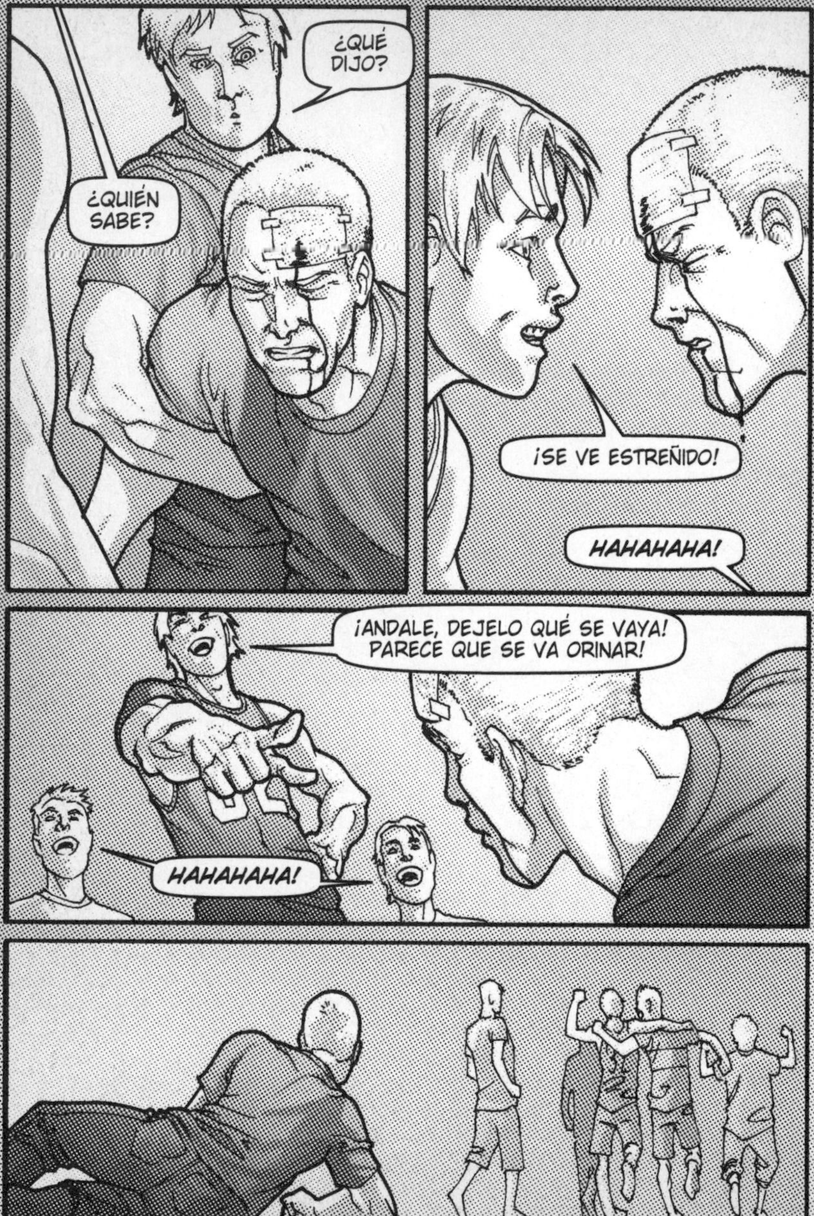
¿QUÉ DIJO?
¿QUIÉN SABE?
¡SE VE ESTREÑIDO!
HAHAHAHA!
¡ANDALE, DEJELO QUÉ SE VAYA! PARECE QUE SE VA ORINAR!
HAHAHAHA!

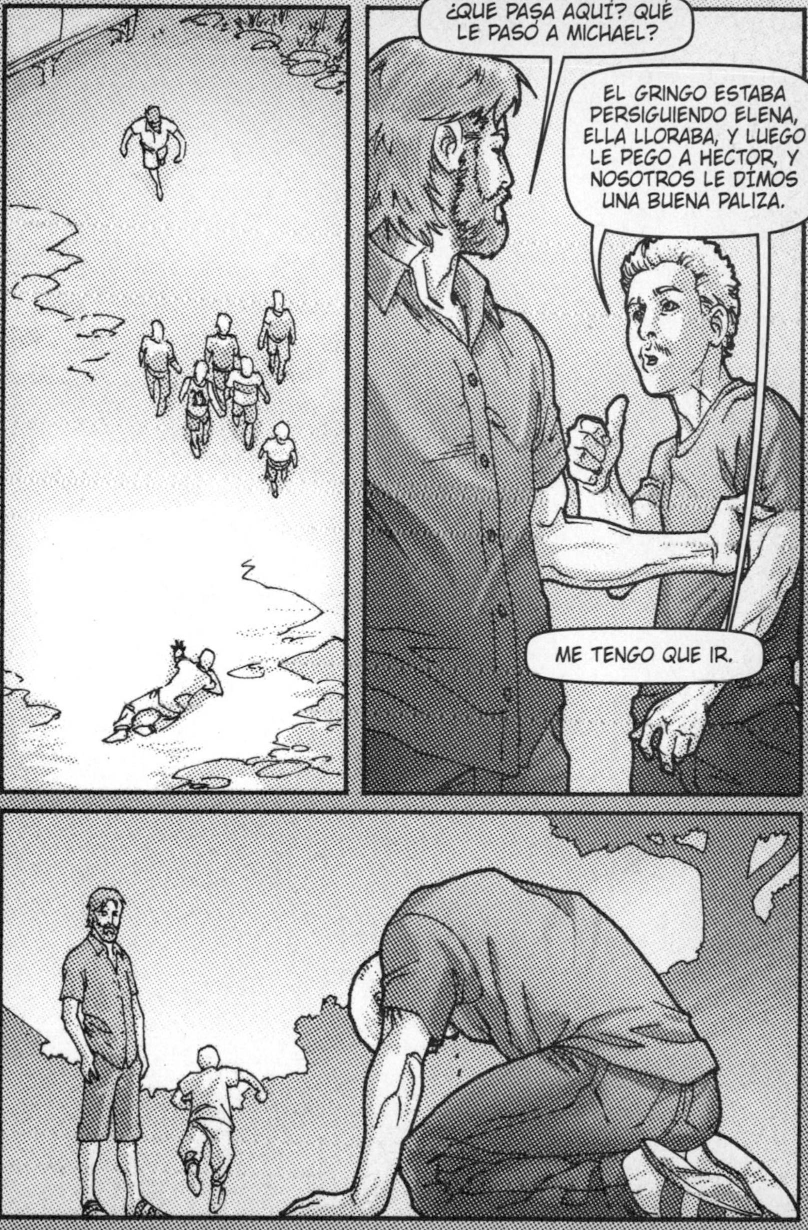
¿QUE PASA AQUÍ? QUÉ LE PASÓ A MICHAEL?
EL GRINGO ESTABA PERSIGUIENDO ELENA, ELLA LLORABA, Y LUEGO LE PEGO A HECTOR, Y NOSOTROS LE DÍMOS UNA BUENA PALIZA.
ME TENGO QUE IR.

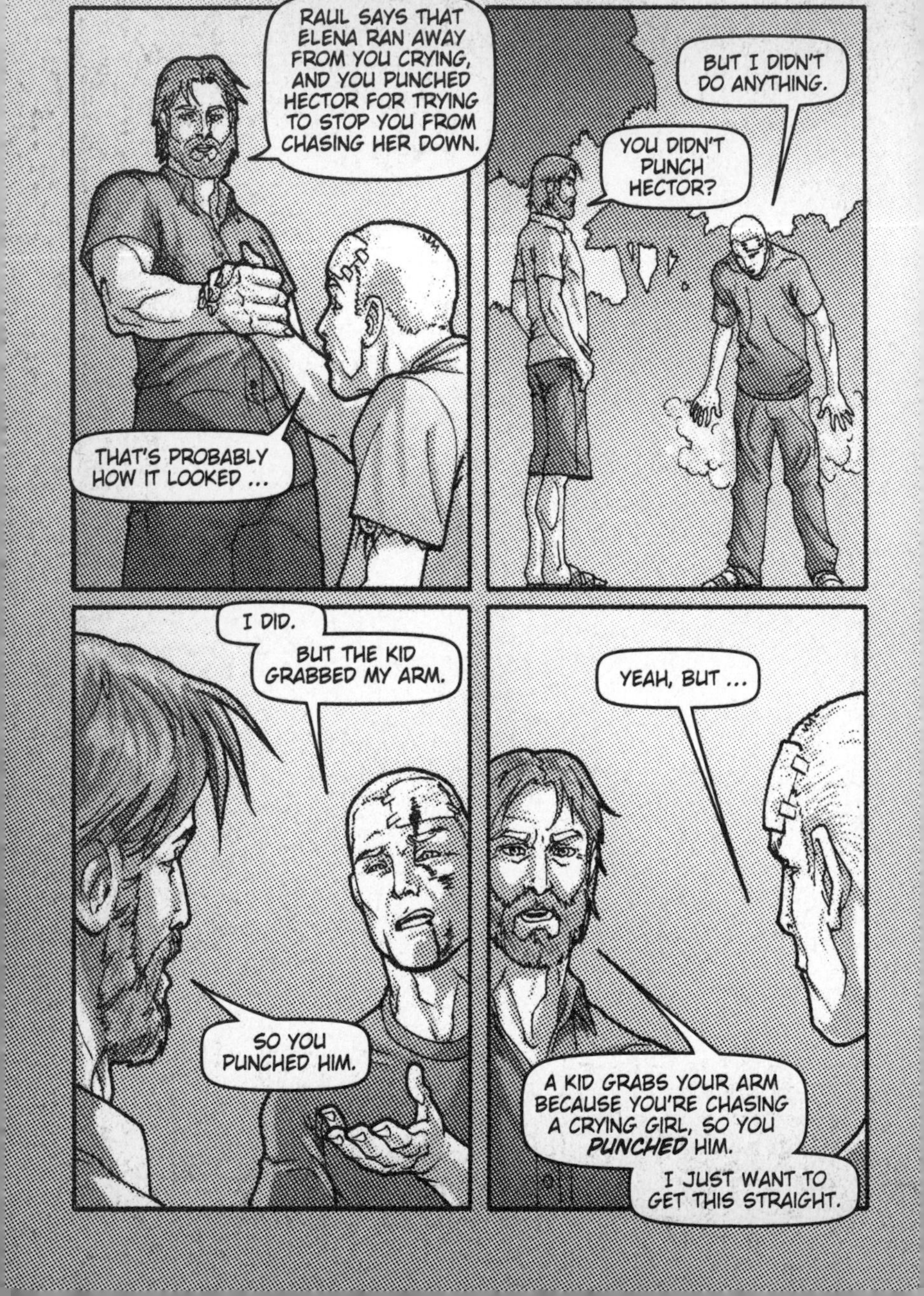
RAUL SAYS THAT ELENA RAN AWAY FROM YOU CRYING, AND YOU PUNCHED HECTOR FOR TRYING TO STOP YOU FROM CHASING HER DOWN.
THAT'S PROBABLY HOW IT LOOKED ...
BUT I DIDN'T DO ANYTHING.
YOU DIDN'T PUNCH HECTOR?
I DID.
BUT THE KID GRABBED MY ARM.
SO YOU PUNCHED HIM.
YEAH, BUT ...
A KID GRABS YOUR ARM BECAUSE YOU'RE CHASING A CRYING GIRL, SO YOU *PUNCHED* HIM.
I JUST WANT TO GET THIS STRAIGHT.

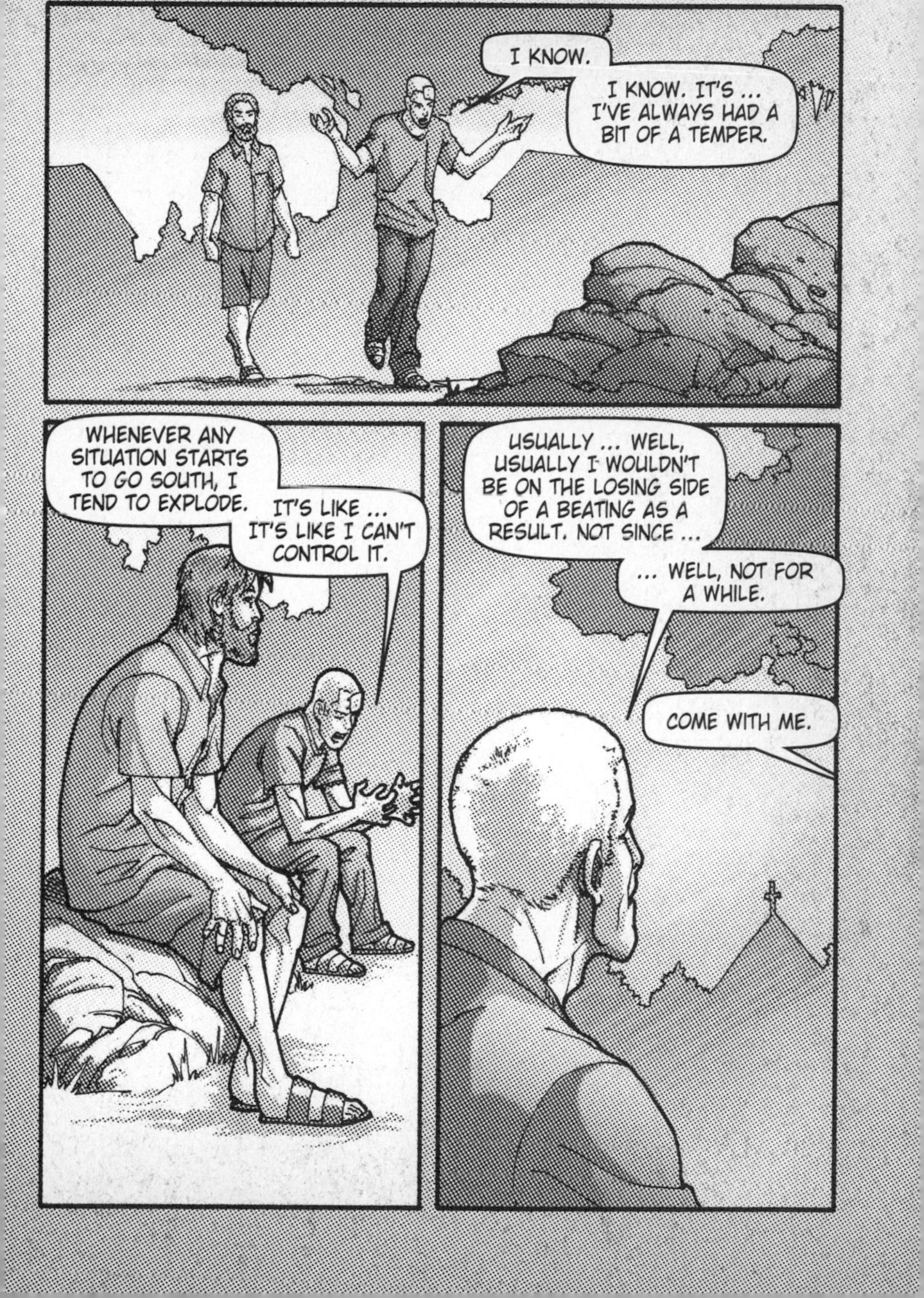
I KNOW.
I KNOW. IT'S ... I'VE ALWAYS HAD A BIT OF A TEMPER.
WHENEVER ANY SITUATION STARTS TO GO SOUTH, I TEND TO EXPLODE.
IT'S LIKE ... IT'S LIKE I CAN'T CONTROL IT.
USUALLY ... WELL, USUALLY I WOULDN'T BE ON THE LOSING SIDE OF A BEATING AS A RESULT. NOT SINCE ...
... WELL, NOT FOR A WHILE.
COME WITH ME.

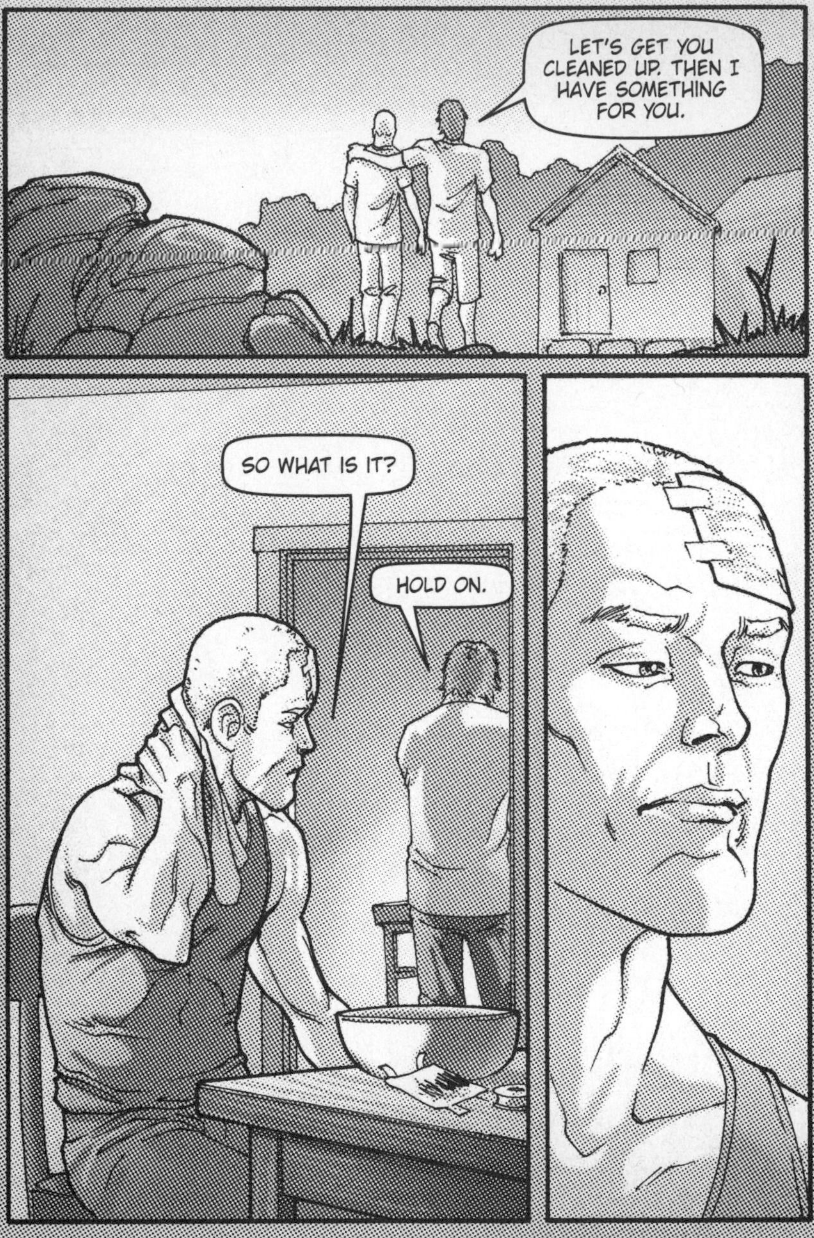
LET'S GET YOU CLEANED UP. THEN I HAVE SOMETHING FOR YOU.
SO WHAT IS IT?
HOLD ON.

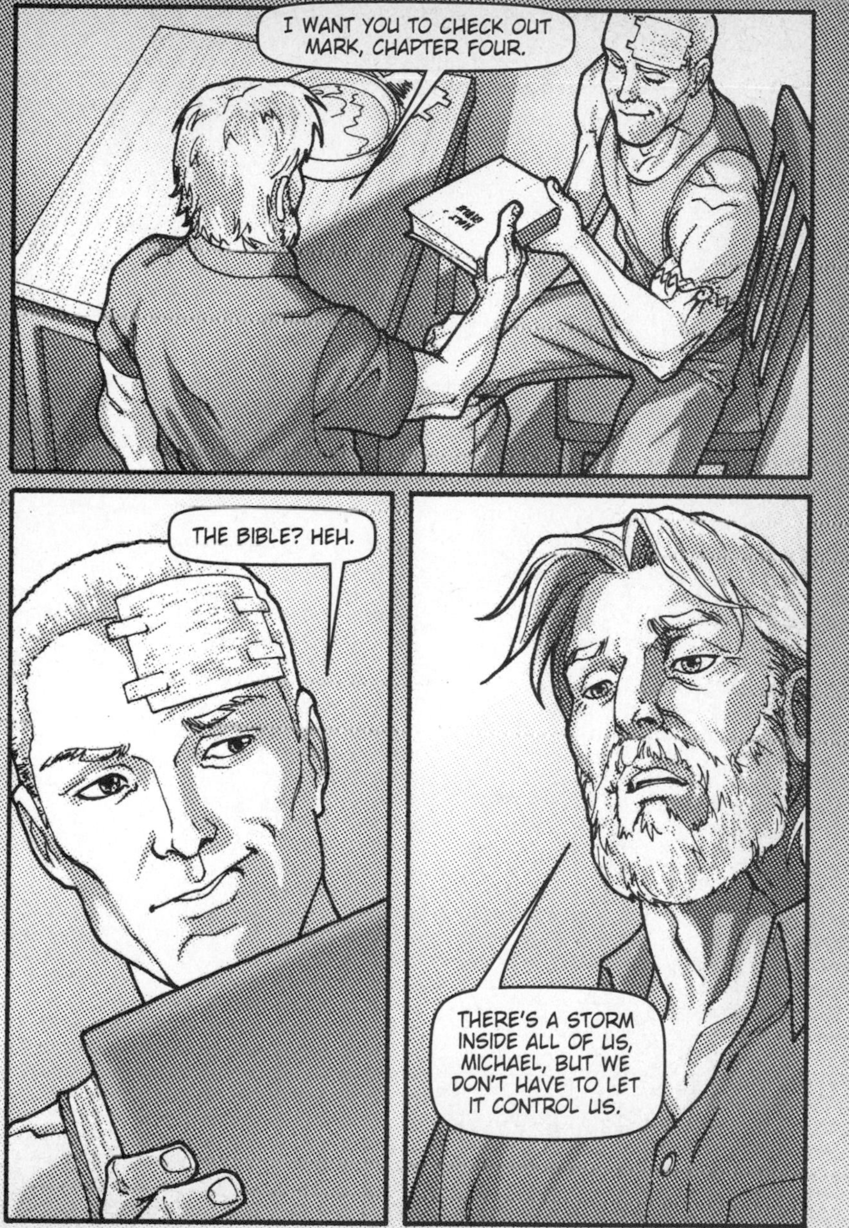

I WANT YOU TO CHECK OUT MARK, CHAPTER FOUR.
THE BIBLE? HEH.
THERE'S A STORM INSIDE ALL OF US, MICHAEL, BUT WE DON'T HAVE TO LET IT CONTROL US.

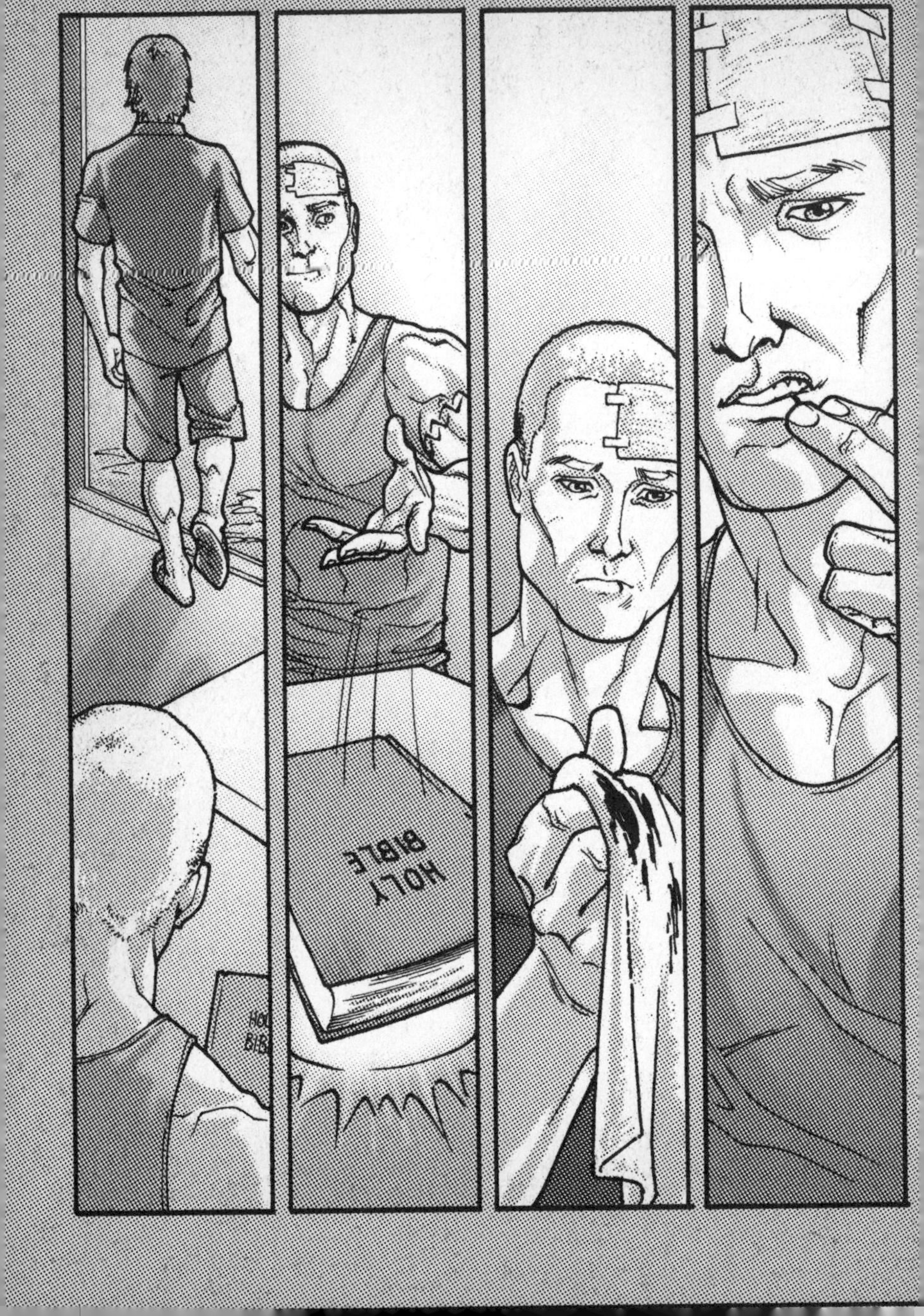
HOLY BIBLE

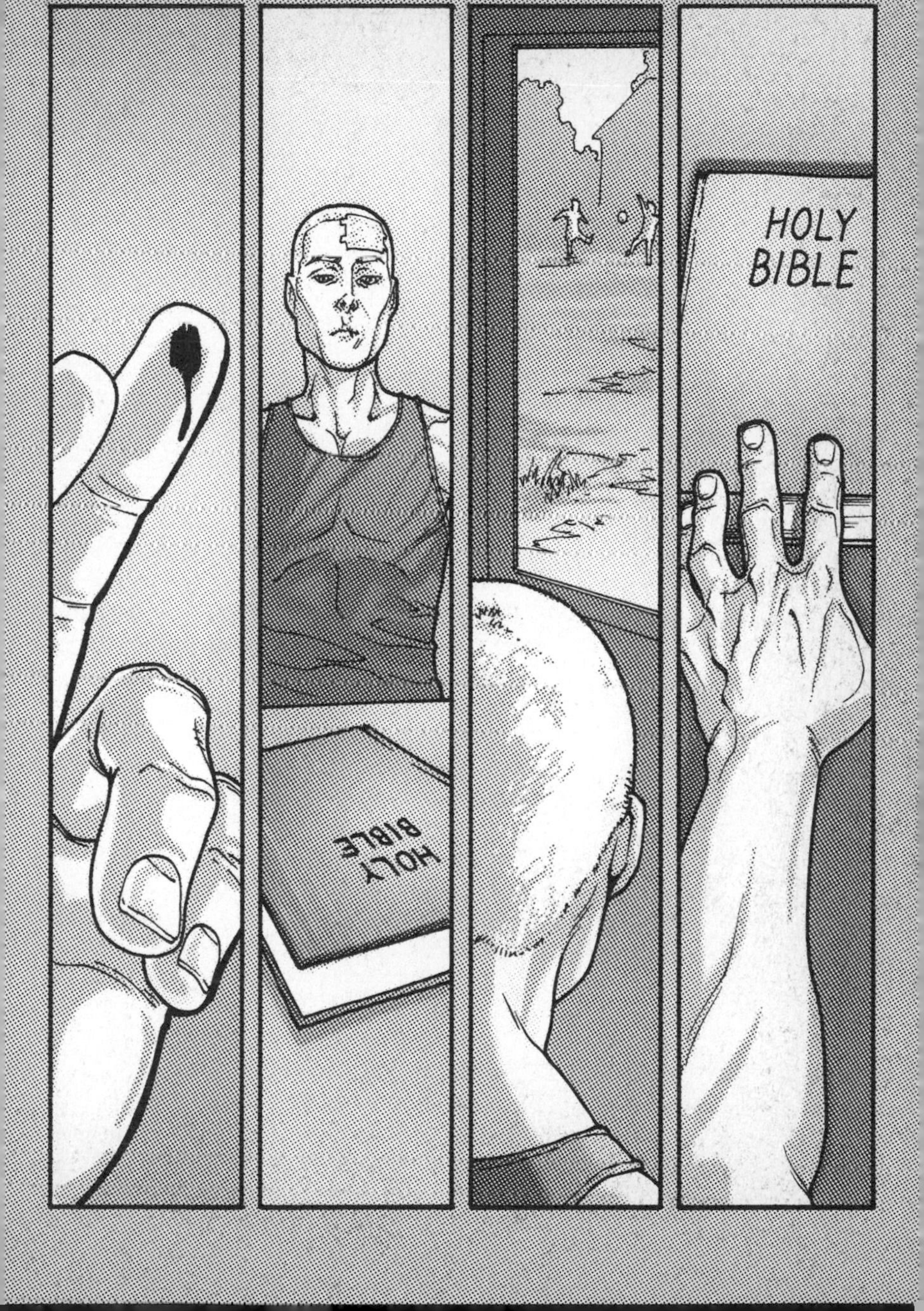
HOLY
BIBLE
HOLY
BIBLE

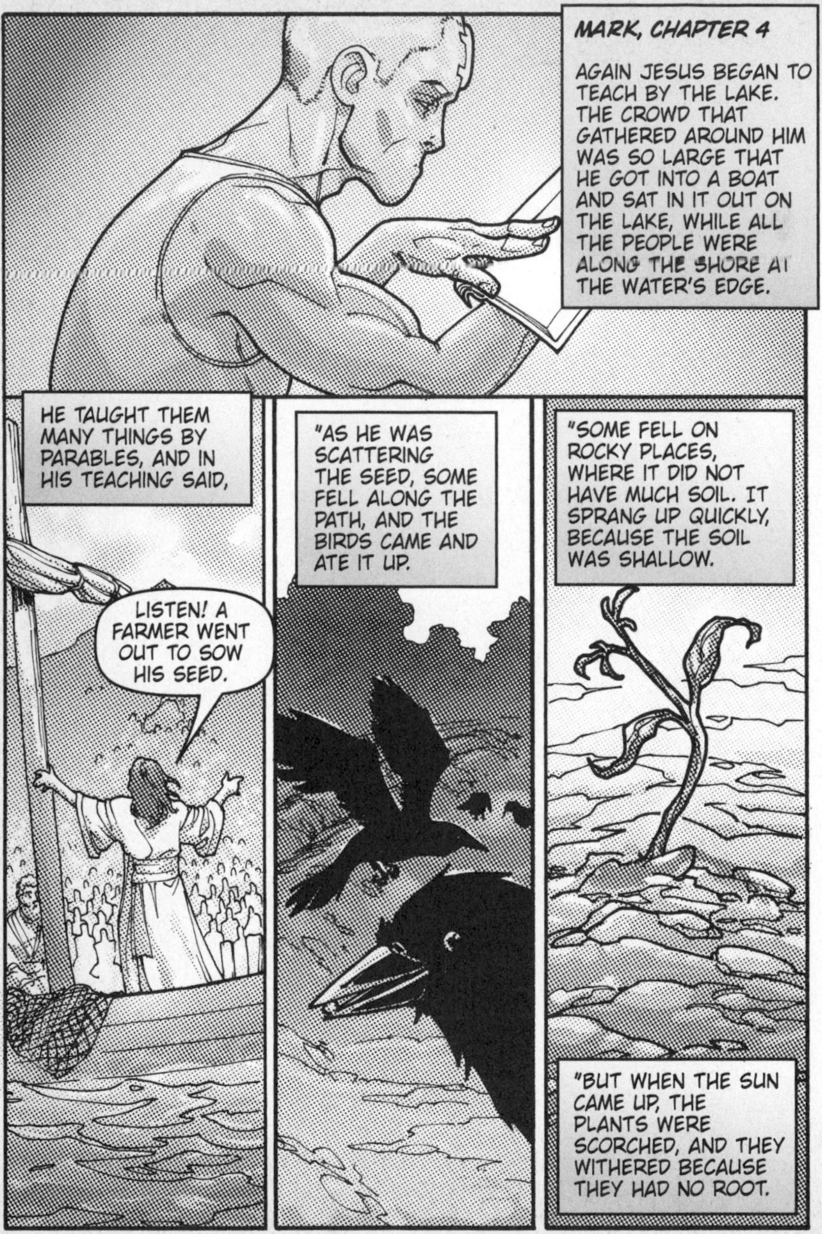
MARK, CHAPTER 4
AGAIN JESUS BEGAN TO TEACH BY THE LAKE. THE CROWD THAT GATHERED AROUND HIM WAS SO LARGE THAT HE GOT INTO A BOAT AND SAT IN IT OUT ON THE LAKE, WHILE ALL THE PEOPLE WERE ALONG THE SHORE AT THE WATER'S EDGE.
HE TAUGHT THEM MANY THINGS BY PARABLES, AND IN HIS TEACHING SAID,
LISTEN! A FARMER WENT OUT TO SOW HIS SEED.
"AS HE WAS SCATTERING THE SEED, SOME FELL ALONG THE PATH, AND THE BIRDS CAME AND ATE IT UP.
"SOME FELL ON ROCKY PLACES, WHERE IT DID NOT HAVE MUCH SOIL. IT SPRANG UP QUICKLY, BECAUSE THE SOIL WAS SHALLOW.
"BUT WHEN THE SUN CAME UP, THE PLANTS WERE SCORCHED, AND THEY WITHERED BECAUSE THEY HAD NO ROOT.

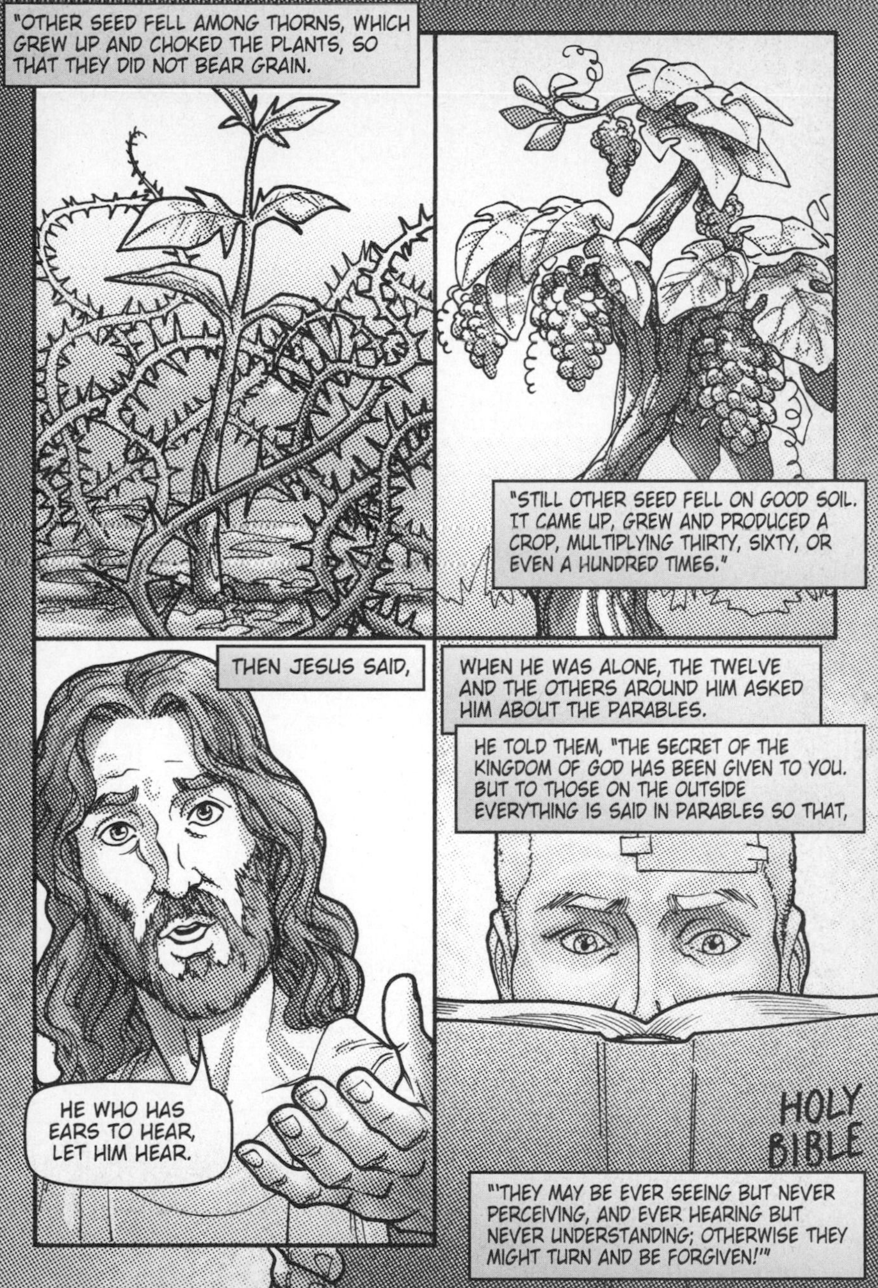
"OTHER SEED FELL AMONG THORNS, WHICH GREW UP AND CHOKED THE PLANTS, SO THAT THEY DID NOT BEAR GRAIN.
"STILL OTHER SEED FELL ON GOOD SOIL. IT CAME UP, GREW AND PRODUCED A CROP, MULTIPLYING THIRTY, SIXTY, OR EVEN A HUNDRED TIMES."
THEN JESUS SAID,
HE WHO HAS EARS TO HEAR, LET HIM HEAR.
WHEN HE WAS ALONE, THE TWELVE AND THE OTHERS AROUND HIM ASKED HIM ABOUT THE PARABLES.
HE TOLD THEM, "THE SECRET OF THE KINGDOM OF GOD HAS BEEN GIVEN TO YOU. BUT TO THOSE ON THE OUTSIDE EVERYTHING IS SAID IN PARABLES SO THAT,
HOLY BIBLE
"'THEY MAY BE EVER SEEING BUT NEVER PERCEIVING, AND EVER HEARING BUT NEVER UNDERSTANDING; OTHERWISE THEY MIGHT TURN AND BE FORGIVEN!'"

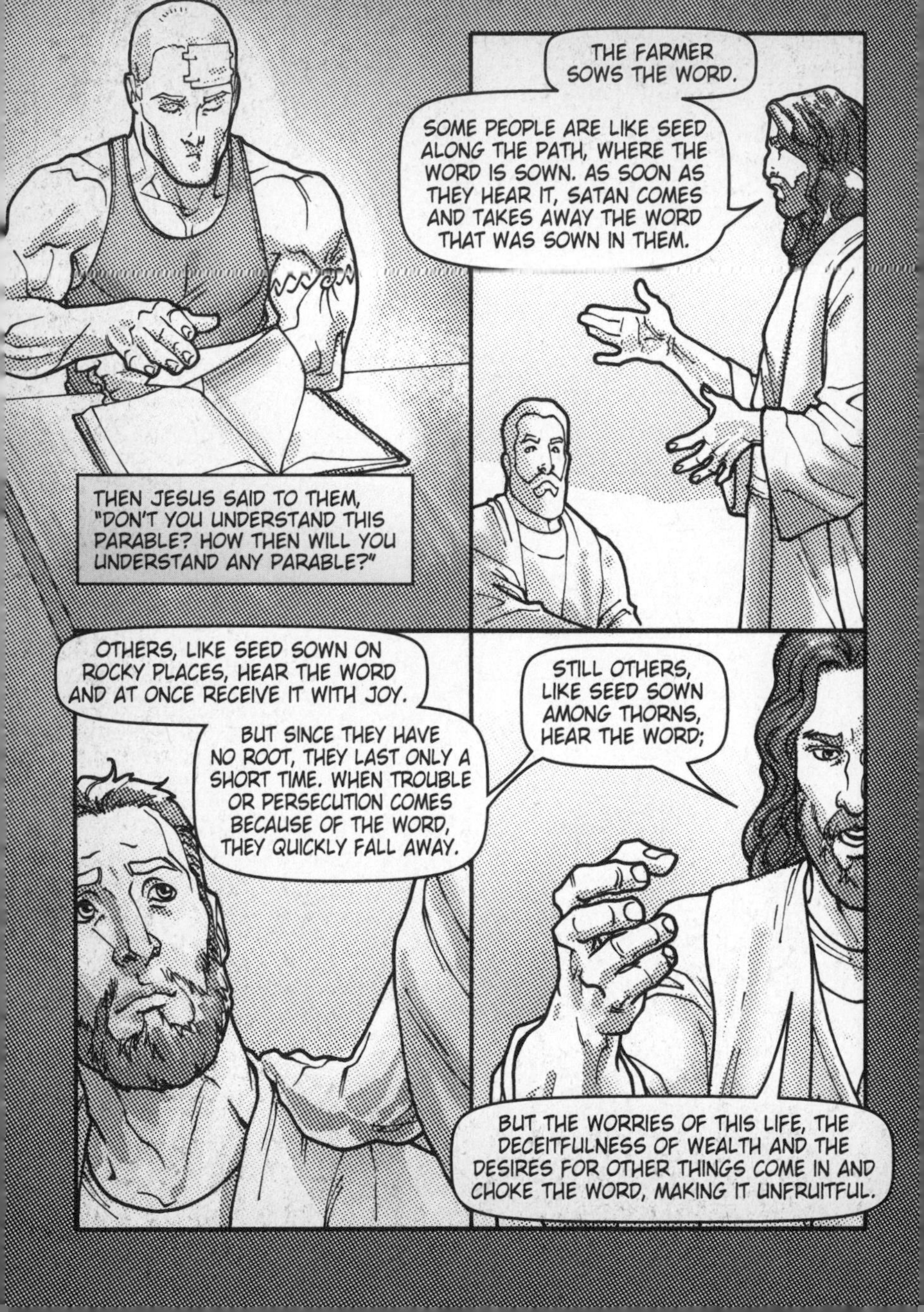
THEN JESUS SAID TO THEM, "DON'T YOU UNDERSTAND THIS PARABLE? HOW THEN WILL YOU UNDERSTAND ANY PARABLE?"
THE FARMER SOWS THE WORD.
SOME PEOPLE ARE LIKE SEED ALONG THE PATH, WHERE THE WORD IS SOWN. AS SOON AS THEY HEAR IT, SATAN COMES AND TAKES AWAY THE WORD THAT WAS SOWN IN THEM.
OTHERS, LIKE SEED SOWN ON ROCKY PLACES, HEAR THE WORD AND AT ONCE RECEIVE IT WITH JOY.
BUT SINCE THEY HAVE NO ROOT, THEY LAST ONLY A SHORT TIME. WHEN TROUBLE OR PERSECUTION COMES BECAUSE OF THE WORD, THEY QUICKLY FALL AWAY.
STILL OTHERS, LIKE SEED SOWN AMONG THORNS, HEAR THE WORD;
BUT THE WORRIES OF THIS LIFE, THE DECEITFULNESS OF WEALTH AND THE DESIRES FOR OTHER THINGS COME IN AND CHOKE THE WORD, MAKING IT UNFRUITFUL.

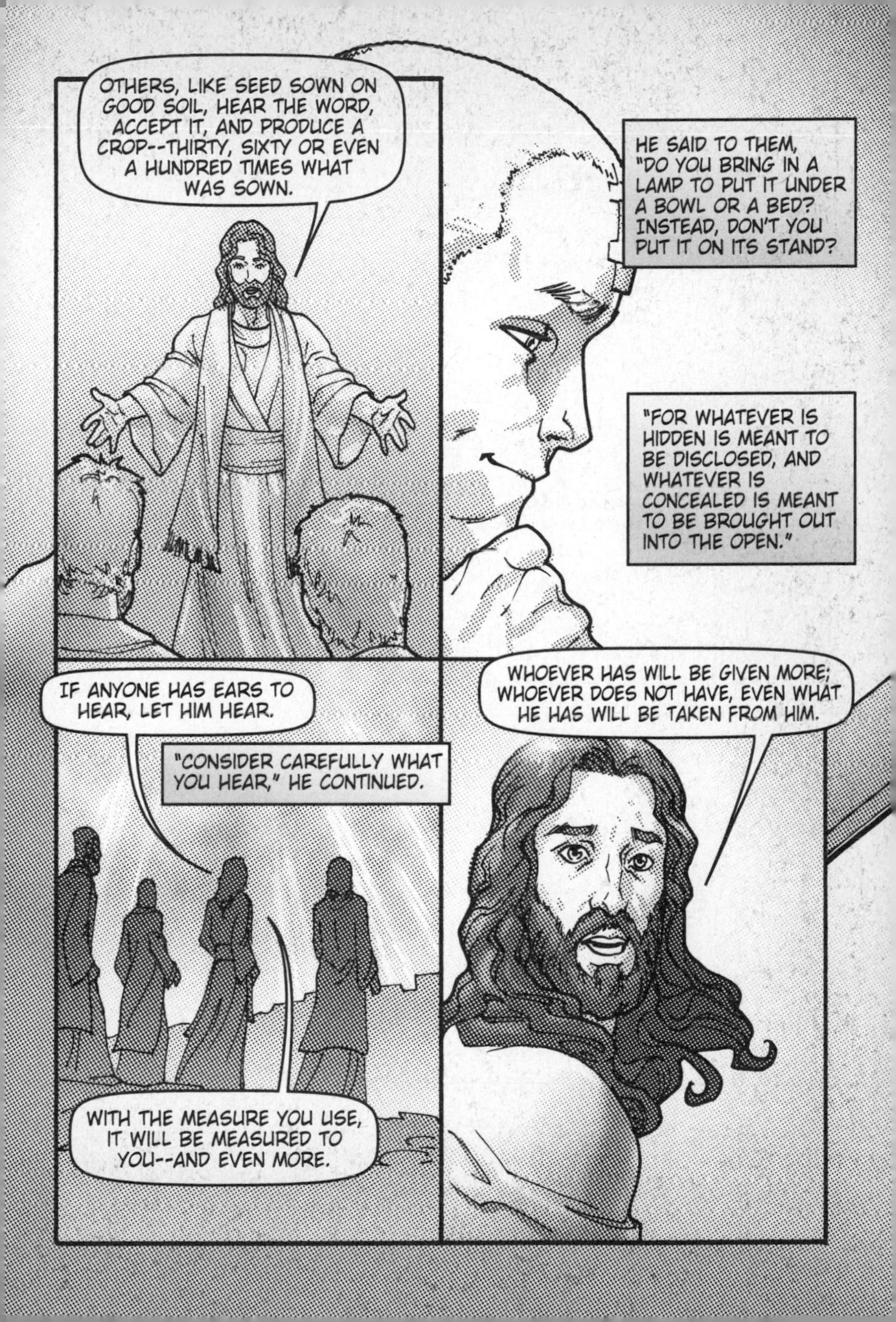
OTHERS, LIKE SEED SOWN ON GOOD SOIL, HEAR THE WORD, ACCEPT IT, AND PRODUCE A CROP--THIRTY, SIXTY OR EVEN A HUNDRED TIMES WHAT WAS SOWN.
HE SAID TO THEM, "DO YOU BRING IN A LAMP TO PUT IT UNDER A BOWL OR A BED? INSTEAD, DON'T YOU PUT IT ON ITS STAND?
"FOR WHATEVER IS HIDDEN IS MEANT TO BE DISCLOSED, AND WHATEVER IS CONCEALED IS MEANT TO BE BROUGHT OUT INTO THE OPEN."
IF ANYONE HAS EARS TO HEAR, LET HIM HEAR.
"CONSIDER CAREFULLY WHAT YOU HEAR," HE CONTINUED.
WITH THE MEASURE YOU USE, IT WILL BE MEASURED TO YOU--AND EVEN MORE.
WHOEVER HAS WILL BE GIVEN MORE; WHOEVER DOES NOT HAVE, EVEN WHAT HE HAS WILL BE TAKEN FROM HIM.

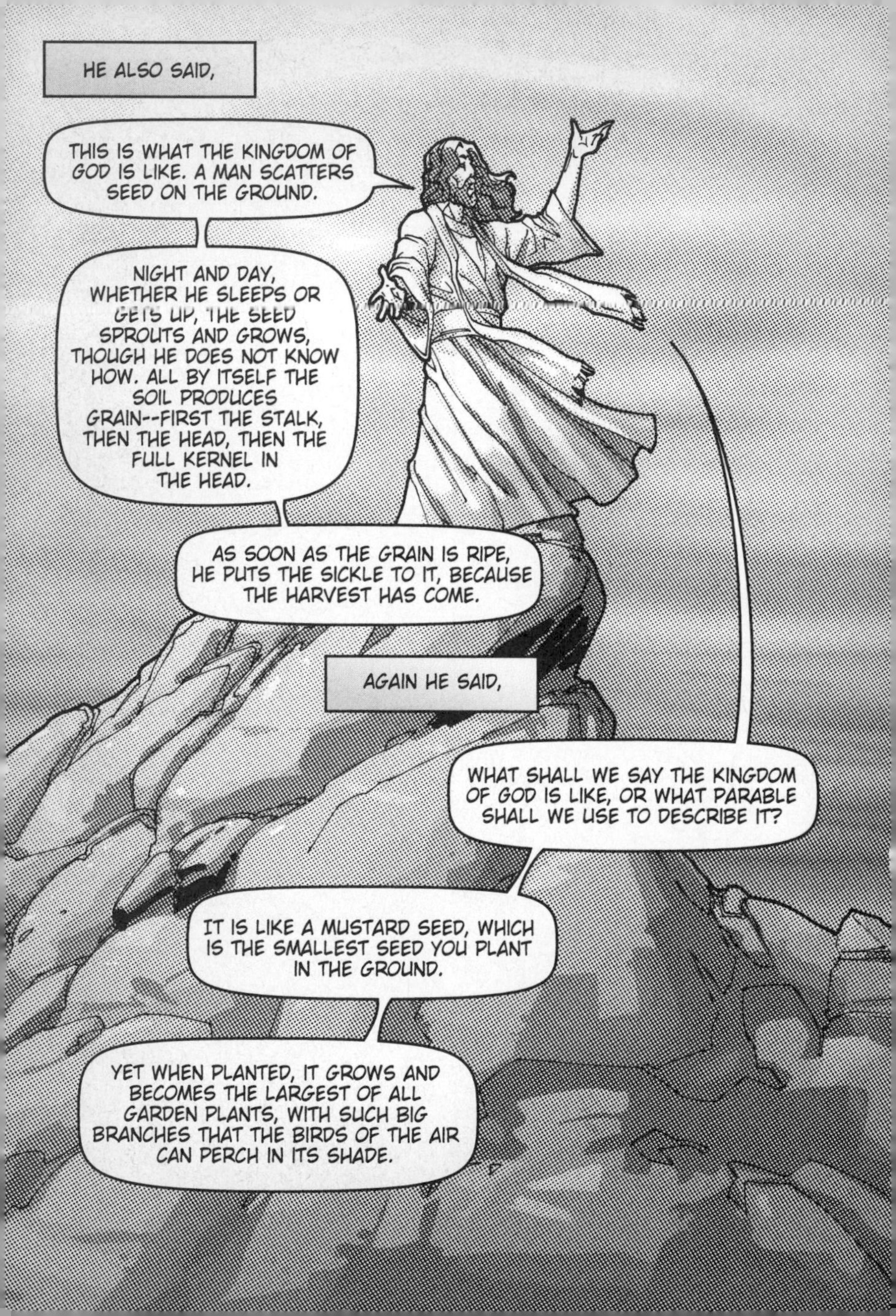
HE ALSO SAID,
THIS IS WHAT THE KINGDOM OF GOD IS LIKE. A MAN SCATTERS SEED ON THE GROUND.
NIGHT AND DAY, WHETHER HE SLEEPS OR GETS UP, THE SEED SPROUTS AND GROWS, THOUGH HE DOES NOT KNOW HOW. ALL BY ITSELF THE SOIL PRODUCES GRAIN--FIRST THE STALK, THEN THE HEAD, THEN THE FULL KERNEL IN THE HEAD.
AS SOON AS THE GRAIN IS RIPE, HE PUTS THE SICKLE TO IT, BECAUSE THE HARVEST HAS COME.
AGAIN HE SAID,
WHAT SHALL WE SAY THE KINGDOM OF GOD IS LIKE, OR WHAT PARABLE SHALL WE USE TO DESCRIBE IT?
IT IS LIKE A MUSTARD SEED, WHICH IS THE SMALLEST SEED YOU PLANT IN THE GROUND.
YET WHEN PLANTED, IT GROWS AND BECOMES THE LARGEST OF ALL GARDEN PLANTS, WITH SUCH BIG BRANCHES THAT THE BIRDS OF THE AIR CAN PERCH IN ITS SHADE.

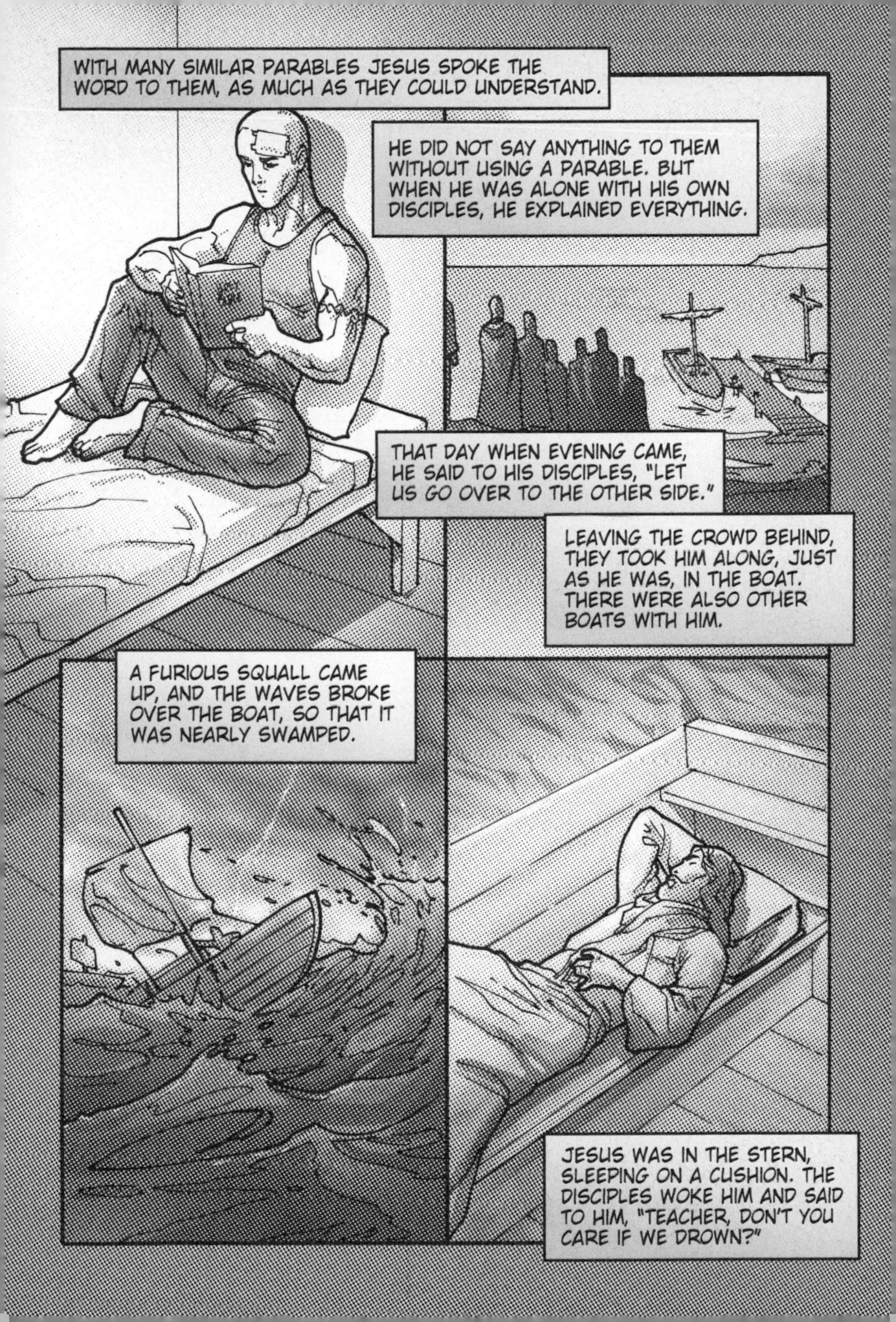
WITH MANY SIMILAR PARABLES JESUS SPOKE THE WORD TO THEM, AS MUCH AS THEY COULD UNDERSTAND.
HE DID NOT SAY ANYTHING TO THEM WITHOUT USING A PARABLE. BUT WHEN HE WAS ALONE WITH HIS OWN DISCIPLES, HE EXPLAINED EVERYTHING.
THAT DAY WHEN EVENING CAME, HE SAID TO HIS DISCIPLES, "LET US GO OVER TO THE OTHER SIDE."
LEAVING THE CROWD BEHIND, THEY TOOK HIM ALONG, JUST AS HE WAS, IN THE BOAT. THERE WERE ALSO OTHER BOATS WITH HIM.
A FURIOUS SQUALL CAME UP, AND THE WAVES BROKE OVER THE BOAT, SO THAT IT WAS NEARLY SWAMPED.
JESUS WAS IN THE STERN, SLEEPING ON A CUSHION. THE DISCIPLES WOKE HIM AND SAID TO HIM, "TEACHER, DON'T YOU CARE IF WE DROWN?"

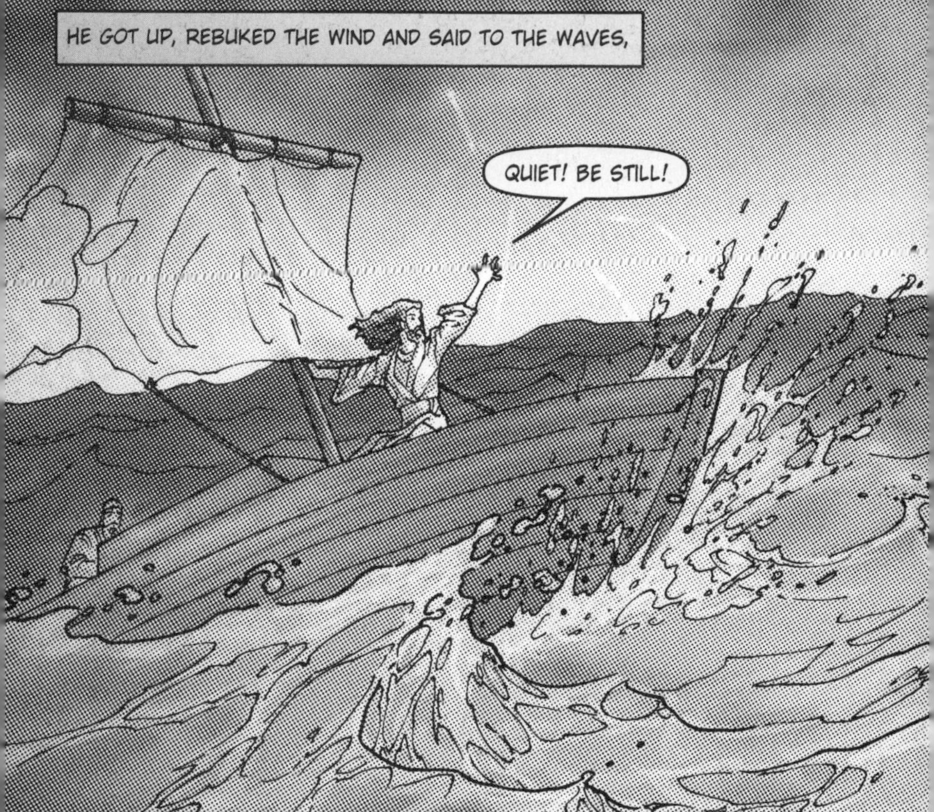
HE GOT UP, REBUKED THE WIND AND SAID TO THE WAVES,
QUIET! BE STILL!

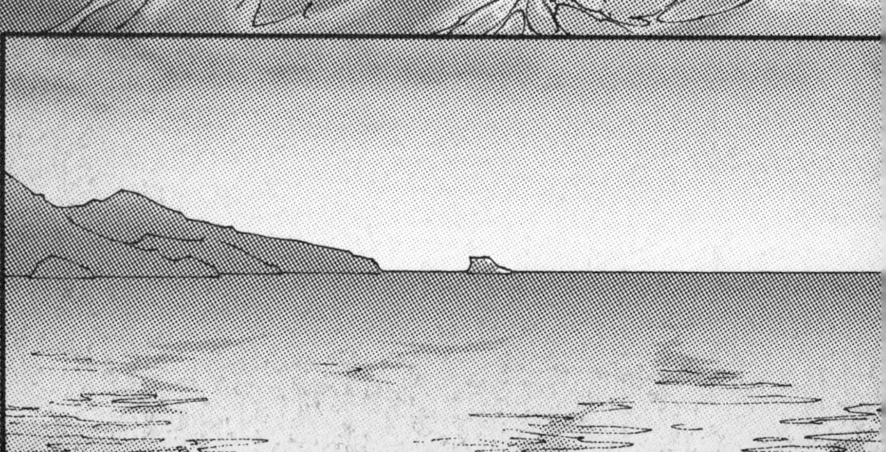

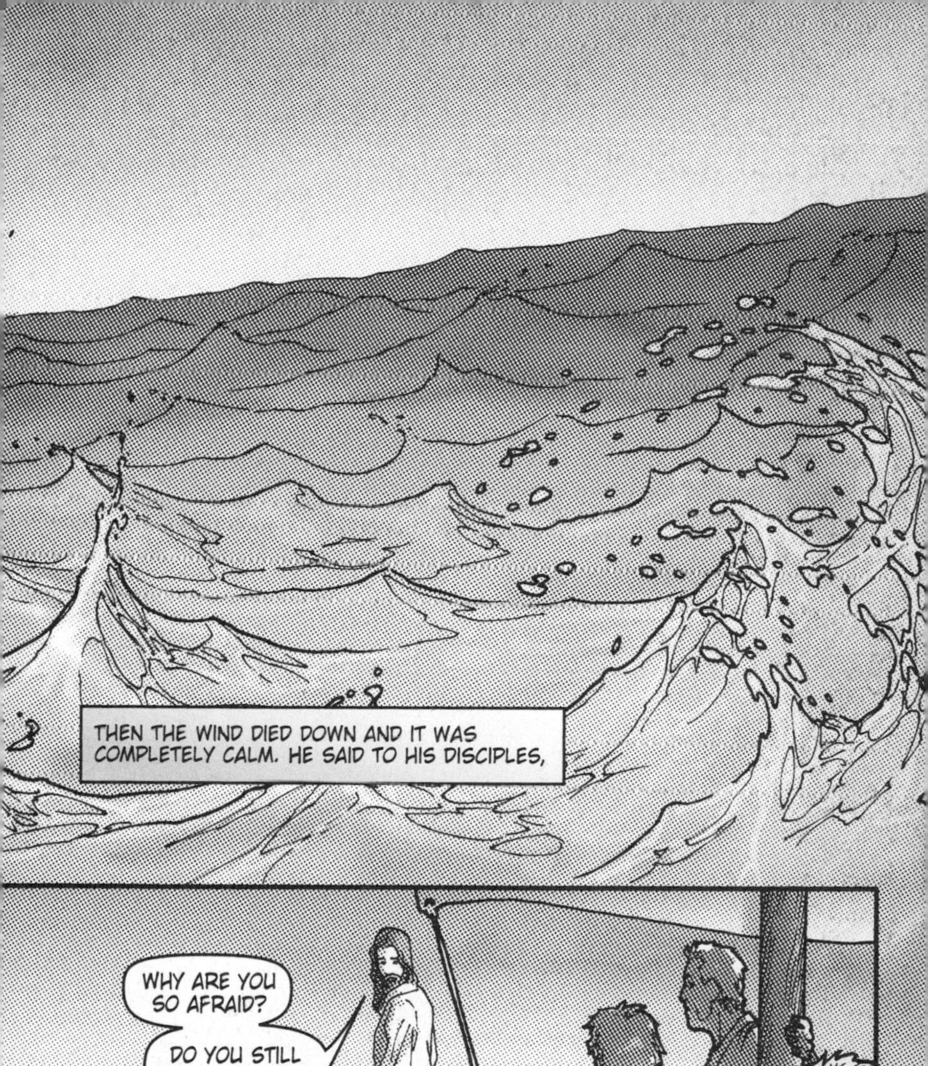
THEN THE WIND DIED DOWN AND IT WAS COMPLETELY CALM. HE SAID TO HIS DISCIPLES,

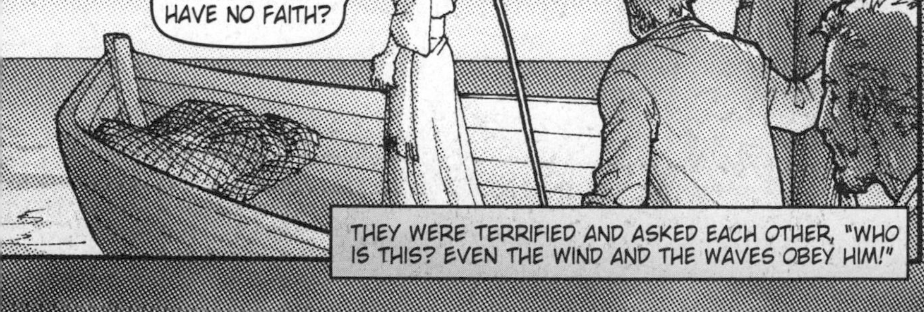
WHY ARE YOU SO AFRAID?
DO YOU STILL HAVE NO FAITH?
THEY WERE TERRIFIED AND ASKED EACH OTHER, "WHO IS THIS? EVEN THE WIND AND THE WAVES OBEY HIM!"

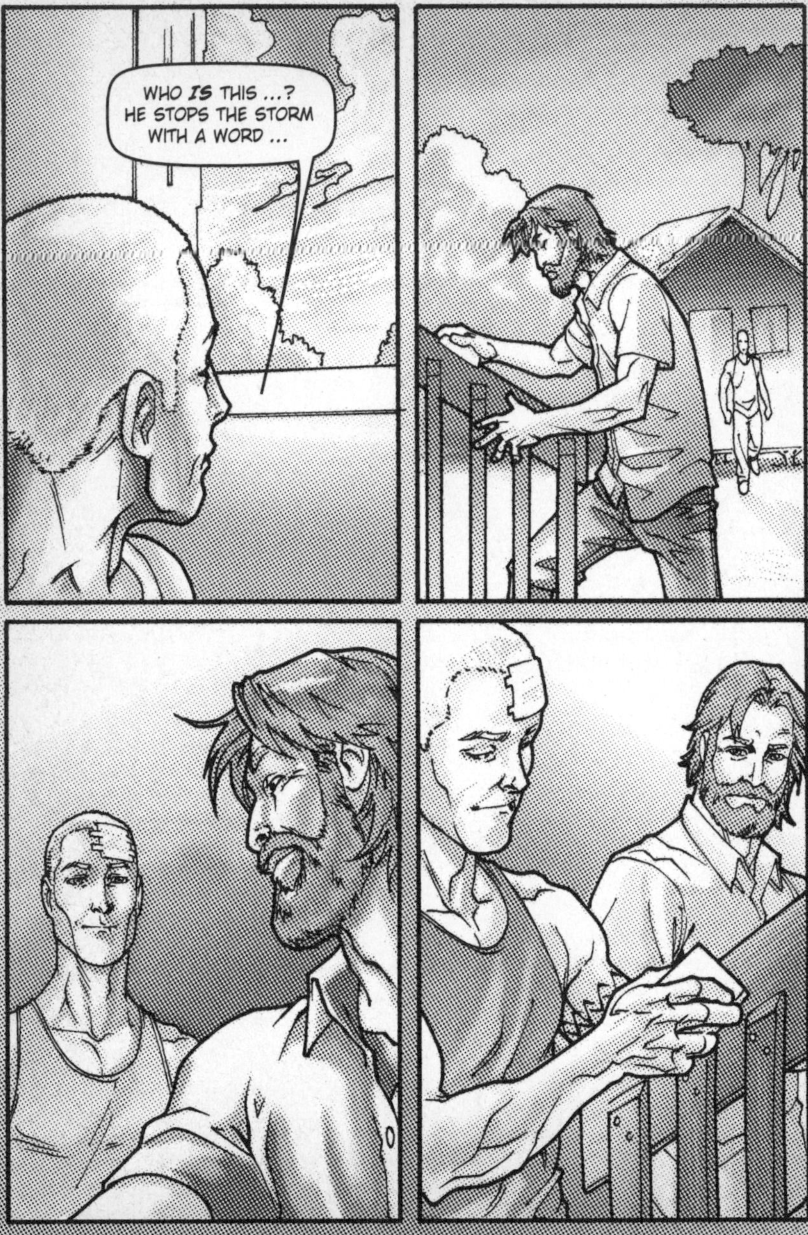
WHO IS THIS ...? HE STOPS THE STORM WITH A WORD ...

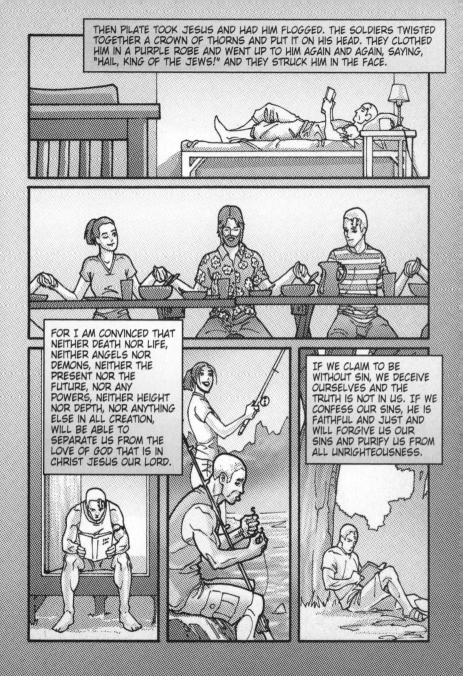

THEN PILATE TOOK JESUS AND HAD HIM FLOGGED. THE SOLDIERS TWISTED TOGETHER A CROWN OF THORNS AND PUT IT ON HIS HEAD. THEY CLOTHED HIM IN A PURPLE ROBE AND WENT UP TO HIM AGAIN AND AGAIN, SAYING, "HAIL, KING OF THE JEWS!" AND THEY STRUCK HIM IN THE FACE.

FOR I AM CONVINCED THAT NEITHER DEATH NOR LIFE, NEITHER ANGELS NOR DEMONS, NEITHER THE PRESENT NOR THE FUTURE, NOR ANY POWERS, NEITHER HEIGHT NOR DEPTH, NOR ANYTHING ELSE IN ALL CREATION, WILL BE ABLE TO SEPARATE US FROM THE LOVE OF GOD THAT IS IN CHRIST JESUS OUR LORD.

IF WE CLAIM TO BE WITHOUT SIN, WE DECEIVE OURSELVES AND THE TRUTH IS NOT IN US. IF WE CONFESS OUR SINS, HE IS FAITHFUL AND JUST AND WILL FORGIVE US OUR SINS AND PURIFY US FROM ALL UNRIGHTEOUSNESS.

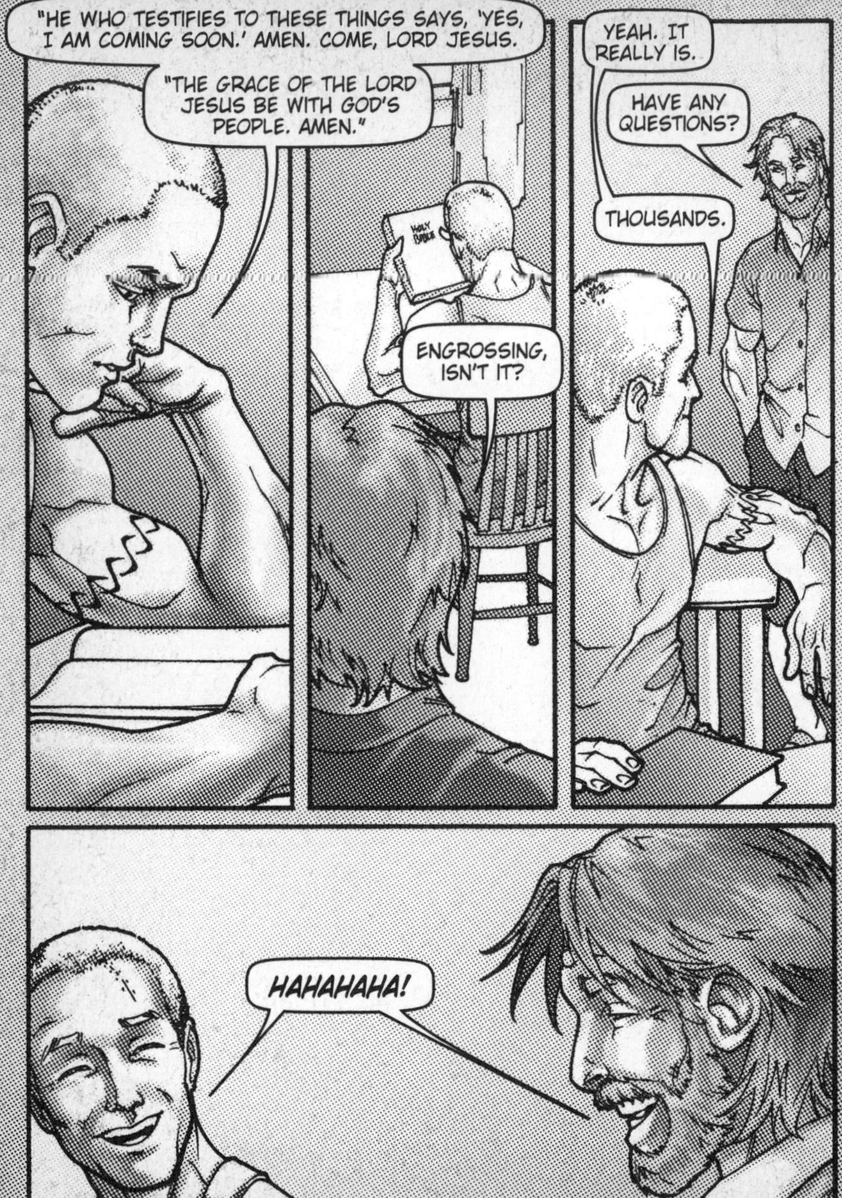
"HE WHO TESTIFIES TO THESE THINGS SAYS, 'YES, I AM COMING SOON.' AMEN. COME, LORD JESUS.
"THE GRACE OF THE LORD JESUS BE WITH GOD'S PEOPLE. AMEN."
HOLY BIBLE
ENGROSSING, ISN'T IT?
YEAH. IT REALLY IS.
HAVE ANY QUESTIONS?
THOUSANDS.
HAHAHAHA!

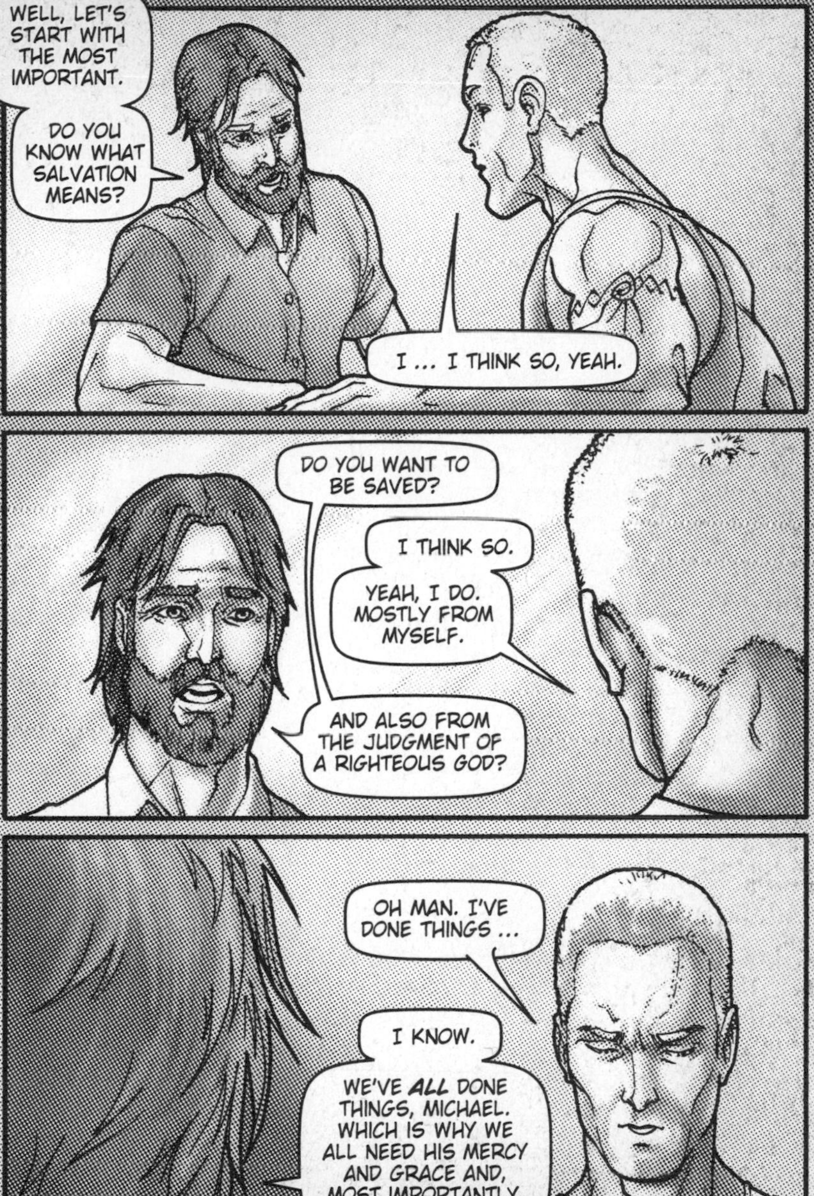
WELL, LET'S START WITH THE MOST IMPORTANT.
DO YOU KNOW WHAT SALVATION MEANS?
I ... I THINK SO, YEAH.
DO YOU WANT TO BE SAVED?
I THINK SO.
YEAH, I DO. MOSTLY FROM MYSELF.
AND ALSO FROM THE JUDGMENT OF A RIGHTEOUS GOD?
OH MAN. I'VE DONE THINGS ...
I KNOW.
WE'VE ALL DONE THINGS, MICHAEL. WHICH IS WHY WE ALL NEED HIS MERCY AND GRACE AND, MOST IMPORTANTLY, HIS FORGIVENESS.

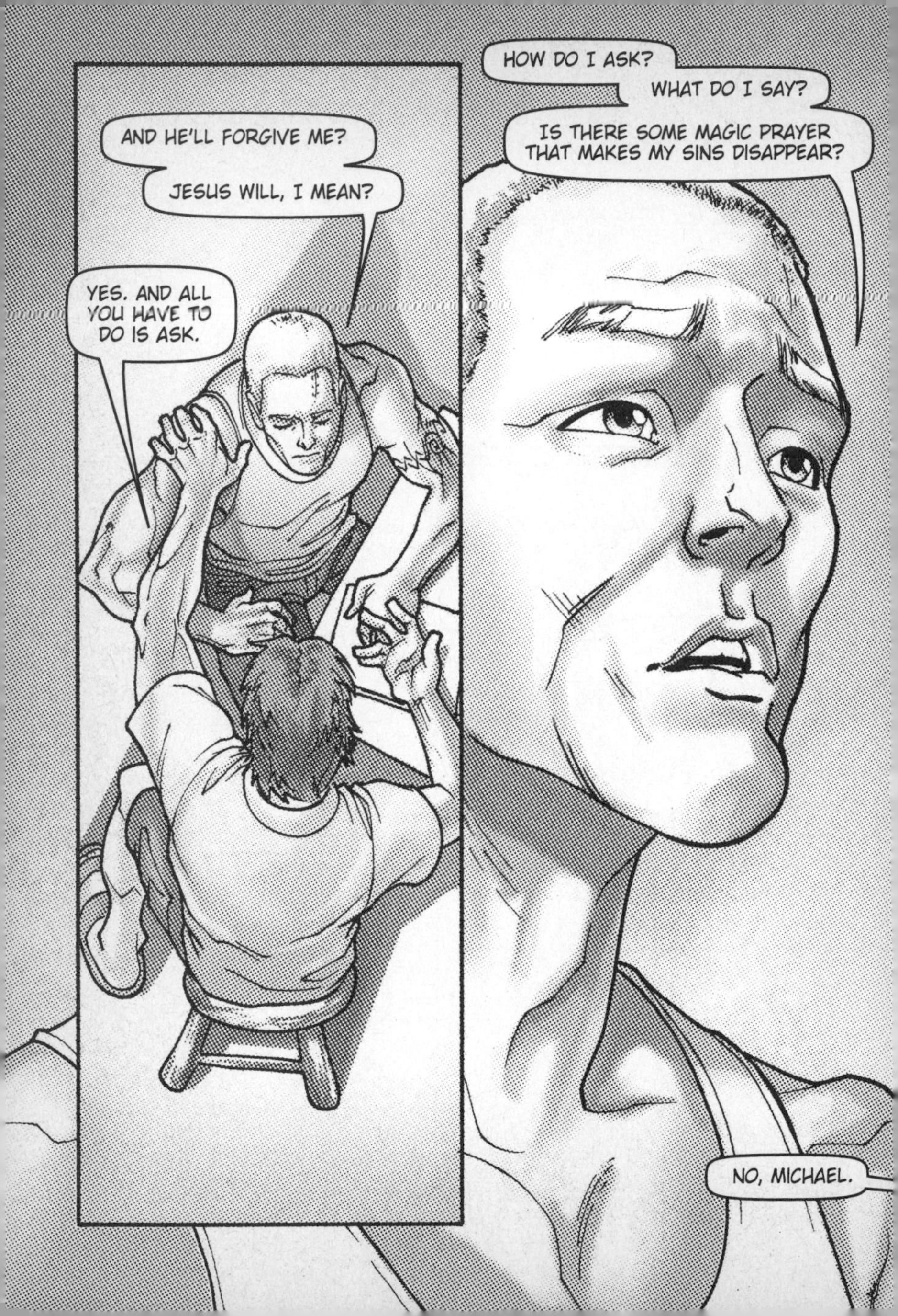

AND HE'LL FORGIVE ME?
JESUS WILL, I MEAN?
YES. AND ALL YOU HAVE TO DO IS ASK.
HOW DO I ASK?
WHAT DO I SAY?
IS THERE SOME MAGIC PRAYER THAT MAKES MY SINS DISAPPEAR?
NO, MICHAEL.

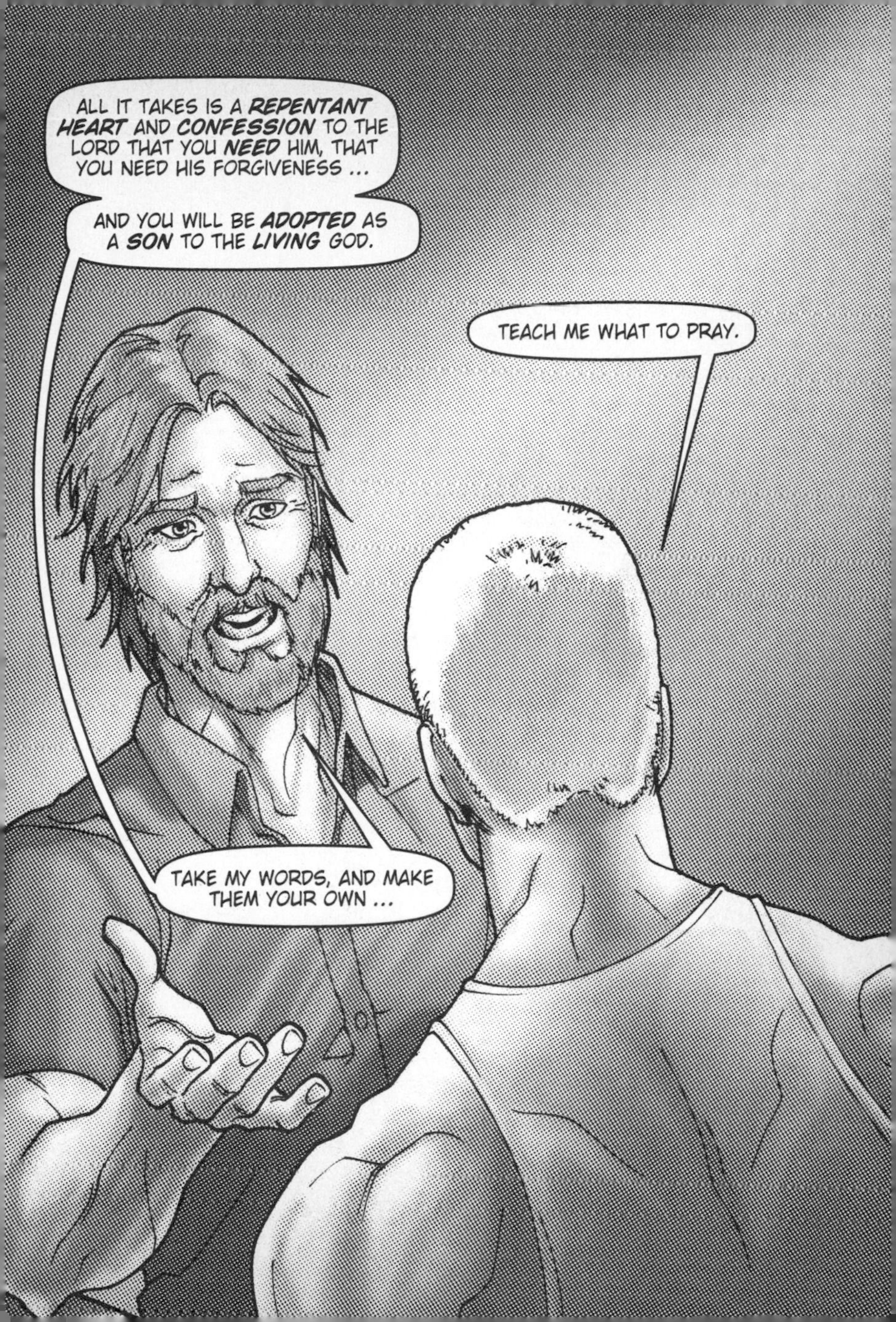
ALL IT TAKES IS A REPENTANT HEART AND CONFESSION TO THE LORD THAT YOU NEED HIM, THAT YOU NEED HIS FORGIVENESS ...
AND YOU WILL BE ADOPTED AS A SON TO THE LIVING GOD.
TEACH ME WHAT TO PRAY.
TAKE MY WORDS, AND MAKE THEM YOUR OWN ...

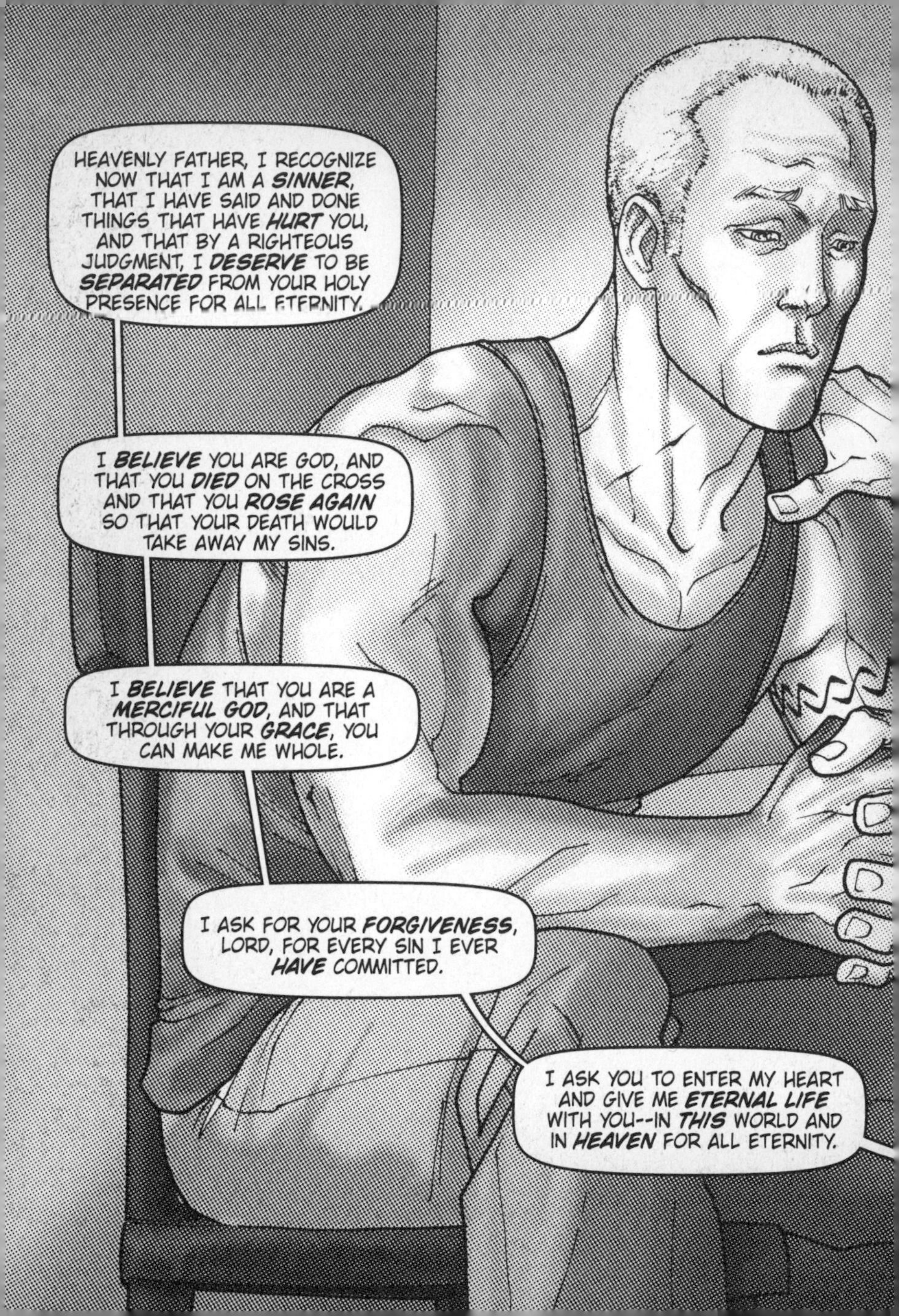

HEAVENLY FATHER, I RECOGNIZE NOW THAT I AM A ***SINNER***, THAT I HAVE SAID AND DONE THINGS THAT HAVE ***HURT*** YOU, AND THAT BY A RIGHTEOUS JUDGMENT, I ***DESERVE*** TO BE ***SEPARATED*** FROM YOUR HOLY PRESENCE FOR ALL ETERNITY.
I ***BELIEVE*** YOU ARE GOD, AND THAT YOU ***DIED*** ON THE CROSS AND THAT YOU ***ROSE AGAIN*** SO THAT YOUR DEATH WOULD TAKE AWAY MY SINS.
I ***BELIEVE*** THAT YOU ARE A ***MERCIFUL GOD***, AND THAT THROUGH YOUR ***GRACE***, YOU CAN MAKE ME WHOLE.
I ASK FOR YOUR ***FORGIVENESS***, LORD, FOR EVERY SIN I EVER ***HAVE*** COMMITTED.
I ASK YOU TO ENTER MY HEART AND GIVE ME ***ETERNAL LIFE*** WITH YOU--IN ***THIS*** WORLD AND IN ***HEAVEN*** FOR ALL ETERNITY.

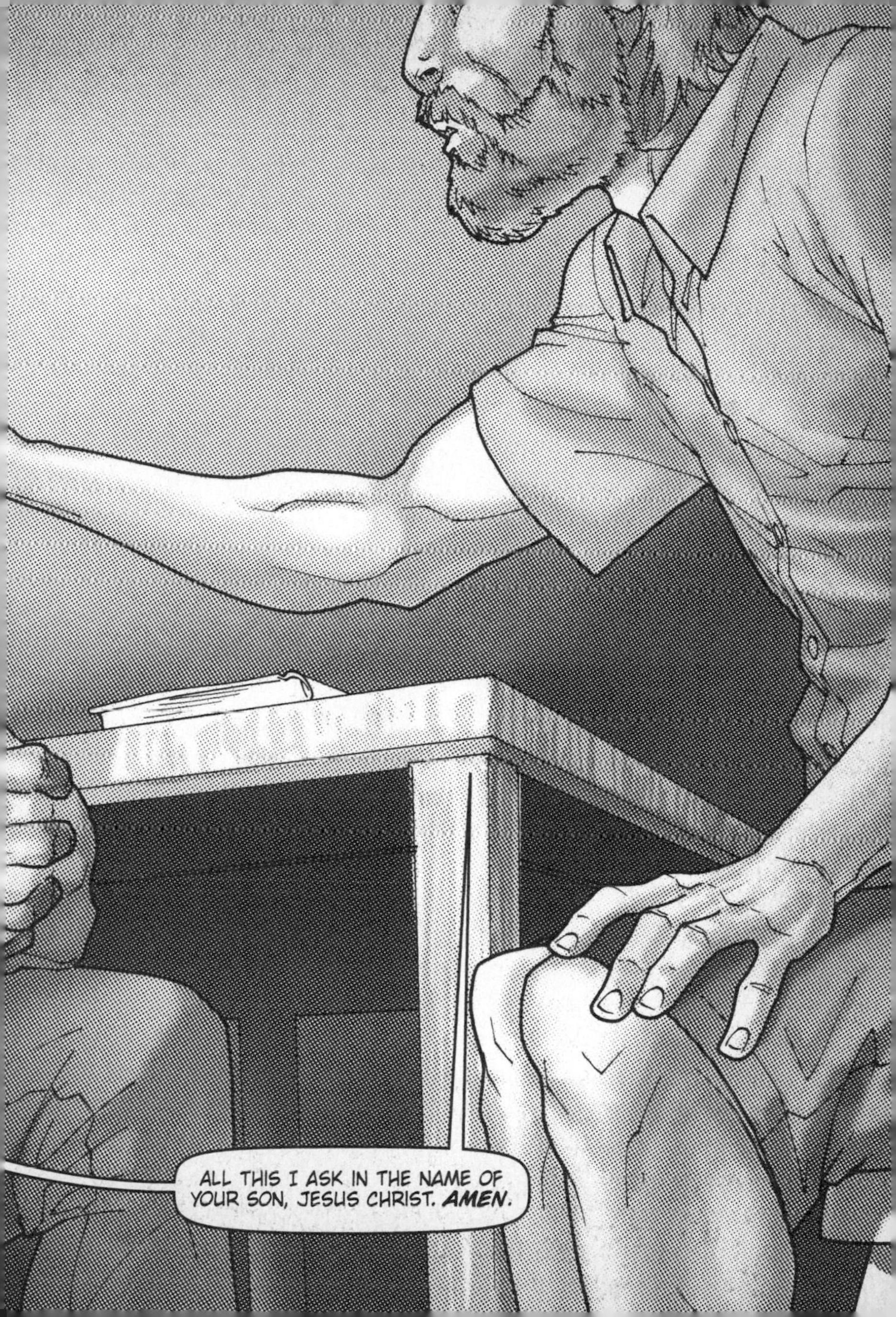
ALL THIS I ASK IN THE NAME OF YOUR SON, JESUS CHRIST. AMEN.

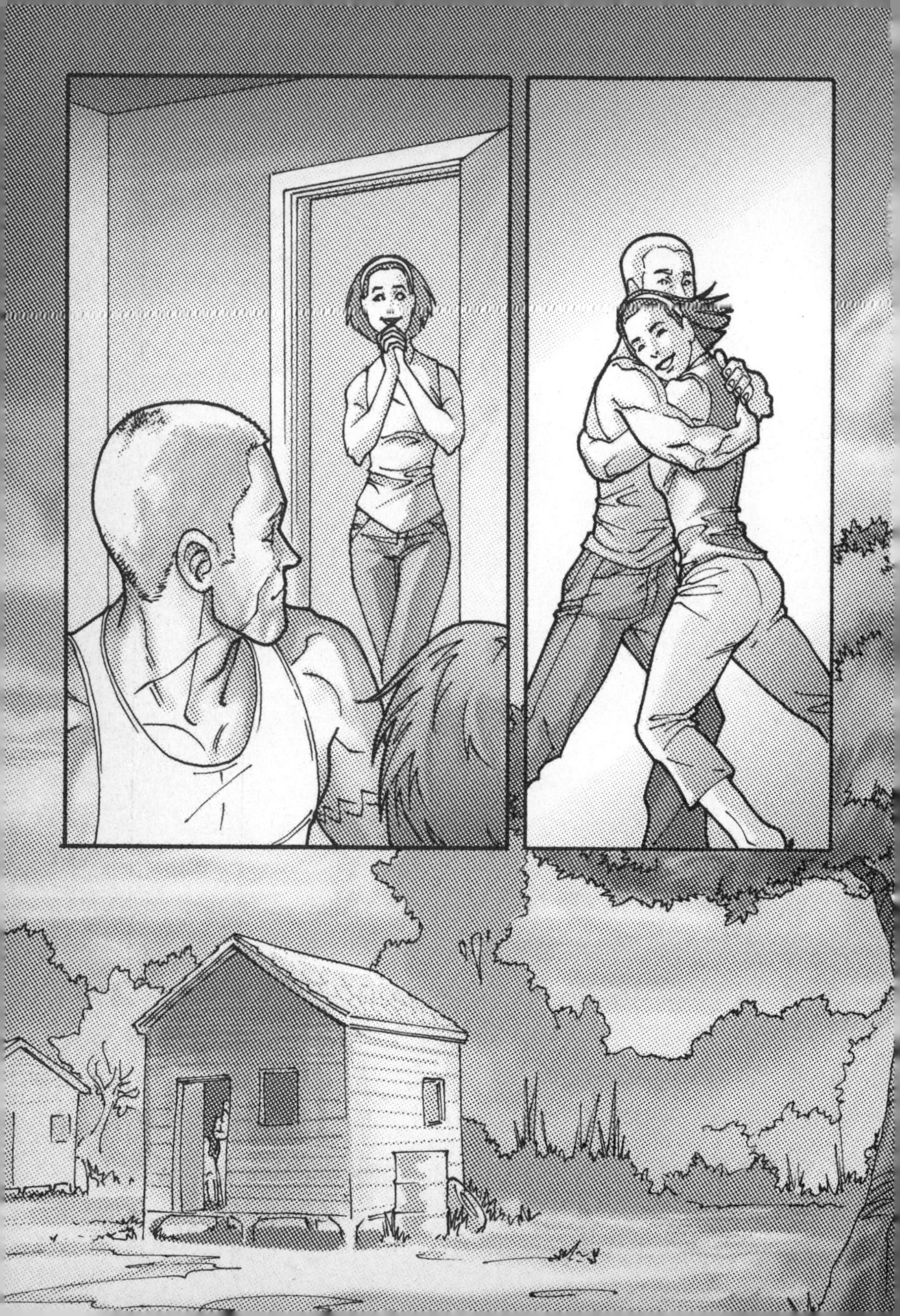

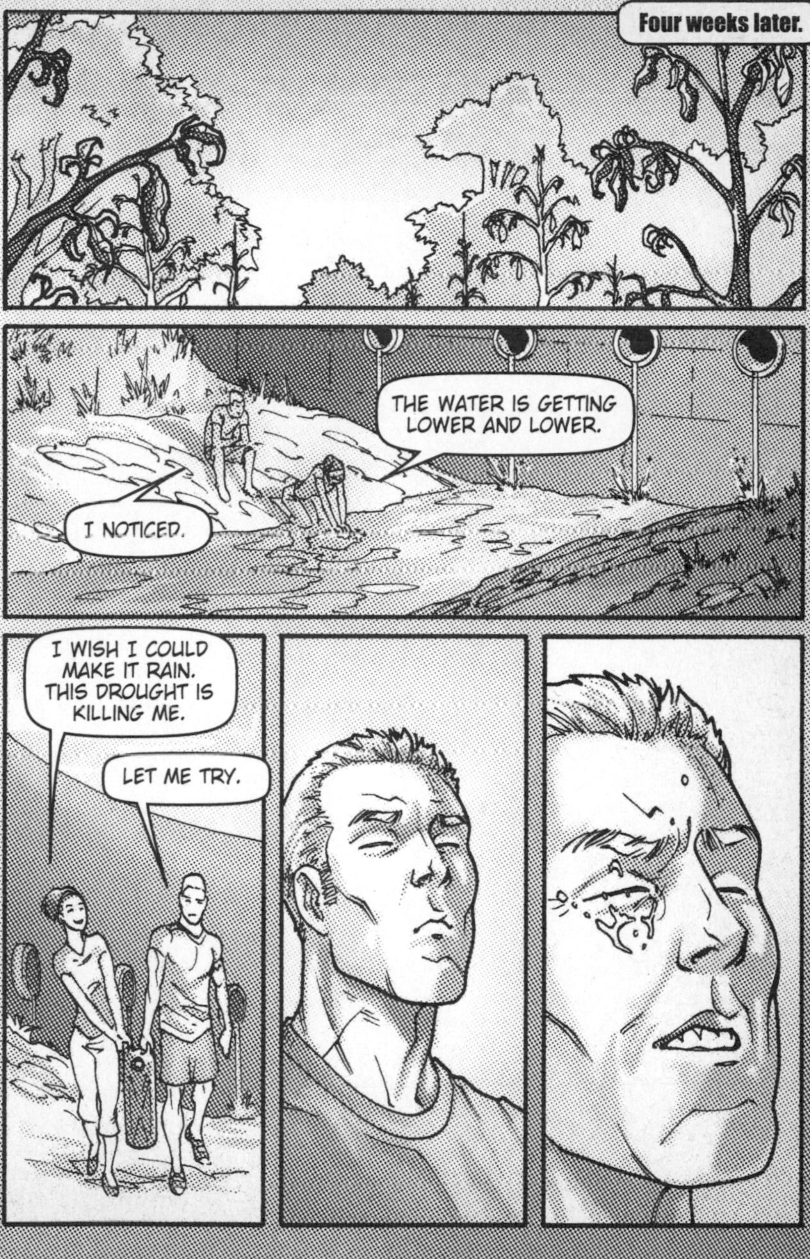

Four weeks later.
THE WATER IS GETTING LOWER AND LOWER.
I NOTICED.
I WISH I COULD MAKE IT RAIN. THIS DROUGHT IS KILLING ME.
LET ME TRY.

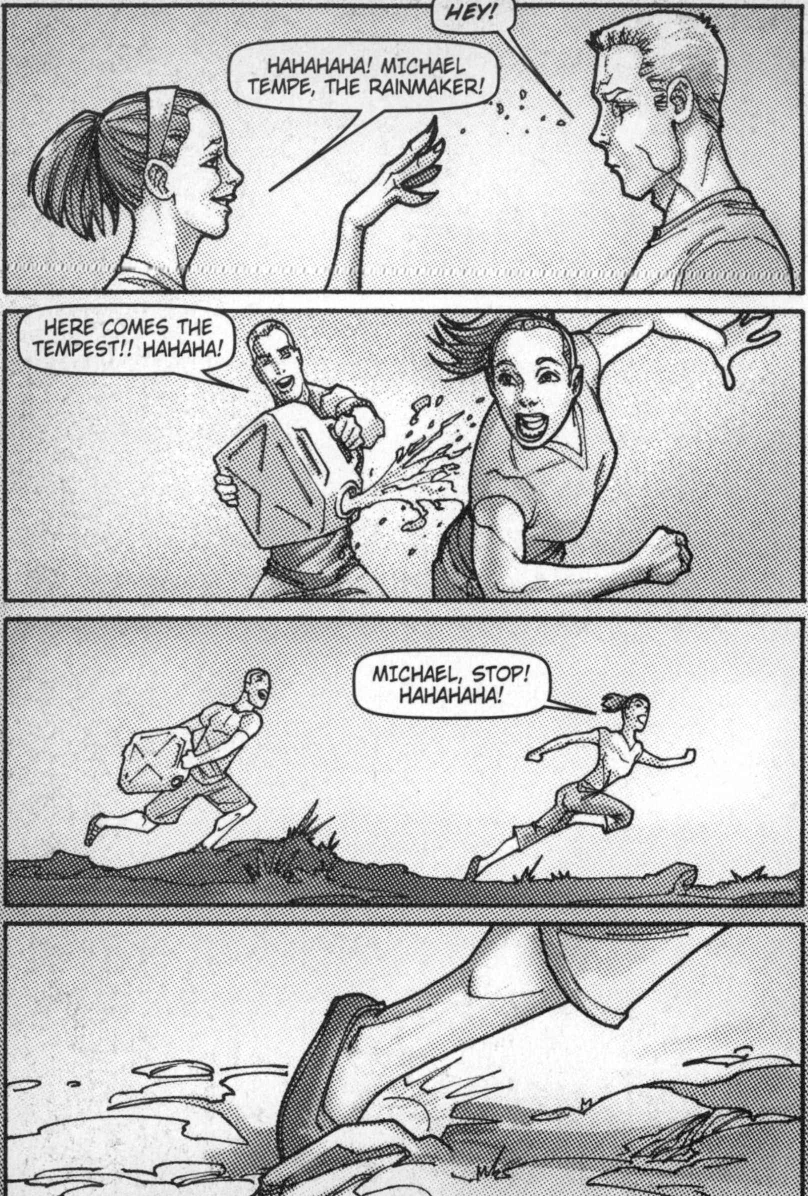
HEY!
HAHAHAHA! MICHAEL TEMPE, THE RAINMAKER!
HERE COMES THE TEMPEST!! HAHAHA!
MICHAEL, STOP! HAHAHAHA!

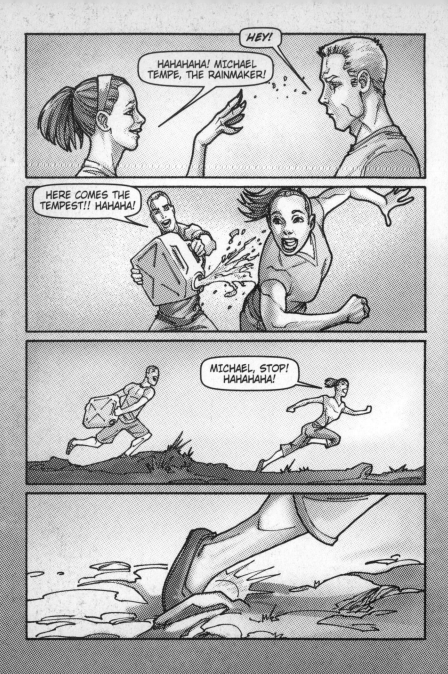

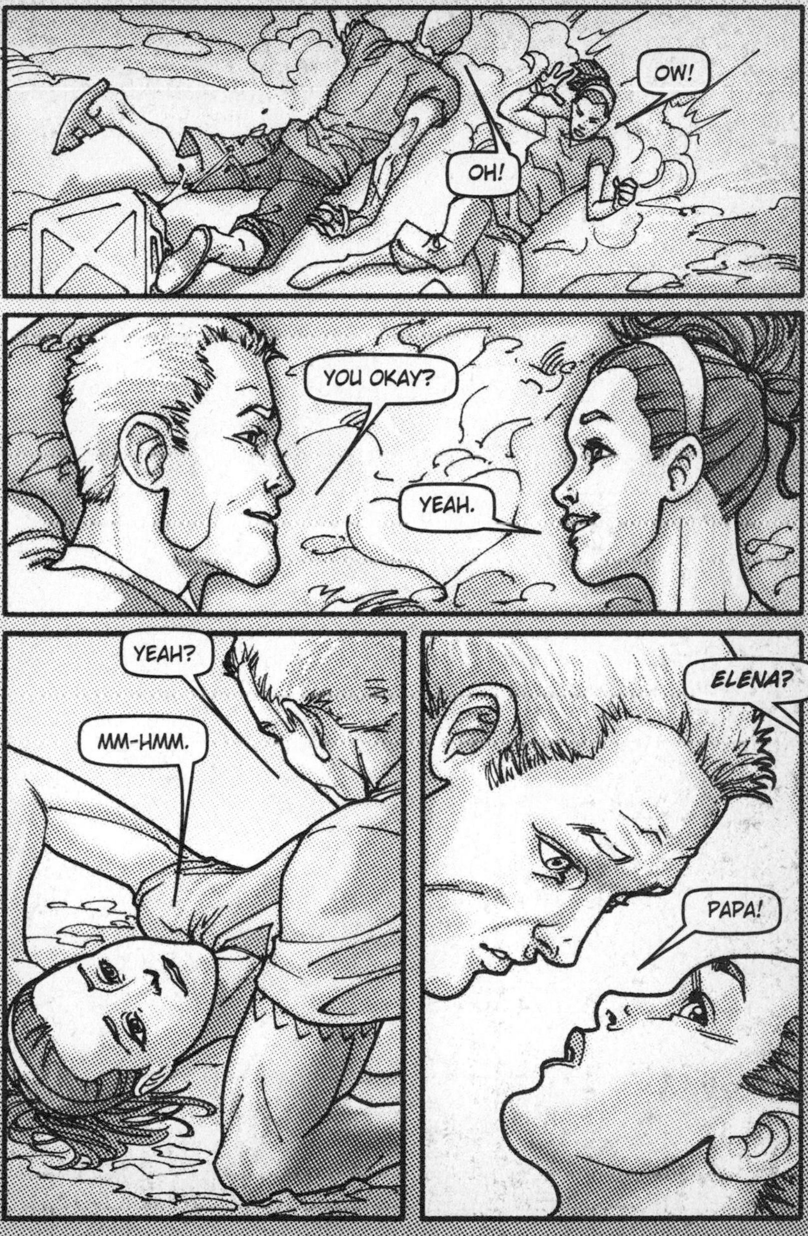
OW!
OH!
YOU OKAY?
YEAH.
YEAH?
MM-HMM.
ELENA?
PAPA!

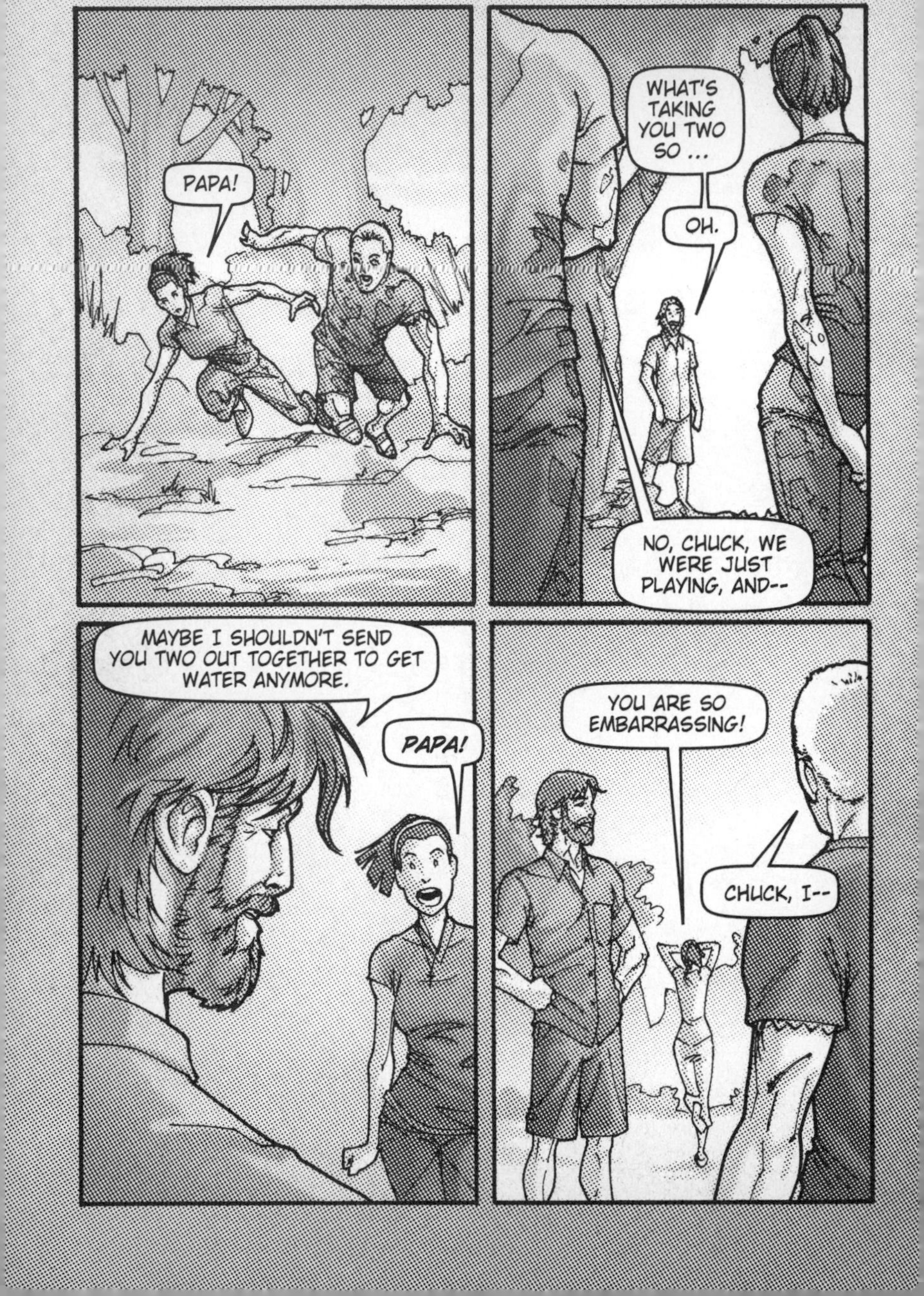
PAPA!
WHAT'S TAKING YOU TWO SO ...
OH.
NO, CHUCK, WE WERE JUST PLAYING, AND--
MAYBE I SHOULDN'T SEND YOU TWO OUT TOGETHER TO GET WATER ANYMORE.
PAPA!
YOU ARE SO EMBARRASSING!
CHUCK, I--

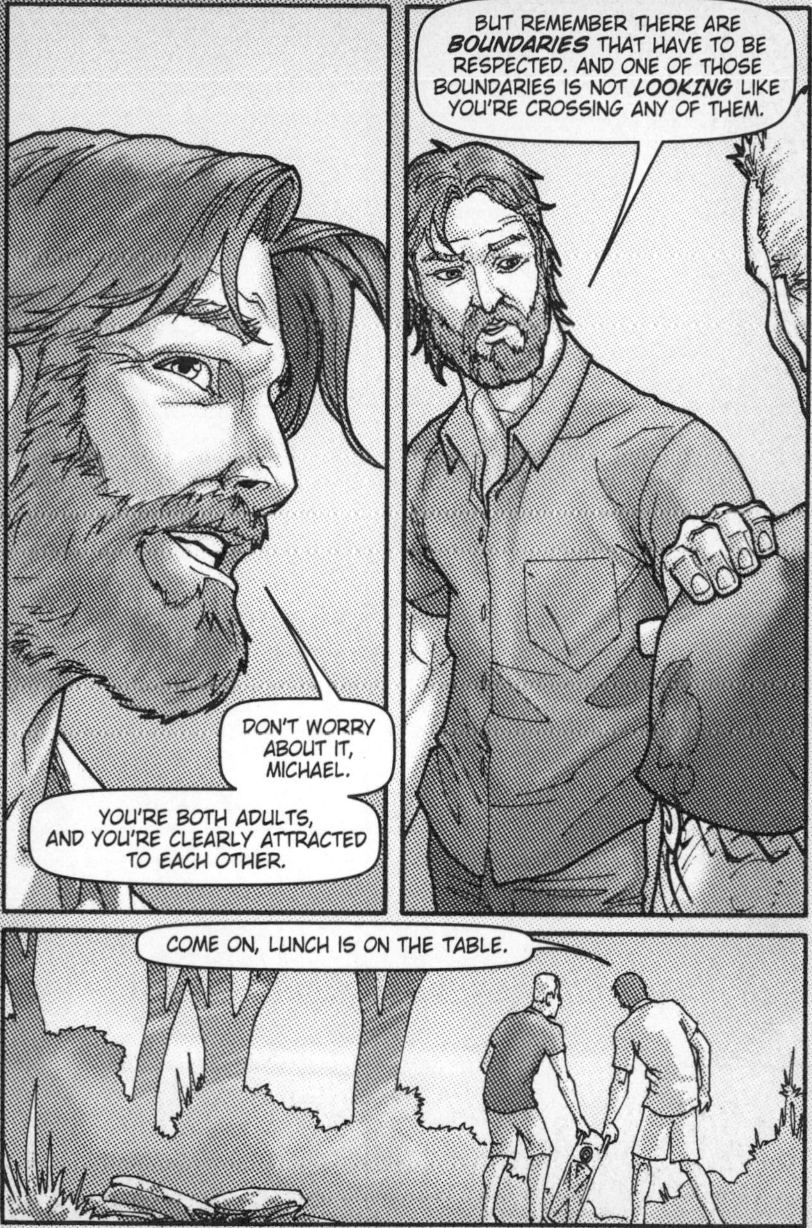
DON'T WORRY ABOUT IT, MICHAEL.
YOU'RE BOTH ADULTS, AND YOU'RE CLEARLY ATTRACTED TO EACH OTHER.
BUT REMEMBER THERE ARE **BOUNDARIES** THAT HAVE TO BE RESPECTED. AND ONE OF THOSE BOUNDARIES IS NOT **LOOKING** LIKE YOU'RE CROSSING ANY OF THEM.
COME ON, LUNCH IS ON THE TABLE.

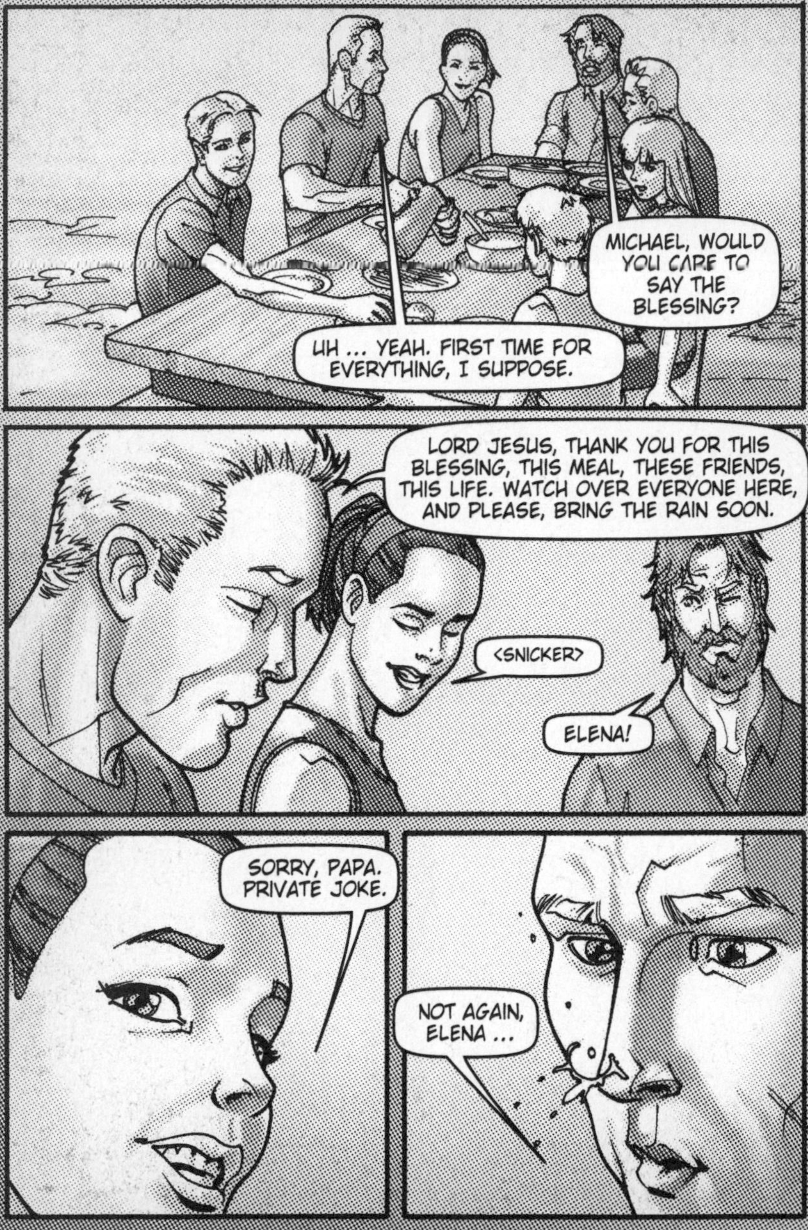
UH ... YEAH. FIRST TIME FOR EVERYTHING, I SUPPOSE.
MICHAEL, WOULD YOU CARE TO SAY THE BLESSING?
LORD JESUS, THANK YOU FOR THIS BLESSING, THIS MEAL, THESE FRIENDS, THIS LIFE. WATCH OVER EVERYONE HERE, AND PLEASE, BRING THE RAIN SOON.
<SNICKER>
ELENA!
SORRY, PAPA. PRIVATE JOKE.
NOT AGAIN, ELENA ...

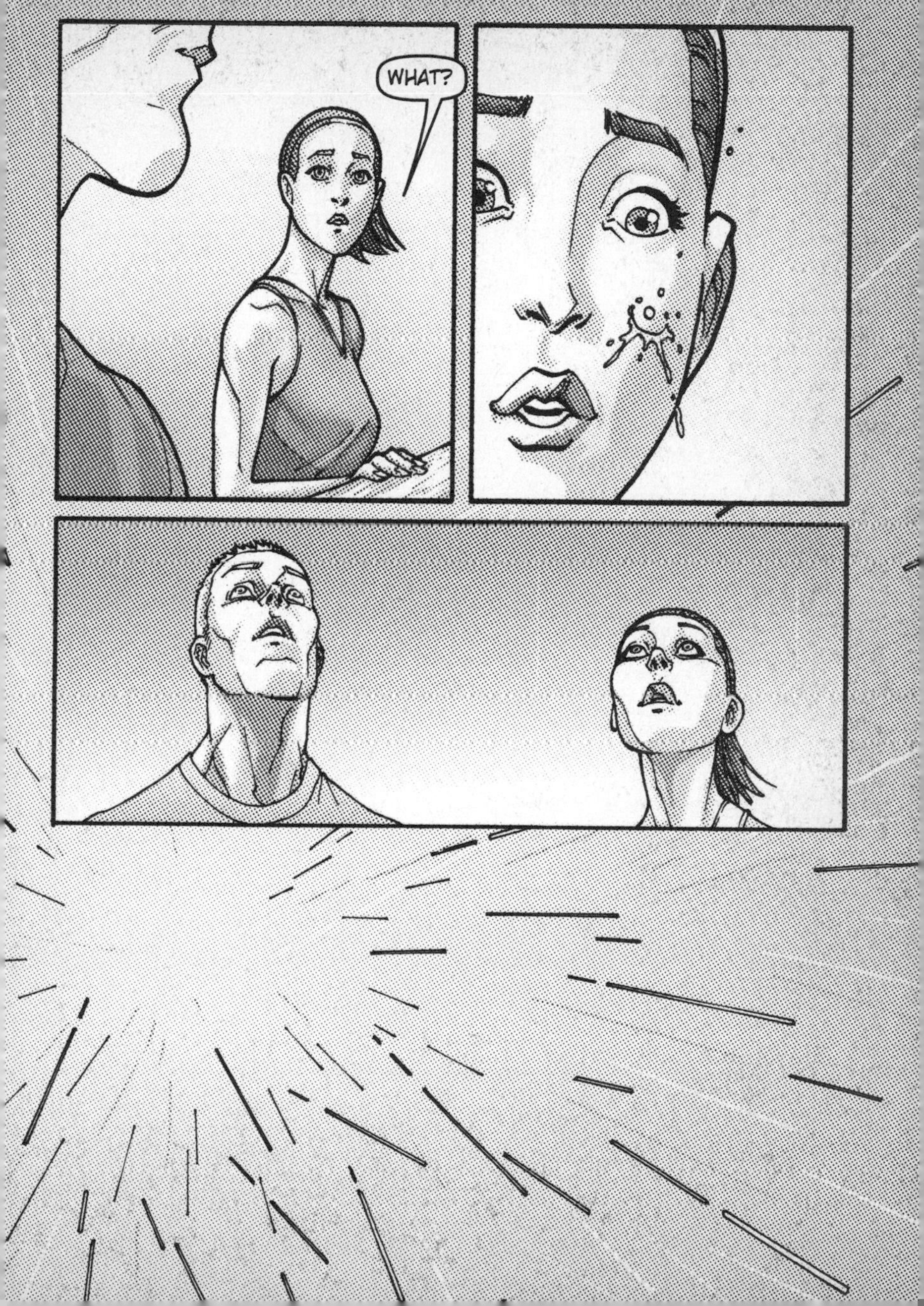
WHAT?

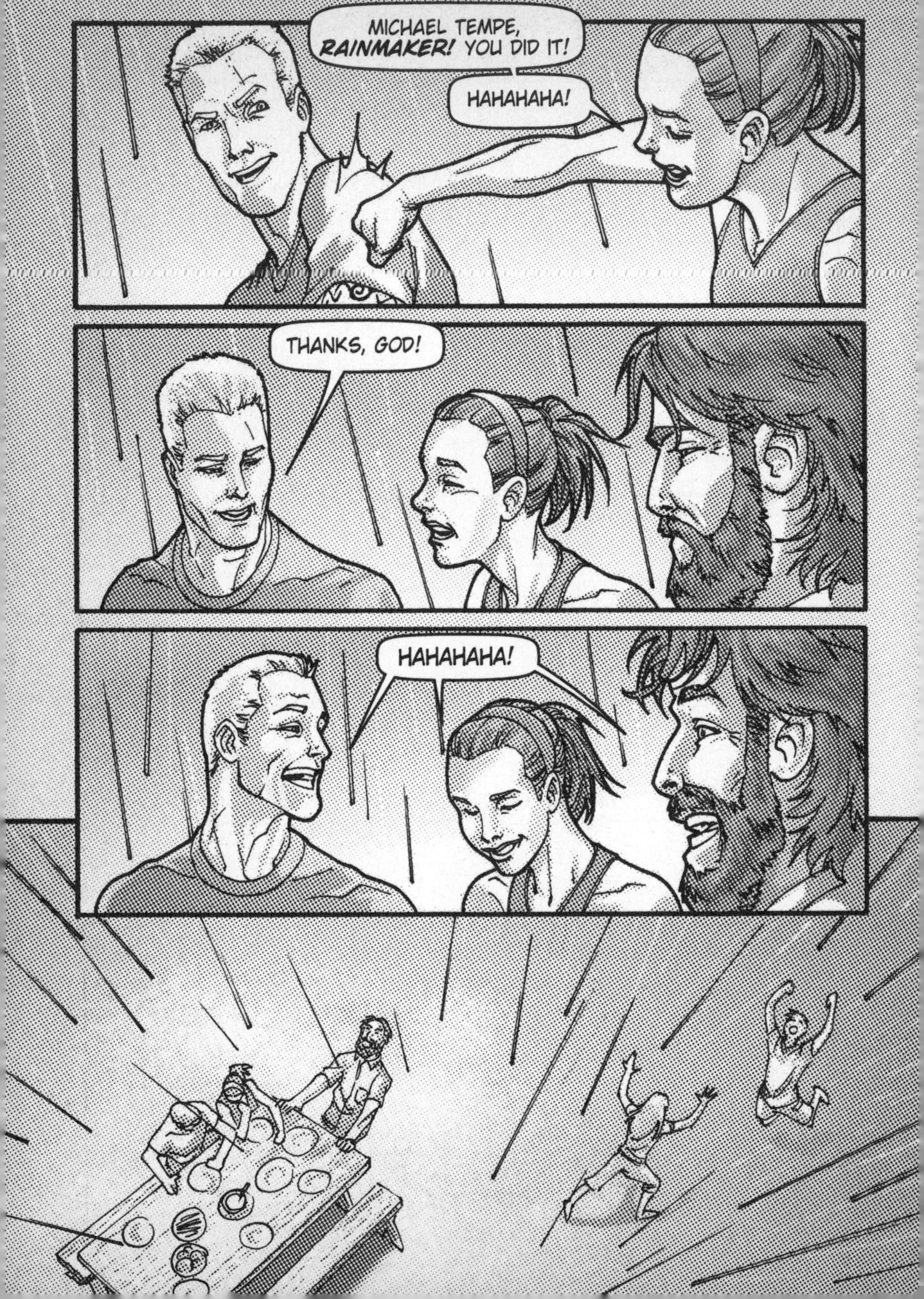

MICHAEL TEMPE, **RAINMAKER!** YOU DID IT!
HAHAHAHA!
THANKS, GOD!
HAHAHAHA!

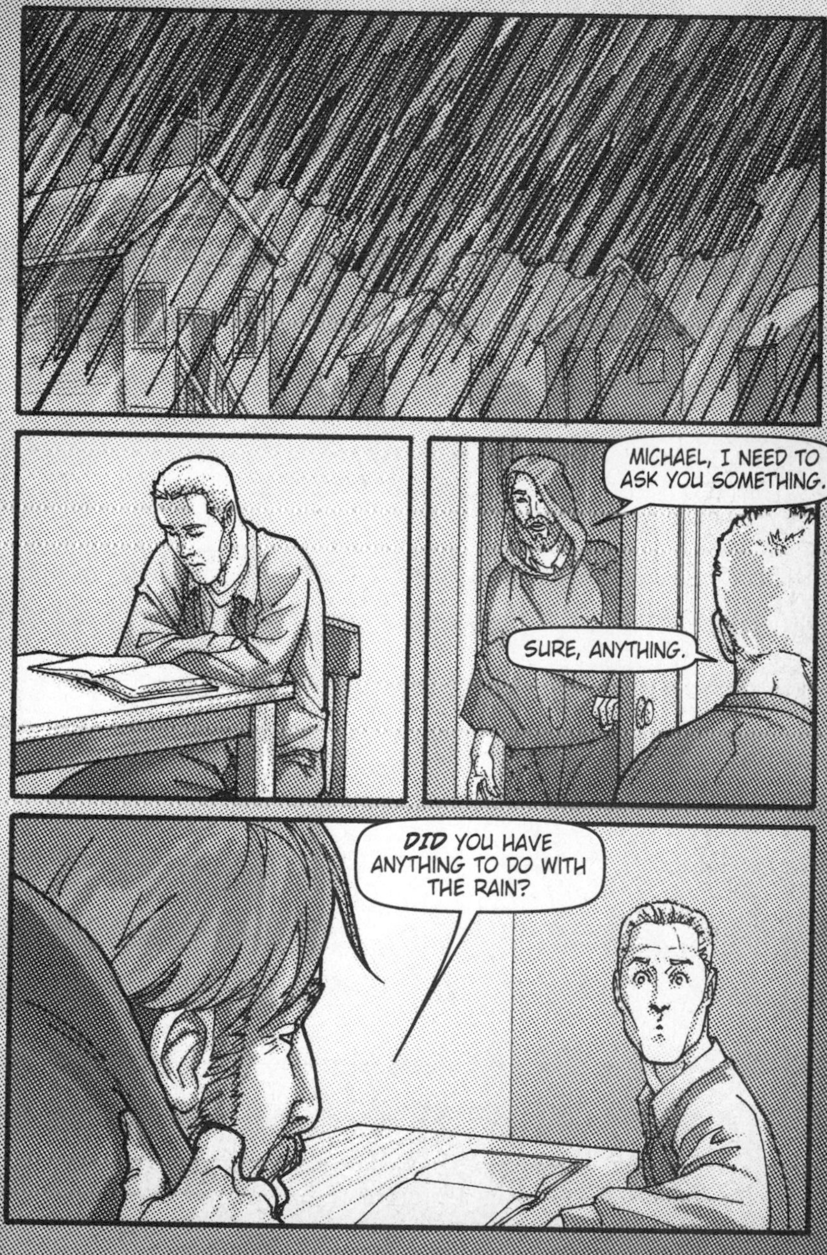
MICHAEL, I NEED TO ASK YOU SOMETHING.
SURE, ANYTHING.
DID YOU HAVE ANYTHING TO DO WITH THE RAIN?

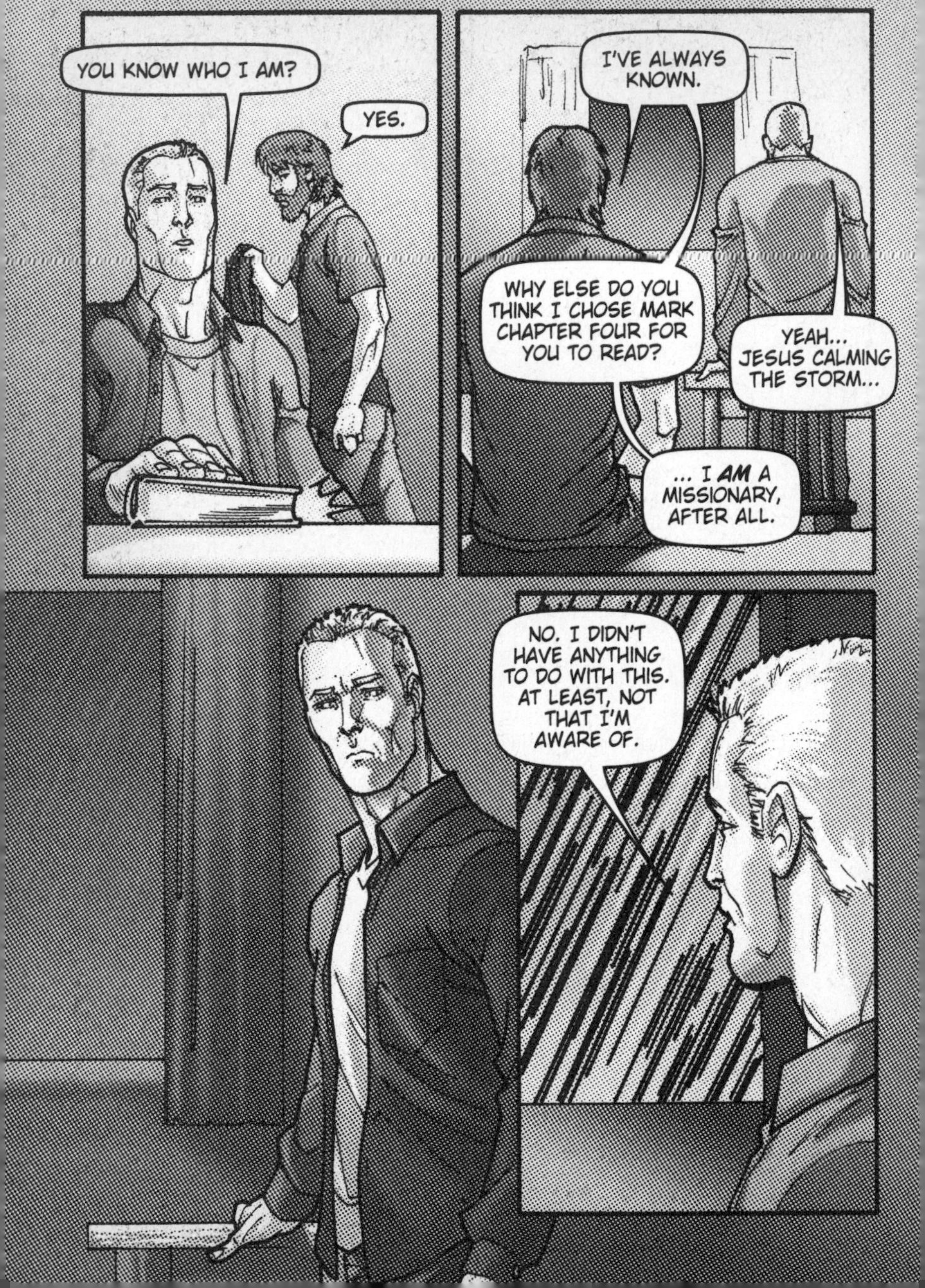
YOU KNOW WHO I AM?
YES.
I'VE ALWAYS KNOWN.
WHY ELSE DO YOU THINK I CHOSE MARK CHAPTER FOUR FOR YOU TO READ?
YEAH... JESUS CALMING THE STORM...
... I *AM* A MISSIONARY, AFTER ALL.
NO. I DIDN'T HAVE ANYTHING TO DO WITH THIS. AT LEAST, NOT THAT I'M AWARE OF.

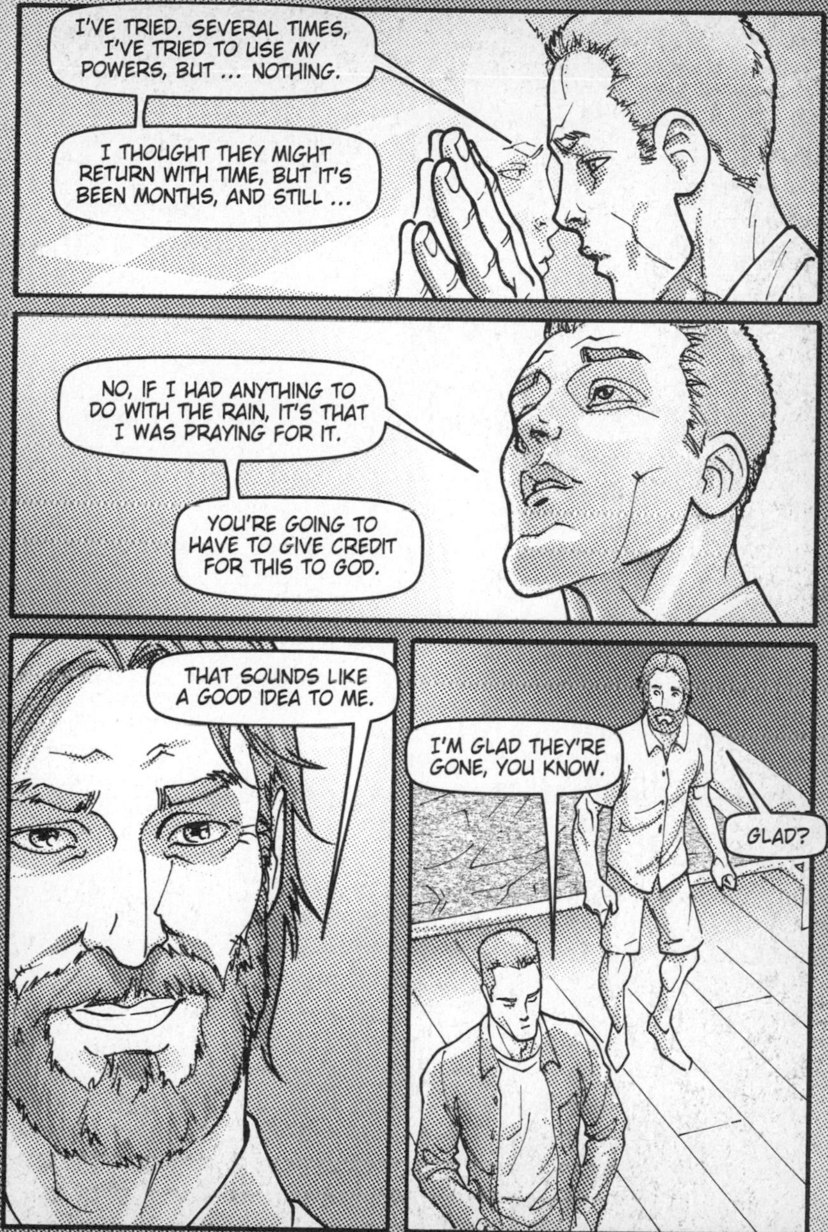
I'VE TRIED. SEVERAL TIMES, I'VE TRIED TO USE MY POWERS, BUT ... NOTHING.
I THOUGHT THEY MIGHT RETURN WITH TIME, BUT IT'S BEEN MONTHS, AND STILL ...
NO, IF I HAD ANYTHING TO DO WITH THE RAIN, IT'S THAT I WAS PRAYING FOR IT.
YOU'RE GOING TO HAVE TO GIVE CREDIT FOR THIS TO GOD.
THAT SOUNDS LIKE A GOOD IDEA TO ME.
I'M GLAD THEY'RE GONE, YOU KNOW.
GLAD?

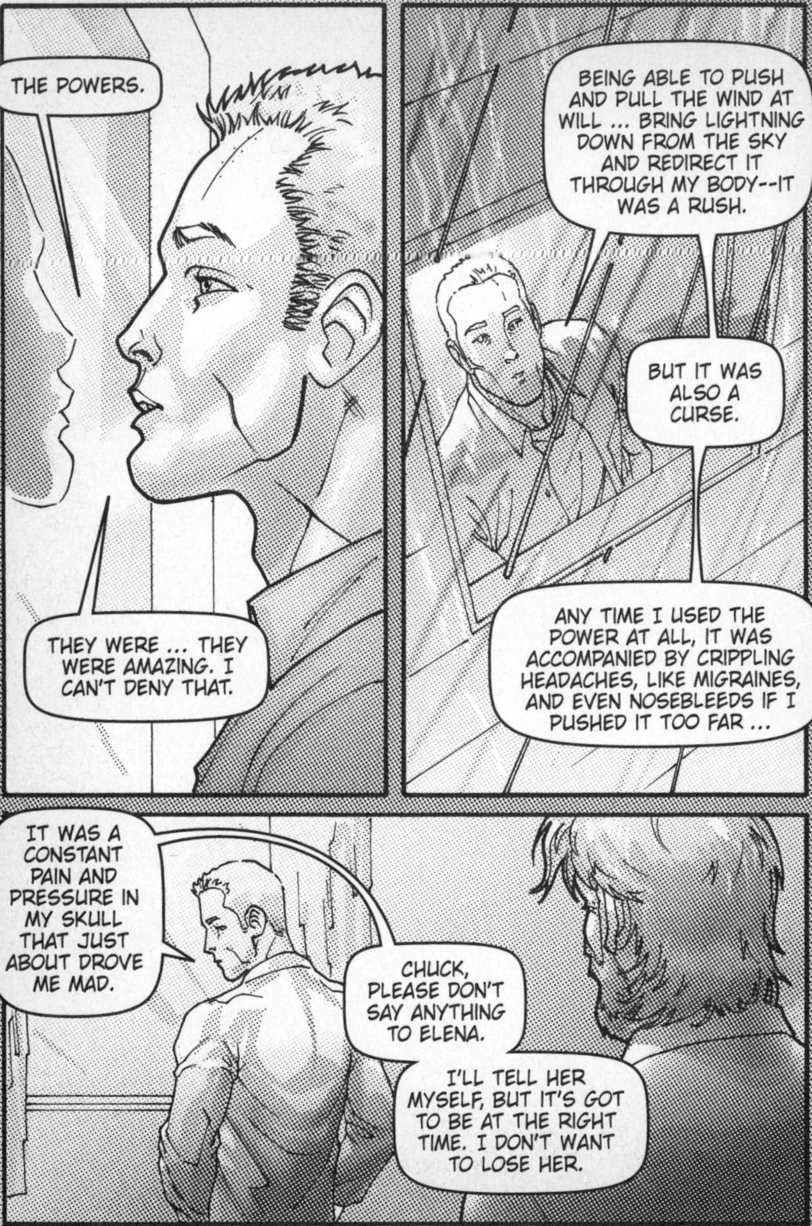
THE POWERS.
THEY WERE ... THEY WERE AMAZING. I CAN'T DENY THAT.
BEING ABLE TO PUSH AND PULL THE WIND AT WILL ... BRING LIGHTNING DOWN FROM THE SKY AND REDIRECT IT THROUGH MY BODY--IT WAS A RUSH.
BUT IT WAS ALSO A CURSE.
ANY TIME I USED THE POWER AT ALL, IT WAS ACCOMPANIED BY CRIPPLING HEADACHES, LIKE MIGRAINES, AND EVEN NOSEBLEEDS IF I PUSHED IT TOO FAR ...
IT WAS A CONSTANT PAIN AND PRESSURE IN MY SKULL THAT JUST ABOUT DROVE ME MAD.
CHUCK, PLEASE DON'T SAY ANYTHING TO ELENA.
I'LL TELL HER MYSELF, BUT IT'S GOT TO BE AT THE RIGHT TIME. I DON'T WANT TO LOSE HER.

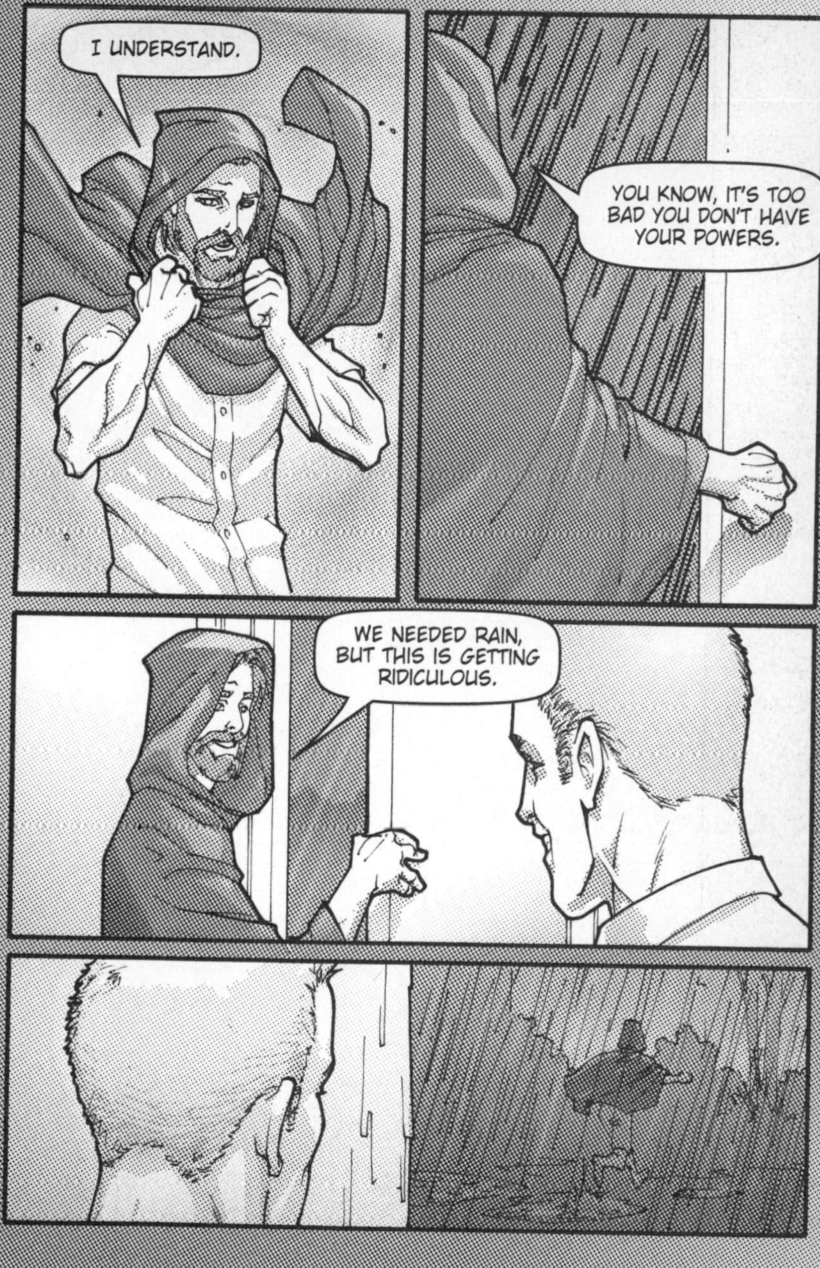
I UNDERSTAND.
YOU KNOW, IT'S TOO BAD YOU DON'T HAVE YOUR POWERS.
WE NEEDED RAIN, BUT THIS IS GETTING RIDICULOUS.

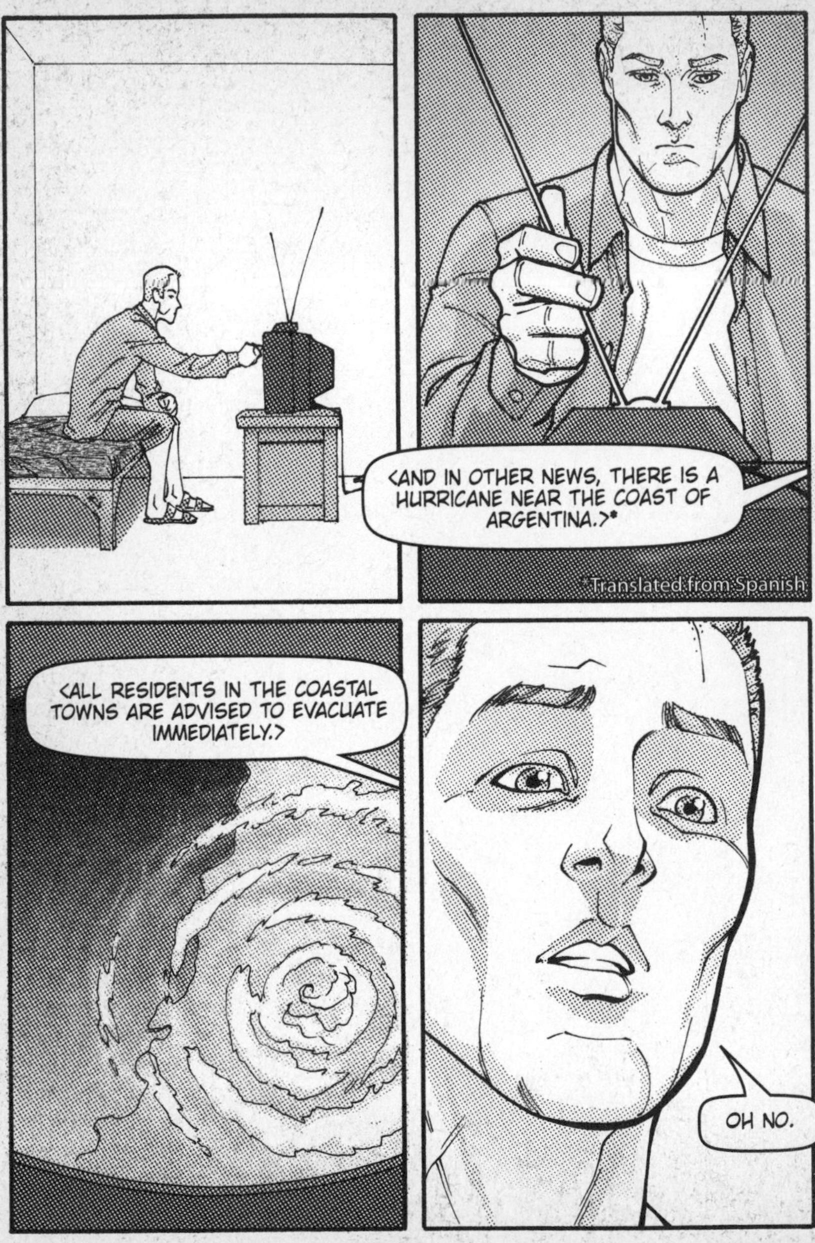
<AND IN OTHER NEWS, THERE IS A HURRICANE NEAR THE COAST OF ARGENTINA.>*
*Translated from Spanish
<ALL RESIDENTS IN THE COASTAL TOWNS ARE ADVISED TO EVACUATE IMMEDIATELY.>
OH NO.

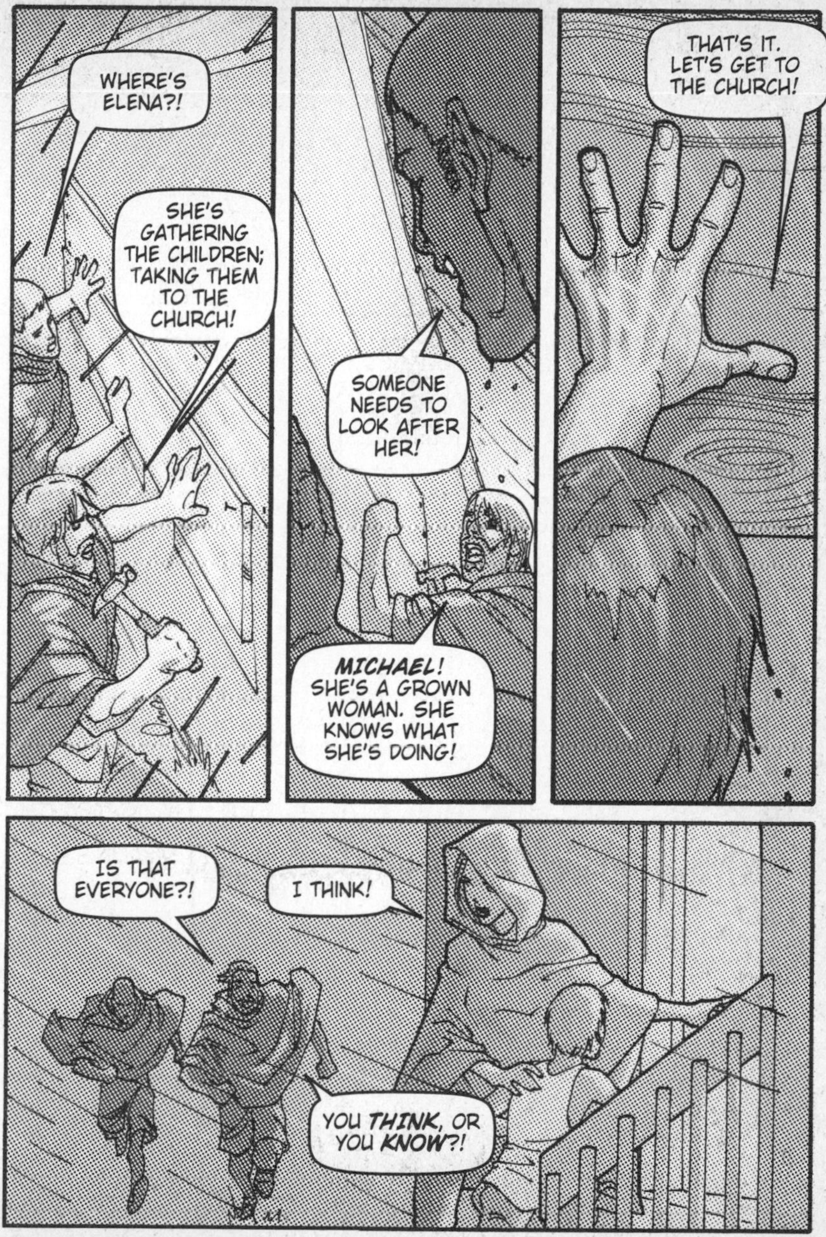
WHERE'S ELENA?!
SHE'S GATHERING THE CHILDREN; TAKING THEM TO THE CHURCH!
SOMEONE NEEDS TO LOOK AFTER HER!
MICHAEL! SHE'S A GROWN WOMAN. SHE KNOWS WHAT SHE'S DOING!
THAT'S IT. LET'S GET TO THE CHURCH!
IS THAT EVERYONE?!
I THINK!
YOU THINK, OR YOU KNOW?!

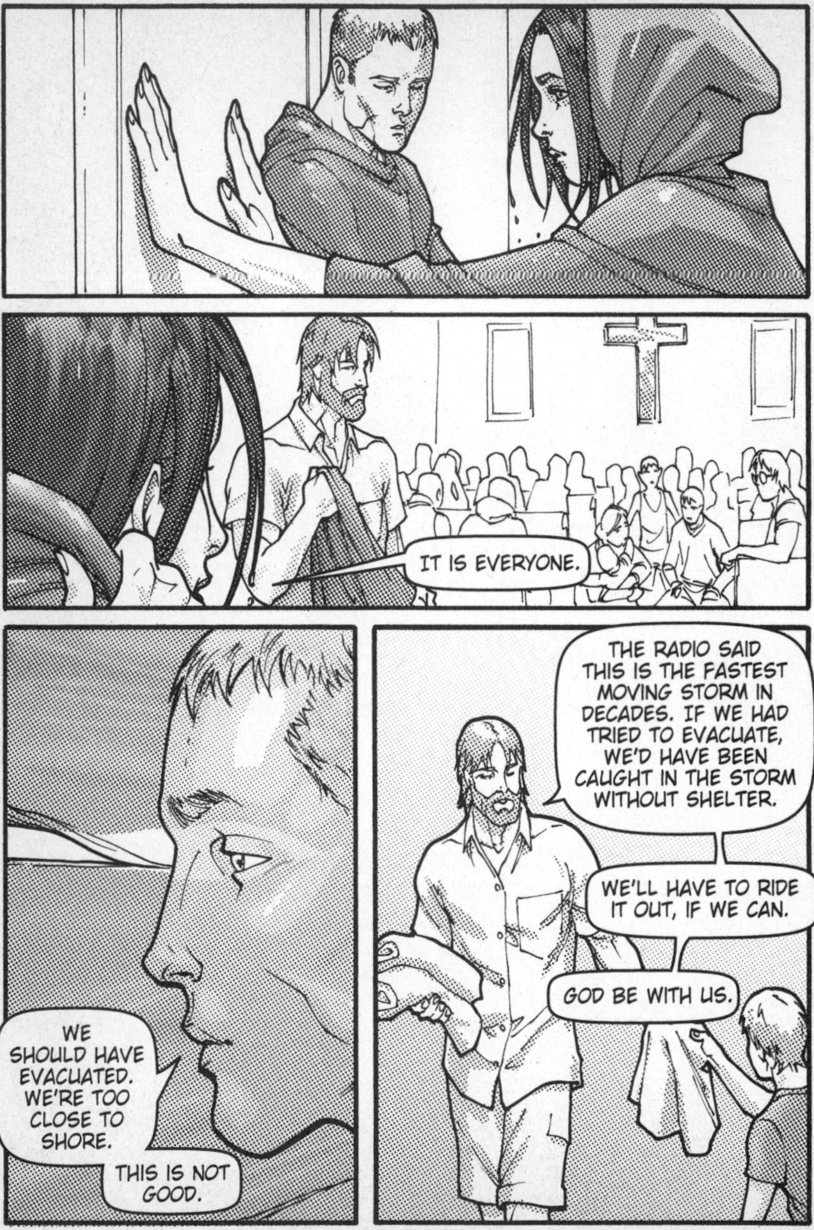
IT IS EVERYONE.
WE SHOULD HAVE EVACUATED. WE'RE TOO CLOSE TO SHORE.
THIS IS NOT GOOD.
THE RADIO SAID THIS IS THE FASTEST MOVING STORM IN DECADES. IF WE HAD TRIED TO EVACUATE, WE'D HAVE BEEN CAUGHT IN THE STORM WITHOUT SHELTER.
WE'LL HAVE TO RIDE IT OUT, IF WE CAN.
GOD BE WITH US.

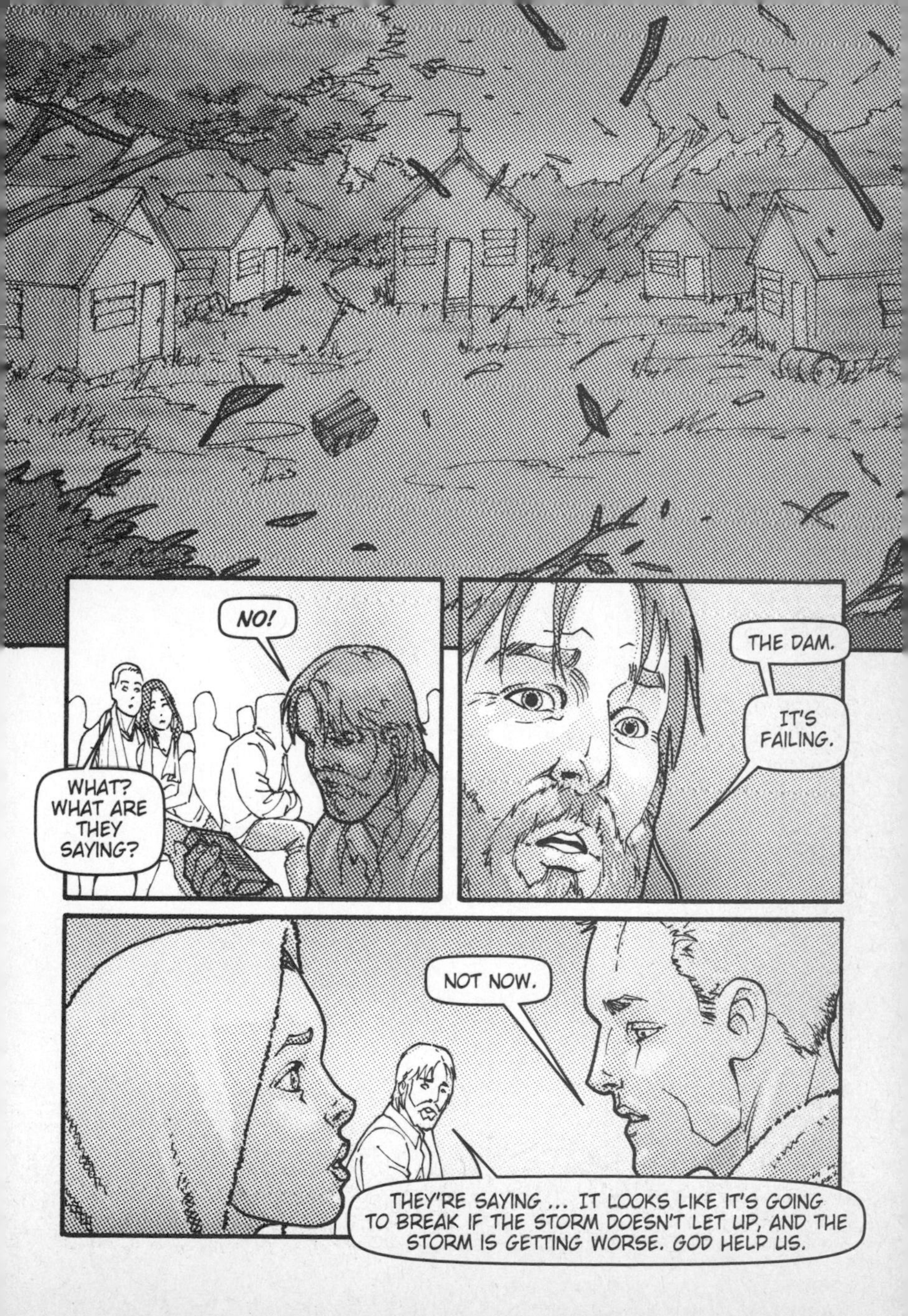
NO!
WHAT? WHAT ARE THEY SAYING?
THE DAM.
IT'S FAILING.
NOT NOW.
THEY'RE SAYING ... IT LOOKS LIKE IT'S GOING TO BREAK IF THE STORM DOESN'T LET UP, AND THE STORM IS GETTING WORSE. GOD HELP US.

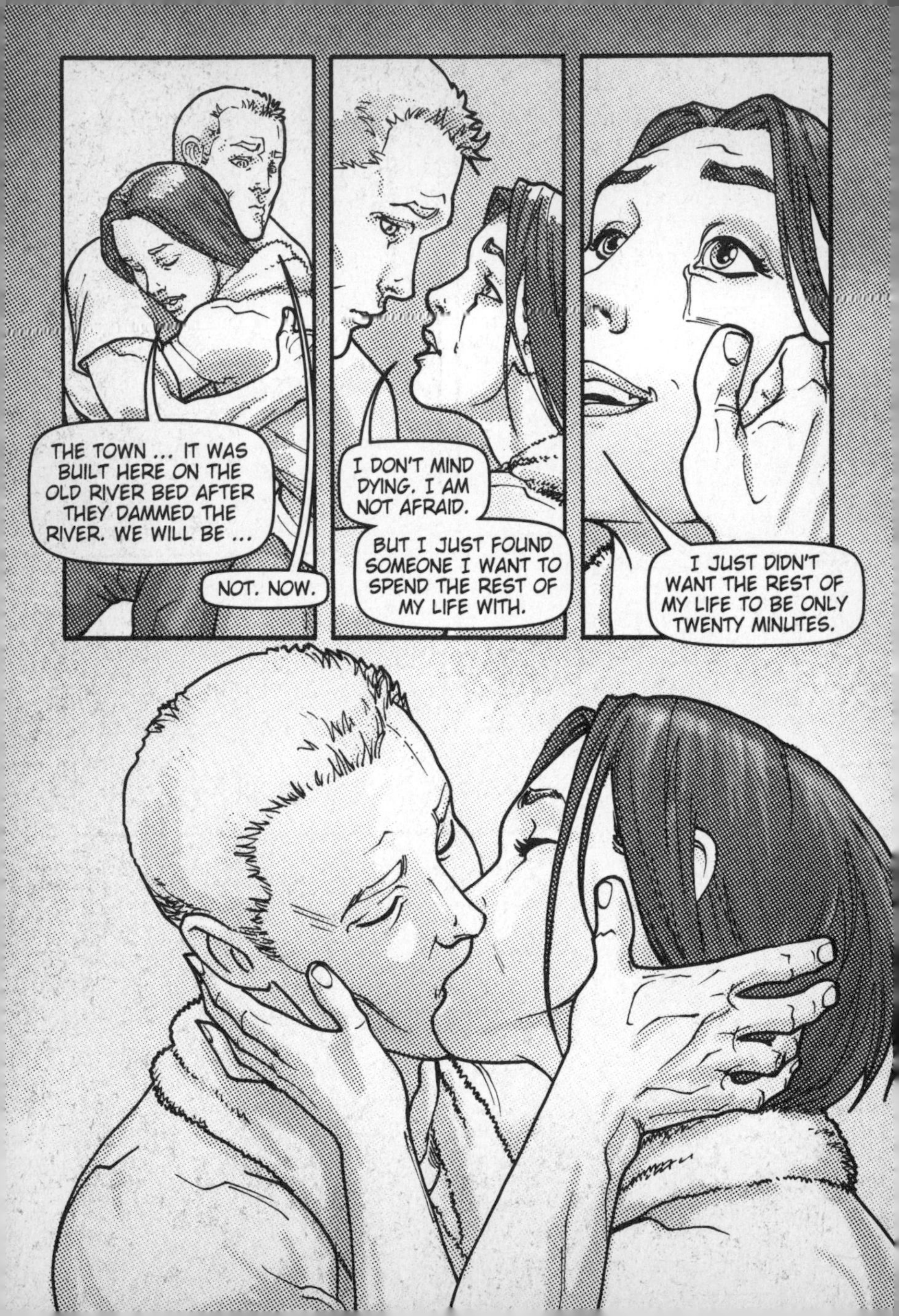
THE TOWN ... IT WAS BUILT HERE ON THE OLD RIVER BED AFTER THEY DAMMED THE RIVER. WE WILL BE ...
NOT. NOW.
I DON'T MIND DYING. I AM NOT AFRAID.
BUT I JUST FOUND SOMEONE I WANT TO SPEND THE REST OF MY LIFE WITH.
I JUST DIDN'T WANT THE REST OF MY LIFE TO BE ONLY TWENTY MINUTES.

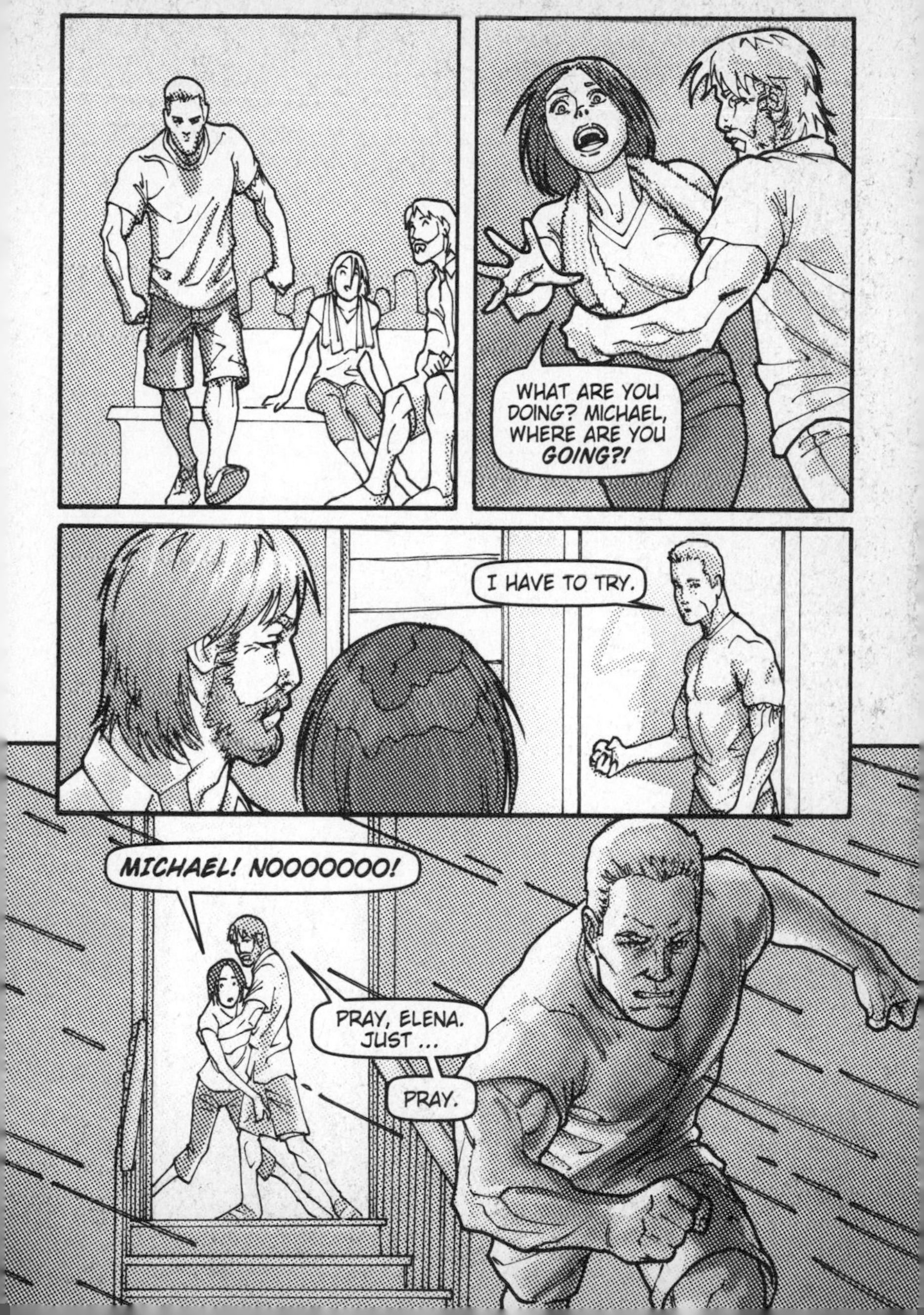
WHAT ARE YOU DOING? MICHAEL, WHERE ARE YOU *GOING?!*
I HAVE TO TRY.
MICHAEL! NOOOOOOO!
PRAY, ELENA. JUST ...
PRAY.

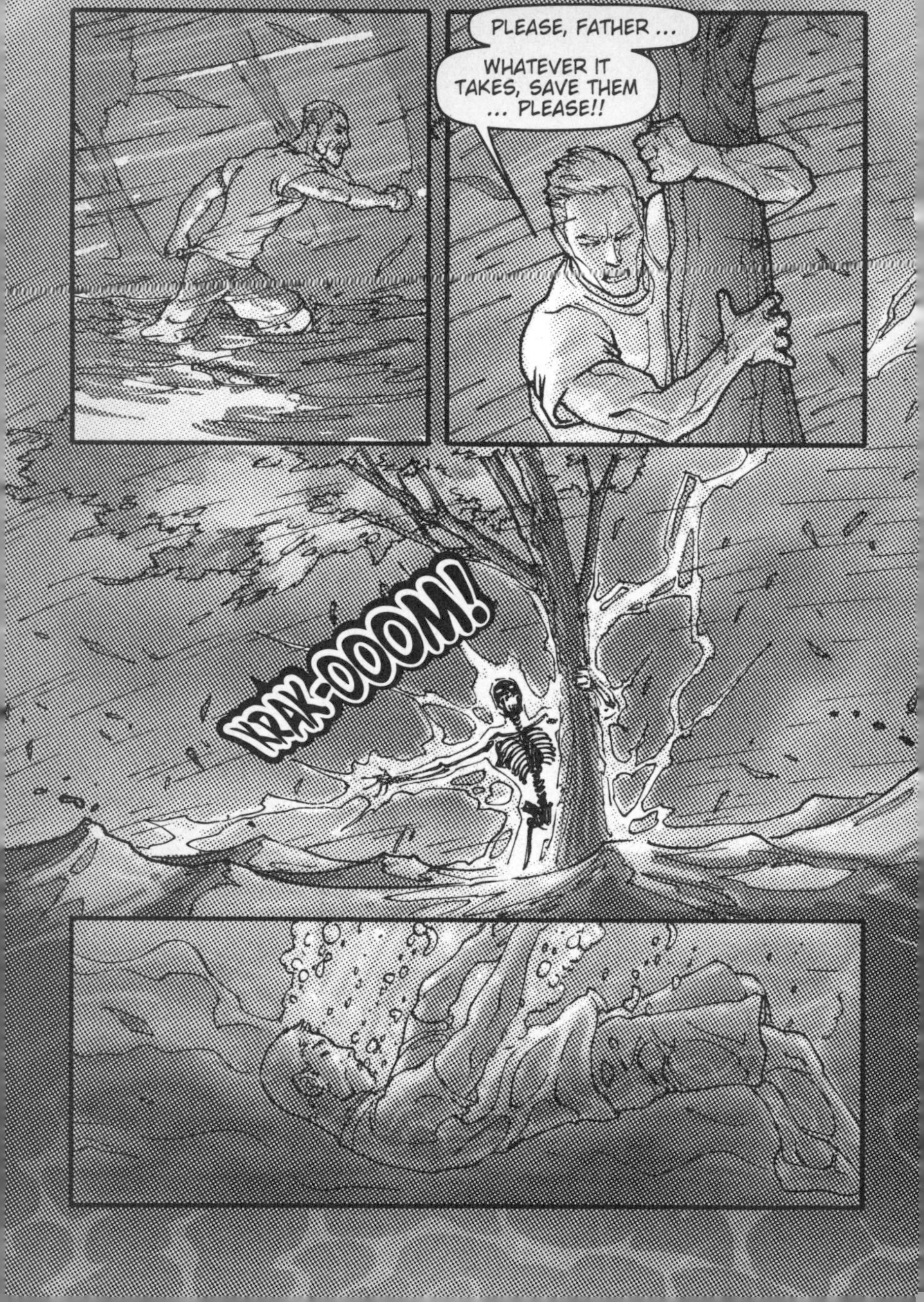
PLEASE, FATHER ...
WHATEVER IT TAKES, SAVE THEM ... PLEASE!!
KRAK-OOOM!

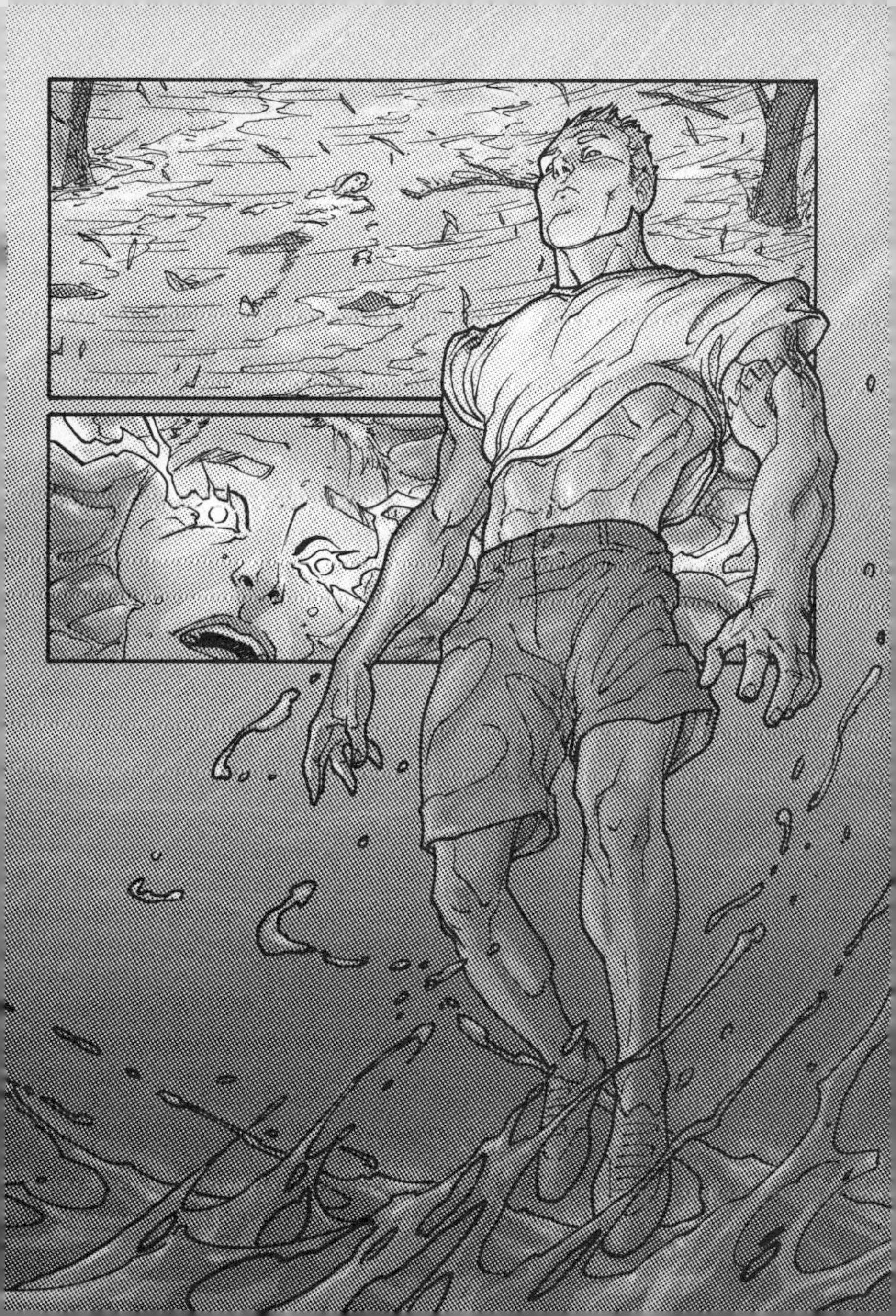

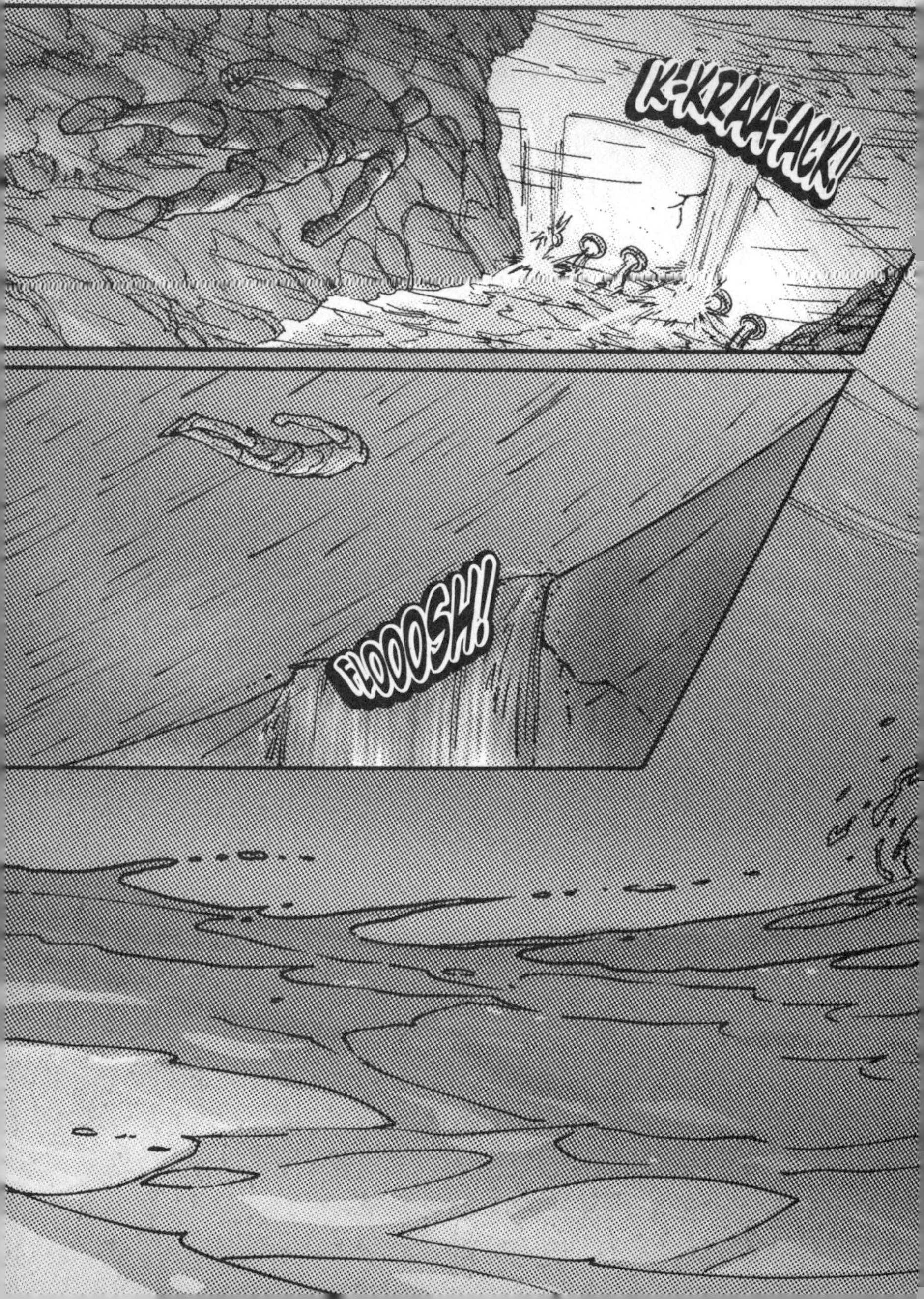
K-KRAA-ACK!
FLOOOSH!

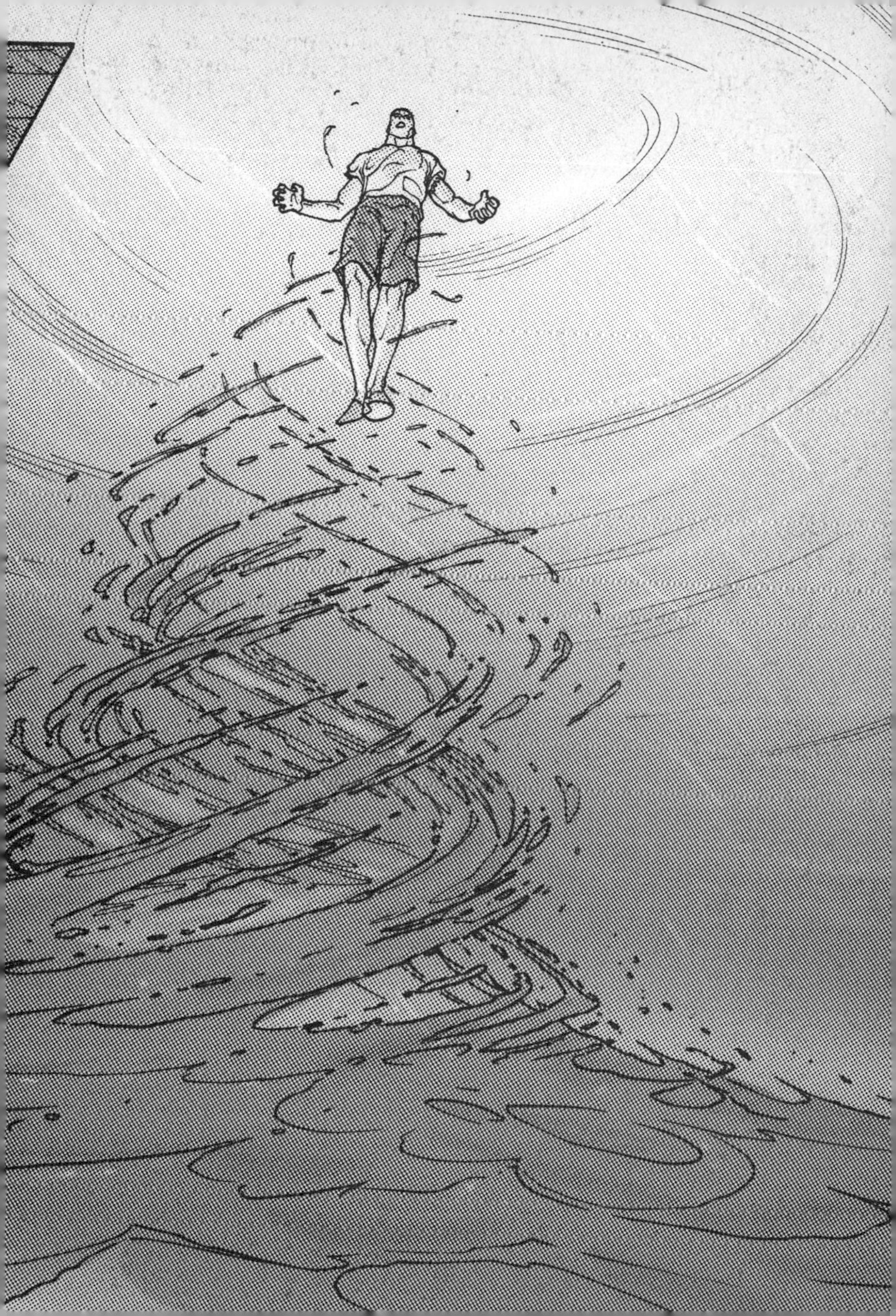

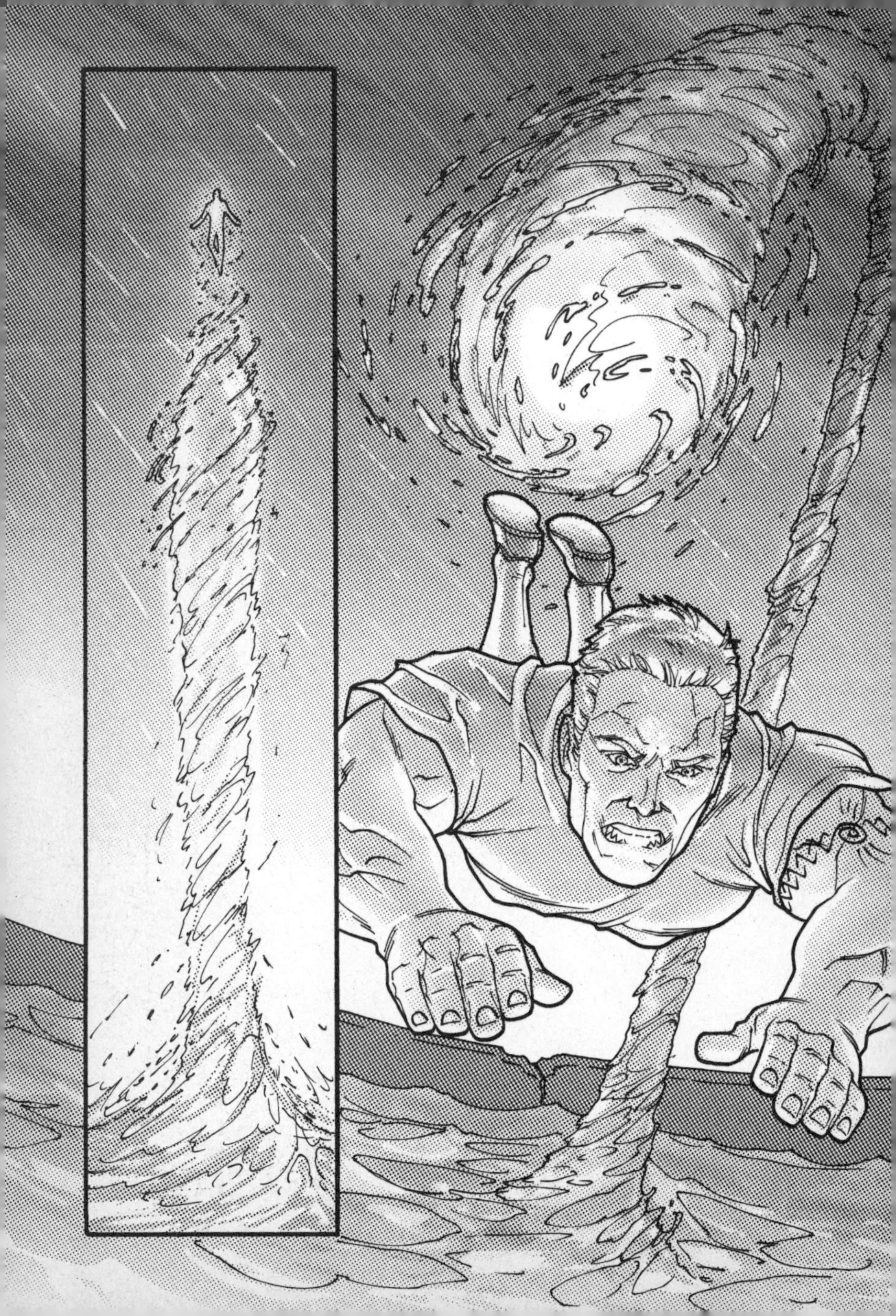

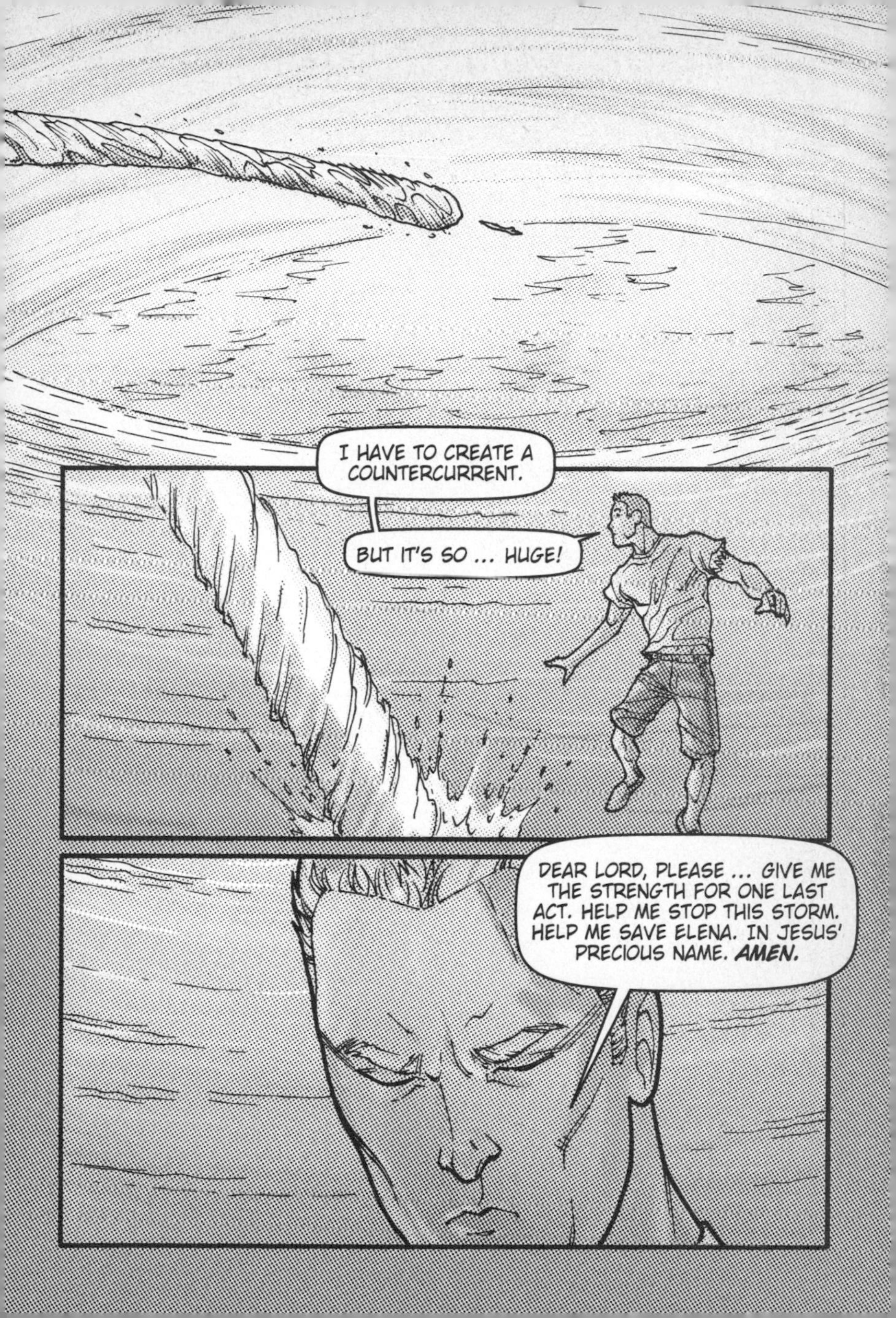
I HAVE TO CREATE A COUNTERCURRENT.
BUT IT'S SO ... HUGE!
DEAR LORD, PLEASE ... GIVE ME THE STRENGTH FOR ONE LAST ACT. HELP ME STOP THIS STORM. HELP ME SAVE ELENA. IN JESUS' PRECIOUS NAME. ***AMEN.***

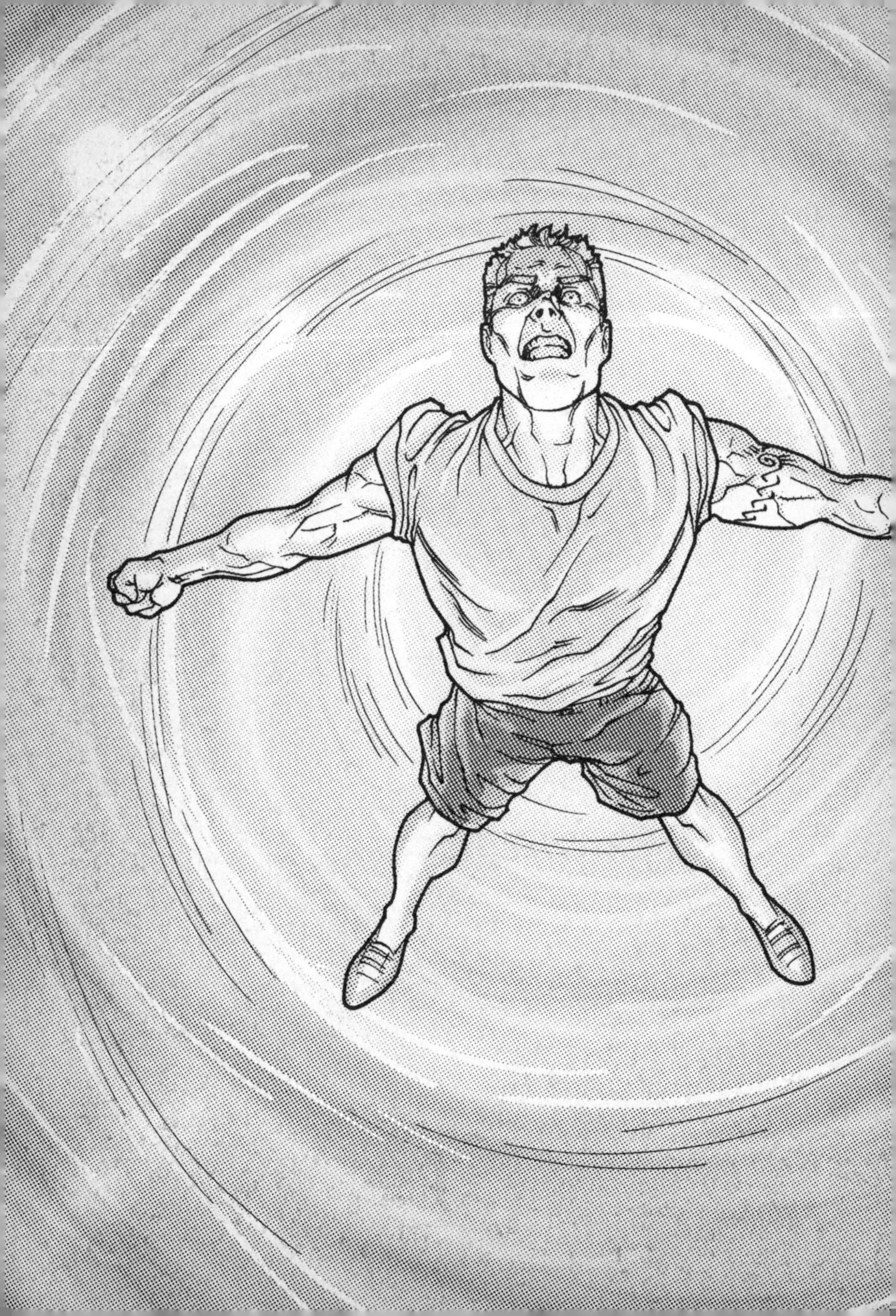

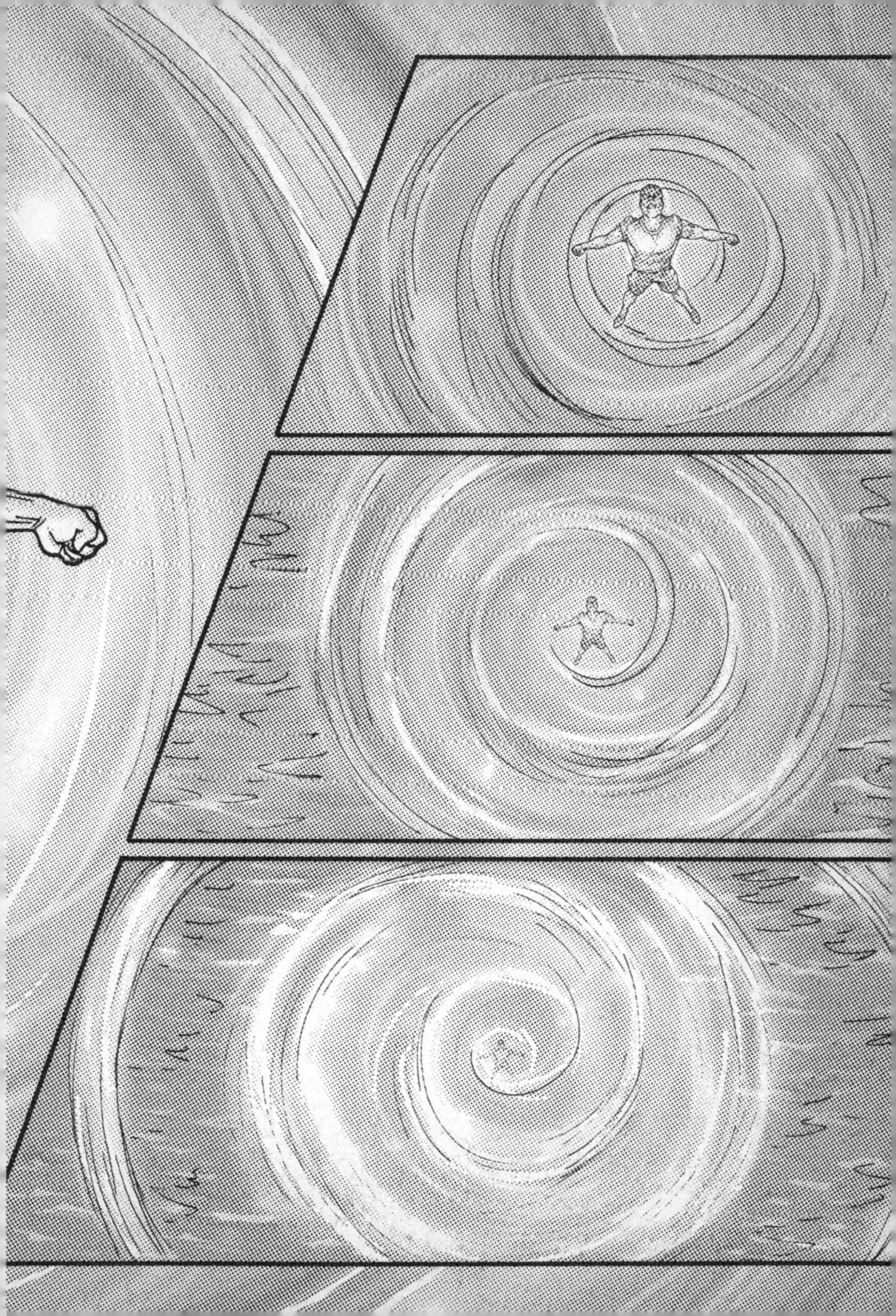

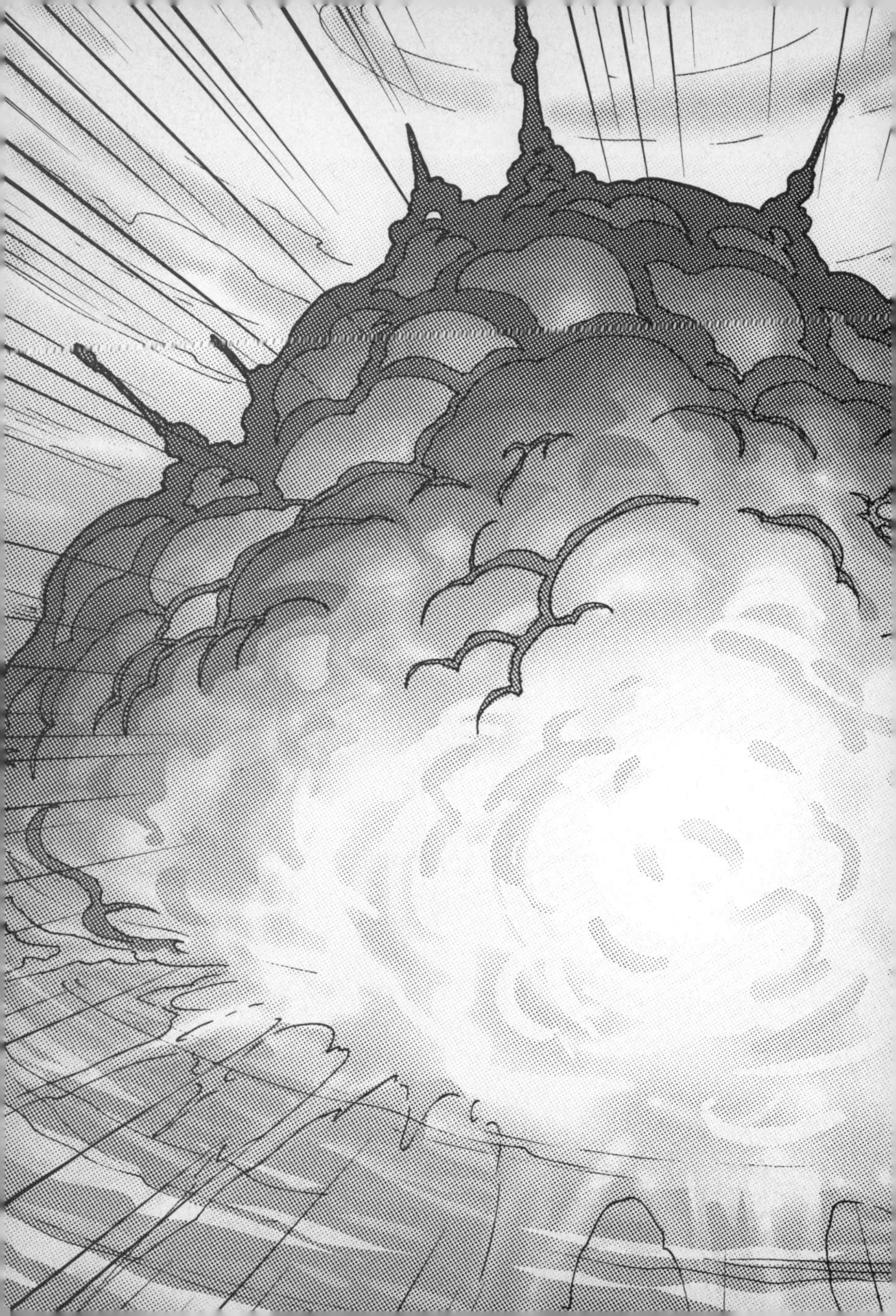

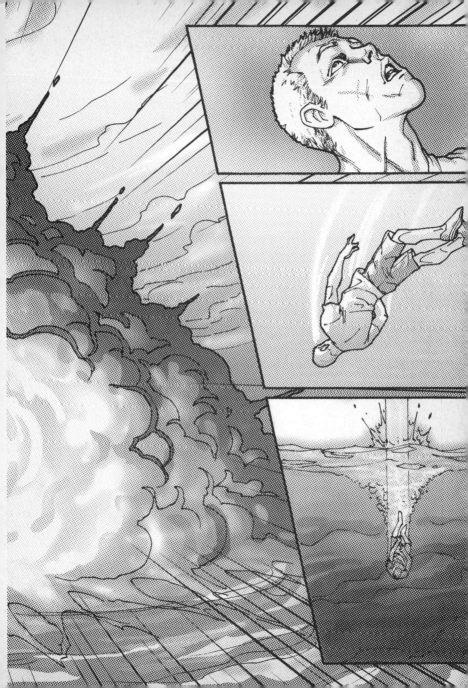

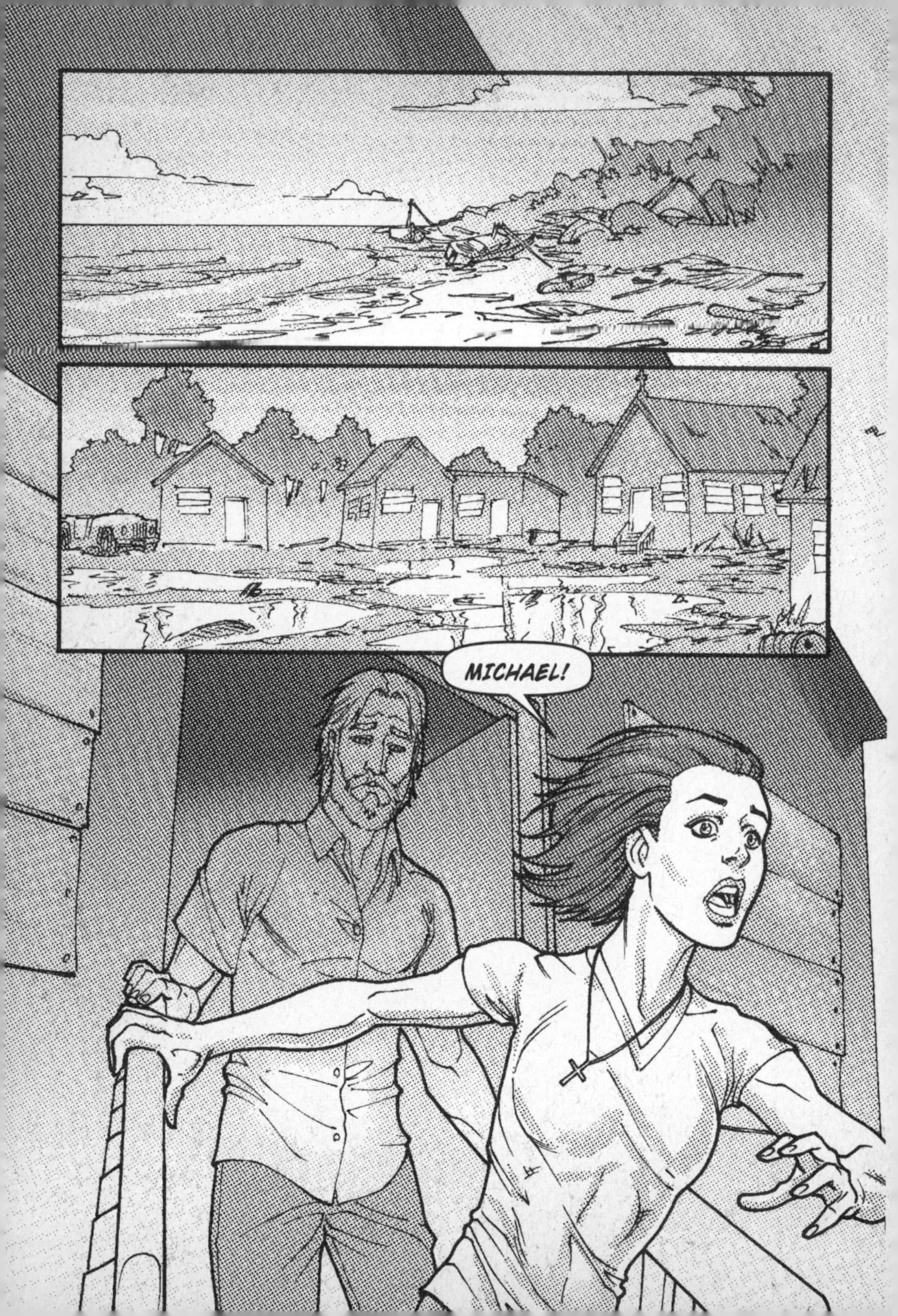
MICHAEL!

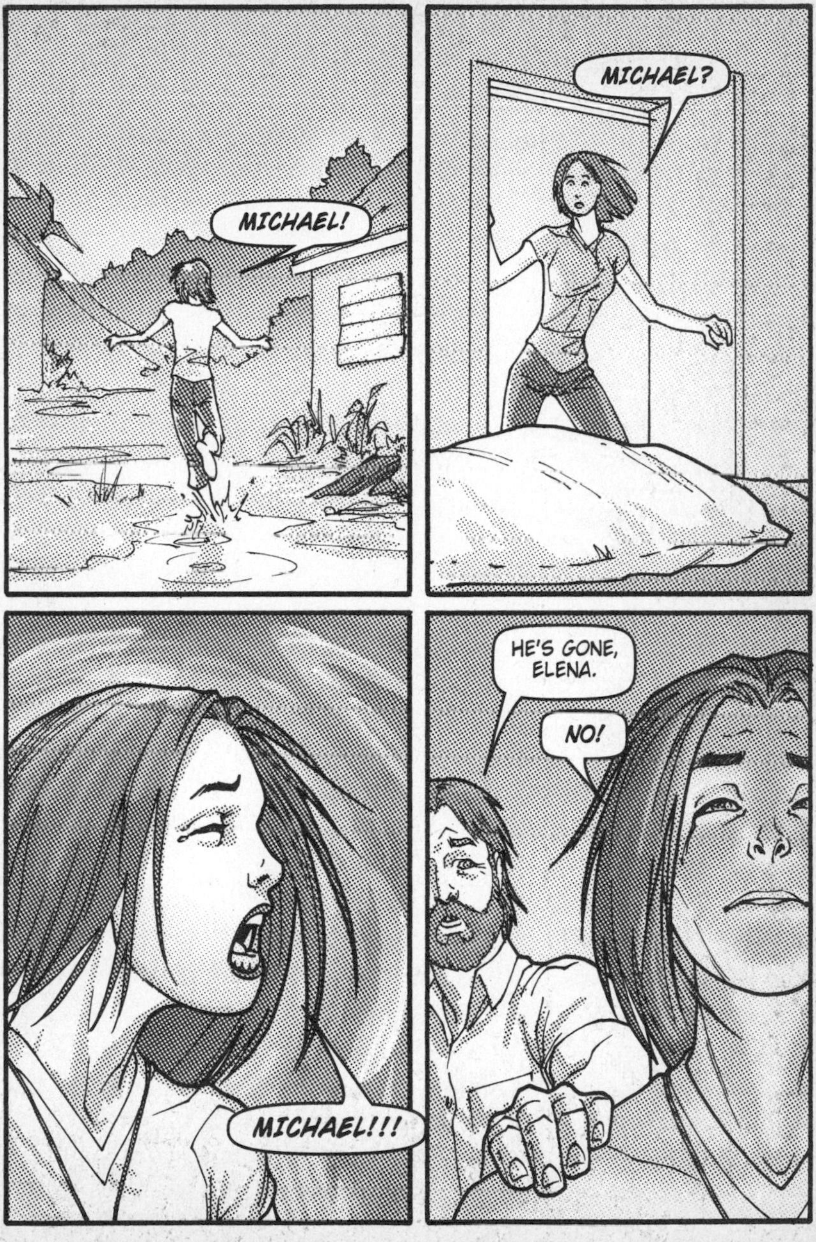
MICHAEL!
MICHAEL?
MICHAEL!!!
HE'S GONE, ELENA.
NO!

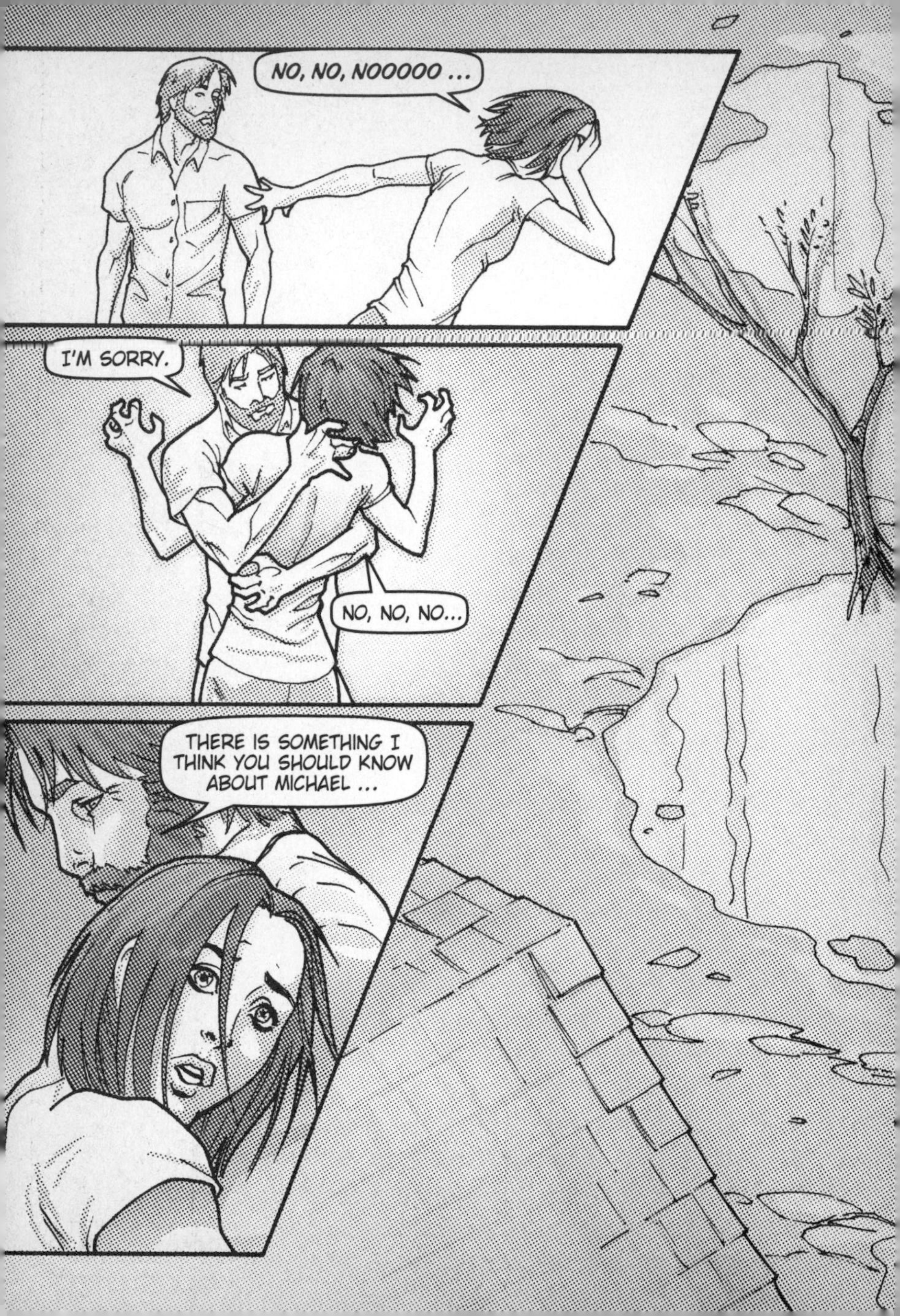
NO, NO, NOOOOO ...
I'M SORRY.
NO, NO, NO...
THERE IS SOMETHING I THINK YOU SHOULD KNOW ABOUT MICHAEL ...

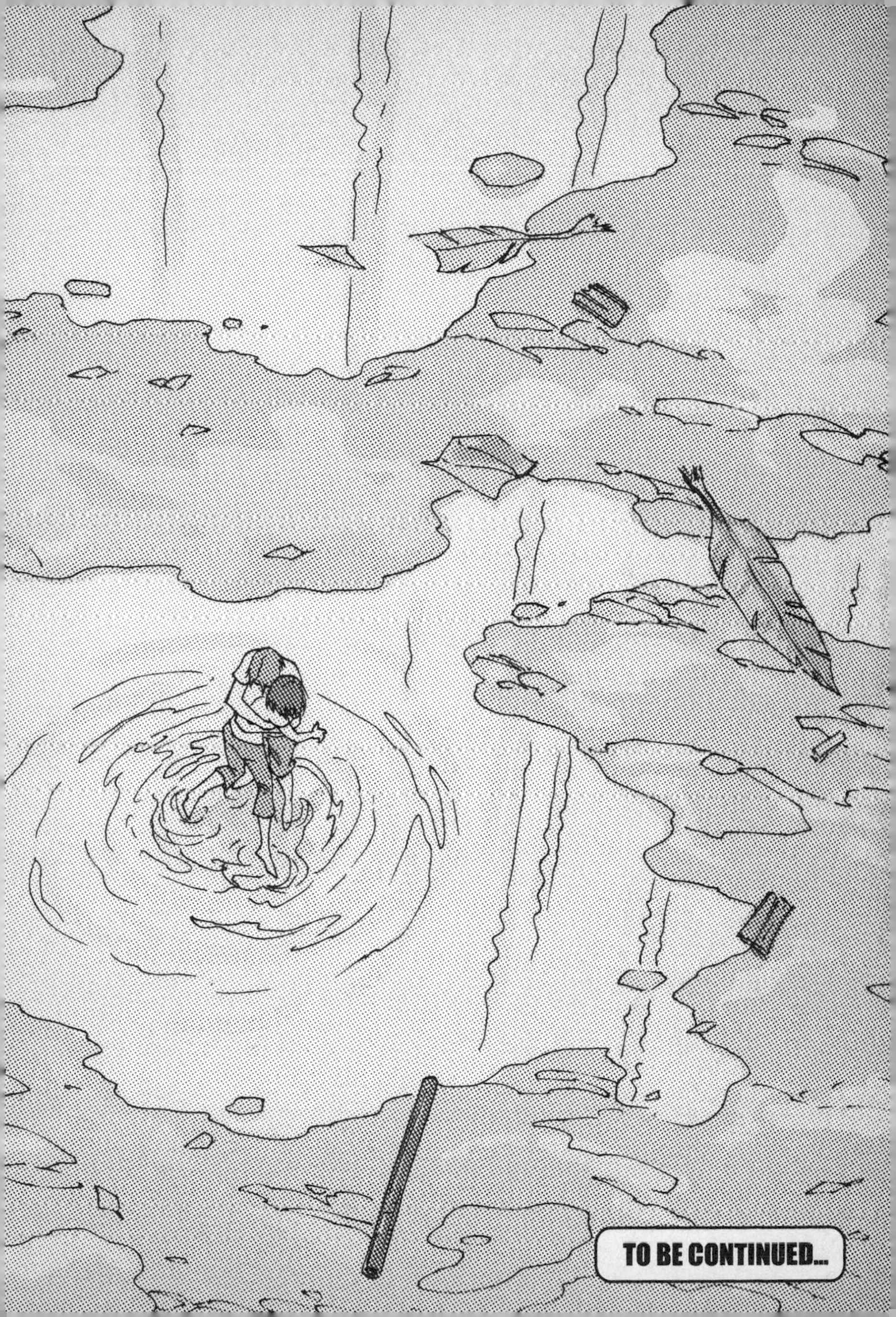
TO BE CONTINUED...

Preliminary Character sketches

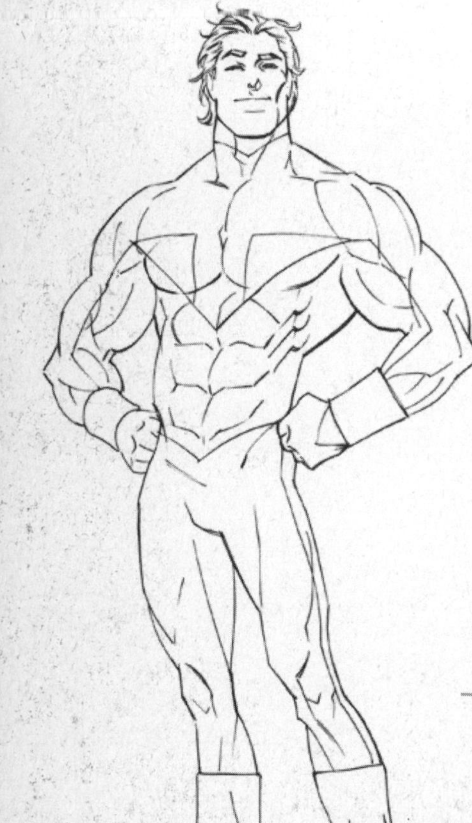

TITAN

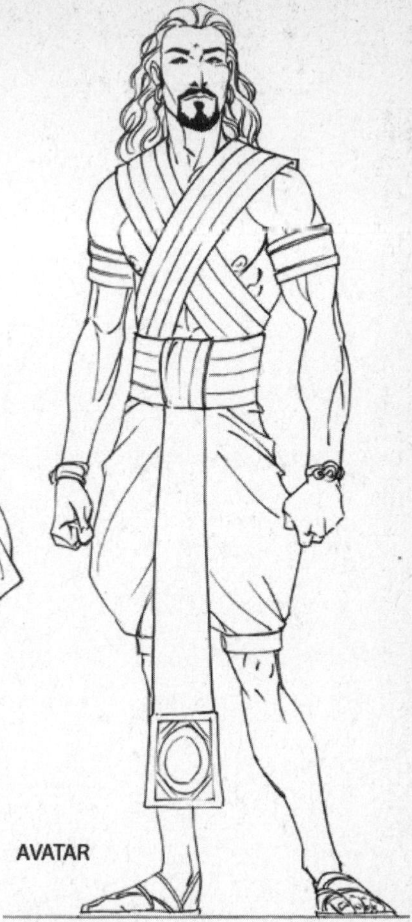

AVATAR

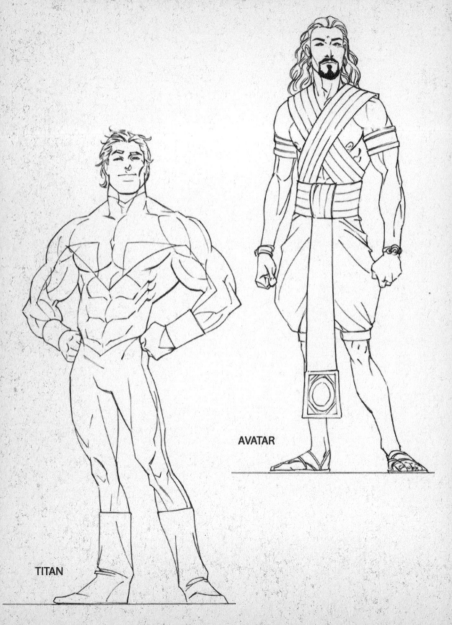

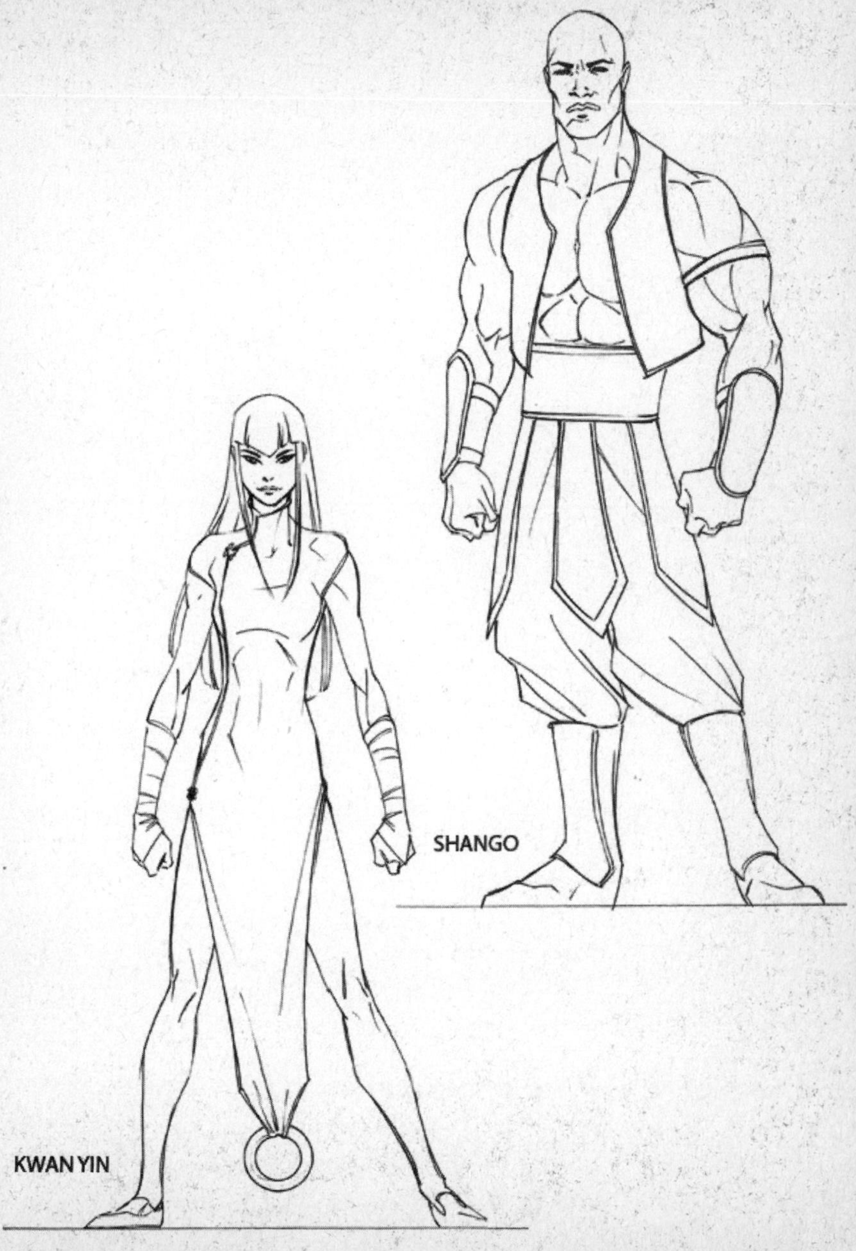
SHANGO
KWAN YIN

Preliminary Character sketches

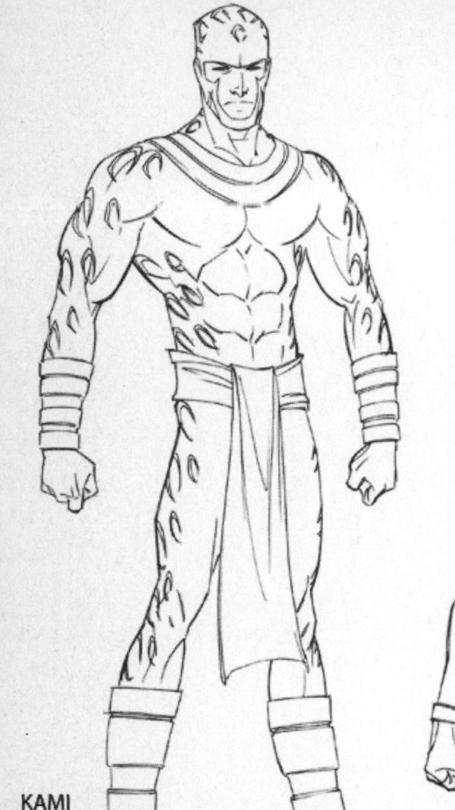

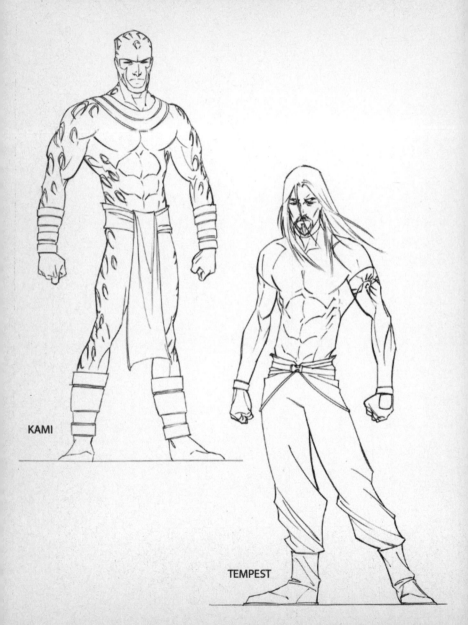

KAMI

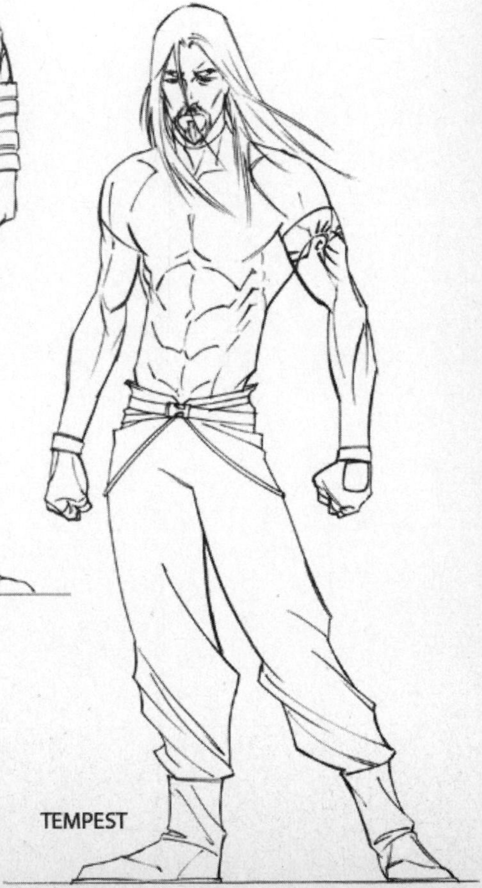

TEMPEST

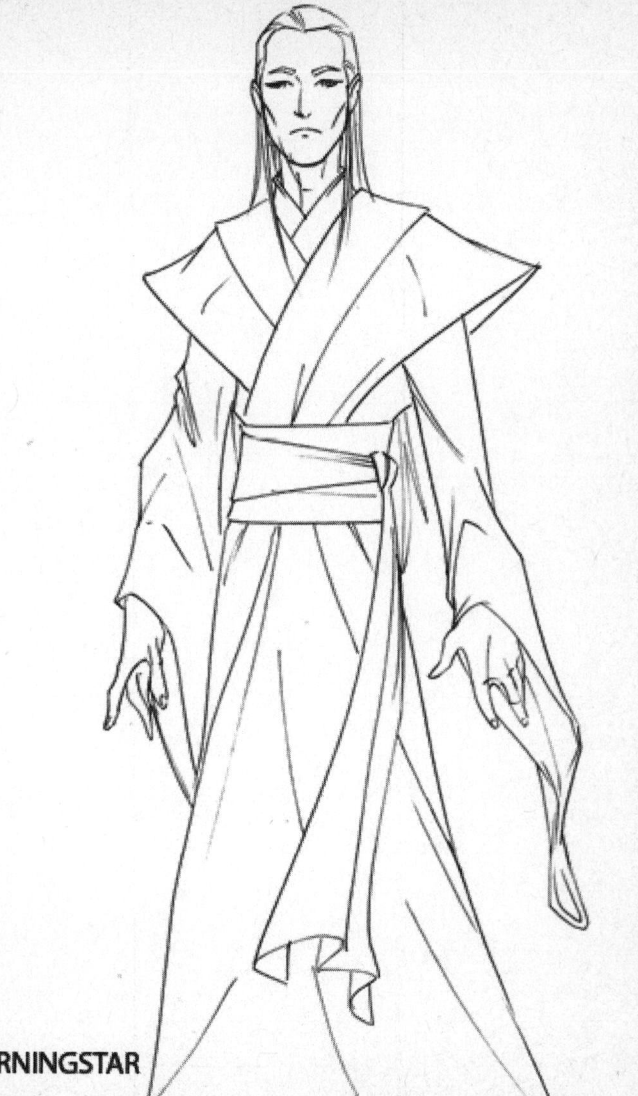

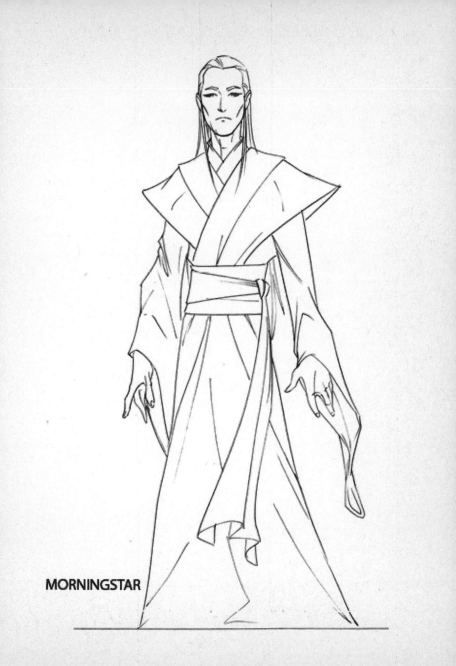

MORNINGSTAR

Preliminary Character sketches

ELENA

CHUCK

MR. ARTEMIS